Close Call

Books by John McEvoy

Blind Switch
Riders Down
Close Call

Nonfiction
Great Horse Racing Mysteries
Women in Racing: In Their Own Words

Close Call

John McEvoy

Poisoned Pen Press

First Edition 2008

10 9 8 7 6 5 4 3 2 1

Library of Congress Catalog Card Number: 2007935724

ISBN: 978-1-59058-495-8 Hardcover

Poisoned Pen Press
6962 E. First Ave., Ste. 103
Scottsdale, AZ 85251
www.poisonedpenpress.com
info@poisonedpenpress.com

To Judy, with thanks
beyond the mere profuse.

Acknowledgments

Making this book possible were the valued contributions of Blathnaid Healy, Eoin Purcell, Carolynn and Bill Sheridan, Randy Rodgers, Mary Summerville, Paddy Walsh, and Barbara Peters and Robert Rosenwald.

"*Your true criminal has two unvarying characteristics, and it is these two characteristics which make him a criminal. Monstrous vanity and colossal selfishness. And they are both as integral, and inerradicable, as the texture of skin.*"
—Josephine Tey
"The Franchise Affair"

"*Trust everybody, but cut the cards.*"
—Finley Peter Dunne
"Mr. Dooley"

Chapter One

When his cell phone rang, Jack Doyle had just slipped his silver Accord onto the Kennedy Expressway at Ohio Street and begun his trip to Monee Park, the aged thoroughbred racetrack located some twenty miles south of Chicago's Loop. The early morning traffic began to thicken in front of him, then coagulated into a bumper-to-bumper morass of frustrated drivers. A weak late March sun had given up its attempt to pierce the city haze.

"Doyle here," he said, guiding the Accord into the left lane so that it wasn't completely surrounded by air-braking trucks and impatient grain traders and stock brokers trying to gun their expensive autos closer to the Jackson Street exit.

"I'm calling to wish you well on the first day of your new job," said the familiar voice of Moe Kellman. Doyle smiled. "Don't jive me, Moe. You're calling to see if I'm punctually on my way to work."

"Jack, Jack, how little you respect my opinion of you. I just thought I'd give you a buzz on my way to the club."

Doyle pictured the diminutive, sixty-eight year old Kellman, with his Don King-like head of frizzed white hair, sitting in the back seat of his chauffeur-driven Lincoln Town Car, tying the laces of his New Balance cross trainers as he neared Fit City. Kellman, reputed to be Chicago's "furrier to the Mob," had a daily workout regimen from which he never varied. He and Doyle had first met three years earlier at Fit City, the popular downtown health club.

Doyle said, "All right, Moe. Thanks for the call. Dinner tomorrow? Sure. I know you've got my best interests in mind. Most of the time," he added, before quickly cutting the connection.

Doyle put the phone down and reached for the radio dial. He turned on 90.9 FM, his favorite local jazz station. Disc jockey Bruce Burnett was promising an upcoming set that would include offerings from John Coltrane, Sarah Vaughn, the Kelly Brand Sextet, and Nicholas Payton. That was fine with Doyle, and he began to relax, accepting the jerky rhythm of the rush hour drive as he passed underneath the Eisenhower Expressway.

Nicholas Payton kicked off the WDCB set with "Way Down Yonder in New Orleans." Hearing the bold, round sound of Payton's trumpet, Doyle recalled the memorable night nearly eighteen years earlier when he had wandered into a Crescent City jazz club in the middle of a rousing jam session involving local musicians. Tired from a day spent with representatives of one of his firm's major marketing accounts, Doyle had felt himself revive as the wave of vibrant music rolled through the brick-walled room. After forty-five minutes or so, in a break between songs, the session's leader motioned toward the rear of the large room. Doyle saw a fresh faced, stocky, African-American youngster spring to his feet, a trumpet in his hand. He was wearing a Hawaiian shirt a gray cloth cap, and an eager look. The cap reminded Doyle of the one worn by one of Doyle's mother's favorite television characters, Jackie Gleason's the Poor Soul. The men that the youngster joined on the grandstand were all many years older and all wore suits and ties over glistening dress shirts.

Any suggested connection to Gleason's Poor Soul was soon washed away when the young man stepped to the microphone, waited respectfully for his signal from the leader, and proceeded to blow the paint off the ceiling. The crowd was stunned by this awesome display of talent, many of them getting to their feet, looks of amazement and delight on their faces. When the set concluded a half-hour later, Doyle said to his waitress, "Who was that?"

"They tell me his name is Payton. Nicholas, I think they said. He's just turned sixteen. He's sure got it, don't he?"

"Could it have been that many years ago?" Doyle muttered to himself. Having recently turned forty-two, he sometimes found it hard to believe that such vivid scenes in his life were nestled so far back in the past. Details of his two failed marriages were less clear in his mind, he thought, and a good thing, too.

A white panel truck with the red logo "Smithereens Pest Control" shifted over one lane, leaving Doyle behind a red Saturn. He could see a small woman at its wheel. The Saturn's bumper was completely covered with slogans. As traffic slowed again Doyle read, from left to right, Who Would Jesus Bomb?... Keep Your Theology Off My Biology...My Kid Brother Sells His Term Papers to Your Honor Student. The last one made Doyle laugh out loud. Then he had to slam on his brakes as a hulking black SUV cut sharply in front of him. Doyle's Accord stopped about the width of a slice of prosciutto from the vehicular mastodon in front of it. Doyle could see the SUV's driver shaking his fist and pounding his horn. "What the hell is he honking at?" Doyle said. "Asshole. He's the one who cut over." The SUV's two bumper stickers were in sharp contrast to those on the red Saturn. One read, Put Christ Back Into Christmas, the other Abortion: Murder of the Innocent. The SUV driver kept banging on his horn for another block.

South of White Sox Park at Thirty-fifth Street, traffic again jammed up. Creeping along now, checking his dashboard clock, Doyle tapped the steering wheel impatiently. He hated being late for anything, much less a new job. A little rim of sweat began to invade the top of his forehead.

Nearing Fifty-seventh Street, the SUV stopped suddenly. Doyle was ready for it this time, but he heard the sound of metal on metal from in front of him. "He must have bumped the red car," Doyle said to himself. Almost immediately, Doyle saw the Saturn pull off onto the left shoulder. Its rear end looked as if it had been sledge hammered. The SUV followed the Saturn, horn blasting away again. Doyle swore aloud as he saw the SUV driver fling open his door. "Uh oh," Doyle said. He started his own hazard lights flashing and eased the Accord onto the shoulder back of the SUV. He didn't like the looks of this.

Doyle saw the driver of the SUV lumber down from his perch. He was a medium tall, overweight white man, about Doyle's age, wearing khaki wash pants, a white sweatshirt declaring him to be a Bob Jones U. Parent, and a look of rage. Even his spiky black buzz cut seemed to be atingle. He moved toward the red Saturn, out of which stepped a short, slim young woman. She had on a tan sweater, brown slacks, and a look of bafflement on her pale face. Before he'd gotten his door completely open, Doyle could hear the Fat Man berating her in a voice that carried over the now resumed Dan Ryan traffic flow.

"Bitch! Why'd you stop that little tin can right in front of me?" Fat Man bellowed. "Shouldn't be allowed on the road, the way you drive."

The young woman bristled, color returning to her face. She said, "If you knew how to handle that big, ugly gas guzzler you wouldn't have rammed into me. You were following too closely. What were you thinking?"

Doyle walked up to where the two were standing now, face to face, Fat Man's complexion having taken on a Heinz 57 hue. He looked like he was either going to slap or belly bump the young woman. Doyle stepped between them. Fat Man, startled, snarled, "Who the hell are you?"

At just under six feet, Doyle was taller than Fat Man, who looked like a one-time high school tackle who had extensively padded his frame with Krispy Kremes, Whoppers, and long necks in the ensuing years. His gut stretched the size XXX white sweatshirt. His meaty hands were bunched into fists.

Doyle spoke loud enough to be heard over the whooshing sound of passing vehicles. "Listen up, Orca, never mind who I am. Just back off until you can get a sheriff's patrol over here to sort this out. You got a cell phone?"

It took Fat Man several seconds to process what Doyle had said. Then he lunged forward and threw a wild right hand that Doyle dodged easily, the Fat Man stumbling past him after his miss. "You don't want to be doing this," Doyle warned. "Now, just calm down and you two can get this straightened out." He glanced at the young woman just as Fat Man let go with another right cross. This one missed by only a couple of inches as Doyle pivoted and ducked. Doyle said, "Mister, you know where you are here? You're out of your goddam element." Fat Man swore loudly. He was starting to get a little bit out of breath already, but his rage propelled him forward again. Doyle sighed, looked resignedly at the young woman, and shrugged. "How did this nitwit get any of his progeny into a university?" he said to her, before turning back to face the onrushing Fat Man.

I don't want to break a knuckle on that bowling ball head, Doyle thought as he got up on the balls of his feet. Seeing Doyle with his fists up, jaw tucked into his left shoulder, shuffling toward him, Fat Man momentarily hesitated. Doyle threw a stiff jab that turned Fat Man's nose sideways, then paused for a second before letting go with a lazy right hand designed to draw attention. Fat Man lifted his hands to protect his face. Doyle stepped in close to Fat Man and quickly hammered three left hooks under the right rib cage, the preferred target area of Doyle's favorite fighter, Julio Cesar Chavez, the Mexican champion renowned for his punishing kidney punches. Doyle's fist dug wrist deep into the layers of flab. Fat Man let out a girlish scream as he fell onto his side.

There was the sound of a distant siren. Doyle said to the wide-eyed young woman, "He won't bother you. The cops are on their way. I'm out of here."

She looked almost as stunned as the fallen Fat Man. She backed away from Doyle. "Are you a boxer?"

Doyle smiled. "Was once," he said. "Until I ran out of people I could beat, and started running into a whole bunch that I couldn't."

She smiled slightly at that before saying, "Well, thanks a lot for keeping that creep away from me. It's your good turn, at least for today."

"Oh, I imagine it'll be for more than today," Doyle smiled. "I don't think they'd find much 'do gooder' in my DNA. It's just that I've never been able to put up with the kind of bully lying over there." Fat Man glowered back at Doyle, but remained sitting on the pavement.

Doyle waved without looking back at her as he turned and hurried to his car, got in, then zipped down the expressway, heading south, not wanting to be late for work.

The morning haze had lifted and the March sun was now a visible presence. Doyle felt pumped. He grinned at himself in the mirror, feeling good in the way he'd felt more than twenty years before, when he was still a factor in AAU boxing. The young woman he'd helped back there certainly wouldn't report him for coming to her aid, and he knew Fatso was too bleary from punches to spot Doyle's rapidly receding license plate. "Doyle to the rescue," he said in a mocking voice, not really understanding the surge of exhilaration he felt, but riding it anyway.

Chapter Two

The main entrance to Monee Park was unattended as Doyle drove through the gate. It was two weeks before the race meeting would begin and there were only a dozen or so cars in the parking lot, most of them in slots marked for "Officials." Looking at the old, brick grandstand that loomed in front of him, Doyle couldn't help but laugh at his irony-laden situation. The only previous time he had taken a job at a racetrack, Heartland Downs northwest of Chicago, it was as a novice groom, intending to fix a race, a plan he had reluctantly carried out. It was a plan that also wound up with him being coerced into cooperating with the FBI in cracking a ring of criminals who were killing horses for their insurance values. Besides helping to bring these vicious crooks to justice, the main benefits for Doyle had been clearing his name with the authorities, winning a major bet on an honest race, and getting to know the beautiful Caroline Cummings. Now, here he was less than a year later, about to begin work as the publicity director of another Chicago area thoroughbred track, this one a small and struggling enterprise that he'd never before set eyes on.

Doyle had returned to Chicago after a three-month stay in New Zealand and, on his first full day back, before he had seen any of the people he knew, he got a phone call from Kellman. "How did you know I was back?"

Moe said, "That's not important. How about if I buy you dinner at Dino's?"

Early that evening Doyle strolled through the crowd of clamoring would-be customers at the entrance of Dino's Ristorante, a Clark Street fixture and Kellman's favorite restaurant. Dino's was a prime destination for the city's movers, shakers, and wannabes in both categories. Angie, the hostess, looked at Doyle in surprise. "Haven't seen you lately," she said. "Go on in. Mr. Kellman is waiting for you."

Kellman was sitting in his usual maroon leather booth at the back of the long room, under the huge photo of Frank Sinatra, the singer's arm around the beaming Dino. There was a Negroni cocktail in front of Kellman. He held a cell phone to his ear. He switched the phone from right to left hand and reached across the table to enthusiastically shake Doyle's hand, all the while continuing to talk on the phone.

"Did I tell you last week or not, that fur won't be in until the end of the month. And the price remains the same." Kellman listened for thirty seconds or so, rolling his eyes. "Feef," he said, "I'm busy. I don't have time to quibble. I know it's late in the season for a fur, but that doesn't make the fur any less valuable to me. There's always next fall. Now, you want it or not?" Kellman nodded and said, "You got it. Good bye."

Kellman took a long drink of his Negroni. "Fifi Bonadio," he said to Doyle. "He's in love again. For about the thirty-ninth time. Some improv actress he met at a Second City benefit for the St. Joseph's League. You couldn't make it up. It's a good thing his wife now spends most of the year with her relatives back in Sicily. And he wants a discount on top of his discount, just because we grew up together on the West Side."

Doyle had heard a good deal about Bonadio but had never met him. That was fine with Doyle. Bonadio owned a huge construction company and several Chicago area banks and car dealerships, but he was not in any Chamber of Commerce. He was known to be a shrewd businessman, avid woman chaser and, more significantly, longtime head of the Chicago Outfit.

Kellman signaled their waiter, who quickly returned with another Negroni plus a Bushmills on the rocks for Doyle. The little man sat back, saying, "Jack, you look good. With that tan you got, all the color you got Down Under, you remind me of Steve McQueen in that prison escape picture. What was it… yeah, 'Papillon.' It's good to see you." They clinked their glasses together. "I was surprised you came back so soon," Kellman said. "I had the impression you might just wind up staying in New Zealand with that Cummings woman."

"Caroline," Doyle amended.

"Yes, Caroline Cummings," Kellman said.

Caroline Cummings, an attractive widow with two young children and sister of horseman Aldous Bolger, a key aide to Doyle in bringing the Kentucky horse killers to justice, had invited Doyle to her home outside of Auckland. Theirs became a satisfactorily social and sexual relationship during Doyle's months there, just as they had enjoyed each other on the Kentucky horse farm the previous summer. But, as Doyle said to Kellman before draining his drink, "Love really never had much to do with it." He hesitated, swirling the ice cubes around in his glass. "I admire and like Caroline a lot. Always will. I think the feeling is mutual. But the more time we spent together, the more obvious it became to both of us that we were never going to be anything more than good friends.…

"It was hard to leave down there," Doyle said. "At the same time, I was pretty damned glad to get back to Chicago. Now," he added, "I've got to go about finding a job."

Kellman's smile gleamed beneath his perfectly trimmed white mustache. "You're in luck again, Jack. I've heard of something that could be just right for you."

Doyle gave Kellman a long look. "Last time you got me a job could hardly be called something that was 'just right for me.'"

"So, yes, there were some ups and downs," Kellman said. "You got drugged, robbed, and came close to being charged with fixing that race. But that was a one-time deal, just as I told you it would be. And, admit it, didn't things work out all right for you in the long run? It was a hell of a lot more interesting than chugging along in life as an advertising account executive."

Doyle shrugged. "I can't argue, I guess. Okay, what plans have you got for me this time around?"

"I don't have any plans for you, Jack," Kellman snapped. "You're, what, forty-two years old. And I'm not your guardian. What I have for you is an opportunity. Which I am bringing to your attention because, for some unknown, continuing reason, I like you. Okay?"

"Okay."

Moe lowered the level of his Negroni by half before saying, "Let's order some food. I'll lay this out for you while we eat." He nodded in the direction of the observant Dino, who immediately sent a waiter hustling over to their booth.

Chapter Three

They had a soup of escarole, white beans, and Italian hot sausage, followed by plates of spinach noodles under mushrooms, asparagus, truffle oil, and shaved Parmesan. At Moe's elbow was his usual large serving of roasted garlic. By the time the chicken Vesuvio was served, Doyle was full. He sat back, took a few more small bites, and watched admiringly as the little man across from him continued to rapidly put away every last morsel on each of his plates before reaching for Doyle's abandoned chicken platter.

"Have you ever weighed more than a hundred and thirty?" Doyle said.

"Right after Korea, when I got out of the Marines and got married. I got up to a hundred fifty by just lying around the house at night and enjoying married life with my Leah. After about a year of that, I went back to the gym and took the weight off. Leah and I are coming up on our forty-sixth wedding anniversary," he added proudly. "But let's get back to the matter at hand. Your job opportunity."

The job, Moe said, was as "publicity director at Monee Park. I know you've never had a job quite like that, but your background in advertising and marketing should make it pretty easy to learn those ropes. Ever been to Monee Park?"

"No, the only Chicago track I've been at is Heartland Downs. Monee, don't they race at night?"

"Right. Night thoroughbred racing during the summer. They've been doing it since the 'thirties. I used to love to take Leah out there for a dinner on hot nights in July and August. It's a neat, little old place. Built back before the Depression. Brick grandstand, third story clubhouse, the stands real close to the racing strip so you'd feel you were close to the action. I cashed some very nice bets there years ago," Moe said, smiling, "some very nice ones indeed." He paused, relishing the memories. Doyle could only imagine what machinations might have resulted in those betting coups back in what Kellman often referred to as "the good old bad days."

Moe said, "Here's the setup. Did you ever hear of Jim Joyce?"

"No."

"He bought Monee Park out of a bankruptcy sale in 1978. He owned and operated it until he died last December. He'd had heart trouble for years, then he got lung cancer. Bang. Three months, then the finish line. It was bad."

Moe took a sip of coffee. "Jim Joyce was a great friend of mine. He was one of the few Micks in our old neighborhood on the West Side. Most of us were Italian or Jewish. His old man ran a saloon that catered to anybody with a buck. Jim and I played basketball together in high school."

Doyle's incredulous look was noticed. "In those days, when I grew up," Moe explained, "they had city high school basketball leagues for guys under five-foot ten. Naturally, I qualified. I think Jimmy slumped his spine down on measurement day, because a year after we graduated he was six feet. We played together for three years.

"Then I went in the Marines. It was during the so-called Korean fucking conflict. Jim got a pass—he was born with only one kidney. Jim stayed here in Chicago and went to work as a runner at the Grain Exchange. By the time I came out of the Marines he'd moved up so fast he'd bought a seat on the Exchange. Ten, twelve years later he'd piled up a huge fortune from his trading. Jim was a genius at it. He used a major part of his capital to buy Monee Park. He renovated the old joint, sold his Exchange firm for a ton of money, and became a racetrack executive. Which he was, until December. Jim was always nuts about horses and racing."

Moe leaned forward, arms on the table, his white shirt cuffs making the linen tablecloth look tawdry. He glanced at his Cartier watch and brushed a crumb away from the sleeve of his immaculate gray suit. "I'm going to tell you a little more about Jimmy Joyce. There were a thousand people at the Cathedral for his funeral. I was a pallbearer. Me and five red faced jumbo Micks sweating out their Bushmills from the wake the night before.

"About a quarter of the crowd was blacks and Mexicans Jim had employed at Monee Park. Even when the track started bleeding money, after the casinos and the lottery came in, Jim never laid off or fired anybody. The rest of the crowd was from City Hall, the legislature, the Grain Exchange, the old neighborhood, plus hundreds of others he'd made friends with. He was awfully damn good at that.

"The Cardinal said the funeral mass. They had a beautiful choir. His niece Celia gave the eulogy. It was funny, and sad, right on the money. One thing she emphasized was that her uncle was a 'man of no pretension.' Perception, yes, but never pretension.

"Leaving the Cathedral there was the Chicago Catholic tradition of pipers walking behind the coffin. I had to laugh. I said to Bernie Flynn, he was across from me on the other side of the coffin we were hauling, 'I'm surprised Jim isn't leaping out of the coffin in protest. He hated bagpipes.'

"'Oh, I know that,' Bernie said back. 'Jimmy always said the Irish invented the damn things and gave them to the Scots as a joke.'"

Moe raised an index finger in the direction of the waiter, who scurried to the booth with two slim liqueur glasses and a carafe of what Doyle knew to be grappa, Moe's favorite after dinner drink and, in Doyle's experience, one of the champion hangover producers in the annals of alcohol. Doyle asked the waiter for more coffee.

Doyle thought about Moe's longtime association with the late Mr. Joyce. After all, Moe had previously convinced Doyle to fix a horse race on behalf of other "dear friends," a contingent Doyle eventually learned was comprised of Moe's boyhood buddies turned Outfit guys. He had no desire to rekindle any association of that sort. "Danger" was by no means Doyle's middle name, having to contend as it did with "bad luck" and "poor choices." His unease must have showed, because Moe smiled before reaching across the linen to pat Doyle's hand.

"Now, Jack," he said, "don't jump to conclusions. Jim Joyce long ago distanced himself from his old neighborhood buddies—except for me. He was an absolutely legit businessman. He never married. There was always a woman in his life, but never one he committed to. Jim had three major passions: making money, horse racing, and his niece Celia, with her coming in first by far. Celia McCann I'm talking about. She was the only child of Jim's older sister Marie, who was killed along with her husband in a car crash years ago. Jim wound up raising Celia from the time she was about ten.

"Jim sent her to a Catholic boarding school in Iowa, but she spent all her summer vacations with him, even when she was in college. Celia learned the racing business from the ground up, starting as a hot walker on the backstretch for a trainer friend of Jim's, then working menial jobs, later lower management jobs at Monee Park. She loved the whole thing from the start. Jim's other sibling, a younger sister named Elizabeth, met and married an Irish citizen and went over there to live more than thirty years ago. She died of cancer several years back, lung, same as her brother. Like her sister Marie, Elizabeth had just the one child, a boy. His name is Niall. Niall Hanratty."

Moe drained his grappa glass, then refilled it from the carafe. Doyle's glass remained untouched. He wanted to keep a clear head. Moe said, "I can see you're still uneasy about our earlier project. Which, if I may remind you, wound up, after some uncomfortable episodes en route, providing you with a fairly decent financial score."

Doyle said, "'Uncomfortable episodes'? That's what you call me being drugged and robbed? Then put in a hammer lock by the FBI? Discovering a friend who was almost battered to death? Not to mention nearly being killed by a goddam helium balloon? You call those 'uncomfortable episodes'? When they get the Masters of Understatement Hall of Fame up and running, you'll be a first-ballot shoe-in." He reached for the grappa.

"Sometimes, Jack, I think you were put on earth just to irritate people." Moe was about to elaborate, but instead put his napkin down and warmly grasped the bejeweled hand of one of Chicago's wealthiest society matrons who had stopped at their booth on her way out of the restaurant, saying in what for years had been her version of a Southern belle's drawl, "Moe, dahlin', how yew tonight?"

Doyle had seen her photo in the Chicago newspapers, especially the one owned by her besotted current husband. She leaned forward and whispered something to Kellman. He whispered back. Then she smiled, waved goodbye, and swept off, trailing Chanel Number Five, never having even glanced at Doyle.

"Lovely woman," Moe said, seated again, grappa glass in hand. "I knew her when she checked hats at the old Mr. Kelly's jazz club. Among other things. She managed to marry very, very well the last three times. A deserved escalation. She's brighter than any of her husbands, past or present, and a hell of a lot nicer. She's been a good customer, too."

"Could we return to this job opportunity you've got for me?"

"Here's the situation," Moe said. "When Jimmy Joyce died, he left Monee Park to two people. Fifty-one percent of it went to his niece, Celia, and forty-nine percent to his nephew, Niall Hanratty, who lives in Ireland. He's a bookmaker. A big one.

"Celia had been Jimmy's assistant general manager. He brought her in to help him a couple of years ago, and I understand she's done very well in the job. But the track hasn't done well. Their business was way, way down at last year's meeting. Monee Park has a serious cash flow problem, which was partly what led to resignations by a lot of Celia's management staff.

Celia was still managing to meet the payroll, but they thought they saw the handwriting on the wall. That the track was doomed to close.

"Among those quitting, and suddenly, was Howie Hagan, her advertising and publicity director. He went to work for an amusement park. When I found out what kind of a jam Celia was in, with Hagan gone and the start of the meeting coming up, I thought of you. You've done advertising and publicity work. You know racing. You can be trusted. And you need a job. Nice fit, to my mind," Moe said, reaching again for the carafe.

Doyle gave Kellman a quizzical look. He said, "It sounds to me like you're boosting me aboard a sinking ship. If Monee Park is doomed, why the hell would I want to go to work there?"

"It's not doomed. On shaky ground, yes. But there are encouraging factors for the owners. For one thing, the land the track sits on is worth a fortune. It's prime property in a booming suburban area. But that's not important."

"Why not?"

"Because Celia will never sell. She loves racing. She's told me she feels she 'owes it to Uncle Jim's memory' to keep the track going. She means it, too. Celia loved her uncle. And she's a very strong, determined young woman."

Doyle said, "But if the track is on the skids, what's the point of keeping it open?"

"Besides the obligation Celia feels to her uncle," Moe answered, "there's hope on the horizon in the form of a gambling bill now in the state legislature. It's in committee down there in Springfield. It would authorize a casino for the city of Chicago. In order to protect horse racing interests from being blown out of the water, the bill would allow the Illinois racetracks to install video slot machines. Even a lot of the downstate legislators see the worth of that. The racetracks are part of a significant agribusiness in this state, one with thousands of farm jobs and suppliers."

"I know this has worked other places," Doyle said. "Video slots have saved tracks on the East Coast, in Iowa, in the Southwest. I guess they'd work here, too. People are suckers for those machines. I read once that each machine kicks back a daily profit of something like $350! Amazing."

"Exactly," Moe said. "You get a thousand of those up and cranking away, your racetrack is golden."

Moe reached into his pocket and pulled out a thick roll of bills wrapped in a beige rubber band. Kellman always paid cash and never carried a wallet. *One of the few like that left in America*, Doyle thought. He had never gotten around to asking Moe why, and he didn't this time, either. He concentrated on the job possibility as Moe peeled off a pair of twenties for the tip. As for the bill, Dino ran a tab for Moe, payable monthly.

"Are there other applicants for this job?" Doyle said.

"No. It's yours if you want it. There's a time element involved here. Celia needs somebody right away. I've known Celia since she was a youngster. She trusts me. I put in a couple of good words for you," he smiled. It was a mischievous look. *If Jews had leprechauns*, Doyle thought, *Moe could pass for one.*

"What did you tell her about me?"

"I gave her a discreetly edited description of you and your various occupations. I didn't mention the race fixing caper. I did tell her you'd had a career in advertising and public relations at some top agencies here in Chicago. A career working, as a good friend of mine once put it, 'in the art of stretching imagination to its elastic limit.' In other words, you could sling the B. S. as fast and far as anyone.

"I told her you had helped the authorities in busting an insurance fraud ring. Celia remembered reading about that case. I told her you were smart, honest, quick on your feet, and with your fists when you had to be.

"I also told her you could be a kind of know-it-all, wise-cracking, authority-hating pain in the ass. In other words, I was truthful."

Doyle's face flushed. He said, "Which of these outstanding qualities of mine impressed her the most?" He picked up his napkin, then tossed it back on the table with a frown. "I'm sure that last part put her solidly in my corner."

Kellman took a final sip of grappa. He carefully wiped his mustache with his napkin, smiling at Doyle and starting to slide out of the booth.

"What impressed Celia the most," Kellman said, "was that you are a friend of mine. And that you are available."

Chapter Four

Doyle parked his Accord in a slot marked Guest just outside the Monee Park clubhouse entrance. It was a warm late March morning and he was tempted to loosen his necktie as he got out of the car. But he thought better of that. "Got to look good from the get go," he reminded himself. He was wearing his best dark blue business suit and his black shoes gleamed.

Inside the building, a maintenance worker directed Doyle to the elevators. He pressed floor five, the highest number showing, where he'd been told the executive offices were located. When the elevator door slid open, Doyle stepped into a carpeted reception area and heard a low, feminine voice say, "So you're the famous Jack Doyle. Right on time, and here to help the damsel in distress."

The statement carried with it a hint of mockery, and the look on the young woman's face affirmed it. "I'm Doyle," he smiled. "Famous, I don't know. And," he added, "my history with damsels has been that I don't so much rescue them from distress, as cause it."

His listener frowned from her chair behind the large desk. She was a thirty-something African American with a no nonsense air about her who proceeded to size him up before saying, "I remember you on TV, and that balloon that crashed at Heartland Downs. That's famous enough for me.

"Welcome to Monee Park," she continued. "I'm Shontanette Hunter, Celia's secretary. I wasn't here the day you came in for your job interview." Shontanette wore a white, open collared blouse and a dark blue skirt. Her hair was close cropped, her smooth complexion the color of cappuccino custard. "Celia's in a meeting. She'll be ready to see you in about ten minutes. Have a seat.

"As for the damsel in distress part, Mr. Doyle," Shontanette said seriously, "you'd better be aware that I've got that girl's back. Celia and I have been friends for a lot of years. I love her like a sister. I'm expecting you to do right by her."

Doyle said, "Look, I'm just here to do a job. And I'll do it right."

He walked over to the long, dark red leather couch. The walnut paneled wall behind it, like the other walls of this reception area, was covered with photos of famous horses and racing people—jockeys, trainers, owners—who had competed in past years at Monee Park, usually on their way up to bigger tracks, sometimes on their way down from them as well.

As he would later learn, Shontanette Hunter first met Celia McCann when they were children. Their friendship formed during summer vacations from high school when Shontantette worked the popcorn stand on the east end of Monee Park's first floor. They were both sixteen that year. Celia was in training with her Uncle Jim, being prepped in track management. The two girls became close and remained so, working at the track the next two summers before Celia went off to college at Saint Mary-of-the-Woods in South Bend, Indiana, from which she would graduate with honors in education. Shontanette, meanwhile, attended a Chicago secretarial school, emerging with a record replete with A grades. When Celia succeeded her uncle as head of Monee Park, she hired her old friend to serve as her executive secretary.

Doyle cleared his throat, and Shontanette looked up from her computer. "Can I ask you something? How old is Ms. McCann?"

Shontanette gave him a searching look. "I'm just curious," Doyle assured her. "I like to know at least something about someone I'm going to work for."

"Celia just turned thirty-four," Shontanette said. "Some people think she looks a bit older than that. Because of those worry lines that show. That's what pain and sorrow can etch into a caring person's face," she said more softly. Instead of elaborating, she continued to regard Doyle warily.

Doyle sighed. "Why is it," he said, "that I seem to arouse suspicion, or at least skepticism, in so many women?"

Shontanette peered at him over the rims of her white-framed glasses. "I would suspect," she said, "that you should be asking yourself that question, not asking me."

"*Touché*," Doyle said, grinning. Shontanette allowed herself a half smile before turning back to her computer.

As he waited on the couch, Doyle thought back to his initial visit to Monee Park the previous Tuesday, when he had been interviewed by Celia McCann. She had been waiting for him in this reception area that morning, sitting behind the large desk. He'd glanced at the nameplate on the desk and said, "Ms. Hunter?"

"No," Celia had replied, smiling. "I'm Celia McCann. You must be Jack Doyle. Good morning." She rose and came out from behind the desk, hand extended. She was a striking looking woman who wore her long red hair pulled back and tied in a bun. Her face was long, with pronounced cheek bones, a wide mouth, nose that curved up slightly, and a delicately molded chin. Her large green eyes were framed by long, reddish lashes. Doyle was disappointed to see that she wore a gold wedding band. As she led him through the office doorway, Doyle noticed that she was tall, within an inch or two of his five-eleven. She was wearing a long-sleeved white wool sweater, gray skirt, black flats. Celia said, "We'll go this way" and led him down a narrow, carpeted hallway filled with unopened boxes. "Office supplies we haven't had a chance to unpack," she said. The walls were lined with more photos, many of them of prominent people from the worlds of politics, show business, and sports, shown during their visits to Monee Park.

Celia looked back over her shoulder and said, "Uncle Jim's great friend Moe Kellman said you were looking for a job and had experience in racing. I am glad you could come in for an interview."

Doyle knew that Moe had told her more than that about him, but all he said was, "I'm glad, too, Ms. McCann."

He couldn't help but gawp as he continued walking in the wake of this long-striding woman. Moe hadn't mentioned to Doyle that his potential new employer was drop dead, then spring eagerly back to life, beautiful.

"Moe, you little rascal," Doyle muttered. Hearing this Ceclia kept walking but looked back over her shoulder inquiringly, right eyebrow raised. Doyle said nothing. He continued to follow her down the long, crowded corridor, checking her out. The flat shoes she wore, Doyle surmised, were probably intended to make her look a bit less tall. He admired her long-legged, graceful advance.

They came to the end of the corridor. Celia reached for the heavy brass handle on the wooden door. Before turning it she said, "My husband would like to meet you, Mr. Doyle."

"Fine. But please make it 'Jack.'"

Pausing at the door, Celia said, "Jack, I don't want you to be shocked when you see him, so I will tell you here that my husband has ALS."

He wasn't so much shocked as surprised by the fact that Moe Kellman, the man who knew so much about so many, was apparently ignorant of this depressing fact.

"ALS," Doyle said. "That's Lou Gehrig's Disease, right?"

"That's what it's commonly known by. The correct term is Amyotrophic Lateral Sclerosis. My husband has had it for more than two years. It's incurable."

"I'm very sorry to hear this," Doyle said as he followed her through the doorway.

They entered the living room of the apartment located on the building's top floor. The drapes were drawn. Doyle noticed book cases, trophy cases, and several paintings of racing scenes.

To the left of a long tan couch sat a man in a wheel chair. Doyle saw him last, for he was just outside the spray of light from the lone floor lamp that was turned on. His pale face was lined. The tendons in his neck stood out as he raised his eyes to Doyle, giving him a look that a pawn broker might aim at a new customer. The man's black hair was neat, as if it had been trimmed that morning. Behind this long-legged, large-framed man in the wheelchair stood a slight, brown-skinned Filipino woman wearing a white nurse's uniform.

Doyle was stunned when Celia introduced the man as "My husband, Bob Zaslow." Stunned because he recognized the name at once. Some twenty years before, on a bitter, winter night at the old Chicago Stadium, Doyle had watched as Northwestern University basketball star Zaslow poured in thirty-eight points against a good Marquette team. Zaslow, a six foot, five inch forward, was all Big Ten in both his junior and senior years at the Evanston school. Doyle recalled that Zaslow had been drafted by the Boston Celtics of the NBA but didn't stick, then disappeared into the business world. Doyle hadn't thought of the man in years.

"And this is Fidelia Rizal," Doyle heard Celia say. "She's our friend and…well…great helpmate." Fidelia came around from behind the wheelchair to shake Doyle's hand. Zaslow didn't move, and it soon became apparent to Doyle that he could not. But his bright blue eyes inspected Doyle from head to toe. Finally, he said in a low, strained, raspy voice, "Hello, Jack Doyle."

Doyle said, "My pleasure, Bob. I remember you well from your playing days at NU. You were terrific." He immediately regretted this reference to Zaslow's healthy past. But the former basketball player looked pleased. He motioned with his head for Doyle to take a seat. It was obvious that Zaslow was almost completely immobilized.

Celia took a chair next to her husband. "Bob's ALS forced him to give up his insurance business over two years ago. He's fought against it as hard as anyone can," she added. "But, Mr.

Doyle…Jack…we're here to discuss you and the possibility of your coming to work at Monee Park. Shall we begin?"

In the course of the next half-hour Doyle described his occupational career, Celia described the job. "You would supervise the press box, be in charge of advertising, write press releases for the media," she said. " Some days, you'd be required to interview winning owners for our in-house television show that's simulcast all over the country on weekends.

"We operate almost seven months of the year, mid-April to early October. We race at nights, except some Saturdays, and your work day would begin long before that. I'm talking twelve hour days, six days a week. Not everyone is interested in a schedule so demanding."

"Which is why I've been invited here," Doyle said. "Naw, scratch that. I'm interested. How about salary?"

Celia said, "$800 a week, a gas allowance, and free meals in any of the track's restaurants. No health insurance, no pension plan. At this stage, that's the best we can do. And I mean it." She looked embarrassed.

Jesus, Doyle thought, I *used to piss away that much night-lifing on a Rush Street weekend.* He said, "I'll take the job if you offer it to me. Do you want to get back to me?"

Celia glanced at her husband. Zaslow gave her some sort of signal Doyle could not discern. She said, "The job is yours if you want it."

"Thanks," Doyle said, getting to his feet. "When do I start?"

Doyle stopped at O'Keefe's Olde Ale House, the Irish saloon near his north side Chicago condo that he had patronized for years, and had a sandwich and a Guinness. But he couldn't get the image of Bob Zaslow out of his mind. He left money on the bar and walked the three blocks to his building, entered, booted up his computer, and Googled ALS.

The web site he accessed described ALS as being characterized by the degeneration and loss of motor neurons, which gradually die, producing progressive weakness and functional loss of muscles. Those neurons affected "…can include muscles of the limbs and trunk, as well as those for speaking and swallowing…The pattern of muscle deterioration varies among people with ALS. Over a period of months or years, they will experience difficulty in walking, using their hands and arms, in talking and swallowing…The mental facilities, however, usually remain intact."

The more Doyle read, the more disheartened he became. Thinking of how physically decimated the one-time star athlete looked, Doyle shook his head. "That poor bastard," he said. He turned off the computer. "And that poor woman. Damn."

Doyle felt a powerful inclination to return to O'Keefe's and get, as he occasionally would describe it, "yellow cab drunk." He resisted, however, knowing that he had to be sharp the next day, his first one on the new job.

He walked into the condo's small living room to the wall shelf with its few liquor bottles and poured himself a Bushmills on the rocks. He turned on the television news. The five o'clock version had just begun. There had been a warehouse fire and the anchor man excitedly announced that "Now we'll go to Hal Hermanson, who is live at the scene." Doyle muttered, "I guess it would be pretty big news if Hal was dead at the scene."

The second "lead" story, Doyle saw to his astonishment, was about two terribly overweight women who'd been denied access to the use of horses at a suburban Chicago riding stable. They were complaining bitterly to the slim, eager, blond interviewer about the "mistreatment" and "discrimination" they had suffered. The stable had a posted rule that no one weighing more than two hundred pounds would be permitted to rent and ride a horse there. This was to "protect the horses from leg and ankle injuries," the rule read. It was a policy deemed highly offensive by the women, each of whom measured barely over five foot, Doyle estimated, and definitely exceeded the two hundred pound weight limit. They were incensed. So was Doyle, who found himself saying to the screen, "Why don't you two rent a couple of Percherons?"

He leaned toward the screen as a representative of the National Association to Advance Fat Acceptance began to read a statement. "Is this fucking 'Saturday Night Live' on a Wednesday?" he said to the set.

Doyle took a long pull on the Bushmills, then sat back in his armchair and breathed deeply, clicking the remote onto off, turning his thoughts to his new job and his first day tomorrow in this, his latest attempt to reinvent himself. The older he got, the more he found himself sitting in solitary silence, trying to fight off pesky questions, like what the hell am I doing here? Have I been doing here? Should I be doing here? He was amazed that he was being plagued by such self scrutiny, he, a man who's always been driven by the belief that he was headed directly to the top. His problem, he knew, was figuring out the top of what.

Chapter Five

"I should have had Shontanette draw me a map," Doyle said to himself. He was walking through the third floor grandstand of Monee Park, toward the west end, looking for a stairway he'd been told led to the press box. The place looked as if it hadn't been swept since the previous year's race meeting. Old newspapers, used drink cups, empty food wrappers lay all over the concrete floor. Flaking paint and dirt-streaked windows added to the evidence of decay, of a budget that was woefully short on maintenance funds. This racetrack was in trouble, Doyle knew, an impression emphasized when he saw two rats scamper from behind an overflowing wastebasket. "Jesus," Doyle said, "they're going to have to clean this joint up in a hurry to be ready for the opener." He thought about suggesting to Celia that she hire the Chicago exterminating company whose name had always impressed him: Smithereens. Writing on their trucks made clear that the Smithereens' employees utilized an anti-vermin weapon described as "Mr. Rat's Last Lunch."

Following Shontanette's directions, Doyle finally came to a heavy, wire screen door. Behind it, a metal stairway rose above the wooden grandstand seats still glistening with morning dew. Most of these seats had not been occupied in recent years during the track's business downturn. Monee Park had a seating capacity of slightly more than 8,000, a remnant of its glory days. Crowds in recent years bordered on 2,000 a night, maybe 5,000 on a good weekend.

He started walking up the first of three flights of metal steps. The first two were straight ahead. The third flight was an elbow bend to the left. Its steps led to a heavy metal door, and they were steep. "Sherpas could train here," he snorted.

Looking down at what he knew would be largely empty seats in the weeks to come, Doyle remembered a story about heavy-weight legend Joe Louis' manager. A major New York boxing promoter was trying to arrange a non-title match for Louis at Yankee Stadium. "We can get 100,000 seats in there, using the baseball field," the promoter enthused. Joe Louis' manager replied, "Yeah. But how many fannies you goin' get in those seats?" The proposed bout never came off.

When Doyle reached the top of the stairs, he saw an in-house phone on the left wall, just about eye height. Shontanette had told him about it. She'd said, "Just pick up the receiver. The phone will beep the press box and the door will be opened by an electronic signal sent by whoever answers the phone up there. It's a security thing," Shontanette had explained. "Years ago," she said, "some broken down horse player went charging up to the press box with a loaded gun intending to shoot Sam Surico, the selector for the *Chicago News*. Claimed he'd gone broke betting Surico's picks. A security guard managed to wrestle the gun away from him before he did any damage. Mr. Joyce decided to secure the area after that incident."

"Surico's retired, right?"

"Right. Just last year," Shontanette answered. "He was a real character. If he had a bad day with his picks, his so-called fans would wait for him at the bottom of the press box stairs, swearing, yelling all kinds of awful things at him. 'Surico, you dumb so-and-so, we should kick your fat butt.' Surico this, Surico that. Sam would just stand there for a minute or two, taking all the abuse, his arms outstretched, smiling. 'These are my people,' he'd say."

Doyle lifted the receiver off the hook. Nothing. He put the phone down for a few seconds, then picked it up and tried again. This time he heard the receiver being lifted, but the connection was broken almost immediately.

Receiver in hand, now pounding with his other hand on the press box door, Doyle was about to begin shouting when he heard a low voice say slowly, "Hellooo."

Fuming, Doyle took a deep breath. He said, "This is Jack Doyle. Will you open the door?"

The low, slow voice answered, "Jack whoooo?"

Doyle turned in a half-circle, receiver in his hand, ready to rip it off its cord. Then he regrouped. "Who am I talking to?" Doyle said, as politely as he could manage.

Silence. Then Doyle heard the low voice say, very, very slowly, "This is Morty Dubinski."

It suddenly occurred to Doyle what this voice reminded him of. His father had been a huge fan of the radio comedy team Bob and Ray, frequently playing their tapes, especially one about the Slow Talkers Club. Doyle senior had broken up with every listening.

Doyle said, "Open the fucking door, Morty. This is your new boss."

In the press box several desks stood spaced out over an old, worn, brown carpet, along with two darkened television sets, a couch and a couple of arm chairs, a small bar and refrigerator and sink. From a cubicle at the end of the room peered a round-faced man in his late sixties, white hair combed straight back on one of the longest heads Doyle had ever seen. Brown framed glasses, possibly the same ones he wore for his high school yearbook photo, perched on his shiny red nose. He wore an old, light blue sport coat and a dark blue bow tie on a white dress shirt dulled gray. His dark trousers were wrinkled but, incongruously, his black brogans gleamed. He pushed his glasses up on his nose as he said, "Hello, there. I'm Morton J. Dubinski. They call me Morty." He gave Doyle a quick once over before adding, "Glad to meet you, Doyle." Then he turned back to his desk.

Without being invited, Doyle entered Morty's cubicle. "Cluttered" would not begin to describe it. Stacks of old *Racing*

Dailies lined two walls from floor level to six feet up. Racing history books were jammed into shelving in the tall book case that stretched along another wall. Morty's desk top was buried beneath a sea of newspapers, racing programs, and magazines and condition books. A cockapoodle could have easily been concealed beneath the mounds. To the left of the desk, on a pull out wood extension, was an Underwood typewriter that Ben Hecht might have pounded. Ignoring Doyle, Morty turned to it, inserted a piece of copy paper, and began rapidly typing. He was interrupted when the phone on his desk rang. Morty picked it up, listened, then said, "My new boss just got here. Guy named Doyle. I don't know a goddam thing about him, except that he's my new boss." He slammed the phone down and resumed typing.

Shontanette had provided Doyle with some background on Morty Dubinski. "He's worked here since he got out of high school in the fifties," she'd said. "He's the son of a good friend of the late Mr. Joyce. He always thinks he's going to get the publicity job you have, but he never does. It's made him somewhat resentful. He can take care of fundamental press box duties, but much beyond that is way over his head. He's not a bad old guy, but you've got to give Celia credit for keeping him on the payroll. They're very loyal here."

"This is my right hand man? Wonderful," Doyle had replied.

Doyle sat down in the chair in front of Morty's desk. He said, "May I ask what you are doing?"

Morty's fingers flew over the Underwood's keys as he answered, "Writing out my resignation."

"From what?"

"From my position here in the Monee Park publicity department," Morty snapped. He continued to type rapidly.

Bemused, Doyle sat back in his chair and watched. After a couple of minutes, when Morty plucked the first piece of paper from the typewriter and quickly inserted another, Jack said, "How long does it take to say 'I quit'?

"And," Doyle added, reaching forward and ripping the second piece of paper out of the typewriter, "why bother?"

He leaned forward, forearms on the desk, hands clasped. Doyle produced his most ingratiating smile, one that had won over most of the toughest sells he'd met in his account executive career. Morty's bushy eyebrows elevated, but he said nothing. "You can't resign, Morty," Jack said. "Celia McCann needs my help. And I need yours. How about the two of us start over?" He extended his hand and Morty, after a brief hesitation, shook it. Morty's scowl was replaced by a look of grateful surprise.

Doyle stood up. "Okay," he said, "let's get to work. I need you to fill me in on the routine here. The deadlines for press releases to the papers and to radio and television people. Ad deadlines. Who's our track photographer, and when I can meet him. The whole megillah. Talk to me, Morty."

Obviously flattered, Morty responded enthusiastically. Three hours later, Doyle, his yellow legal notepad nearly filled, sat back in the chair. "How about some lunch?" he said.

Morty reached into his lower desk drawer and extracted a brown bag.

"No thanks," he said, "I brought mine. Then I can stay here and answer the phone."

"The phone hasn't rung since I got here. But suit yourself." Doyle got up from the chair, prepared to leave.

Morty cleared his throat, he thrust his glasses back up the bumpy slope of his nose, looking at Doyle appraisingly. "Can I ask you something, Mr. Doyle?"

Doyle nodded. "Call me Jack."

"What is your background in racing?"

Doyle paused before replying, "I've been involved in a number of aspects of it."

Morty looked dubious. "Oh, yeah? Tell me, Jack, who was the last horse to win the Triple Crown?"

Doyle shot him a look. "Don't start trying to yank my chain here, Morty. It was Affirmed. I can also name the number of years between Affirmed and the first Triple Crown winner, Sir

Barton, faster than you can zip your fly. Which is something I suggest you do."

He turned to leave. Morty, mortified, quickly adjusted his zipper, blushing almost the color of the press box's burgundy wallpaper. But he recovered. As Doyle neared the door, Morty said loudly, "Okay, Mr. Doyle...Mr. Boss. What about other horses if you think you know so much? You ever hear of Gene Autry?"

"The old cowboy singer and actor? I think he owned one of the California major league baseball teams years ago. What about him?"

"What was his horse's name? In the movies?"

Doyle said, "You sneaky little bastard. It started with a C, right? Was it Cyclone?"

Morty's eyes gleamed. "Champion, Mr. Doyle, Champion," he said triumphantly. "Shoot, just about everybody knows that. I got you that time." He hurried back to his cubicle. Doyle left, laughing.

Chapter Six

Tony Rourke, office manager at Shamrock Off-Course Wagering headquarters in the Dublin suburb of Dun Laoghaire, brought the Wednesday mail into his boss' office. He said to Niall Hanratty, "Letter from the States for you. There, on top." Hanratty thanked him as Rourke turned to leave. He reached for the thick envelope, noting the Chicago return address under the name of Arthur P. Riley, Esq.

Hanratty pushed aside the pile of betting account printouts he had been reviewing. He opened the envelope and read:

"Dear Mr. Hanratty,

"I am writing to offer my sincere condolences for your loss of your Uncle Jim Joyce, a dear, dear friend of mine. Be assured that numerous Masses will be offered on his behalf.

"I feel an obligation to inform you of some specifics regarding your Uncle's will and they may prove to be of great benefit to you. I realize that, so far removed from the Chicago scene while in your beautiful native land, you may not be aware of some of that document's ramifications. Please feel free to call me at the following number at any time. I believe I have information that you will find to be very, very valuable.

"Wishing you all the best, I am…"

The letter was signed Arthur P. Riley. The letterhead bore an address on South LaSalle Street in Chicago. Hanratty tossed it back on the desk, a frown on his darkly handsome face. He had received a copy of his Uncle Jim's will the previous week and been surprised to find himself named a beneficiary since he had never met his mother's brother in all of his thirty-eight years. Heard much about him, of course, and received a Christmas gift check every year since he was a boy, but never once a meeting. The fact that he'd been left forty-nine percent of an American racetrack called Monee Park had stunned him. Niall had learned of his uncle's death in a phone call from his cousin Celia. Days later he'd received from Celia, who was the executor of their uncle's estate, a copy of the will. Hanratty had no way of estimating the value of this bequest out of the blue, though Celia, in an accompanying letter, wrote that she would be forwarding to him "all the relevant financial details regarding our shared inheritance." He had yet to receive that letter. Maybe lawyer Riley could be of some help in that area.

Hanratty rose and stretched his lean, lanky frame, long arms in his blue Oxford shirt reaching toward the sound-proofed ceiling of the large office. He loosened his red tie before sitting back down in his desk chair and reaching for the phone. "Riley," he said aloud. "Now, here's one that's popped out of the rat hole, his nose twitching. Or maybe he's just one of those American super Micks, the Irish wannebes, patronizing us while they praise us." He smiled wryly. "Can't hurt to find out what's up this rascal's sleeve." He calculated the time difference, Ireland was six hours ahead of Chicago, and decided to wait until late afternoon to make his call.

Riley picked up on the first ring. *Must be a small law practice if your man's answering his own phone*, Niall thought. He said, "Mr. Riley? This is Niall Hanratty, calling from Ireland."

"Mr. Hanratty, how good to talk to you. I take it you've received my letter about Jim Joyce. Now one with the dust," Riley added dramatically. "Passed away in his sleep, you know, peaceful as a Meadow in Meath."

Hanratty, rolling his eyes at this bit of blather, said, "That's a comfort, to be sure. Now, Mr. Riley, about your letter, and my uncle's will. What 'great benefits' are you referring to?" Riley cleared his throat. Hanratty sat back in his chair. He'd never known a barrister who'd gotten anywhere near the point in the first furlong or so, and he doubted the American would be any different.

After describing in detail his great admiration for Jim Joyce, and a snide comment or two about cousin Celia's business acumen, Riley finally arrived at the point, saying, "I believe there's money to be made from that racetrack that you, perhaps, have not been apprised of."

"Go on, man."

Riley assumed, he said, that Hanratty had been informed of Monee Park's current "dismal financial condition. It's an old dump, getting dumpier. There's no money for badly needed capital improvements. What your cousin Celia is pinning her hopes on is a bill in our state legislature that would legalize a Chicago casino. To lessen the effect of damaging competition to existing racetracks, the thinking is to give the Illinois racetracks the right to put video slot machines on their properties."

Hanratty said, "Besides Monee Park, what other tracks are near Chicago?"

"The big one is Heartland Downs, out north and west of the city," Riley said. "It'll survive with or without video slots. Then there are three smaller harness racing tracks. Two of those, like Monee Park, could surely use the revenue from slot machines."

"What are the chances of this bill passing?"

Riley paused. "Perhaps fifty-fifty at this point," he said. "The state is desperately in need of new revenues, and casinos are guaranteed to produce them. Look at the states that have legalized them in recent years. Huge financial successes for the casino owners, the state, the taxpayers."

"Not so much for the gambling addicts, I presume," Hanratty interjected.

"True, true Mr. Hanratty. You being in the gaming business yourself over there, I'm sure you're well aware of that problem plaguing a tiny minority."

"When might such a law be passed? And go into effect?"

"Ah," Riley said, "this state being what it is, which is quite conservative on gambling issues, a bill such as this would only have a chance in a non-election year, which this is. That's when the boys down there in Springfield get brave, churning out laws they hope nobody will hold them responsible for when they run for office next time.

"The timing, then," Riley continued, "is favorable for such a bill. But that in itself doesn't guarantee its passage, not by any means. There's a very conservative faction in the House that's staunchly against any expansion of gambling. The bill's sponsors are going to have to clear that hurdle." He chuckled at his reference to racing.

Hanratty groaned softly, wondering how much faith to put in the opinions of this long distance opportunist.

"Assume the thing passes, Mr. Riley. How long before the video slots are up and running then?"

"At least a year from now," Riley estimated, "before any new money could come flooding into old Monee Park."

Without elaborating, Hanratty said, "Well, that's not ideal by any means, as far as I'm concerned." He was not inclined to inform Riley that he was planning a major expansion of Shamrock Off-Course Betting Corp., both its Irish operation as well as creating two offices in Spain, one in Portugal. He had been laying the groundwork for this project for three years. Getting it off the ground would require some major borrowing as well as a significant infusion of his own cash. The news of Uncle Jim's will had encouraged Niall to think that new money would be available relatively soon. Now, according to Riley, that would not be the case.

"I'm damned sorry to hear that," Hanratty said softly. "I was under the impression that the disbursement would be much sooner."

Riley laughed, then caught himself. "Oh, disburse they may well do," he said. "Except for the fact that there's nothing to disburse at this particular point."

Hanratty sat back in his chair, mulling this over. He'd always tended to sift carefully through information even before the time when, as a young clerk in a down country off-track betting shop, eager to learn the bookmaking business, he'd made a huge score wagering on a longshot winner of England's Grand National Steeplechase. He'd used the winnings to buy the small shop in which he worked. Its aging owner, eager to sell and retire, had offered advice as he signed over the papers. "This is a beautiful, ould, steady business, Niall. If you don't get adventurous, or caught up in the booze or the cooz, you can't fookin' lose."

A tireless, ambitious man, Hanratty in subsequent years had expanded his holdings by opening shops in locations other bookmaking firms had avoided, or sometimes using the power of slightly veiled threats to help in the purchase of existing independent shops. There had been murmured complaints about his methods of acquisition. None hindered the growth of his thriving company. "That Hanratty, he's a hard man entirely," was whispered about him.

Niall said to Riley, "Can you tell me this, man: why are you so interested in this matter if there's no immediate return in sight?"

Riley chuckled, then began talking so softly Hanratty strained to hear him. "Your cousin Celia is a very determined person," Riley said. "She's got her heart set on keeping Monee Park going until the video slots relief arrives. But," he continued, voice even softer now, "it's quite possible she could be convinced to recognize the advantage of selling the land now. Reaping immediate profits. Profits that you, of course, would be receiving almost half of. This could conceivably happen within the next few months."

"How is it, Mr. Riley, that you know all these details about Uncle Jim's will?"

"Why, because my former partner Frank Foley wrote the will years ago. He and Jim were high school classmates."

Tony Rourke peeked his head into the office. Hanratty put his hand over the phone, and said, "Tony, be a good man now and run down to that new Starbucks and get us a couple of expensive coffees." He winked. Rourke smiled and went back out the office door.

"I take it, Mr. Riley," Hanratty said, "that you yourself would be in charge of whatever persuading that needs to be done over there."

Riley said, "That could certainly be arranged. Your cousin is a charming, smart, and very stubborn woman. She'll not just be talked off her current stance. She'll need some convincing. I've given this a great deal of thought, and I'm confident the plans I've made will get her to see the light. If you get my drift."

"Yes, counselor, I'm getting your drift. About what might that drift cost me?"

"Fifteen percent of the sale price of Monee Park," Riley shot back.

Hanratty hesitated, then said, "I'll give you ten percent of my net, Mr. Riley. And that's that. And I don't want anymore phone calls regarding your fee. My word is good. I'll be tracking your progress.

"Go on with it then, man," Hanratty said, and hung up.

Thousands of mile away, Riley smiled as he put his phone down. Born and raised in the working class Chicago neighborhood called Canaryville, he still had strong ties there even though he'd married a woman from Winnetka and had lived in that northern suburb for years. He and his wife had seven children, four of them already in college. Riley was straining to finance their educations, and this with another three to go. He'd always kept his eye out for the main chance, and in the Monee Park situation he believed he'd found it.

Although he'd moved fifteen miles and a world away from Canaryville, Riley was remembered there, both envied and respected for his departure from the insular old neighborhood where families had known each other and intermarried for generations. He knew who to call if he wanted to tap into the small talent pool of toughs always ready to create mayhem, whether they were paid for it or not.

Had Hanratty pressed him for details, Riley would have described the two young men he was now planning to contact: "Brutal bastards who don't like people, or working, but love money, especially if they've stolen it. They're tougher than your granddad's toenails," he'd have said, with a satisfied smile.

Chapter Seven

Aiden Lucarelli walked out of Ogden's Funeral Home first, a step or two in advance of Denny Shannon. From a distance the two of them, each a blocky five-foot six, wearing jackets with tavern softball team names on the back, looked almost identical. Up close, not so. Lucarelli's dark eyes were widely spaced, his complexion carrying a Mediterranean tinge. He wore his black hair slicked back and sported one of the trimmed goatee/mustache combinations favored by many Major League baseball pitchers.

Shannon's skin was the color of printer paper, his closely set light blue eyes almost slits above cheek bones that stuck out like little shelves. The two of them walked with the thigh-bulging strides of the steroid-using amateur weight lifters they were, their black half boots clicking on the pavement. They were twenty-six years old, first cousins, and best friends since first grade at Holy Rosary parochial school in Canaryville. It was at Holy Rosary that they'd early on became known as "vicious little shits," a reputation they'd done nothing to diminish in the two decades since.

Unlike many of their fellow Canaryville residents, Lucarelli and Shannon had not been granted prized employment in the City of Chicago's Department of Streets and Sanitation, notorious for its paternalism and phantom payrollers, while at the same time home to thousands of hard working citizens. "Streets and San" was replete with patronage sponsored Canaryville men, but Shannon and Lucarelli had been blackballed by the local political powers who deemed them to be too dangerous.

The cousins worked during Chicago's warm months on road construction crews. Laid off the rest of the year, they collected unemployment and indulged in pastimes that suited their personalities: house breaking and burglary in some of the ritzy Chicago suburbs, some strong arm work for a local bookie, visits to Rush Street bars where they frequently amused themselves harassing other patrons. They had been permanently barred from three such saloons thus far. The girls they'd occasionally managed to pick up in the bars and take to a nearby motel were usually naive tourists visiting the city.

Of the two, Shannon had the most severe case of class envy directed toward the well-dressed, college educated young people populating these bars and restaurants. He loved walking down the sidewalk behind women who were talking on their cell phones, brushing them with his shoulder, saying, "Let me talk to him when you're done." He had Lucarelli laughing so hard he had to hang on to a parking meter the time Shannon shouted at a startled female pedestrian whose angry phone conversation he'd interrupted, "That's right, give it to the bastard. I wouldn't take that from him, either." The woman had first regarded Shannon with astonishment. Getting an even closer look at this grinning goof who pressing his face closer to hers, his beer breath blasting, she paled and dropped her cell phone. Shannon kicked it onto Division Street before he and Lucarelli strutted away.

A few steps outside the funeral home, Lucarelli stopped to light a Marlboro. "I hate those fucking places," he said. As he waved the flame off his match, the night sky exploded six blocks to their north. "Hey, one of the Sox hit one out," Denny Shannon said, smiling, fist in the air. "Old Fuzzy would have liked that, man."

"Maybe he'll sit up in his damned chair in there," Lucarelli replied bitterly. They walked to Lucarelli's nine-year-old faded blue Taurus that sat in the middle of the small, crowded Ogden's Funeral Home parking lot. Shannon said, "Fuck's the matter with you?" Lucarelli waited until they were in the car before answering.

"The scene in there, in Ogden's. Too fuckin' weird for me, man. I hated it." Lucarelli slammed his door shut and turned on the ignition. The old motor roared to life and he pressed down hard on the accelerator as he drove north on Parnell.

Shannon sat back in the passenger seat and lighted a Pall Mall. "It didn't bother me none," he said. "I heard they wouldn't let the family set Fuzzy up like that over by McIlhenny's," the neighborhood's major funeral home. "That's why they sent him over here to Ogden's. It's new, Ogden's, they're looking for business."

The viewing they had just left was that of Howard "Fuzzy" Fitzpatrick whose liver, under heavy alcohol attack since his high school days, had finally given out on him at age fifty-seven. A lifelong White Sox fanatic, Fuzzy had celebrated in earnest the previous October when the team won its first World Series since 1917. His celebrating continued almost unabated into the following year, such dedicated drinking resulting in an even earlier death than had been anticipated by Fuzzy's family, friends, and neighbors.

At his request, Fuzzy's remains had been dressed in his regular jeans and a black 2005 Champion Chicago White Sox jersey, then placed in his favorite arm chair, hauled from the basement of his bungalow to Ogden's by dedicated fellow fans. A White Sox cap sat atop Fuzzy's head. A can of Bud Light had been taped into his left hand, a Kool affixed between rigid fingers of his right. It looked, at first glance in the funeral home, that Fuzzy could be sleeping in his basement rec room facing his wide screen TV, his head back in the chair as if, like thousands of nights in the past, he had merely passed out, not away. Mourners were taken aback when they entered the viewing room and observed this sight.

"Freaks," Lucarelli said.

"Who you talkin' about?"

"Fuzzy. Him and his crazy family that would go for a set up like that in there. The people in there gawking at him. All freaks."

Lucarelli drove on in angry silence. Shannon didn't look at him, knowing that a terrible temper eruption might be sitting precariously on his volatile cousin's emotional cusp. It was funny, Shannon sometimes thought, how alike they were, but also how different. Shannon's mom, Molly McIlhenny, was the most placid, even-tempered woman he knew—except for her sister, Bridgett, Aiden's mother. But whereas the normally laid back Shannon took after his mother's side, Aiden had inherited his close to the surface boiling point from his late father, Jimmy Lucarelli, the low level Outfit guy Bridgett McIlhenny had married much against the wishes of both sets of parents. Neighborhood people still remembered the brouhaha over Bridgett insisting on giving their only child an Irish name, Jimmy Lucarelli angrily conceding to his wife's demand, then charging outside their basement flat and destroying her car with a sledgehammer.

Shannon finally broke the silence, saying "Didn't get a chance to tell you before at Ogden's, but I got a call from Art Riley this afternoon." No response. Shannon, himself starting to get a little wound up now, said, "So, you want to hear about it or not?"

"I'm not sure," Lucarelli said, gunning through a red light at Roosevelt Road, thinking about Riley, the lawyer who had represented them in the past, the man he always referred to as Art the Fart because of a gaseous incident one afternoon in the courthouse at Twenty-sixth and California, the product of Riley's hastily consumed beer and burrito lunch across the street. The expulsion had seen Riley's fellow passengers flatten themselves against the three gray elevator walls en route to floor five.

Shannon said, "Didn't he get us off every fuckin' time? Put us on to some of our biggest scores to get the money to pay him? Am I right or am I right?"

Aiden couldn't argue with that. He and Denny had been arrested dozens of times but charged just twice, resulting in a lone assault conviction and suspended sentence for Shannon. The other assaults and the mixed bag of burglary raps they'd beaten, frequently aided by "Canaryville amnesia," a condition that overtook witnesses who lived only a few perilous blocks removed from the accused, and found themselves the targets of seriously believable threats prior to the scheduled start of trials.

Riley had been their lawyer each time and, being from the neighborhood, was an old hand at such matters. Once he'd gotten to know Aiden and Denny, Riley had been able to steer some work their way, muscle jobs involving tardy debtors in need of motivation to satisfy their obligations. Riley knew the cousins to be eager for such work. Providing these two chunky brutes with such opportunities was like waving a lamb shank in front of a pit bull.

"So, tell me what Riley wanted," Lucarelli said.

Chapter Eight

On Wednesday of his second week at Monee Park, Doyle entered the Finish Line dining room on the building's fourth floor, hungry for lunch. He'd already put in five hours of his working day, trying to get the feel of his new job. He planned to stay around until the start of that night's racing program, at 7:30, another six hours away. Doyle figured his first couple of weeks here, he'd better come in early and remain late until he'd managed to define his role to his own satisfaction and become comfortable with it.

He said hello to Marilyn, the dining room hostess, then heard himself being hailed by Steve Holland, a retired investment banker and current racehorse owner and breeder he had met at the track's opening night reception. Doyle walked to Holland's table and they shook hands. "Want to join me, Jack?" Holland said. Doyle said, "Thanks, but no. I've got some reading to do." He hefted the bulky manila envelope in his right hand.

Holland had papers spread out all over his table. He looked perplexed. "What are you working on?" Doyle said.

"I'm trying to come up with names for my yearlings. I've got six this year. And naming horses is getting harder and harder to do each year," Holland complained. "I came here to get away from the office and to get some peace and quiet while I work on this project. Maybe me doing it at a racetrack will make it inspire me. It's gotten just so darned hard."

"Why is that?"

"Look," Holland replied, "according to The Jockey Club, which is in charge of all this, you can only use eighteen letters and spaces in a horse's name. You can't use the names of past champions. You can't have two horses with the same name. You can't use commercial products—I couldn't name a horse after anything connected to my former bank. You can't use infamous persons' names. If you want to name a horse after a living person, you have to get that person's written permission. Remember, there are thousands of other breeders and owners submitting names every year. And there are 35,000 new horses to be named every year. So, you might think you've come up with a terrific name, then you're told that somebody else has already beaten you to it."

Doyle said, "It seems to me a lot of the horse namers could use some help. There's been a lot of nutty names given racehorses. Look at some of them running here tonight," he said, pointing to pages in the Monee Park track program. "The Barking Shark. What the hell kind of name is that for a thoroughbred racehorse? Formal Mouse. Rats on Ice is in the same race with Formal Mouse. Maybe we should play a rodent exacta. These are terrible names."

Holland said, "I agree. But at least those horses have names. Mine are currently incognito. And the deadline is approaching."

"I'll leave you to it," Doyle said. "Good luck."

He walked to an empty table near the window overlooking the racing strip. An aged waiter shuffled up and politely handed him a menu. Doyle ordered an iced tea before reading the menu. The waiter was one of the numerous elderly employees Doyle had noticed on his inspection of Monee Park. When he'd mentioned this to Shontanette Hunter, she said, "Oh, Mr. Joyce was very loyal to his work force. Didn't like to fire any of them if he could avoid it. That's how you wound up with Morty Dubinski," she laughed, before commenting, "We've got some real dinosaurs positioned around here."

Waiting for his tea to arrive, Doyle saw that, except for the presence of the frowning, head-scratching Steve Holland, and a table of jockeys' agents drinking coffee and playing cards, he was alone in the large, table-filled, carpeted room overlooking the track's finish line. This was where the higher level track employees took their meals during non-racing hours. As he looked out the window at the track's green infield and blue, man-made lake glistening in the sun, Doyle couldn't help but marvel at this latest chapter in his life. Here he was, after a string of well-paying, hype-laden account executive positions, two disappointing marriages, and one failed international love affair, churning out ad copy and publicity releases for a troubled racetrack on the edge of southern Cook County.

Doyle's reverie was interrupted when he looked up to see Celia McCann slipping into a chair across from him. "Do you mind if I join you, Jack?" Smiling, he said, "My pleasure." Celia was wearing a light green, short-sleeved dress, nearly the color of her eyes. The afternoon sun over her shoulder highlighted glints in her dark red hair. Doyle looked at her appreciatively.

The old waiter put a bit of a spring in his step as he approached with Doyle's iced tea wobbling on a saucer, saying, "Good afternoon, Ms. Celia." She smiled back. "Hello, Hugo. I'll have my regular."

"I'll have the same," Doyle said, and the waiter smiled and shuffled away. "By the way, Celia, what's your 'regular'?"

"It depends on the day. Wednesday and Friday, I have the Cobb salad. Thursday and Saturday, a Reuben sandwich. They're terrific. Sunday, if I have time, I zip through the buffet line. I've been coming here for years. I know what I like."

"Cobb salads, Reuben sandwiches, buffets…I'm impressed," Doyle said.

Celia cracked a breadstick in two before saying, "Impressed with what?"

"With how well you've, well, managed to stay in terrific shape." *Jesus*, Doyle thought, *you'd think I was saying something to a well-conditioned boxer instead of this beautiful woman.* Celia sensed his unease. She sat back in her chair, giving him a mischievous look. Doyle tried to rebound. "Are you musical?" he said. This was met with a puzzled look. "What with Celia being the patron saint of music," he quickly added, thinking, *I'm digging an even deeper hole.*

Celia tried to muffle a giggle before replying, "Oh, you know your saints then, do you Jack?"

"I know *of* them. Thanks to Sister Mary Theresa back at Saint Nicholas grade school. But, to my knowledge, I've never met one." He sipped his tea, relaxing a bit now.

As they waited for their food, Celia asked how Jack was adjusting to his new job. He assured her that all was going well, that he'd even made peace with, if not a friend of, his assistant Morty. Celia nodded. "I've gotten the impression that you're starting to settle in nicely here," she said.

"Well, it's early days, of course, but I think you're correct. The work interests me. I'm enjoying it. And I'm enjoying the people here, too."

Celia raised an eyebrow. "Even Morty? I know he can sometimes be difficult."

Doyle shrugged. "First day or so, it was tough going. Morty's got a bit of an inferiority complex, it seems to me, that makes him both resentful and kind of hostile at times. And he's a terrible dresser. But Morty's actually not such a bad little guy. Once in awhile, I'll look over and see him struggling to finish some simple assignment I've given him, and I can't help but think he's often out of his league in life. But he tries hard.

"I'm a little concerned about Morty's betting. I know what his salary is. Seems to me he's got a good chunk of it riding every night. And not riding very well."

Celia said, "Oh, I wouldn't worry about that, Jack. Morty's been a bettor all the time I've known hm. He's a bachelor, living at home with his mother, so he doesn't have much in the way of expenses. Betting horses is his major interest. He just enjoys it."

Doyle drained his glass of iced tea. "You'd know better than me. Anyway, he and I are getting along okay. I've worked with far worse people than Morty Dubinski, I can guarantee you that."

As they lunched, Doyle did one of the things that he did best: ask questions, all the while looking sincerely interested in the answers, which in this case he actually was. He learned where and when Celia had met her husband Bob, details of her long friendship with Shontanette Hunter. Working backward, he asked Celia about her college years. "I had a wonderful experience at St. Mary's," she said. "And after graduation, I taught third grade for three years. That still left me free to help Uncle Jim here at the track during the summers."

"Ah," Doyle said, "an elementary school teacher. Usually one of the gentler souls. Excellent Cobb salad, by the way," he remarked before asking, "How did you happen to switch from blackboards to odds boards? Why a career as a racing executive?"

"It was because of Uncle Jim. His health was deteriorating rapidly. I knew that the track, and he, were in financial trouble. He'd put most of his money into it." She turned her face away, glancing out the window. "I owe him so much," she said. "He practically raised me, paid for all my education, doted on me, spoiled me. I couldn't have wished for a kinder, more generous relative. When I saw that he needed my help, there was no way I was not going to give it to him. So, the racetrack became my career."

The waiter placed the bill at Celia's elbow. She scribbled her signature on it. "Thanks, Hugo," she said. "Thank you, Ms. Celia," Hugo said, eyes alight as they spotted the generous tip.

Celia turned back to Jack. "You know, it all went well for a few years. I liked the work. Uncle Jim was both appreciative of my efforts and generous with his time in teaching me the workings of the track. And Bob, well, he was extremely supportive. His insurance business was going well. We built a new house. I wasn't home as much as during the years that I taught school, but Bob was very understanding. And we started thinking about planning a family."

She paused, mouth slightly trembling before continuing. "Track business started to pick up. Things were looking great. Then Bob started showing signs of illness. He stopped playing pick up basketball games at our health club. He cut back on his golf, then stopped completely. I could see all these changes, how, suddenly, he'd fall into these morose periods. I'd ask him what was going on and, for the first time since I'd known him, he said 'I don't want to talk about it right now.' Finally, one morning when we were having breakfast, he said, 'Celia, there's something seriously wrong with my body. I've got to find out what it is.'

"I could hardly believe my ears. This big, strong, vibrant guy who had never been sick a minute in all the years I'd known him, all of a sudden hit by one of the cruelest diseases there is. We got second and third opinions, but there was no getting around the fact that the initial diagnosis was correct. Bob has Lou Gehrig's disease.

"That was a little more than two years ago. Our lives have never been the same since. They never will be."

There was a long silence. Doyle hated it. He said, "Celia, I can't imagine how hard this all must be. Dealing with your husband's illness on top of running this racetrack."

"Nobody ever said it was going to be easy, Jack Doyle," she said. "Not my parents before they were taken from me. Not the nuns. Not Uncle Jim. Not anybody I knew."

She took a sip of her coffee. "Actually, my job here has been a blessing in a way. I set my own hours, so I can spend as much time with Bob as need be. At the same time, it serves to distract me from concentrating full time on his horribly progressive decline. A double-edged blessing I guess you'd call it." She gave a short, bitter laugh.

"Irony," she said, "it seems my life is thick with it."

"How so?"

Celia said, "Another woman track executive I know—there aren't many of us—once compared the sexes when it comes to positions of power. I'll never forget what she said. 'If a man in the position does his job correctly and efficiently, he's considered a strong administrator. Women handling the same assignment exactly the same way are considered bitches.' Unfortunately, I've found her to be correct when it comes to a lot of people I've had dealings with in this business."

For a moment she looked so dejected that Doyle almost reached across the table to take her hand. But then she shook her head, as if shrugging off a punch. "Enough of my war stories."

"All right," Doyle said. "But I'd like to ask you something. How have you kept on fighting to keep the track going, following your uncle's wish, with all you have to deal with concerning your husband?"

"Oh, it's not just a selfless act of obligation to Uncle Jim's memory. Bob and I need the money from this place. Bob will never work again. A teacher's salary wouldn't begin to cover our expenses, not with his medical bills. His health insurance is not adequate. It's like the physician who keels over, never having had a physical. Bob was in the insurance business, but was badly underinsured himself for health problems. Another sad irony.

"But," she added confidently, "this track will eventually make a lot of money. It'll be very, very profitable once the video slots bill passes. That's what we're counting on."

"Aren't you tempted just to sell the place?" Doyle said. "You'd come out well financially, there's no doubt about that."

"Sure, I'm tempted," she said, her green eyes flashing. "And my cousin Niall, the minority shareholder, would love to have me do it. But I look at that as a giving in, a surrender. Maybe I am, as some people have said, too stubborn. But selling this property for real estate development would go against Uncle Jim's wishes. It would disrespect his memory. And it would be an admission of defeat. I'd be seen in some quarters as being incapable of running a racetrack. I'm not going to give in to that temptation, no matter how my cousin in Ireland feels about it."

She glanced at her watch. "I have a 2:30 appointment," she said as she stood up, adding, "It was very nice talking to you, Jack." She swiftly walked toward the door, his eyes on her. "Beauty and acuity," he said to himself, "all in one choice package."

Hugo the waiter brought Doyle out of his reverie when he came to clear away the dishes. He was at the same time also watching Celia move off, a fond look on his creased old face. When the door closed behind her, Doyle said to Hugo, "So, you've known Ms. McCann a long time?"

"Most of her life and a good portion of mine," Hugo said. "A lovely, lovely woman."

"You'll get no argument from me on that."

Chapter Nine

Minutes before Saturday night's seventh race, Morty said, "Take a look at the No. 6 horse in here. Rambling Rosie."

Doyle looked down at the track from his press box window where number six, a copper colored chestnut filly, was prancing toward the starting gate, swishing her tail, bobbing her head, obviously feeling good. Doyle opened his *Racing Daily* for a look at the filly's credentials. Examining her pedigree, he remarked, "She's by Nothing out of Nothing." Her sire had won just two races in his life, her dam none, though both were themselves products of high class parents.

"Yeah," Morty said, "but she's won five straight races while climbing straight up the class ladder. She's special fast. Believe me."

Doyle closely examined Rambling Rosie's past performances. She had lost her only two starts as a two-year-old the previous season. This year, as Doyle commented with a smile, she'd been "a horse of a different choler." After winning for the first time in a $10,000 maiden claiming event, Rosie had scored for $20,000, then $30,000. Moved up into allowance company, from which she could not be claimed, or bought, she had reeled off another pair of easy wins. All of her victories had come at sprint distances: five furlongs, five and a half, then six furlongs.

"Who's this Tom Eckrosh? The guy who owns and trains her," Doyle said.

"You never heard of old Tom? He's been around the racetrack almost all of his life, and he's nearly eighty now. He served in the Army during World War II, was a jockey for awhile after he got out of the service, then took up training. He's raced mainly here at Monee during the summers, then New Orleans in the winters. Never had a real top horse, but he's always had some useful runners. But he'll tell you Rambling Rosie is the best he's ever had his hands on. He claimed her for $8,000 at Devon Downs in southern Illinois late last year. She'd lost her only two races. What he saw in her, with that obscure pedigree, I do not know. But he saw something. Can she run!" Morty enthused. "I understand old Tom has turned down some big bucks for her. I mean major, major money."

Doyle said, "But he won't sell?"

"He will not. One day, I asked him why. He said, 'Morty, at my age, what would I do with all that money? I waited a long, long time for a horse like Rosie. I'm going to keep her all for myself.' And, you know, I can see his point," Morty said.

Doyle glanced at the in-house television, which had zeroed in on Rambling Rosie as she moved toward the starting gate. "Uh oh," he said. "She's got four white feet."

"So what?" Morty said.

"Don't you know the old racetrack saying about a horse with white feet? I heard it more than once when I was working at a breeding farm down in Kentucky."

Doyle immediately regretted mentioning that segment of his career when Morty responded, "You did? When was that?"

"A year or so ago. It's a long story. But this is my point. The saying goes

Two white feet, try him.
Three white feet, deny him.
Four white feet and
A white nose,
Feed him to the crows."

Morty said, "Well, Rambling Rosie doesn't have any white on her nose. And when you see here four white feet flying over this track, you'll forget about that old saying. Wait and see."

"Did you bet her?"

"Naw," Morty said. "I never bet favorites."

They walked out onto the press box porch to watch the seventh race. A field of eight was led into the starting gate. Rambling Rosie was the even-money favorite. As soon as the bell rang and the gate opened, she shot to the lead. After a quarter mile, she was three lengths in front of her nearest pursuer. Turning into the homestretch, she had opened up by five lengths and was apparently going easily. Her jockey, Ramon Garcia, wrapped up on her during the final sixteenth of a mile. Throttling down her speed, Garcia hand rode her under the wire to a three-length victory. Her time of 1:09 3-5 was only a fifth of a second off the Monee Park record. Rambling Rosie came bouncing back to the winner's circle amid waves of applause from happy bettors.

Doyle said, "Wow! I'm impressed. She put on quite a show." He watched as Garcia, grinning, talked excitedly to a short, stockily built, brown-skinned woman who clipped a shank onto Rambling Rosie's halter and was leading her into the winner's circle. The woman wore a gray sweatshirt, blue jeans, and a broad, white smile. She turned Rambling Rosie toward the waiting track photographer just as an elderly man approached. "That's Tom Eckrosh," Morty said. Eckrosh was dressed in khaki pants, a blue and white checked shirt, and a threadbare navy blue sport coat. He wore a battered gray fedora which, Doyle was to learn, was his ever present head piece. Eckrosh exhibited none of the jubilation evidenced by jockey Garcia and the female groom.

"Why is Eckrosh so glum?" Doyle said. "You'd think he'd be pretty damn happy, the way his filly ran tonight."

Morty said, "He probably is happy, but he'd never let on. That's just his way. He's a pretty nice fellow, once you get to know him."

"How long does that take?"

"Oh, not more than five or ten years," Morty said as he opened the press box door.

Doyle said, "I think I'll start with him tomorrow morning. His filly makes a heck of a good story for Monee Park."

It was just after seven on a beautiful, late spring morning when the clatter of feed buckets, chatter of workers, and the music blaring from one of Chicago's Spanish-speaking AM stations greeted Doyle as he walked the dusty path between Barns C and D on the Monee Park backstretch. He was on his way to meet Tom Eckrosh. Monee Park's racing secretary Gary Gabriel had informed him that "Old Tom is stabled in Barn D," but Gabriel hadn't told him the Eckrosh stable stall numbers in the long wooden building that housed more than a hundred horses for various trainers. Doyle did not speak Spanish, so he passed by several Mexican grooms and hotwalkers without attempting an inquiry. He walked on until he recognized Alex Graff, a young trainer he'd met, to ask exactly where Eckrosh was located. "At the end of the barn, on the opposite side," Graff said. "That's where you'll find Grouchy," he added with a smile.

Walking past the section of Barn C where Kristina Jenkins' horses were stabled, Jack waved to the trainer. He had met Kristina earlier in the meeting at a breakfast the track hosted for all the trainers with horses on Monee grounds. Jenkins was currently third in the trainer standings. Kristina was Monee Park's version of Maggie Collins, the similarly young horsewoman who annually ranked high at Heartland Downs the other side of Chicago. Doyle was suddenly brought up short by something he heard. He stopped and looked back. Kristina nodded to him but continued talking on her cell phone, undoubtedly to one of the two dozen or so owners she trained for. It hadn't been Kristina's voice that made Jack halt in his tracks. It was what he thought was the bleating of a goat.

Sure enough, there in stall twenty-one, standing beneath the outstretched head of Jenkins' best runner, Wicklow Brian, was a small, dirty-white, male goat, replete with horns and a bell that was tinkling rhythmically. Wicklow Brian and the goat were swaying from side to side, in unison, the big brown thorough-bred dwarfing his bearded companion poised under him. Doyle stared at them. Jenkins clicked off her phone and walked over to Doyle. "Isn't that something?" she said ruefully.

Jack said, "What the hell's going on with these two?"

Kristina said, "Wicklow Brian is a weaver." Seeing the puzzled expression on Doyle's face, she went to explain that "It's a nervous habit some horses develop. Not very many, thank heavens, but some. Instead of standing still they move, or weave, shifting their weight from side to side. They do it hour after hour, day after day."

"What's the problem with that?"

Kristina said, "It's an energy waster. Why would you want your horse to be wasting energy he could be using in a race?"

"Well, I guess you wouldn't. But what's the deal with shorty there, the goat?"

"Actually," Kristina said, "his name is Sylvester. He's a fairly friendly little creature. I bought him because usually the presence of a goat can calm down nervous horses like Wicklow Brian. Get them to stop their weaving. Horses and goats get along great, as you can see. Look how contented they look," she said resignedly.

"The problem here," Kristina continued, "is that Sylvester not only didn't get Wicklow Brian to stop his darned weaving, Wicklow Brian has now got Sylvester weaving right along with him."

They turned to look again at this synchronized odd couple.

"You trainers have to put up with some of the damndest things," Doyle said.

"Tell me about it," Kristina said.

Fifty yards from Kristina's barn, Doyle saw a Mexican woman meticulously raking the dirt in front of the five stalls assigned to horses trained by Tom Eckrosh. He recognized her as Rambling Rosie's groom, the woman he had seen in the winner's circle the previous night. She was working her rake around some sparkling clean water buckets that had been set out to dry in the morning sun. Geranium baskets hung overhead, attached under the barn eaves. Doyle could hear the hum of an electric fan in one of the horse's stalls. The woman wore a gray tee-shirt, jeans, white running shoes. She was humming softly to herself as she worked. The muscles in her brown forearms stood out like cords as she moved the rake.

"Excuse me," Doyle said. "Miss?"

The woman, deep in thought, looked up, startled, the long, dark braid down her back swinging as she turned to face him. "Yes?"

"*Buenos dias,*" Doyle said. "I'm looking for Mr. Eckrosh."

"Oh," the woman replied, her brown face transformed by a bright smile. "*Buenos dias. Si*, Mr. Tom is there in his office at the end of the barn," she said, motioning with the hand not holding the rake handle. "He may be taking a small siesta. Knock on the door, *por favor.*"

Doyle said, "*Gracias,*" and nodded at the watchful horses, heads sticking out over their stall doors, as he passed them on his way to the far end of the barn.

Eckrosh was awake when Jack poked his head in the doorway. He looked up at Doyle through thick bifocals, his battered fedora on his head. He had his feet up on the corner of the desk atop an old copy of *Racing Daily* and was busy fitting together a piece of horse equipment. He waited for Doyle to speak. "I'm Jack Doyle, Mr. Eckrosh. What's that you're working on?"

Eckrosh said, "It's a bit. A special one. I use it on my old hard headed gelding Editorialist. It's called a Springsteen bit. You don't see them around much anymore."

Doyle laughed. "A Springsteen bit? Not named after 'The Boss,' I guess."

Eckrosh frowned. "Whose boss? This here item is for horses with real hard jaws. There's a spoon-shaped prong that jabs the horse's jaw when he lugs in or bears out. It works pretty good on Editorialist. He's brought a check back every time I've run him this year. What did you say again about somebody's boss?"

Doyle sidestepped having to explain his reference to rock star Bruce Springsteen, instead using the next few minutes to present his reasons for wanting to interview Eckrosh and write about his sensational filly. "Rambling Rosie could provide a pretty good publicity boost for this track, which certainly needs it," he said. Eckrosh listened intently. Finally, he said, "Okay." He got up from behind his desk. "How long you been working here, son?" Doyle said "a little more than three weeks." Eckrosh nodded. He said, "You want to see Rosie?"

Eckrosh led the way to the second stall from the end of the barn. The groom had finished her raking and was sitting on an equipment trunk, cleaning a bridle. The trainer said to Jack, "This is Maria Martinez." Doyle smiled at her, adding, "We've already met." She nodded. Eckrosh said, "Maria, bring out Rosie." Doyle thought he saw Eckrosh give her a wink. Does this old fart have something going with the senorita? He wondered. Maria, looking slightly embarrassed and struggling to hide a smile, got to her feet and entered the stall. Seconds later she led out a tall brown animal that whinnied with delight at being released from his twenty-two hour per day confinement. Doyle could feel the eyes of Eckrosh and Maria trained on him as he appraised this gawky creature.

"Nice," Doyle said, and Eckrosh nodded expectantly, trying to keep a straight face. "Nice try, that is." Doyle kicked at the dirt. "Jesus, Eckrosh," he said, "I may have been born at night, but it wasn't last night. I'm not a racetrack lifer like you, but I've been around enough to tell a six or seven-year-old gelding from a three-year-old filly. Why are you trying to pass off this sickle hocked old item as Rambling Rosie?"

The old man's face flushed. Marie turned the horse around and led him back into his stall, her eyes averted. Eckrosh said, "Now, don't get all huffy, son. I just wanted to see if you knew which end was which. I've had writers coming around here the last few years, bothering me, that couldn't pick out Secretariat in a herd of buffalo. They're annoying as hell. They read their damned statistics sheets, and past performances, and figure they know horses and horse racing. I just wanted to see if you were one of that crowd." He paused before admitting, "You know more than I was about to give you credit for."

With another signal to Maria, out came Rambling Rosie, nickering and nudging the groom's shoulder. Maria led her out of the barn a few feet onto the grassy patch that bordered the building. She turned the filly around for Doyle, who looked her over from head to toe. The first impression he had was how small she was. Eckrosh must have expected that reaction, for he said, "She can't weigh more than eight hundred and fifty pounds, a couple hundred less than your average horse. And," he went on, "usually your top horses are the tall, big-bodied ones. But there are exceptions to every rule. And you're looking at one of them," Eckrosh said proudly. Doyle was making notes as the trainer continued his assessment. "When you look at her, nothing really stands out except her head and eye. She's got a very intelligent eye. But then you look again and you see, even though she's on the small side, everything she's got is in balance. She's the quickest horse I've ever had. That, and her will to win, is what makes her stand out."

Doyle patted the friendly filly on her neck. He didn't have to reach up to do it. "I don't even think she's fifteen hands tall, is she?" he said. "Probably not," Eckrosh said. "But I've never measured her."

Doyle smiled and made another note. "The 'Pocket Battleship.' That'll be a good nickname for her." He saw what he thought was an actual smile on the old trainer's face. "C'mon into the office," Eckrosh said gruffly. "I see you know something about what you're doing. At my age, I don't have time to put up with nitwits."

Doyle said, "How old are you?"

"None of your business."

"Great," Doyle said, "a publicity man's dream." Eckrosh pretended he hadn't heard that.

An hour later Doyle had Eckrosh's story, or at least enough for that day's purposes. Eckrosh, he'd learned, had started as a teenager on a small racetrack in his native Nebraska. "I was a jockey, and a lousy one," Eckrosh said. "Then I got too big to ride anyway, and I switched to grooming horses for a great trainer out there named Marion H. Van Berg. A few years later, I went out on my own. I've had horses now for more than fifty years. Rambling Rosie is twenty lengths better than any one I had before.

"Yes, I was married," Eckrosh said in response to Doyle's question. "My wife worked with me for years. Died of a heart attack right here at Monee Park five summers ago. Never sick a day in her life," he said bitterly. Eckrosh clammed up after that statement, and Doyle clicked off his tape recorder and put his notebook in his pocket. Then he thought to ask, "How many people do you have working here?"

"Two. And I'm one of them. The woman out there, Maria, she's the other one. Hell of a worker. Takes care of all five horses I've got and turns them out happy, healthy, shiny, and relaxed. I couldn't get along without her. Before Rambling Rosie started earning some good purse money, I couldn't have afforded any other workers. Now that I can, Maria says, 'No, you don't have to get no more. I can do this job.' And she can.

"I'll tell you, son, she's a hard working, honest person who's damned good with horses. She doesn't drink, she's here early and smiling every morning, and she doesn't mind working late. You know how hard it is to find somebody like that these days? I don't care that she's a woman, or a Mex, or any of that crap. Plus," Eckrosh admitted, "I have a hard time keeping help. I'm kind of tough on them if they don't do things the right way."

Doyle smiled as he said, "Old school?"

"Old school, hell," Eckrosh growled. "Just do it right is all I ask. My horses deserve that. So do I."

Doyle said, "I'd like to talk to Maria, get some background on her."

"She's not much of a talker," Eckrosh said. "Besides," he said, looking at his watch, "she's gone by now. She goes home to make an early lunch for her kids before coming back here in the afternoon. She lives about a mile down the road, in that trailer park."

"Can you tell me anything about her? Where she's from? How she got started on the racetrack?"

Eckrosh shook his head. "It's up to her to tell you about herself, not me. Come back some other morning."

It wasn't until the following Monday that Doyle could fit another visit to the Eckrosh barn into his schedule. In the meantime, he'd done some research. He'd found that the backstretches of American racetracks dramatically reflect the tremendous recent influx of Hispanics into the U. S. population. His interview subject that morning, Maria Martinez, was part of a Chicago racetrack work force that now was more than ninety percent Hispanic, more than half of them women, many with families.

Monee Park provided rudimentary housing for some of these workers; others lived in cheap apartments nearby, or rented in the trailer court. Grooms earned an average of $325 a week—"Jesus," Doyle said to himself, "that's not even minimum wage with these hours they put in"—and worked six days a week. At Monee, they started their jobs at six, continued until late morning, then were off until the races began that night if the horses they groomed were entered to run. If so, they would usually remain at the track until nearly midnight. Then, it was back to work by six o'clock the next morning. Doyle shuddered at the thought of such a schedule.

Walking past Tom Eckrosh's office, Doyle waved a hello. The old man grumped an inaudible reply. Doyle found Maria at the end of the shed row, feeding carrots to Rambling Rosie. Marie agreed to sit down with him at a nearby picnic bench. She brought with her two exercise riders' saddles, a tin of saddle soap, and some rags. She worked while she talked, first softly and haltingly, then more openly. Doyle found that the less he said, the more Maria told him things he wanted to know.

Maria hailed, she said, from Guerrero, Mexico. Twelve years earlier, she'd snuck across the border to Tucson with a cousin, leaving her two young children at home with her mother. "I never went to school," she said. "I don't know how to read. I struggled a lot in Mexico. That's why I decided to come here. My husband never helped me at all with the kids before he just went away one day and never came back. He was a bum most his life, drinking and gambling and all that. When I left Mexico in 1994 I had to leave my children behind. I brought them here five years later. My son was a month-old baby when I left. That was very hard for me. But we had no money. I had to find a way to get money. I listened to what people told me about jobs in America."

After arriving in Arizona, Maria said, she and her cousin made their way to Florida "to work in the fields. I worked on picking tomatoes, picking cucumbers, sweet peppers, squash, picking watermelon. The work is very hard, and it's very hot there. I started at seven in the morning, and one day I didn't drink any water until one in the afternoon, just so I don't waste time. I was running all the time. When I finally went for a glass of water, I fell down. At 2:30 in the afternoon, I woke up in the hospital. They took me there from work, half dead. Ever since, I've been bothered by the heat."

Doyle said, "What brought you to Chicago?"

She gave him a quizzical look. "The bus."

"No," he laughed, "I mean, why did you come here? What made you decide to work at the racetrack?"

"Oh," Maria smiled, "I know what you mean. Okay, there was some people from Florida who were coming here, a family also from Guerrero. They came to Monee Park because they had friends working here. I came with them. First, I worked for a man, a very bad man I did not like, for a long time. Then one of my cousins brought my children to me one summer. That was the same summer I got a job here with Mr. Tom. He is a good man to work for," she beamed, "a very good man."

Maria had been rubbing saddle soap into a bridle as she talked, her dark head down, but she looked up when she talked about Eckrosh. "I was a hot walker for this other bad trainer, and I finally quit one day because he was so mean. To me, to his horses. My friend told me Mr. Tom needed a groom. I went and talked to Mr. Tom and told him I could be one, that I was a hard worker. He said, 'Okay, we'll see. You start tomorrow.' I was very happy to get a job with him. He has taught me much about horses."

She leaned forward. "He pays me more than other grooms get paid, I know that," she confided. "And I get a bonus when Rosie wins.

"I get to the barn at 5:30 every morning. I come shouting to my fillies and my horses, 'Mama' to the fillies, 'Papa' to the horses. I teach my horses to be very gentle. I like them as though they were my children."

Doyle was curious about Maria's status as an immigrant. Did she have permanent resident status, as some backstretchers did, or was she like many others, an "illegal," living under the constant threat of an INS raid? He was reluctant to ask her, but she saved him the trouble. "I have a green card," she said proudly. "Mr. Tom helped me get it. And both my children are doing very well in school here.

"I don't know much except about horses," Maria added, "and I wanted my children to learn, and they are learning. My life was very hard, but I thank God I am here."

Chapter Ten

Art Riley had provided them with a detailed plan of Monee Park in a meeting at his downtown office. His instructions to Aiden Lucarelli and Denny Shannon were simple. The equipment they would need for the assignment they already possessed.

Following the floor plan, the two men easily located the locked door that led to the Monee Park money room. This large space, at the rear of the first floor grandstand area, was, as they had been advised by Riley, unguarded from the outside. It contained large amounts of cash, the difference between what people bet on the races and what they won. At the end of each night of racing, a security firm truck picked up what was not needed for the next night and brought it to the bank.

Producing this money was the eighteen to twenty-five percent deducted from each buck bet, depending on whether it was a "straight" wager (win, place, show) or an "exotic" bet (exacta, trifecta, superperfecta, pick four). From this "bite" the track paid horsemen's purses, taxes to the state of Illinois, and covered operating expenses. Many bettors were unaware that the track owners don't give a hoot what horses win the races. The bettors are in competition with each other under this pari-mutuel system, with the track taking out the same percentages regardless of whether favorites or long shots win. On any given night at Monee Park, the money room housed hundreds of thousands of dollars in cash.

Lucarelli and Shannon spent nearly two hours that Friday night in a bar across from the steel door of the money room, an area termed the Winners' Lounge. They watched as a variety of pari-mutuel employees, carrying cloth bags of cash collected from the mutuel windows around the building, walked to the door, pressed a buzzer to the right side of the door frame, and were immediately admitted. They emerged minutes later, their bags empty.

Nursing only his second Bud Light of the night—he had to be at the top of his game for this—Shannon said softly, "They're fucking asking for it. The guards must be inside."

"Guard," Lucarelli said. "That's what Riley found out. One guard, for all that money. They've never had a robbery, and they must think they never will." He laughed as he lighted a Marlboro. They were standing at an island table in the rear corner of the small room. An opened copy of *Racing Daily* was laid out in front of them alongside a track program. They looked like engaged bettors. Underneath the table was a brown satchel, the kind that some serious horse players brought with them on track visits, containing statistics, charts of past races, notes they'd made, graphs of recent betting trends. This satchel was empty. Lucarelli looked at his watch, then up at the television screens on the wall behind the nearly empty wooden bar. Horses were parading postward for the sixth race of the night. "When this race goes off," he murmured to Shannon.

Seven minutes later, an elderly mutuel department employee named Ray Lokvam stepped out of the elevator some thirty feet from the money room door. He carried a bulging cloth bag over his shoulder and was struggling under the weight of it. Lucarelli and Shannon quietly fell in behind him. As Lokvam tapped the buzzer, they took ski masks out of their dark windbreakers and yanked them over their faces, Lucarelli finishing first, then reaching for his pistol. The door began to open. Lucarelli moved forward and shoved Lokvam through it. Shannon followed, slamming the door closed behind him.

On an old wooden chair propped against the right wall, security guard Paxton Brownlee looked up in astonishment at the two masked men. Before he could move, Lucarelli was on him. He smashed Brownlee across the right side of his head with the gun barrel, sending him crashing to the floor. Lucarelli turned to survey the ceiling of the small room, swinging his gun from one corner to the next. "Not a fucking security camera in here either," he said with satisfaction, having confirmed Riley's prediction. "Talk about running a place on the cheap."

Lucarelli reached down and yanked Brownlee's revolver from its holster. He tossed it to Shannon, who had backed the bewildered Lokvam against the wall and sat him down next to the unconscious, bleeding Brownlee. Shannon waved the gun under Lokvam's trembling chin. "Turn to the wall, you old fart. Quick!" Lokvam paled, sweat popping out on his wrinkled forehead. He moved to obey. Shannon took handcuffs from Brownlee's belt and roughly put them on Lokvam. "Sit on the floor, facing that wall," he ordered.

Lucarelli had vaulted over the long wooden counter to the aisle fronting shelves stacked with currency. The shortest shelf was packed with $50 and $100 bills. He concentrated on it, shoveling packets into the brown satchel, glancing at his watch, saying "thirty more seconds and we're out of here." Shannon grunted his assent, keeping his eye on Brownlee, who was still out. When he noticed Lokvam trying to look over his shoulder at them, Shannon shoved the old man's face against the wall. He looked at his watch. Then he brought the butt of the gun down on Lokvam's head. The old man crumpled onto his side.

At the door, satchel in Lucarelli's hand, they ripped off their ski masks and put them in their pockets. Shannon peered out. No one was close. The small group of patrons of the Winners' Lounge, as well as the bartender, had their eyes riveted on the televised showing of the seventh race. None of them took their eyes off the screen as, heads averted, Lucarelli and Shannon, Lucarelli with the heavy, money-filled brown satchel, hurried out of Monee Park's east grandstand exit to the parking lot. Three minutes later Lucarelli's Taurus was on the nearby highway, heading north to Chicago. The car jerked from side to side as the two men high-fived each other repeatedly, hollering in triumph. They didn't start to count the money until a half-hour later when they sat at the scruffy old poker table in the paneled basement of Lucarelli's mother's home, open cans of beer in front of them. When the count was completed, their high-fiving resumed.

Chapter Eleven

Word of the money room robbery was all over Monee Park the next morning, most of which Doyle spent on the phone, answering questions from various media outlets. He assured one and all that, despite this damaging incident, the track would be "open for business as usual tonight."

During a brief lull between calls, Morty said, "Jack, how will there be enough money here to operate tonight? From all I've heard, the track is pretty strapped for cash. And credit, for that matter."

Doyle said, "You've heard right. Celia told me a couple of hours ago that her bank won't give her a short term loan even at a larcenous rate. Her equity line is stretched. The thieves got away with $127,000. That doesn't sound like a lot to me when you think of a racetrack's holdings. But, and this is just between you and me, Celia said she's already scraped the bottom of the financial barrel. She's in a tough spot."

Morty scratched his head. "So, where's the money coming from?"

"A friend of mine," Doyle said. "That's all I can tell you."

Doyle had phoned Moe Kellman at his north Michigan Avenue penthouse just before midnight, or two hours after he'd learned of the money room robbery.

Trying to jocularly ease his way toward his request, Doyle had said, "How are you fixed for cash?"

"Comfortably. Why are you calling me at this hour to ask?"

Doyle told Moe what had happened, describing the alarming consequences facing Monee Park. When he'd finished, there was a short silence on the other end of the line. Then Moe said, "Any idea who pulled this off?"

"Not a clue. The money room guards said there were two guys, short, husky, wearing ski masks. And brutal. They gave our men a pretty good going over."

Moe said, "This couldn't have happened at a worse time. The proposed video slots bill won't mean anything to Celia if she doesn't have an operating racetrack in order to qualify for the license. Jack, hold on a minute. I've got to go into my den."

When Moe picked up the phone in the den he said, "I'll call Celia in the morning. Later this morning, I should say. You tell her my driver, Pete Dunleavy, will be bringing her a briefcase around noon. Tell her this is a loan, interest free, from me to her. Nothing on paper. Just the way her Uncle Jim and I used to do business in the old days. Naturally, I'll expect to be paid back once the video slots get up and going."

"You know," Doyle reminded, "what Celia needs is nearly a hundred and thirty grand."

Moe sighed. "Jack, I'm neither deaf, nor forgetful. You already told me that. What I am, though, is tired. Have Celia call me after she gets the money from Pete. Good night, Jack."

Pete Dunleavy was on time and Celia immediately called Jack to let him know the briefcase had arrived. "God bless Moe Kellman," she said. "And thank you, Jack, for thinking Moe would help. I'll call Moe right now."

The press box clock showed 12:11 p.m. He heard Morty say, "Jack, I'm hungry. How about some lunch?" Doyle stood up, stretched, and reached for his sport coat. "Sounds good. Lead the way."

"Follow me. I'll introduce you to the best chef in the Midwest."

Doyle stopped walking. He said, "Morty, I haven't got time to drive into the city. I've got a busy afternoon."

Morty laughed. "We don't have to go into Chicago. We're going right downstairs to the jockeys' room kitchen. I'll introduce you to the great Clarence Meaux."

In the elevator, Morty said "Clarence is a retired jockey from Louisiana. I guess he was a pretty good little rider as a kid. Then he got too big, too heavy. You're not going to believe it when you see him, but Clarence won more races than any apprentice rider in the country when he was sixteen. That was twenty or so years ago. He rode at a hundred and eight pounds and won more than 300 races. Today, he weighs about one-eighty. He loves to eat. He carries the evidence of that around on him," Morty laughed.

They entered through the jockeys' room side door, passing the pool and ping pong tables and the exercise room with its tread mills, cycles, bar bells, weight machines, and jump ropes. Several riders were working out on the equipment. More were lounging on couches, reading *Racing Daily*, or watching television. Others were gathered around a card table where an intense game of Racetrack Rummy was underway, comments loudly being offered not only by participants ("You still the sucker you always been, Julian,") but also by onlookers ("Aw, shit, don't do that, man.")

There was a lunch counter with a half-dozen stools at the rear of the large room. Two wooden tables were placed near the south wall, each with four chairs. Behind the counter was a large refrigerator, two sinks, and a sizeable grill, in front of which sat a short, stocky man with black, slicked-back hair and a pencil thin mustache. Morty said, "Dammit, Clarence, ever since you grew that 'stache you're looking more and more like a Bourbon Street pimp. What's today's special?"

Clarence Meaux uncrossed his arms and extended a hand. "You must be Mr. Doyle, the publicity guy. You have my sympathies," he smiled, " having to work with Mr. Morty here." He turned to Morty and said "Crawfish étouffée." Doyle noticed two young apprentices sitting on stools at the end of the counter. "They're liking it," Meaux said, as the weight conscious youngsters ate slowly from small cups containing the rich food. "I won't serve them boys more than that," Meaux said. "No need for them to eat their way out of a job like I did."

Once Jack and Morty were seated at one of the tables, Meaux brought over their orders of the day's special in large bowls, accompanied by a plate of hot French bread. "Baked it just a bit ago," Meaux said. "Can't let these jocks see or smell it, though, it'd drive them crazy."

Doyle dipped his spoon into the steaming étouffée. He said, "Clarence, this is terrific. Where'd you learn to cook like this?"

"Down home in New Iberia," Meaux replied. "Nearly everybody around there can cook. After my apprentice year was over, I rode three more years, starving myself, winning just a few dozen races every year, and getting heavier all the time. You remember years ago that old Boston Red Sox pitcher name of Frank Sullivan, or O'Sullivan? I heard he talked about himself one time as being 'in the twilight of a mediocre career.' One of them northern jockey agents told me that. Cracked me up. I knew exactly what that pitcher meant. I wasn't going nowhere anymore as a rider. So I hung up my tack, started hanging around the New Orleans Fair Grounds. Made a little money putting on crawfish boils and barbeques on the backstretch on weekends. Then one day, Mr. Louie LaCombe, he ran the track then, told me they needed a man to do the cooking in the jocks' room. Was I interested? Damn right! I work Fair Grounds in the winters, then come up here to Monee in the summers. Want some more étouffée?"

Doyle said he would if he could, "But I'm full. It was great. I'll have to put in an extra hour in the gym tomorrow to make up for it." Morty said, "I wouldn't mind." Meaux got up and went behind the counter.

"Clarence is a good guy," Morty said appreciatively. "And you should taste some of the other stuff he makes when he's in the mood. Not just the crawfish étouffée, like today, but things like peppered shrimp, one of the best things I've ever had. And he's always got a great pot of gumbo on the simmer back there."

Meaux had overheard Morty. Placing the étouffée in front of Morty and sitting down at the table again, he said, "Special occasions I maybe do some catfish remoulade, crawfish casserole, maybe creole chicken…."

Doyle said, "Clarence, I've got to get on your mailing list."

Meaux sat back in his chair, obviously pleased. He patted his rounded, white aproned stomach. "You like all that stuff?"

"I surely do."

"Good," Meaux said. "I'll let you know next time I put together a little feast down here. Course," he added, winking at Morty but so Jack could see it, "you got to be prepared to eat, well, a lot of things. Am I right, Mr. Morty?"

Morty laughed before dipping another piece of the hot bread into his now nearly empty étouffée bowl. "Tell Jack that Cajun story you always tell people," Morty said.

Leaning back expansively, rounded midsection straining the white apron, Meaux said, "This baby crawfish is out walkin' with his mamma along a ditch outside New Iberia. The baby crawfish goes on ahead, but pretty quick he comes flyin' back down the ditch to mama. She says to him, 'What's the matter?' He says, 'Look at the big thing over there!' Mama says, 'Don't worry none about that, no. It's just a cow.'

"They keep on walkin' along that ditch, the baby crawfish up ahead again. Pretty soon, back he comes again in a big hurry. His mama says, 'What now?' He says, 'Look at the big thing right there.' His mama says, 'That's just a dog. He won't hurt you none.'"

Meaux's eyes were crinkling up as he smiled. He patted his stomach and paused, holding back a little, until Doyle said, "So?"

"So, these two move on ahead, the mama going in front for awhile. All of a sudden the mama crawfish turns around and heads back in a hurry, speedin' right up to the baby crawfish.

"Baby crawfish, all scarified now, asks his mama's what's wrong. The mama crawfish says, 'Just start runnin'. That's one of them Cajuns up there ahead. They'll eat anything!"

Doyle laughed and Morty did, too, although he was familiar with the story. After Clarence signaled to the dishwasher to bring over the coffee pot, Doyle said, "Clarence, I'll bet you've got some good stories from your riding days down there in Louisiana."

"Oh, yeah, but I couldn't have you writin' about none of the best ones, no."

"Why not?"

Clarence said, "There was some stuff went on down there in my day, 'specially at the little bush tracks, that you wouldn't want to be tellin' racing fans about."

Doyle grinned. He said, "Like what?"

"Well, at some of them small tracks down there in those old days, everybody took their best shot most all the time. What stewards they had was either half blind or all the way asleep. Us boys'd try 'bout anything to win a race. There'd be trainers lightin' up their horses with coke, jocks hittin' 'em batteries. The motto was 'Hop 'em. Shock 'em. Bet 'em and brag on 'em.'"

"Naw, Mr. Jack," Clarence said, "no need for you to be tellin' those old stories to anybody." He got to his feet. "How 'bout you fellas tryin' some of my bread puddin' just came out of the oven?"

Chapter Twelve

Illinois House Representative Lew Langmeyer (D-Palatine) closed up his cell phone when his breakfast order arrived— toasted onion bagel, cream cheese, black coffee, the same trio every time he visited Cozy Corner, the restaurant near his Main Street office. Across the table, his legislative assistant Randi Rickert picked up a spoon and began idly stirring her bowl of plain yogurt. She was very thin and intended to stay that way. "Any progress with Wilgis?" she asked, referring to Langmeyer's fellow representative, William "Willy" Wilgis (D-Kankakee).

"Hard to tell," Langmeyer replied. "He's a crafty old son of a gun. Nearly thirty years in the Illinois House, and still nobody can ever confidently predict which way he'll go on any given bill. He's been anti-abortion, but pro gun control. For an increase in taxes for schools, against teacher evaluation. You just never know with Wilgis. But I need him to be with me on the video slots bill. He is a powerful force, particulary with his downstate colleagues. They call him Wily Willy.

"You'll meet Wilgis later this morning," Langmeyer added. "He's agreed to see me at his hotel downtown. He's in Chicago for his annual physical at University of Chicago Hospital. Wilgis is seventy-eight years old and apparently indestructible. He's a widower and also a terrible old lecher, so keep your distance. Your dad wouldn't even want you to be in the same building with Wilgis."

"My guard will be up," Randi said.

Langmeyer, a fifty-seven year old attorney, had been representing his district for sixteen years. It included several new business parks, a growing bedroom community of white collar workers who commuted to Chicago, and giant Heartland Downs Racetrack. Owners of the latter were among his major financial supporters. They were solidly behind his proposed bill to permit the installation of video slot machines at all the state's racetracks. Horse racing in Illinois had been hard hit by competition from the state lottery and the nine privately owned riverboat casinos. This billion dollar agribusiness was under financial siege. Langmeyer's bill was intended to help save it, not only the thousands of racetrack workers, but the many other thousands engaged in horse breeding, feeding, and housing at farms all over the Prairie State.

A first year law student at Northwestern University, Randi Rickert was interning with Rep. Langmeyer for the summer. Her father Harold and Langmeyer were partners in a small but politically connected law firm. Randi had worked for the firm in its Palatine office the three previous summers. She had decided to devote this one to learning first hand about state politics from her father's partner and friend. Young enough to be Langmeyer's daughter, she was smart, pretty, and ultra ambitious. As Langmeyer had confided to Harold Rickert, "Randi's the best intern I've ever had. But don't tell her that. It might give her ideas about running against me some day. I wouldn't look forward to facing her in an election," he said, only half-jokingly.

Randi took a sip of water before asking Langmeyer, "Tell me more about Wilgis. I know he's a downstate farmer. About every time I've ever seen him on television, he starts out saying, 'I'm just a country boy, but....'"

Langmeyer said, "He's from the country, all right, but don't fall for that American Gothic guise he affects. He's played that role to perfection for years. When he first ran for office and won, he attacked the whole Springfield establishment. Voters ate it up.

"Willy's father owned miles of good farm land near Kankakee," Langmeyer continued. "Right after Willy got out of the Army after World War II, his father died. Willy inherited everything and proceeded to build it up further. Way up. He's a major factor in growing Illinois corn for ethanol production.

"And," Langmeyer said, "he's a notorious lady's man. His wife died many years ago. He's never remarried, but he's had a longtime association with his secretary. That hasn't stopped him from sticking his snoot under many a marital tent, both in Springfield and back in Kankakee County."

"Wasn't he under investigation a few years back? Allegedly for taking bribes to influence legislation?"

"Yes. Both by a committee of his fellow legislators, believe it or not, and by the feds. But nothing ever came of it. Nobody had a provable case. I think it all started with a disgruntled staffer Wilgis dismissed, a guy with a grudge but nothing else. Wilgis just made fun of the whole thing. 'You think I'm another Paul Powell?' he'd say. He was talking about a one-time Illinois secretary of state who kept shoe boxes full of cash in his closet, discovered after his death. Powell was the guy who used to say, when he was on the verge of something beneficial to him, 'I can smell the meat a cookin'.' Wilgis said one time that Powell was a 'poor boy possibly gone wrong. On the other hand, I'm a lucky boy who grew up to do good.' That's been his mantra over the years. It works. Like I said, he's been indestructible, both physically and politically.

"And," Langmeyer said with a laugh, "he's famous for his cornball sayings."

Randi looked puzzled. Langmeyer said, "You know, so-called down home expressions. When he first ran for office, Willy's campaign slogan was Run the Squirrels Out of Office—Keep the State Safe for Nuts. People down in his district loved it."

Langmeyer reached into his briefcase and extracted an old sheet of paper that had small newspaper clippings pasted to it. He laughed as he looked at it before handing it to Randi. "Here," he said, "these are some examples of the wit and wisdom of Willy Wilgis that I've collected over the years. I can't help it, the old rascal just makes me laugh. There's nobody like him that I know."

Randi began reading the clips. Langmeyer had hand written above each of the quotations from Wilgis a description of their origin.

—From a campaign speech in his initial run for the State House: *They've been sweeping so much dirt under the rug in Springfield it'd take a Swiss mountain climber to get across the room.*

—On his memory not being as sharp as it had been: *Your cheek is right up on the firebox door; mine has cooled off.*

Even the cool, hip Randi was grinning when she came to Wilgis' description of a triumphant foe who had managed to kill a favorite Wilgis bill: *He looked as pleased as a possum sittin' in a pan of pork chops.*

Randi did have to ask Langmeyer the meaning of the word firebox.

Twenty-seven miles away, on the ninth floor of Chicago's Bolden Hotel, Representative Willy Wilgis also was breakfasting. Two room service carts had been pulled up to the arm chair in which he sat, eating with methodical ferocity, while also glancing out the window at the nearby Water Tower, listening to the "Today" show on television, and admiring the impressive bust line of his longtime secretary and paramour, a fifty-two year old divorcee named Evelyn Stortz. She was examining herself in the full length mirror on the back of their suite's walk-in closet doors.

"You get any better looking than you are," Wilgis said, "and I won't be able to turn my back for fear they'll steal you away from me." She glanced over at him, smiling. He sat with a fork-ful of blueberry pancake in one hand, a glass of buttermilk in the other, round shouldered, his sizeable paunch expanding his blue dress shirt under a gray wool vest, grinning back. Wilgis had a full head of white hair, a pug nose, and an undershot jaw. His stubby legs pressed against the sides of the food table as he leaned forward to fill another plate. Evelyn had long believed him to be the most attractive man she'd ever known.

"Not to worry, Willy," she replied. "I'm your gal. Or," she murmured to herself, "at least one of them." Over the course of nearly a decade together, Evelyn had come to accept Willy's roving eye and other bodily parts. She was grateful for the Springfield condo he'd bought her, the numerous gifts he'd given her, for their extensive travels together. She was philosophical about his infidelities. "Willy strays," she told her best girlfriend, "but he always comes back bearing gifts, looking sheepish, looking lovable. There's only one Willy Wilgis and, for the most part, he's mine."

Wilgis finished off his eggs Benedict, then a stack of pecan waffles. As Evelyn nibbling on a croissant, said, "What time is Representative Langeyer coming up?"

"About ten."

"What does he want to see you about?"

Wilgis said, "That pending bill he's so hot about. The one that'd put video slot machines at the racetracks plus a casino here in Chicago. He introduced it in the last session, but it didn't get too far. I figured he'd introduce it again.

"He's got some fire power this time," Wilgis continued. "R. L. Duncan, the man who owns Heartland Downs, is strongly behind it. And he's strongly behind Lew. The other state tracks also say they need those machines in order to compete with the casinos on what they call 'a level playing field.'"

"What do you think?"

"You know, I voted against the casinos before they got in nine years ago. My constituents aren't much for gambling. Hell, even our Catholic churches don't have bingo. But," Wilgis added, pushing the table away and standing up to his full five-foot four, "I'll listen to Lew anyway. There's a connection between these horse tracks and some of the breeding farms down my way. I know some of the horse people pretty good. But the bill has got too much in it as far as I'm concerned. I'm going to tell Lew there's too many peas on that knife.

"Besides," Wilgis grinned, "you know I like to surprise people. Keep 'em on their toes. I'm not going to commit to anything today."

◇◇◇

It was nearly noon when Langmeyer rose from his chair in Wilgis' suite and prepared to leave. Randi got up, too, listening as her boss said, "Thanks for your time, Willy. I'm glad you heard me out about the benefits to everybody of this bill."

Wilgis shook Langmeyer's hand. "I'll give it my most serious consideration," he said, his face crinkling into the jovial politico's mask he had perfected over the years.

The phone rang. After Evelyn answered it, she said to Wilgis, "It's that Reverend Simpkins. The anti-gambling man." Langmeyer's face reddened when he heard the name. He was somewhat mollified when he heard Wilgis respond, "Evelyn, put that four flusher on hold." Wilgis opened the door for Langmeyer and Randi, patting her fondly on the back as he did so.

In the elevator Randi said, "Well, how did you think that went?"

"As expected," Langmeyer said. "Wilgis isn't tipping his hand at this point. But I'm not discouraged. Non-committal is better than an outright rejection. I can understand his reservations about selling this thing to the conservative Christians down in his bailiwick. But he has on occasion gone against their grain and gotten away with it. He carries his district by a huge majority every time."

At his suite window, Wilgis looked out appreciatively at Michigan Avenue's Magnificent Mile. Evelyn came to stand next to him, linking her arm in his. He said, "What a great city this is." She nodded in agreement.

"Tell you what," Wilgis said, "it looks like a beautiful summer day out there. How about you and I sashay down a few blocks to see an old friend of mine?"

"Who would that be?" Evelyn asked.

"Moe Kellman."

"The furrier? Oh, I've heard you talk about him."

"That's the fellow, honey," Wilgis said, giving her a squeeze. "Winter will be here before we know it. Let's go see about a new fur coat for you."

Chapter Thirteen

It took them less than nineteen hours to lose nearly all their racetrack haul.

Bursting with the feeling of power their heist gave them, Lucarelli and Shannon had driven into the Loop to a Wabash Avenue steak house and proceeded to feast: jumbo shrimp cocktails, New York strips, baked potatoes, creamed spinach, two baskets of rolls, all washed down with three bottles of expensive Cristal champagne. "Just like those NBA guys," Shannon gloated, "and those rap assholes. This is what they drink. It's all right with me, man."

They finished their desserts just before midnight. Lucarelli said, "Whadda you say we hit the boats?"

Shannon leaned back in his chair and burped loudly. He'd just paid the largest restaurant bill he'd ever seen, adding a huge tip that had their astounded waitress suddenly beaming after two hours of semi-sullen serving. He said, "Sure. Let's do it."

At the intersection of State and Congress, Lucarelli waited impatiently at a red light. He opened his window and unleashed a huge gob of spit that splattered off the passenger side window of the black Lexus next to him. The driver of the Lexus looked at the trickling liquid, then at Lucarelli, with disbelief. He started to roll down the marred window but thought better of it after Lucarelli shot him a menacing look. The light changed and Lucarelli hit the accelerator. Shannon gleefully pounded the dash board as they sped away.

Less than twenty-five minutes later, first driving on the Dan Ryan Expressway, then the Skyway, they reached the massive Horseshoe Casino right across the state line in Hammond, Indiana. The two men had made this trip many times in the past, almost invariably leaving behind most of the money they'd brought, just as they did on their annual January trips to Las Vegas, visits marked by multi-day debauchery involving booze, grass, and hookers, with numerous hours of gambling interspersed. Aiden's mother Bridgett, well aware of her son's earmarking "three grand for Vegas," which he usually came home without, once said to him, "You work hard on construction for your money, when you're working. Why don't you just mail the cash out to Nevada and save your air fare?"

"You don't get it, Ma," Aiden had replied, relishing the thought of Vegas' well advertised promise, "What happens here, stays here."

After lighting up jumbo cigars, Shannon and Lucarelli elbowed their way to one of the Horseshoe's blackjack tables with a $10 minimum. In the car, on the way there, Shannon had said, "Let me do the blackjack. That's my game. Whatever we win over here, we'll split."

"Since when do you know so much about blackjack?" Lucarelli said.

"I been reading some books about it. Playing it on the internet at my cousin's house. No shit, man, I've got some good angles to play. Let me handle it."

The first dealer they faced was a young Asian woman, Korean maybe, perhaps Vietnamese, who zipped the cards in a brown handed blur across the green baize. Shannon took a half step back from the table before again leaning his hands on its rim. He shook his head, as if he'd just taken a good punch. Concentrated.

Shannon was to the dealer's immediate left, the "first base" position, and had to lead the betting. The dealer prodded him into action, forcing him to play much faster than he wanted. Uncomfortable, struggling to keep up, Shannon hit seventeen one time, eighteen another, stayed on fourteen twice, double downed on sixes, playing $40, then $50 and $100 a hand, all the while working his way through a succession of Courvosiers and a huge chunk of his bankroll.

He keeps smiling that stupid smile, like he knows what he's doing, Lucarelli thought, frowning at his buddy through a haze of cigar smoke. Lucarelli stood back occasionally, walking over to observe the action at other tables, then returning to find Shannon's initial buy-in mounds of chips almost all gone. Then Shannon shoved another wad of their cash forward, buying replacements. After nearly three hours of this, the Asian woman having been succeeded by a young black man, then a middle aged white woman dealer, "every goddam one of them throwing me shit cards," according to Shannon, the bankroll had dwindled by nearly $27,000.

There was a commotion at one of the crowded wheels in the nearby roulette area. Several young men were whooping and high fiving each other, evidently having hit a number or numbers in a big way. "About fucking time," one of them shouted. Another, a tall guy in a Yale sweatshirt who looked like he'd been drinking heavily for hours, dropped his empty beer bottle on the carpet and lurched toward the tray of a passing waitress. He bumped her arm hard. The tray and its glasses went airborne. More laughter from his group. Furious, the waitress turned on the tall man, but a casino manager grabbed her elbow and led her away, talking earnestly. The waitress listened, then hurried to the bar, got a Beck's, and brought it back to the lout who'd caused the accident. He grinned as he grabbed the bottle out of her hand.

A casually dressed, white-haired gambler standing next to Lucarelli said, "Those punks are having somebody's bachelor party here. Ever since last night they've been throwing money around like they were printing it. I guess management is going to keep them going in that direction as long as possible." He shook his head, smiling. "What a racket this is," he said. "Unfortunately, I love it." He turned back to the $5 slot machine he'd been playing with limited success for the last five hours.

Shannon was semi-drunk by now, not giving a damn about his losing streak, when Lucarelli tugged him off his stool and walked him away from the blackjack table. "Hey, it's only money, man," Danny said, words slurred. "We got plenty of that."

"Shut up," Lucarelli snarled. He walked Shannon into the casino's Village Square Buffet, advertised as "All you can eat…food stations that take you around the globe…China Town, Little Italy, Home Cooking." Lucarelli ate voraciously. Shannon said he wasn't hungry. Later, they walked outside the casino and sat on a bench overlooking a parking lot that, at almost 4:30 a.m., contained more than a thousand cars, their hopeful owners inside butting their heads and their bankrolls against an opponent that kicked ninety percent of them in the pocketbook each night. A cool breeze drifted over the marina. Lucarelli checked to see if the Saturn was where he'd parked it, with nearly $100,000 still in the trunk.

Lucarelli reached into his jacket for another of the $25 cigars they'd purchased from the sexy coat check girl at the steak house in Chicago. He said, "This ain't the place for us right now. Plus, I'm beat."

Shannon reared up. "I'm not going fucking home," he said. "Not with all the money we got. Not tonight. No way."

The statement seemed to exhaust him and he slumped back down onto the bench. Lucarelli said, "We'll get a room over in the hotel. We'll get some sleep. Have another crack at 'em later today."

Lucarelli watched a pay-per-view pro wrestling program in their hotel room, "$59 per night." Shannon slept on one of the double beds, his snores nearly rattling the frames of the generic prints on the walls. Finally, Lucarelli did a hundred push ups and sit ups and lay down on top of the coverlet of the other bed. He was antsy and had a hard time drifting off, which was very unusual for him. He thought about going down to the Taurus and bringing the satchel up to the room. He'd meant to do that, but forgot. He fell asleep instead.

◇◇◇

Sunlight slapped them square in the face when they walked out of the hotel just after noon. Lucarelli opened the trunk. The money was all there. "Okay," he said, "now we can go back and get some breakfast. Or lunch." He stretched, feeling good, and gave Shannon a playful punch on the shoulder. Shannon, still bleary eyed, appeared not to notice.

They switched to the slots when they went back into the Horseshoe, both playing now, starting with the $25 machines. "I got a system for this, too," Shannon had announced, and early in the afternoon he hit two $500 jackpots within minutes of each other. They high fived each other and a couple of cocktail waitresses. Lucarelli, not drinking but taking several crystal meth hits as the day wore on, left to shoot craps.

He blew more than $28,000 in ninety minutes. That called for another trip to the Taurus trunk. Aiden took out a bundle of bills for Shannon, too, who was now playing the two-coin $25 slot, making plays every five seconds. At 1:47 p.m., a woman next to Shannon hit a five grand jackpot. Shannon cursed her, his bad luck, and resumed his frantic play. When he staggered from his seat at a quarter to four, he'd dropped another $45,000. Denny found Aiden at a nearby bar, drinking rum and Coke. The pile of swizzle sticks in front of him indicated he'd been knocking them back at a good pace. Shannon said, "The hell with this dump. Let's go over to Trump's."

Four hours in Trump's Lake Michigan Casino, interrupted only by a hurried lunch in the Top Deck Deli, served to empty out the satchel that had once sat, full, in the Taurus' trunk. Near the end, down to their last few thousand, both Shannon and Lucarelli attacked the $100 slots, then, finally, the $500 machine, assuring each other, "We're bound to hit one soon."

"This place sucks," Lucarelli said, thumb pointed back over his shoulder at the giant river boat in the Taurus' rear view mirror. The late afternoon sun was in his eyes as he drove back to Chicago. He reached for his sun glasses before remembering he'd put them down on a shelf in the men's room when he'd snuck in for his last meth hit. "They can sink fucking Trump and his fucking boat, too, far as I'm concerned."

Looking as depressed as he felt, Shannon slumped in his seat, head back, eyes closed. "I was figuring we wouldn't have to work for at least a year. I was going to call Boots (Robert "Boots" Lee, the foreman of their Bonadio Construction Company crew) and tell him to shove the fucking job. Good thing I didn't," he sighed.

Lucarelli reached into the glove compartment for the only cigar left. He gave Shannon a withering look. "You and your fuckin' gambling systems."

Shannon, eyes closed, muttered, "What a couple of losers we are."

Lucarelli swung his fist against Shannon's left arm. His eyes were wild. He nearly sideswiped a dilapidated looking landscaper's truck, its back filled with tired looking Latino laborers. "Don't you ever fuckin' say that," he screamed at Shannon. "Not fuckin' ever. We're not fuckin' losers."

Shannon sat up in his seat, eyes wide open, startled by his friend's fury. "Yeah, okay, Aiden," he said. "I got it."

The two sat silently until, back in the neighborhood, Lucarelli pulled into the parking lot of Haller's Pub. "We've got enough drinking money left for a week," he said. "Let's get to using it. I'll call Riley tomorrow. Maybe he's got something else for us."

Chapter Fourteen

Riley had really reamed them out. Lucarelli and Shannon rode the elevator down from his law office in silence. Shannon was about to say something before the doors opened to the lobby. But one look at his buddy, and he knew better. He knew Aiden was furious, a condition that, in Denny's experience, did not bode well for anyone.

A heavy Loop haze, the combination of early evening heat and the residue of day-long pollution-spewing auto traffic, hung over south LaSalle Street. Pedestrians immediately began to sweat as they hurried away from their air-conditioned work places. Shannon's forehead was gleaming before they'd walked the two blocks to where Lucarelli had parked his car, in a loading zone around the corner on Van Buren, directly across the street from a private lot that charged $12 an hour. There was a $100 parking ticket under the windshield wiper on the driver's side. Lucarelli yanked it off and ripped it apart before unlocking his door.

Inside, motor going, air-conditioner laboring, Lucarelli sat for several minutes, staring straight ahead. He could still hear that fuckin' Riley, his doughy face red with anger, lecturing them. They were in Riley's small office in one of the older, more casually maintained LaSalle Street office buildings. The view out of the dust streaked window was of the gritty, gray brick building just across the air shaft next door. "I don't give a damn that you blew all that racetrack money you stole," Riley had said, pacing back and forth in the small room. "Any garden variety idiots could have done that. But it takes a special brand of idiot to do it so quickly, and in one weekend, at just two casinos in the same area."

He wiped his forehead with his handkerchief. He said, "You'd think somebody might notice a couple of guys who were dropping nearly a hundred thirty grand in less time than it'd take you to drive to Florida. Honest to God, boys, what were you thinking?"

They sat there, silent. Finally, Aiden asked, "How do you know this?"

Riley said, "My brother-in-law Marty is a shift manager at the Trump. You two were pointed out to him as first division losers. They'll probably send a limo for you the next time you want to go gambling there. Jesus," Riley said, "a hundred thirty grand down the tubes so fast. You don't have much respect for money, do you?"

Riley had sat down then, Lucarelli, his head down, watching out of the tops of his eyes, listening to the old leather chair creak as Riley plumped his fat ass onto it. Shannon had his head down too, sitting in a chair before the desk alongside Lucarelli, like bad boys in the principal's office. Lucarelli looked up, sneering at the attorney, "Well, so what? It was our goddam money. At least it was at that point," he'd added, laughing at his own cleverness, jabbing Shannon with his elbow.

"You still don't get it, Aiden," Riley barked. "The last thing you'd want to do after pulling off a job like Monee Park is get noticed. The way you get noticed? You throw money around in public places in a hurry. That's how." Riley shook his head. "You're just damned lucky there was a bachelor party for some young, hot shot Chicago trader going on at those casinos last weekend. That group went from one boat to another and back, drinking, raising hell, losing their asses. One of those cocaine-fueled nitwits lost a quarter of a million dollars in three hours at a roulette table. These jerkos drew all the attention. You can be thankful for that."

Riley's lecture had continued for another ten minutes, Lucarelli really starting to steam as it went on. Finally, he leaned forward and banged his fist on Riley's desk. "Can we move on to something else?" he snarled. "This ain't working for me."

Riley stifled a sharp retort. He said, "Do you get my point, boys?" They said yes. Riley didn't offer to shake hands with them, and they didn't reach for his. Walking to the office door Shannon kept his head down, like a chastised juvenile. Before closing the door behind them, Riley said, "We'll work through this, lads. Remember the other times I've helped you out. I'll be in touch."

Exhausted from his confrontation with these two galoots, Riley sat down in his creaky chair. He took the Wild Turkey bottle out of the lower right hand drawer and didn't cheat himself. Sighing, he reviewed that day's depressing news, that Monee Park, despite being robbed, was not going to miss a night's racing, having somehow come up with the badly needed money. He sighed again, knowing he'd have to reach out and call on the two cousins another time in the near future. Unfortunately, they were the best he had to work with. Their predecessors, a half-dozen or so Canaryville punks, had unfortunately fallen within the grasp of the justice system.

Still sitting on Van Buren in the Taurus, Lucarelli bitterly quoted the attorney. "'Remember the other times I've helped you.' Big fuckin' deal. It wasn't just Art the Fart's efforts got us off."

"What do you mean?"

"Don't forget Canaryville Amnesia," Aiden said, starting to feel a little better, especially when he heard Denny laugh and say, "You're right about that, man."

It wasn't getting any cooler in the Taurus. Lucarelli was about to pull out into traffic when he looked in the side view mirror and stopped. One of Chicago's mounted police officers was coming up on his left. The cop stopped and peered down from his horse at the scraps of parking ticket on the concrete. Lucarelli gave him a dirty look, aiming another one at the horse. Horse and rider continued on their way. Lucarelli, smirking at Shannon, said, "Let's go get a pop." He put the car in motion. Shannon was relieved at the lowered level of tension now emanating from his volatile cousin. "Go for it, man," he said.

Lucarelli at first drove east on Van Buren. Then he said, "I don't feel like Rush Street tonight." He turned right on Wells.

They left the Taurus in an unattended, self-pay parking lot on South Dearborn and entered Mackie's, a long established saloon featuring great hamburgers and, since the gentrification of the old loft buildings in the South Loop area, a popular place for young professionals. This was a neighborhood that years before had seen Hollywood movie stars stop between trains at the Dearborn Street Station and be photographed for the Chicago newspapers. That impressive old structure today was an indoor mall, surrounded by recently developed condo buildings.

"I was here for my cousin Lily's birthday party last month," Aiden said to Shannon as they walked in. "She lives around here." Shannon, dressed like Aiden in jeans and work shirt, looked around uneasily. "Not our type in here, Aiden," he said. Aiden paid no attention to him. He muscled his way through the crowd to the bar and told the bartender "Jack Daniel's shots, a couple of taps back." Chris, an Art Institute student who'd only recently taken up bartending at nights, said, "What should be back?" He looked so puzzled that Aiden had to laugh. "Taps," Aiden said. "Tap beer. Beer on tap. Draft beer," he explained, grinning, but still kind of pissed that this yoyo acted like he was hearing a fuckin' foreign language. "Pull a couple of beers and put them behind the shots. My man," he added, jabbing Shannon in the side.

They had four quick rounds, Aiden working some of the few remaining Monee Park twenties out of his back pocket. Half an hour into it, Aiden offered to buy a round for the party of six to their right, two guys and three decent looking girls, one outstanding one. The men hesitated. But Aiden gave them one of his looks, suggesting they'd be better off goddam well accepting his generous offer, and they did. The outstanding looking girl at the end lit a cigarette. Aiden could see her eyeing him in the long mirror behind the bar. She was tall and tanned with a body she wasn't shy about displaying, tank top and shorts, like she'd just come from tennis on a nearby Grant Park court. Aiden figured his head probably came up no farther than her clavicle, a spot both lower and higher than from where he wouldn't mind starting on her. He flexed his forearm as he reached for his beer, muscles jumping underneath his snake tattoo. She didn't appear to notice.

While Chris worked up another round for the two of them, one of the guys they bought now buying for them, Aiden patted his jeans jacket pocket. He said to Denny, "You want a little bump?" Denny, eyes semi-glazed, said, "No, man, I'm already flying along here. I've got to order some food. You want a burger?"

Aiden didn't reply. He was in motion now, brushing past these stuck up yuppies on his way to the washroom, fondling his stash of meth. Into one of the men's room stalls, out with the pocket mirror, laying the precious powder onto the glass. A careful inhale. Magic time! The click hit him before he'd even finished washing his hands. He looked at the "Employees Must Wash Hands" sign. "No shit they should," he said, feeling frisky now. Suddenly he lashed out at the towel machine with his right hand, putting a pretty good dent in the metal. He was rolling now. He yanked the washroom door open so violently it nearly left its hinges.

Denny was talking to some guy about the White Sox current pitching woes when Aiden returned to the bar. He sidled over next to the outstanding looking chick. She was smoking another cigarette. He said, "Want a drink?" She didn't turn, didn't respond, didn't even look at him out of the corner of her eye. For a second he wondered if maybe she was deaf. Then she turned to the girl next to her and said something in a low, cool voice that Aiden couldn't hear. They both laughed.

He could feel his face burning when the young woman turned back to look at him in the mirror back of the bar, a faint smile on her lips. She still didn't say anything. Aiden snatched the Virginia Slim out of her hand and plunged it into her half-filled cranberry martini glass. It made a hissing noise. She looked at him in astonishment. "Should learn to answer when you're talked to, bitch," he said. A guy behind him said, "Hey, watch that talk." Lucarelli shoved him aside as he grabbed Shannon's arm with his other hand and headed for the door. "Let's blow this fag joint," he said loudly.

"I was having a good time in there, Aiden," Shannon complained as they walked to the car. Lucarelli didn't answer him. Approaching the Taurus, Lucarelli suddenly stopped. There was a figure on the ground next to the car's left rear wheel. "What the hell?" Lucarelli said, running forward. "Get the fuck away from there," he shouted.

It was an old man, apparently a wino who had wandered away from the mission facility a block over on State Street. He grasped an empty pint of Thunderbird ("What's the word? Thunderbird. What's the price? Sixty twice.") in one hand. The other arm lay across his forehead as if he was shielding his eyes from the distant street light. He was snoring softly, head propped against the outside of the tire. Lucarelli kicked him in the ribs with his right boot. The old man cried out. Shifting his weight, Lucarelli drove his left foot into the man's face. There was a cracking sound. Blood spurted from his nose and mouth, and he passed out again.

Lucarelli grunted with satisfaction. Leaning down, he grabbed the wino's legs, pulled him away from the car, and dragged him over into the shadows near the parking lot fence. Shannon followed. He gave the old guy a kick with the side of his boot, kind of half-hearted, but enough, he thought, to keep up his cred with his dangerous cousin.

Chapter Fifteen

In the days after the track robbery, things started quieting down for Doyle, his routine resembling that of his uneventful first week on the job. He fell into the rhythm of his lengthy work days that began when he toured the stable area early each morning to gather material for the Barn Notes that he wrote, then e-mailed by noon to local media outlets. The hope was the Notes would serve as a basis of publicity for the track. Most Chicago area sports departments these days, Doyle knew, had pretty much chosen to ignore horse racing on a daily basis, though they still reserved some coverage for the big weekend races. With the exception of *Racing Daily*, the industry's trade journal, the newspapers only staffed Monee Park on Saturdays. Doyle tried to break through this barricade by making his Notes as unusual as possible. He enjoyed his conversations with most of the trainers and jockeys he met on the Monee Park backstretch, though there were some rude bastards he learned to avoid.

The smooth nature of his week came to an abrupt halt just before the final race Saturday night. That was when two middle-aged press box stalwarts, Hollis Randolph of the *Chicago News* and Randy Hicks of *Metro Daily*, got into what they considered to be a fist fight.

For some reason, the press box vibes had been bad for most of the evening, beginning when Randolph asked Doyle "turn down that damn jazz you're playing on the radio." Doyle looked

up, startled. He'd never heard Randolph say anything so forcefully.

"What, you don't like jazz?" Doyle said. "What kind of
American are you?" Still, he reached over to his CD player and
lowered the volume on John Coltrane's "Giant Steps."

"Too damn squawky," Randolph answered. "If there has to
be music playing in here, make it classical," he sniffed, turning
back to his computer keyboard.

"I'm going to take umbrage at that, Hollis," Doyle
responded.

"Take all you want."

"You're telling me you dig that classical mush, the tedious,
predictable repetition of the same note patterns in different keys
for minutes at a time? Where, after you've heard the first few
notes, you can accurately predict the next fifty or so? Where
you look around at the audience and there isn't a toe to be seen
tapping? Where the only display of movement in the dead serious crowd is that of guys nodding off to sleep? An old buddy of
mine termed it SFB music. So Fucking Boring. Not for mine,
my friend. However, in the spirit of cooperation, I will lower
the sound over here."

His mustache twitching, Adam's apple bobbing behind his
navy blue bow tie, Randolph grunted an indiscernable reply.

But the squabble that erupted a couple of hours later did not
involve musical tastes. Source of this conflict was the traditional
press box handicapping pool. That night, Randolph and Hicks
were in the contest, along with three television camera men,
Morty Dubinski, Alvin the press box mutuel clerk, Rudy the bartender, and two radio station reporters. The contestants each put
$10 into the pot. The person with the most points accumulated
by the end of the night (five points for picking a winner, three
for second, one for third) got the money. Doyle had decided to
stay out of it until he got to know this crew better.

This night, everyone in the contest blew their chances early in
the program—except the voluble Hicks. He was, as he chortled
loudly, "hotter than a bowl of Terlingua, Texas chili." He kept

rubbing it in, especially irritating Hollis Randolph who was holding the pool money. Hollis had managed to come up with just one winner through the first eight races. Hicks, who had tabbed five, rode him unmercifully as the night went on. "You couldn't pick your nose tonight, Hollis," was one of the least offensive Hicks jibes.

To Hollis Randolph's irritation, Hicks announced that he wanted to "get away early to beat the traffic." Because of that, he asked Randolph to pay him off so he could leave. Randolph refused. He worked at his computer, not looking up as he said, "You know the rules, Hicks. The winner of the pool doesn't get paid off until after the last race is run."

"Yeah, but nobody can win the last race and beat me," Hicks protested. "I'm too far ahead. I'm the winner, you idiot. Now pay me!"

As Randolph continued to ignore him, the enraged Hicks reached around from behind him and slapped him across the cheek. The tall, spindly Randolph sprang out of his chair like a startled heron. The two then began flailing away ineffectually at each other as the other press box denizens gawked.

Doyle could hardly believe what he was seeing as Randolph and the squat, overweight Hicks stood no more than three feet apart, missing each other with both hands, puffing and sweating. He roughly stepped between them, shouting, "I'm not going to watch any more of this bitch slapping from you two. If you can't fight like men, return to your seats. And," he added, "Randolph, give Hicks his goddam money."

The two responded to these commands with relief. Randolph, hands shaking, eye glasses askew on his long nose, got out his wallet and handed some bills to Hicks, whose round face was now glistening with sweat. Hicks took the money without saying a word. He went to his desk, packed up his portable computer, and scuttled out the door.

Doyle gave Rudy the bartender the high sign for a round of drinks on his tab. Rudy quickly produced a Bushmills on the rocks for Doyle, then started filling the rest of the orders. Doyle said to Morty, "How often does this kind of crap go on here?"

"I've never seen a fight in a press box in my life."

"Well," Doyle said, "you sure as hell couldn't say you saw one here tonight. That hardly qualifies as even a minor fracas. What a couple of nudniks."

He walked to his desk and sat down. Susan Lane-Barker, the tall, slim young woman who covered the weekend races for one of the major press services, looked over at him. "Why are you smiling, Jack?" she said reproachfully. "I thought that was disgraceful."

"Oh, I don't know," he said, smiling back at her. "Sometimes, seeing people making fools of themselves tends to lighten my mood. As long as they don't harm anyone but themselves," he added. "It's a weakness of mine." Susan, far from mollified, turned back to her keyboard.

Doyle asked Morty to lower the volume of the televised White Sox game. It was Morty's turn to look aggrieved. "I take it you're not a Sox fan, Jack?"

"That's right."

Morty sighed, forcing himself to come to grips with a dreadful new possibility. He said, "A Cubs fan, I suppose."

"Nope."

Morty was surprised. He sat back in his chair, giving Jack a long, speculative look. "You mean you're not a baseball fan? What kind of American are *you*?"

Doyle let a little of the smoky Bushmills roll around in his mouth, "grace his gums" as he had once described the feeling, before he answered. "I gave up on the so-called national pastime several years ago, Morty. Starting when mediocre major league infielders started making more money in a single year than all the teachers in a mid-size elementary school. Since sluggers turned into grotesque masses of muscle and started to hit six-hundred foot home runs. That's when I scrubbed baseball off my blackboard. C'mon," he said, "let me make a bet with Alvin and we'll go outside and watch the last race."

It was Doyle's first bet at Monee Park. The race was for older horses going a mile and a sixteenth. He used the first two favorites and a 7-1 shot in a straight trifecta, needing them to finish one-two-three in that order. They ran one-two-four. He crumpled up his mutuel ticket. They walked back into the now nearly empty press box. Morty said, "Can I leave now?"

"Did you e-mail that press release about Monday night's special events?"

"Done."

"Okay," Doyle said. "Take off. See you tomorrow."

Morty turned around when he'd reached the door. He had a sly grin on his face. "One more thing," he said. "Hopalong Cassidy. What was the name of his horse?"

Doyle said, "You're a devious little bastard. Hopalong Cassidy? How the hell would I know the name of his horse? That was way before my time."

"Topper," Morty said triumphantly, then exited, chuckling.

Chapter Sixteen

Aiden Lucarelli was sitting at the bar working on a Bud Light when Denny Shannon stumbled into Haller's Pub on Thirty-third and Parnell. As usual, there was an empty stool on either side of Aiden. Everyone in the neighborhood knew him as an anger-packed, argumentative, combative collection of complexes in "great need of avoidance," as old Donal Corcoran, a Haller's regular, put it. Corcoran also said of Aiden that "He's like a nightmare combination of the Al Capone-Dion O'Banion criminal lines, just as lethal and eager as each."

Haller's Pub was one of Chicago's oldest saloons. Located a half block south of Democratic ward headquarters, for decades it had been a popular hangout for politicians, cops, firemen, city workers, tradesmen, and senior retirees. It smelled of cigarette and cigar smoke, beer, and grilled onions. It was known in the neighborhood as a "goddamn gold mine." The loudest sound on south Parnell early every morning was the cascade of beer kegs down delivery truck ramps at Haller's service door.

At age twenty-six, Denny and Aiden were Haller's Men, having played Little League baseball on Haller's sponsored teams, years later sixteen-inch softball, in between making their rite of passage from soda pop swillers to dedicated adult drinkers. Patrons of Haller's often held bachelor parties in the tavern's large back room. A few permitted their wives to join them in this male-dominated sanctum on the occasion of post-funeral receptions.

Shannon was late. Lucarelli had amused himself by asking Marge Duffy, the afternoon bartender, for perhaps the sixtieth time, to "go out with me some night." Her regular reply was, "As soon as my fifth child clears kindergarten, I'll start considering it, Aiden." Her laughter trailed behind her as she moved to the far end of the long mahogany bar to welcome two thirsty fire captains just off duty. Marge was a forty-one year old divorcee with two young children, a great body, and absolutely no inclination to expose it to the likes of Aiden Lucarelli. Her rejection of his advances was an ongoing joke between them, at least the way Marge saw it. Lucarelli frequently envisioned the moment he'd jump her outside of Haller's after she'd worked a night shift and fuck her silly, a mask on, her never knowing it was him.

It was twenty after one in the afternoon. Lucarelli and Shannon had agreed to meet for lunch at noon to talk over Art Riley's newest plan for them to put into effect at Monee Park. Lucarelli looked at his cousin with disgust. "Christ, man," he said, "you're stoned. And drunk. And late. What the hell happened?"

Shannon rested his thick forearms on the bar. He shook his head from side to side. He was wearing his most recently favored tee-shirt. On the back it read, "Drink Til You Want Me!" Lucarelli noticed drops of dried blood on the front of the shirt.

"Saw my old man early this morning," Shannon mumbled as he gingerly sat down on the bar stool. "He came around for the first time in three years. Right before I walked into the house, he started beating on Ma again. I beat the shit out of him. Just like he used to beat the shit out of me all those years. He got in a few licks himself."

"Bastard had it coming," Lucarelli said. He held up two fingers and Marge popped open two more bottles of beer.

"I know *that*," Shannon said irritably. "But I still don't feel great about it, even if the old man had it coming. He got this kind of pitiful, scared look on his face when I was whaling away on him. Made me sick to see him that way. I don't know why I had to have a pa like him, I really don't."

The White Sox-Detroit Tigers game was on the big television up behind the bar. They watched a half inning in silence. Conversation among the other dozen or so patrons of Haller's was muted, the noise level nothing like it would be after five o'clock when the working men came in ready to raise their glasses, voices, and a little bit of hell if the opportunity arose. Marge had specifically requested a transfer to the day shift so she wouldn't have to face what she described to owner Butch Haller as "that motley crew" every evening. "With them trying to hit on me, plus running me ragged pulling draft beers like a robot, and listening to the same old arguments, this shift is shortening my life," she'd complained to Haller. He granted her request. Her only regret was the occasional dealings she had with the cousins on the days they got off of work early.

When the commercials began before the start of the third inning, Lucarelli broke their silence. "At least you got a pa," he said morosely. "You're ahead of me there."

Shannon stared straight ahead, thinking of the stories he'd heard about Aiden's late father Jimmy, a "made man" in the Chicago Outfit who had been shot to death during a police raid on an Elmwood Park bookie joint. Aiden was two at the time. His mother Bridgett never remarried. The fatherless child was spoiled rotten by both the Italian and Irish sides, raised "like a young prince," as Bridgett proudly put it. This lack of discipline served to smoothly develop him into the arrogant prick he always would be.

Lucarelli said, "Let's eat." He walked over to a corner table near the window looking out on the tavern's parking lot. Across the street was the Holy Rosary school yard, where he and Shannon had terrorized their classmates for most of eight years. Haller's property had also been the scene of numerous fights matching the cousins against usually hapless, outmatched foes. Lucarelli grinned. "We've spilled a lot of blood over these two blocks."

"Yeah," Shannon said, "usually other peoples'." They gave the young waitress their orders for sandwiches and "a couple more Buds." Then they got down to discussing their latest assignment from Art Riley.

Chapter Seventeen

Doyle came down out of the press box with a bounce in his step. It was a beautiful July Fourth evening at old Monee Park. Mid-day rains had been heavy but short-lived and, though turning the racing strip into a sea of slop, were followed by cloudless skies starting in late afternoon. Thousands of south side horse racing fans had chosen to come out for the twilight racing program that would be followed by a fireworks display, then a concert by some area country and western bands. This annual event had been inaugurated by Jim Joyce years earlier and Celia was determined to keep it on the schedule, cost be damned. From his press box perch Doyle had watched as the Monee parking lots began filling up well before six p.m. He knew this was something rarely observed, like seeing a fat cyclist, or a skinny Hell's Angel.

Now, making his way through the crowded grandstand, Jack could feel and hear the buzz of an assemblage eager to be entertained, and to bet. There were long lines at the mutuel windows, and the bars and concession stands were busier than he'd ever seen them. *There must be 10,000 people here already*, he thought as he sidestepped a man who was walking with his head buried in the tabloid *Racing Daily*, the so-called bible of thoroughbred racing. The air was rich with the smell of grilling Italian and Polish sausages, hot dogs, popcorn.

One of the longest lines was in front of the small booth of Madame Fran, Forecaster Supreme. Madame Fran was a short, hefty woman with lively eyes and a ready smile. Doyle watched as Madame Fran, dressed in her usual working outfit of long sleeved orange caftan, white turban, a sparkling ring on every finger, waved forward the next customer, a pants suit wearing matron eager to pay the $5 fee for Fran's list of predicted winners on the night's racing program. In addition to the printed cards containing her horse picks that she sold before the races began, Madame Fran offered private consultations at considerably higher fees. She was usually busy with those later in the night, her prognostications encompassing not only horse racing but the stock market, crop futures, and, occasionally, domestic dilemmas. She had been doing a thriving business at Monee Park for years, having been hired by Jim Joyce, then retained by Celia. When the racing season ended, Madame Fran put her booth in storage and herself in her Sarasota, Florida condo.

Shontanette Hunter had introduced Jack to Madame Fran when, right after he'd started work there, she gave him an extensive tour of Monee Park. Jack had picked up one of the printed cards Madame Fran provided, gratis, to Monee Park patrons. They contained what she described in bold face type as "Rules to Bet By."

"A happy bettor is more likely to be a winning bettor."

"Do not approach the mutuel windows with a frown on your face, or with fear of defeat in your heart."

"Your intuitive powers function best when channeled through a corridor of optimism."

Doyle had asked Shontanette, out of Madame Fran's hearing, "Does she believe this stuff? She gives the impression that she does."

Shontanette said, "I know, I know, it sounds like a lot of other hustles. But I'll say this about Madame Fran: every year for about the last ten or so she's picked more winners on her little tip sheet than any other handicapping expert in Chicago. You can check it out, Jack."

Madame Fran, originally Freda Finklestein, was beaming as she advised a client sitting in a chair alongside the table at her booth. She looked like a woman who was enjoying work she had been doing for more than two decades since, at age twenty-two, she dropped out of her pre-med course at Northwestern University and morphed into Madame Fran. The only disconcerting part of that career change was telling her horrified parents. But she won them over after declaring "There has to be a better way for me to help people, have fun, and make a living besides looking at lesions."

Doyle stepped to the side of Madame Fran's table. "What's in the forecast?" he said, smiling. "It's crystal clear," she replied, round cheeks dimpling and her brown eyes alight, "I'll have at least five winners. But," she added with a frown, "I feel there's something not quite right about tonight. I don't know what it is, but I can feel it." She shuddered slightly, just enough to set into motion her double chins. Doyle knew this kind of pessimism was completely out of character for her.

"What's different," Doyle said, attempting to reassure her, "is the great business we're doing for a change. Enjoy it," he advised, patting her on the shoulder before moving away.

Just outside Madame Fran's booth there was a line of a dozen waiting customers. Near the back, not in the line but talking earnestly to a middle-aged man who was, stood a tall, skinny, old man. He wore a tattered, long-sleeved white shirt, wrinkled khakis, and a new ball cap that said Monee Park. Doyle recognized it as last week's featured track give-away item (Free Caps to the First 2,000 Paying Customers).

Doyle felt a tap on his back. He looked around at Karl Mortenson, Monee Park's director of security. The two men had met for the first time the previous week, Mortenson eager to impress Doyle with the fact that he was "retired from the Chicago PD," now engaged in a second career at the racetrack. Mortenson was a big, beefy, middle-aged man, redolent of a powerful pine-scented after shave lotion that failed to mask his breath, which smelled rather strongly of moth balls. He had the kind of glad handing style Doyle despised. Nodding toward the skinny oldster, Mortenson confided, "He's at it again. We can't seem to stop him. We bar him, but he somehow manages to get in. I'll have to throw him out again."

"Who is he?"

Mortenson said, "A guy named Slim Wallace. Been around the racetrack all of his life, in one capacity or another. His capacity in recent years has been tout."

"He's touting a horse to that man now?"

Mortenson grinned. "Bet on it," he said. "The race coming up has a ten-horse field. Slim has probably given a different one of those horses to each of ten people. All he asks is, 'Buy a win ticket for me.' Naturally, one of the ten horses he recommends will be the winner. And Slim will track down the winning bettor and ask for his winning ticket, and maybe a bonus. I've seen a lot of racetrack touts. Slim is one of the slickest. Here, let's move up a little closer. You can listen to him."

"Will a drying out track bother him? Flinty McGinty? Not a chance," they heard the old man saying in a strong, confident voice. His listener was apparently not fully convinced. Slim pressed on. "Flinty McGinty's the class of this field. This horse could win running over cobblestones. Or hot coals. In sleet or snow. He'll run through fire. Bet him good for me, will you?" Slim pleaded.

The mark still looked a bit skeptical. He said to Slim, "If Flinty McGinty is so good, why is he twenty-two to one on that odds board?"

"Mister," Slim said, "that's because his trainer, an old friend of mine, has been hiding this speedball. Working him in the early morning dark so he couldn't be timed by the clockers. Believe me, he's a stick of dynamite about to go off and make us rich."

Mortenson intervened at this point, grasping Slim by the elbow and pulling him roughly to the side. "Caught you at it again, old man," he said. Slim grimaced in Mortenson's powerful grip. Glaring at the security chief, he said, "You mean I can't give my handicapping opinions to this friend of mine here? What happened to free speech in this country?"

Mortenson started marching Slim toward the exit. "Friend of yours?" he said. "Hell, you never saw that man until five minutes ago."

"Well, if Flinty McGinty wins he'll be a friend of mine."

Doyle watched them traipse away, thinking *there's as many characters per square foot around the racetrack as there are divorcees in Vegas.*

Immediately after the second race, back at his desk now, Doyle received a call from Roger Bullard, the Monee Park manager of pari-mutuels. Bullard was excited. "Jack," he said, "I just wanted to tell you we've had more money bet on the first two races tonight than any time in the last ten years. Almost a new record on the daily double. I thought you'd like to know because we might be on our way to a season's high for the nine races."

Doyle said, "Thanks, Roger. That's great news." He was going to add, "Give me a running total through the night, will you?" when the infield tote board abruptly went dark, followed by all the lights that were spaced around the racing strip. Lighting in the building remained on. Doyle closed his eyes for an instant, thinking he'd imagined it. But when he opened them and again looked out his window, darkness still enveloped the track and the tote board remained blank. Twenty minutes later, when it became apparent the problem could not be quickly remedied, the announcement was made that the rest of the nights' races were cancelled. Monee Park admissions employees began issuing rain checks to departing customers. Betting was over for the night and the hard core players were disgruntled. Thousands of people with their families remained, however, for the fireworks show which went on as planned.

Doyle tapped out a short news story about the partial blackout for the media and e-mailed it. Depressed, the glow having been ripped off this once promising night, he was about to leave and head for O'Keefe's Olde Ale House when his phone rang. Shontanette said, "Jack, will you come upstairs for a few minutes? Celia needs to talk to you."

He walked into the apartment, saying hello to Shontanette, Bob, and Celia, who was talking on her cell phone. They sat around the dining room table, coffee cups before them.

"Damn," said Doyle, "what an unlucky break that was. Any report on what caused the malfunction?" He pulled out a chair and sat down as Shontanette said, "Of all nights for this to happen! Things were going so great. Our biggest crowd in years, betting like crazy. Talk about bad luck!"

Celia put her phone on the table. She looked stunned. "There was no luck involved," she said slowly. "That was Chuck Lipman, the head electrician. He says part of the lighting system was sabotaged. He said that's evident from the damage done. He has no idea how whoever did it knew how to attack the system. Swears it couldn't have been any of his crew, and I believe him. It'll take at least a day to repair," she said. She put her head down on her folded arms that lay on the table. Doyle looked at Bob, sitting immobilized in his wheelchair next to his wife, Doyle knowing that both of them wanted to move to Celia and comfort her, but were unable to do so.

Shontanette broke the silence. "Damn, we're on a bad roll here. First the money room robbery, now this."

Doyle said, "I'm starting to think we're under siege."

Bob Zaslow whispered something Doyle couldn't hear. Celia, sitting next to Bob, shook her head. Bob said nothing more. He just stared at Doyle, who was feeling uncomfortably left out. Doyle looked at Celia. "What did Bob say?" he asked.

Celia said, "Nothing important, really." She patted her husband's hand. He looked back at her, anger in his eyes. She gave into him then, saying, "Okay, what Bob said was 'We were never under siege before Jack Doyle got here.'"

Chapter Eighteen

Doyle stood at the clubhouse rail, cup of coffee in hand, notebook in the pocket of his tan windbreaker, watching the horses go past in their morning workouts, when he felt a hand on his elbow. He turned to see Celia. With the sun at her back she looked a picture, he thought, her red hair glistening in the glow of morning, green eyes full of life. She wore a blue sweatshirt, the words Monee Park on its front, blue jeans, and a White Sox ball cap, its brim pulled low. "Caught you daydreaming, Jack. Looking at horses down here instead of upstairs writing about them." She smiled to assure him that she was kidding.

"I like watching the workouts," Doyle replied, turning back to the track and leaning his arms on the rail. "You know what Winston Churchill said. 'There's something about the outside of a horse that's good for the inside of a man.' I couldn't agree more."

They stood without talking for a few minutes. The sounds filling the cool air were those of pounding hooves, hard-breathing animals, the chirps of their riders. Then Jack said, "So, Celia, what brings you down here this morning? Looking for a hot horse?"

She laughed. "Hardly. Actually, I was hoping to talk to you. I need to ask a favor."

Doyle finished his coffee, then tossed the cup into a nearby metal waste basket. "What kind of favor?"

"A pretty big one," Celia admitted. "Walk with me over to those empty grandstand seats. I want to keep this just between us for now," she said, as she waved to a couple of trainers who had called out greetings to her.

In the next quarter hour, Celia laid it out for him. Her attempt to persuade her cousin Niall Hanratty to sell her his interest in Monee Park had failed. So had her attempt to convince him that the value of the stock would soar once video slots were approved, that Monee Park would be a viable, profitable entity. "Niall doesn't seem to understand how much we both have to gain if we hang on to this property," Celia complained, voice rising. "For a man supposedly so smart about money, well, he's thick on this subject. It's so stupid, his attitude. 'Money now, money quickly,' that's all Niall's interested in. It's all that's been mentioned in the two letters to me from his lawyer here, this Art Riley, and in the one brief, long distance phone conversation I had with Niall. In the last letter, Riley even hinted that Niall might try to challenge Uncle Jim's will, try to break it! That's ridiculous. He has no grounds for that."

Celia frowned as she looked out over the track. "I'm sure," she said, "that he's disgusted with having to deal with a woman on an equal basis."

"Naw," Doyle said, unable to resist, "maybe just a really stubborn woman, like you."

"Not funny, Jack Doyle."

"Oh, I know that. But when you think about it, your cousin does have a decent argument. The land here is like gold. Sell it for townhouses and a golf course and what have you, you've got easy money in the bank in a hurry. Holding off, waiting for the video slots bill to pass, well, I can see how that might not appeal to Hanratty."

"It doesn't make any sense to him," Celia shot back, "because he knows nothing about Monee Park. Or Uncle Jim. Or how Uncle Jim loved this place. How could a Niall Hanratty, living thousands of miles away, know anything about that?"

A track siren signaled the start of a fifteen minute "break" during which horses were not permitted on the loam surface while tractors pulled harrows over it, smoothing it out. Most of the horse trainers and owners walked from the rail or stands inside the building for new supplies of coffee and doughnuts. A staple of racetrack mornings, Doyle had learned, was caffeine accompanied by some form of fried dough.

Celia remained where she was seated, the brim of her cap pulled down over her forehead. When she finally looked up at him, Doyle saw tears in her eyes. He felt a catch in his throat. He started to put a hand on hers, but she got to her feet. Arms crossed, she composed herself, then looked down at him.

"I'll get to the favor now, Jack."

"Fire away."

"I'd very much appreciate it if you would make a quick trip to Ireland to talk to Niall Hanratty for me."

Doyle's jaw dropped. He rubbed his hand through his hair as he got to his feet. "Kind of came out of left field with that one, didn't you?" he said. "Well, I have a one word answer. Why? Why me?"

"That's three. The answer is, *I* can't go. I can't leave Bob for a trip like that. And I can't seem to get Niall to see my side of things by phone or mail. I need someone to talk this out with him. To persuasively present my side. You're the best person I know that could do this for me. The only one," she repeated, pressing a tissue to her nose.

"Aw, c'mon," Doyle said, conceding, "no crying, okay?" Celia turned away for a few seconds, her shoulders shaking, then turned back to him. He saw that she was struggling to control a laugh. She failed, and it rolled out, making him laugh, too.

"You'll do it for me then?"

He nodded yes.

"Was that...pretty...good?" she managed as she resumed laughing.

"Oh, yes," he admitted, "that was a first rate hustle. I didn't know you were such a capable actress."

"But you'll still respect me," she said with a giggle.

"This morning, and all others."

Celia turned serious again. Looking straight at him, the sun now full fledged and out of its cloud coverlet behind her, she said, "I have a ticket for you on tonight's Aer Lingus flight from O'Hare to Dublin."

Doyle said, "Why the hell not? It would be all new to me. My forebearers managed to get their butts out of there before the famine got them. Their descendants never evidenced any desire to return that I know of. Funny, I've always been curious as to what the 'ould sod' is like. I'll do this favor for you, Celia."

Doyle wrapped up his morning's work in a hurry. He called Morty over to his desk, explaining that he'd be "gone for a few days. You're in charge." Morty blanched. "Where to?" he asked. But Doyle was already on the phone, saying, loud enough for Morty to hear, "Moe, I'm leaving town tonight. For Ireland. Yeah, on very short notice. How about a farewell lunch?" He listened for a few seconds before saying, "I'll see you there." Morty said, "Ireland?" Doyle nodded, patted Morty on the shoulder, and walked out.

By 12:30 Doyle was seated in Moe Kellman's regular back booth at Dino's Ristorante, beneath the owner's most prized possession—the large, framed photo of Frank Sinatra, inscribed, "Dino, Keep on Swingin'." Moe glanced up, said, "Hello, Jack," then back down at the front page of that day's *Wall Street Journal*. Seconds later he folded up the paper and disgustedly pushed it aside. "Another ring of corporate crooks found guilty," he said. "Insiders scooping the cream off the top before their company goes under. Every other week there's a story like this. It's amazing to me. Hell, some of the guys from my old neighborhood had more ethics than these blue suited jackals.

"You know what I'd like to see, Jack?" Moe said earnestly. "Instead of putting these guys' ages in the paper, who cares about that, they should put in their alma maters, what universities they came out of. I think the public has a right to know where these thieves are being trained."

"I'd drink to that," Doyle said, "if I had a drink."

"Patience, Jack, patience," Kellman said, just as a waiter arrived at the booth with Kellman's Negroni, a bottle of Pilsener Urquel beer for Doyle. They clinked glasses, Kellman smiling now, finished at least for the time being with concern over corporate corruption. "So tell me," he said, "what's with this Ireland caper?"

Doyle described the mission he was going on for Celia, telling him how she "foxed me into it, I've got to admit. She's not a bad actress for an education major," he said with a grin.

Moe sipped his Negroni, then patted his neat white mustache with his napkin. He looked speculatively at Jack. He said, "You haven't fallen for Ms. McCann, have you Jack?"

"Forget that idea," Doyle snapped. "She's a very, very attractive woman. But she's married, for one thing, and married to a nice guy who is trapped in his own body. I'm not going down that path."

Moe said, "How do you plan to handle things over there?"

"I hope to meet with this Hanratty the day after tomorrow. I'm going to try to convince him to go along with Celia's plan for the track. You know, keep it running until the slots become a reality. As I've said, Hanratty wants to sell the place right away and cash out his forty-nine percent. I may spend ten minutes with this guy and wrap up the agreement Celia wants, or walk out of a disagreeable situation. We'll see."

"What do you know about Hanratty?"

"His name, occupation, and relationship to Celia. That's it."

"I made some inquiries about him," Moe said. Doyle smiled. "I'll bet you did. I've got to admit it, sometimes you amaze me, what you get interested in, who you know. Actually," he added, "I do know that Hanratty has hired a lawyer here to represent him. Guy named Art Riley."

Kellman's eyebrows elevated. He took a sip of his Negroni. "Not good," he said, "not good at all."

"What do you know about Art Riley?"

Moe said, "He's got a reputation shakier than a penniless junkie. Been around for years, working with hack politicians, bent labor leaders, picking up good-sized pieces of deals here and there. He's big in the Fourteenth Ward Democratic organizations, where clout is king."

"Have you had any dealings with him?"

"Just once, years ago. I had been led to believe Riley could do a favor for a friend of mine. So I met with him. He's a smarmy, hustling type, probably smarter than he lets on. A lot of nudging, winking, fake joviality. All I could think, watching Riley's phony act, was that this guy's probably got a heart colder than a Nome park bench. Our association, if you could call it that, was short-lived. And not repeated. After I'd met him I didn't want to get anywhere near the guy ever again.

"A couple of years later," Moe continued, "I went to a wake for a good friend of mine, Owen Mahony. Years before he had hired, then quickly fired Riley from the law firm he started. Owen was a south side alderman for years. He and Riley grew up in Canaryville. Then they had a bitter falling out.

"Anyway, Art Riley shows up at the funeral home for Mahoney's visitation. When Riley gets up to the coffin, he starts carrying on loudly about his 'dear lost friend.' He looked like he was going to collapse from grief. When Riley bends over the coffin for a final look, a guy behind me says, 'I know that phony bastard Riley. Watch his hands. He's probably going through poor Owen's pockets, looking for loose change.'"

The waiter set down their food, a platter of shrimp and garlic pasta for Moe, a chicken parmesan sandwich for Doyle. Dino himself appeared carrying another Negroni for Moe. Doyle said he'd like another beer to go with his sandwich and Dino sent the waiter off to get it before asking, "How is everything, Mr. Kellman?" Moe gave Dino a thumbs up with his left hand, his right in use forking a rapid stream of food into his mouth. The only thing Doyle had ever seen Kellman do in a hurry was eat. "It's from my childhood," the little man had once told him. "I was the youngest, and smallest, of six kids with a father who struggled to put food on the table. He didn't put much. We ate like starving wolves."

Within minutes, Kellman had polished off his pasta platter and was sitting back in the booth, relaxing, Negroni in hand. He said, "Maybe you'll hit it off with this Hanratty, convince him to go along with Celia. Maybe it'll all go smoothly. Though, you got to admit, things rarely do for you." He smiled as Jack's face reddened.

"I'm only joshing you, kid," Moe said. "Take it easy. Don't get mad."

"I'm not mad."

Moe said, "Just be on your toes when you're over there among your own kind."

"I'm well aware that 'my kind' aren't to be trusted any more or less than any other kind. That's not news to me."

Moe took a long drink of Negroni. "Sometimes our 'own kind' need more watching than anybody else, that's all I'm saying. I'm not talking about just you Micks. Did I ever tell you about the two young rabbis, twin brothers mind you, Isaac and Isadore Epstein, and the ecumenical conference?"

"I am certain I would have remembered if you had. Go on."

Moe said, "The brothers had been invited to attend this important religious gathering here in Chicago, at the Hilton. Naturally, they wanted to look their best for this occasion. So they decided to order new suits, black, from Pincus, the neighborhood tailor they'd gone to since they were bar mitzva-hed. Pincus greeted them warmly. Told of their plans and the upcoming conference, he said, 'Young men, you are in luck. I am having a big sale on black cloth. I'll give you a great deal on these suits and have you fixed up in a week.' The brothers thank him and leave.

"A week later they go back to try on the new suits, which fit them perfectly. But Isadore looks closely at his jacket. And he says to Pincus, 'Are you sure this cloth is black? I'm not color blind, but this looks more like midnight blue to me.'

"'Ha ha,' says Pincus, dismissing this notion. Pincus rings up the sales and ushers the twins out the door.

"A couple of days later there they are, in the lobby of the Hilton, all set for the big conference. But Isadore is still kvetching about the color of their new suits. Isaac says to him, 'Look, there's a group of Catholic nuns over there, wearing their black habits. Go over, say hello, and ask one of them if your suit isn't the same color as what she's wearing.'

"Isadore goes over, introduces himself, and strikes up a conversation with one of the sisters. Isaac watches as they talk for a few minutes. Then Isadore holds his arm next to the nun's habit. She says something to him, shaking her head. Isadore bids her goodbye and, looking very depressed, goes back over to where his brother is standing.

"'Well,' Isaac says, 'what did the sister say about the color of our suits?'

"Isadore said, 'It was an expression that sounded like Latin.'

"'What was it?'

"'Pincus fucked us.'"

Doyle, laughing, raised his beer glass in a toast to Kellman. Moe laughed, too, before returning to the subject of Niall Hanratty. He said, "Well, at least you've got some things in common. He's Irish, so he probably likes to drink and gamble like you."

"Hanratty might be a teetotaler for all I know," Doyle said, "there are plenty of them over there. And he's a bookmaker, not a gambler. If they've got any smarts at all, bookmakers don't lose money." He looked at Kellman over the rim of his nearly empty beer glass. "And another thing. Your ethnic generalization reeks of political incorrectness. Not to mention startling ignorance."

"I didn't say all Irishmen drink and gamble. But I think a great many of them do, or would like to be able to do so without ruining their psyches, families, and livers. I'm well aware many of the men have 'taken the pledge' not to drink, as they put it. It's just that I, personally, have never known a non-drinking Irishman. Just like I've never known a combative barber," he added, "or a reticent lawyer."

Doyle pushed his empty beer glass to the side and signaled the attentive waiter. "Bushmills on the rocks, please," he said. Turning back to Moe, Doyle grinned. "Mark Twain put it best: 'beer corrodes an Irishman's stomach. Whiskey polishes it.'"

"Twain put a lot of things best," Moe said. "Cheers. Have a great trip, Jack."

Chapter Nineteen

Doyle's cab dropped him off at the bustling International Terminal of O'Hare Airport. It was early evening. The heat of the blistering Chicago summer day lingered. After checking his bag and displaying his passport, he joined the long line leading to the security entrance. It was moving very, very slowly.

Starting to sweat a little bit, even in the cavernous, air-conditioned area, Doyle listened with growing irritation as several of the people in both his and the adjacent lines talked on their cell phones. Like many users of those devices in public places, they did not murmur. As a result, Jack and the other phone-less people in the area were forced to listen to a woman arguing loudly with husband about how often he ("Ron, she's on a schedule") should walk their darling dog Cindy while she was away; an all-business looking guy barking instructions to an underling about an upcoming Golden Tier Salespersons' Weekend Retreat; and an excited teenage girl, wearing low slung jeans revealing her fat-rimmed waist, describing how she had "just, like, coming through the terminal," nearly bumped into a retired Chicago basketball legend, one of the world's most famous athletes, going the opposite way. The girl was shifting her weight from foot to foot, revealing a vivid tattoo riding her lower spine. Doyle thought of comedian George Carlin's wise warning: "Just because your tattoo has Chinese characters in it doesn't make you spiritual. It's right above the crack of your ass. And it translates to 'beef with broccoli.'"

The girl talked rapidly as she struggled to nudge her bulging carry-on case forward with her foot. "No," she said, "I couldn't, like, ask him for an autograph. He was with a bunch of guys and they walked past, like, really fast. But he is soooo fine! I heard them talking about Vegas, I think they were coming back from there."

Doyle smiled at that, remembering Moe Kellman's description of this famed athlete's betting habits. "He loves to gamble, and he's not real good at it," Moe had said. "He also fancies himself as a golfer. A few years back he got roped into some very high stakes golf matches at a country club up on the north shore. Some of the fellows I grew up with on the old West Side set him up like a ball on a tee."

Doyle knew who the fellows were, since he had a few years earlier been apprised of Kellman's boyhood spent among people who today ran what was left of the Chicago Outfit. "They brought in a very good golfer, a guy who could have been a pro but who worked for them in other capacities," Moe had continued, "and arranged for him to play the local star every day for almost two weeks. Every day the imported golfer won by a stroke or two. Just enough to keep the big fish on the line. No matter how good or how bad the star athlete played, no matter what score he shot, he always just barely lost. To a man with a competitive nature like his, pride like his, it was torture. He kept increasing the bets, coming back for more, convinced he could beat the imported shooter. He wound up getting taken for about a half-million, in cash. Which, of course, with his salary and endorsements, he could well afford," Moe said.

It wasn't until the passenger line had reached the conveyor belt and wand waving security people that the cell phone users shut up. On the other side of the check point, Doyle hurriedly put on his shoes. The dog-owning woman had resumed berating her husband as Doyle hustled past her and into one of the numerous airport bars. There were cell phone users in there, too, but at least he could sit near a television and watch and listen to the local news while he sipped a Bushmills. The cell phone annoyance made Doyle recall the comment made by one of his former bosses in advertising, a notorious lecher, who'd said that the "best thing cell phones are for is arranging adulterous meetings."

He felt comfortable now, in air-conditioning, out of range of the phone yappers. He felt himself relaxing. Thinking about his impending trip, he marveled at how quickly he'd acquiesced to Celia's request. It wasn't like him to give in so readily to anything of that nature. He smiled, remembering Celia's lovely face, but the smile disappeared when he thought of her husband's pitiful plight. "How mixed our days can be," he said to himself.

That thought triggered a memory of one of the young men on Doyle's AAU boxing team more than twenty years earlier. Horace Knox was a lanky, slow talking, tow-headed light heavyweight who had grown up in a small Kentucky mining town before moving north with his family as a high school student. Horace was frequently stunned by aspects of life in Chicago, turns of events involving weather, crime, the vagaries of humanity in a big city. Horace would shake his head at unusual happenings and comment, "Life's a funny old dog, ain't it?" Doyle and the other boxers would laugh hearing the man they called Hillbilly Horace say that. But Doyle wasn't laughing now as he waited for his first flight to Ireland, thinking of how Horace's observation applied to this mission he was about to embark upon.

The Aer Lingus flight from Chicago to the Dublin and Shannon airports was, as usual, full. Many of the passengers were Irish-Americans excited about visiting the home of their ancestors. There was also a sprinkling of Irish citizens, most of them happy to be going back after visits to the States. Doyle had a window seat next to a shy, quiet, middle-aged nun, who worked her rosary beads all the way across the Atlantic. The only thing she said to Doyle for hours was while they were still on the tarmac in Chicago. Glancing briefly at him, she whispered, "Hello, this the first time I've ever flown."

"There's nothing to be worried about," Doyle assured her. She nodded, far from convinced, and looked straight ahead from then on, fingers on her beads, lips moving in silent prayer. She declined all food and drink and attempts by the friendly flight crew to engage in her conversation. She was dressed in one of the traditional nun's habits now only worn by a few orders. Doyle couldn't help but think of the twin rabbis and the "midnight blue" hustle by Pincus the tailor.

After a surprisingly decent airline dinner, Doyle read the newspaper and magazine articles that he'd printed out of his computer before departing Monee Park. They dealt with contemporary Ireland, a country transformed in the last decade or so from economic laggard into the Celtic Tiger. A very good educational system producing an eager work force, combined with major tax breaks for business investors, had resulted in newly thriving computer, pharmaceutical and auto production industries. The number of people employed had doubled and the gross national product mushroomed four hundred percent. Ireland, Doyle was surprised to learn, ranked second only to Japan in the percentage of engineers and scientists in its population. A fifth of America's investment abroad was flowing into the Erin Isle. This onset of wealth had undoubtedly aided Niall Hanratty's business, Doyle thought, for the Irish were mad about horses, and betting on them. Now, they had more money than ever before with which to do so.

Doyle had also extracted from the great internet repository of information details about Hanratty's bookmaking operation. It was headquartered in the Dublin suburb of Dun Laoghaire, he read, a town whose name was pronounced "Done Leery." Hanratty also owned shops in Dublin as well as others in small towns scattered around many of the two dozen counties of Ireland's south. Hanratty's chain did not rival the giant Paddy Powers company, but it was extensive. According to a brief biography, Hanratty had grown up in subsidized housing in a poor section of Dun Laoghaire. He now owned a very upscale seaside residence located near that of Irish rocker Bono in his hometown, as well as a country house near Kinsale in County Cork. The rise of this ambitious, self-made man had obviously been rapid. "A hard man entirely." Wasn't that how Moe had heard Hanratty described?

There was an attractive Vacation Planner on Ireland in the pocket of the seat in front of Doyle. He examined it thoroughly, being particularly struck by the page pointing out that the native Irish language, Gaelic, did not "historically include the words 'yes' or 'no.'" That fact, the brochure continued, "explains a lot," including the roundabout ways many Irish citizens deal with such matters as the offer of a drink. "Ah, ye will! Ah, I'd better not. Ah, go on…Well, maybe a small one." The travel writer speculated that this fact "could also explain Ireland's tremendous success in the literary world, with such giants as Yeats, Joyce, Wilde, and Beckett, because if you can't say 'yes' or 'no' in your own language, when you come to speak and write in another one you've already got a head start in playing around with words."

Doyle smiled as he pondered this theory, thinking, *Hanratty and I won't be chatting in Gaelic. I'll settle for a resounding "yes" from him in good old English.*

At seven a.m. Dublin time, an hour before the scheduled landing and five and a half hours after departing O'Hare, the brightly efficient Aer Lingus flight crew began to serve a light breakfast, even offering coffee along with tea, croissants, and scones. Doyle was thankful he'd had three solid hours of sleep. In recent weeks, Monee Park problems on his mind, he had, in the words of the old blues song, not gotten much rest in his slumber. He felt great this morning approaching the small island which his forebearers had been forced to flee so many years before.

The plane crossed the shoreline near Bray, then circled north to begin its approach to Dublin Airport. Looking out his window, Doyle was surprised to see hundreds of small lakes, like tears formed on a green blanket, dotting this part of the island. The hues of green varied, but all the flecks of water glistened in the early sun. These numerous shining surfaces reminded him of what he'd seen during a flight over northern Minnesota.

Doyle looked at his seatmate. Though she had stayed awake praying through the dark Atlantic night, the nun appeared to be rested. He was glad to see she had accepted tea and a scone from the stewardess and put her rosary beads down next to the little jam packet on the plastic tray. She smiled at Jack as she leaned forward to look out his window. "Not so bad at all," she said, voice full of confidence and relief.

Some of Doyle's fellow passengers were barely half awake as they approached Customs in the Dublin Airport. Soon, however, they were alert and responding to the enthusiastic, loud-voiced official whose function it was to steer them into either the line for returning Irish citizens, or the line for others. He was a tall, lanky, brown haired man wearing a baggy, light brown suit, a laminated badge on its left lapel, and a yellow knit tie on a white shirt that had seen its prime. He stood at the dividing point between the two lines, dispensing warm welcomes, a huge smile never leaving his long, animated face. His name tag read F. Flynn.

Doyle watched and listened with amusement as Flynn energetically greeted the arrivals. To a chunkily built young woman in the Irish citizens line, Flynn said, "Ah, it must be Miss Ireland, returned from her vacation. Welcome back, darling." The woman beamed, a blush the color of a pink carnation spreading across her plain features. "Ah, go on with you," she said, playfully nudging Flynn with her elbow as she moved forward. A grumpy businessman couldn't help but grin when Flynn patted him on the shoulder, saying, "You're a sight for sore eyes, you are. Travel must agree with you, sir."

Flynn occasionally asked to see a passport before waving the person through to Customs. He asked Doyle for his. "Mr. Doyle, is it? Comin' from the States. Welcome home," Flynn said, reaching to shake Doyle's hand.

Waiting for his suitcase at carousel two, Doyle heard an elderly woman say to her husband, "That fella Flynn is a lively item, is he not? Talk about blarney!"

Smiling as he reached down for his suitcase, Doyle thought, *I don't know about blarney, but I can certainly appreciate bullshit of a very high caliber.*

Doyle took a taxi to the city. In contrast to his experiences in Chicago, the driver, after asking Doyle's destination, politely inquired if Doyle would mind him making a call on his cell phone. Doyle was startled at this request, having frequently sat behind Chicago cabbies who *never* stopped talking on their phones, even when accepting fares and tips.

Before pulling away into traffic exiting the airport, the cabbie asked, "Is it time you'll be needing to save?" He was a broad shouldered man, mostly bald, with a neatly trimmed fringe of brown hair on his large head. "I'm in no great hurry," Doyle said.

"That being the case, I'll drive you through the city instead of bypassing on the M50. Same fare, of course."

"Fine with me," Doyle said. "This is my first time in Dublin. I'd like to get a good look at it."

Riding down crowded city streets, Doyle was surprised to see many non-white faces. Then he remembered reading that the population boom was being fed by a significant influx of immigrants from various parts of the world. He was amused to see a Chinese grocery, then a Russian delicatessen, two Polish bakeries within blocks of each other. His cabbie, meanwhile, was on the phone, although driving carefully and well with one hand.

The cabbie's phone conversation lasted nearly five minutes. Conducted in low tones, it was comprised primarily of questions and oaths, with the occasional interspersing of a heartfelt "Jaayzus," or "the gobshite," or "you're having me on now." When he finally replaced the phone in its cradle next to him, he was shaking his head. He glanced at Doyle in the rear view mirror. "Honest to God," he said, "if he weren't me own brother I'd kill him."

"What went on there?" Doyle asked.

The cabbie took a deep breath. "I've got an older brother, Liam, who drinks. Too much and too often. He did so last night. After he stumbled out of the local, Regan's Pub, he gets in a cab. Halfway to home, Liam realizes he's out of money. He's spent it all on drink." He paused to downshift and smoothly cruise through an intersection just as the light changed.

"So," he continued, "Liam tells your man, not a driver from this company by the way, thank God, or I'd never hear the end of it, that he'll have to wait when they arrive so Liam can run in and borrow some Euros from our Mam. That's where Liam lives, at home, with her.

"Apparently, now, the cabbie has had a rough night prior to this. He's not about to go along with this idea of Liam's. So he stops the cab, gets out, opens the back door, and yanks Liam out. As I said to my brother just now, 'I don't blame the man.' I had a fare not pay me two nights back, and then throw up all over the back seat as well. A real gobshite. We put up with a lot in this business, you know," he said, making eye contact with Doyle in the rear view mirror.

"Anyway, Liam's real indignant, like. He says, 'I'll report you for this.' 'Report away,' the cabbie says, 'I should be the one reporting you,' and he drives off. Liam's about two miles away from home at this point." The cabbie paused, pointing ahead. "We're just coming up on Trinity College," he said, interrupting his narrative so Doyle could get a look at Dublin's educational landmark as they drove past.

Doyle said, "Thanks. Very impressive layout." He settled back in his seat. "But tell me, what happened with your brother?"

"Well, Liam starts walking home, or staggering was probably more like it, when he suddenly hears Garda sirens blaring, heading his way. As potted as he is, Liam thinks the cabbie has gone and reported him for not paying his fare. He's thinking the Garda, that's our police, are after him. So he veers off the sidewalk and ducks down behind some bushes of this big house. It takes him a minute or so to realize he's not alone. There's a couple of young fellas hiding there close to him in the same set of bushes, one of them with a big gunny sack, the other with a flashlight that's turned off. Fierce looking fellas.

"The sirens are getting closer. Liam's in a sweat now. He says, 'I can't believe they'd be on me so quick like.'

"Your flashlight man says, 'Shut the fook up and keep your head down.' Or words to that effect. He then whispers to Liam that he and his mate have just burgled a mansion two streets over! Says the flashlight man to me brother, 'You think they're lookin' for you? Don't flatter your fookin' self. They're after us.'"

Doyle leaned forward. "So, what happened?"

The driver executed a neat right turn across oncoming traffic before replying, "The three of them lay on their bellies in the bushes for about a half hour, quiet as cod, waiting for the guards to leave the area. Then they went their separate ways. Ah, Jaayzus," he concluded, "that Liam tops them all."

The cab pulled up at the curb. Doyle paid and tipped well, evidently well enough that the driver turned in his seat, smiled at Doyle, and extended his hand, saying, "Enjoy your stay here now. And tanks."

Chapter Twenty

With the famous Shelbourne closed for renovation, Shontanette Hunter had booked Doyle into a more modestly priced hotel, the Kenney, in Dublin's Temple Bar. "On our budget, it's just as well they're working on the Shelbourne," she'd said to Jack, adding, "but we're not skimping on you." This section of the city, he'd read, was thought of as Dublin's Times Square, but he found it to be much less garish and noisy, though similarly crowded.

After checking in, Doyle napped for an hour, then rose refreshed to begin a walking tour of the neighborhood, a routine that always helped him combat jet lag. A stroll, an early dinner, a couple of drinks, and a solid night of slumber, he figured, would set him up nicely for his next morning's meeting with Hanratty at the bookmaker's Dun Laoghaire headquarters.

It was a cool, sunny afternoon, and Doyle walked down Dame Street to Trinity College. Opting to give the school's library, housing the famous Book of Kells, a respectful pass, he walked through the beautiful campus before pulling up for a pint of beer in the Pavilion Bar. He next ventured into St. Stephen's Green where he spent nearly two hours ambling about, occasionally stopping to sit on a bench and observe the numerous passersby, breathing in the scents of summer in this 2,000 year old city.

Back in his hotel room, Doyle listened to a message on his phone's voice mail. It was from Barry Hoy, who described himself as "one of Mr. Hanratty's assistants." Hoy was calling to inform Doyle that his meeting with Hanratty the next day would take place "down at Kinsale. Urgent business took the boss there. He apologizes for the change in plans and looks forward to seeing you tomorrow. Oh, and he says bring your luggage along, you can overnight at his house near Kinsale. I'll pick you up at your hotel at ten in the morning." Doyle had to re-run the message twice, struggling to understand Hoy's frequently impenetrable Cork accent. Finally, he slammed down the phone. "So, the one upsmanship begins," he muttered.

Too tired now to maintain his anger for long, he went downstairs to the hotel's recently refurbished bar. Doyle was surprised to be handed a cocktail hour menu comprised of Spanish tapas, "our newest wrinkle in the hors d'oeuvres line," the bartender said. The tapas selection was varied and delicious. Doyle's reaction must have been obvious, for the bartender smiled, saying, "Oh, yes, we've come a long way from just fish 'n chips now. And how's your drink holdin'?" An hour later, Doyle paid his bill, left a ten Euro tip, and went off to bed.

Hoy was right on time the next morning. At the front desk, the Kenney cashier informed Doyle that Hoy had already checked him out and paid the bill. "He's waiting for you in front," the young woman said. Hoy stepped forward to shake his hand, mumble a greeting, and put Doyle's suitcase in the trunk of the dark blue BMW Sedan. He opened the right rear door, but Doyle said, "I'll ride up front if you don't mind." Hoy opened the passenger side door. "Foin," he said.

City traffic was thick and slow moving. They made better time on the highway as they headed southwest toward, first, Cork City, then on to the Kinsale area. It took Doyle several miles before he could adjust and become comfortable seeing oncoming traffic to the right side of his door.

Hoy was an excellent driver, not much of a conversationalist. Doyle asked how long the drive would take. "You'll be there for loonch," Hoy said, which Doyle had to think about before he realized the reference was to the mid-day meal. Doyle tried a few more salient questions. How long had Hoy worked for Hanratty? "Quite awhile now." Did he enjoy his work? "Ah, sure." Did his boss like racing? "The harses are fine with him, dogs too, other bets. They all bring in the mooney."

Doyle gave up and fell silent. Hoy, seemingly relieved, turned on the radio to a program of traditional Irish music. They drove through several small patches of what the reticent Hoy muttered was "a bit of lashin' rain." Each of these brief, moist interludes was followed by vivid sunlight. Doyle sat back in the car's very comfortable seat, enjoying the music and the view of the lush countryside. Hefty black and white cows, some appearing round as balloons, dotted the distant hillsides. Waiting at a stop light in one of the small towns on their route, Doyle glanced out at a store with a window displaying a variety of roasts and chops. He laughed aloud when he read the wooden sign that hung above this establishment. It read, "The Seriously Good Meat Shop." On the main streets of several of these small towns, Doyle admired impressive old churches, some of which now, incongruously, were bordered by new petrol stations and convenience stores.

When Doyle attempted a question about Hanratty's family, Hoy answered with a sharp look. Doyle looked at Hoy's big fisted hands on the wheel of the speeding auto, at his large, set jaw. The man had wrists like axe handles. His knuckles were disfigured in a way that a former boxer like Doyle could understand.

They rode without speaking for most of the next four hours. Again, Doyle resorted to closely observing the countryside. Besides the herds of milk cows, there were numerous, paint-marked flocks of fat sheep under the watchful supervision of border collies. Nearing Kinsale, Doyle saw a number of new homes. Some were very modern looking. The construction of many others was apparently designed to reflect that of nearby houses that were more than a century old.

Doyle was surprised when, as they entered the outskirts of Kinsale, Hoy broke his silence. He announced, "That's Charles Fort," pointing across the lovely harbor to a large set of stone buildings on a hillside. "They built that fort before 1700 even,"

Hoy volunteered. "The old courthouse there, down by Market Square, was there a hundred years before that. It was right off Kinsale that the Lusitania was sunk," he added, before resuming his silent driving.

Kinsale's long waterfront was crowded with slowly moving cars, looming, growling, tour buses, the narrow sidewalks packed with people. Dozens of moored boats bobbed in the blue green water. It was from this port, Doyle knew, that countless thousands of Irish emigrants had sailed on jam-packed boats to America, fleeing famine, religious persecution, and absentee landlords with their long history of imposing economic deprivation. Those that were able to leave were referred to as Wild Geese by families and friends left behind. Doyle wondered if his ancestors hadn't walked, frightened and reluctant but desperately determined, onto sailing ships in this very harbor, ships that would tear them away from all they'd known.

Hoy eased the blue BMW through the crowded, narrow streets, pulling up before Kinsale's Shamrock Off-Course Wagering Shop.

"I'll leave you here then," Hoy said. "The boss'll be expecting you upstairs. Just tell the lad at the door who you are. Don't worry about your luggage."

Niall Hanratty came around from his large, paper-strewn desk, his hand extended. He was an inch or two taller than Doyle, perhaps twenty pounds heavier, in apparently good shape. The sleeves of his white dress shirt were rolled up, revealing thickly muscled forearms, much like those of Doyle's maternal grandfather, who had been a Wisconsin cheesemaker. Hanratty's eyes and eyebrows were black, as was his combed back, carefully trimmed hair. "Mr. Doyle," he said, "it's a pleasure to meet you. Sorry to have changed the place of our meeting, but it could not be avoided."

Doyle said, "It worked out okay. I enjoyed the trip down from Dublin. This is my first time in your country."

"But not the last, I hope," Hanratty answered. "Now, could you do with some lunch?"

On their way out the front entrance of the betting shop, Hanratty stopped at the top of a wooden ramp. Coming up it in a wheelchair was a heavy set young man who smiled at them, saying, "Good day to you, Niall."

"Hello, Maurice," Hanratty replied, reaching down to shake the man's hand. "Have you done your research on today's races, then?"

"Indeed I have," beamed the man, beginning to roll himself through the doorway.

As they walked down the street Doyle said, "Are all of the betting shops here handicapped accessible?"

"All mine are," Hanratty said. He grinned at Doyle. "That lad back there? Maurice Banion? Sure, I'd build a highway if I had to in order to get him into the shop. He's one of my biggest volume customers. And he's among the very best for losing money to me."

Maurice Banion, Hanratty went on to explain, had been stricken with Parkinson's Disease "a few years back. He's on some medication for it that his Da, one of the richest men in Cork, tells me has helped Maurice somewhat physically while at the same time turning him into a gambling addict. The medication contains something called dopamine agonist. I'm not sure if I'm pronouncing that right.

"All I know," Hanratty continued, "is that Maurice showed up one day about two years ago. His chauffeur struggled to get the lad's wheelchair up the steps and through the door of the shop. Maurice lost 29,000 Euros to me that afternoon. He was betting wild—dog races in England, 'chasers in Scotland, some soccer matches in England. And having a hell of a good time doing so, I might add.

"Oh, he was an obvious treasure. Especially after his dear old Da showed up the following week to tell me that any losses incurred by Maurice were guaranteed by him. 'The poor lad has only a few years to go,' Da says to me, 'and I want him to enjoy them as best he can.' We shook hands, then, me thinking, 'Christ, let's do all we can to prolong this valuable life. I quickly had the wheelchair ramp in place. We serve Maurice lunch and dinner. He's happy as a lark. And one of the worst gamblers on this or any other island, I would venture to say."

Doyle was ordinarily hard to shock, but this approach to commerce struck him as being beyond the border of callous. He looked at Hanratty with new disrespect.

They approached a small restaurant overlooking the harbor. It was crowded with a combination of tourists and locals. The hostess greeted them by saying, "Your table's ready, Niall." He said, "Thanks, Mairead. And how are you keeping?" She said, "Not too bad at all" as she led them to a corner table at the back window overlooking a small courtyard.

They ordered drinks, iced tea for both, and food—"all the fish is grand here," Hanratty advised—before they got down to business. A slight smile appeared on Hanratty's long face when he said, "I'm impressed that cousin Celia decided to dispatch an emissary to talk to me."

Doyle let the "emissary" go by. He said, "I think she did it out of respect for you, as a relative and minority stockholder. I know she's written to you about her plans for Monee Park, but maybe not in the detail I can provide. Let me tell you what the situation is over there."

Over the next hour, and a superb lunch, Doyle carefully presented Celia's argument for not selling Monee Park. Facts and figures came trippingly off his tongue. Hanratty asked a question now and then, but for the most part listened silently. He occasionally made a notation in a small notebook he'd placed on the table.

They'd finished their coffees when Hanratty said, "Well, you've given me a lot to think on, Mr. Doyle."

"C'mon, Niall, let's drop the mister."

"All right, Jack," Hanratty said, eyes briefly alight in his dark, handsome face, "I can do that. What I can't do is give you an answer right off the reel. I suggest this: you stay at my house tonight. It's very near. Tomorrow, we'll go up to the Curragh, and see the racing, and do a bit of talking there."

Disappointed at the delay, but not wanting to show it, Doyle said, "I've always wanted to see that racetrack. All right."

Hanratty said, "I'll call ahead and tell the wife you'll be coming. She'll set you up. I'll join you out there for drinks by five or so." They shook hands outside the restaurant before Hanratty began walking to his office. Doyle watched as the blue BMW drove up to the curb almost at once, the stoic Hoy at the wheel.

The Hanratty residence was located some six miles outside of Kinsale, north, along the coast. Hidden from the road by a tree-lined berm, it sat on a small cliff that jutted out toward the sea. It was a three-story beige brick house, liberally windowed, with a swimming pool on its south side, and a large atrium on the ocean side facing a manicured lawn that ran to the cliff's edge. Hanratty's wife Sheila met Doyle in the atrium after a maid had shown him up to his second floor room and he'd unpacked and freshened up.

Sheila Hanratty was a short, plump, blond woman whose bangs bounced above her blue eyes as she rose from a couch to greet him. Her round cheeks were heavily freckled, as were her forearms. She wore a short-sleeved, navy blue blouse over white pants. Her handshake was firm, and while she looked at Jack appraisingly, it was not in a cold manner.

"You've come a long way, Mr. Doyle," Sheila said. "Welcome to Ireland. Welcome to our home." He told her how impressed he was by the house, and she then gave him a tour of the first floor. It was, throughout, expensively but comfortably furnished. It was obvious that she took pride in showing it to Doyle, noting that "we had it built for us nearly four years ago now." After a few moments, she added, "I'm from Bray, a town right over from Niall's Dun Laoghaire. We've come a long way from there," she added softly.

They spent the next hour talking in the atrium with its view of the sparkling, restless sea. Doyle asked about their family.

"Three boys," she answered, "two off at summer camps, the youngest visiting my parents over near Kilbrittain. They're retired there, in a house Niall had built for them." Sheila asked about Celia and Bob. Her eyes widened when Doyle described Bob Zaslow's deteriorating physical condition. "I had no idea that was going on," Sheila said. "That must be an awful thing to be facing each day."

Hanratty arrived at five, as promised, and they had drinks on the long, low terrace outside the atrium. Dinner was roast lamb, new potatoes, a salad of organic vegetables, then plates of fruit and cheeses. Doyle pronounced himself "satisfied beyond satiated. That was a wonderful meal, Sheila," he said, noticing how Niall nodded slightly in appreciation of the compliment.

It was still light when the two men walked down the two flights of wooden stairs to the beach. Sheila stayed in the house, helping the maid as she cleared the dinner dishes, then calling her parents to check on her son. "To tell you the truth," she'd confided to Doyle, "I'm uncomfortable having servants. I don't like even calling them that."

The dark waters of the Irish Sea touched gently on the shore and the night sky was speckled with stars. "One of our finer nights, Jack," Hanratty said. "Our summer at its best." As they continued walking, Hanratty asked about Doyle's career background. Doyle responded with a very summarized, somewhat sanitized version, Hanratty watching him out of the corner of his eye as they walked.

In turn, Doyle asked Hanratty how he'd "gotten so far, so fast, in such a tough business?" The bookmaker replied, "Long hours spent outthinking the competition. Longer hours putting my plans to work." He offered no more.

"Do you know where any of your folks hailed from over here?" Hanratty asked.

"No," Doyle said, "I'm sorry to say I don't. People on my father's side fought in our Civil War, I know that. One of my great-great-great uncles, Pete Trainor, 'gave a leg for the Union cause,' as family lore has it."

Hanratty said, "So, they were probably Famine People."

"That's probably the case. But I don't have any idea how those early relatives even entered the U. S. An aunt of mine could find no written records of their entrance. She speculated that they were probably what was called Two Boaters."

"And what's that?" Hanratty said.

"Many people from Ireland took ships that landed them in Canada. Later, they crossed over into New England, or upstate New York, by taking canoes or small boats on the St. Lawrence River."

"Two Boaters," Hanratty laughed. "That's a new one."

He turned serious a few minutes later when he pointed up the cliff to what he said was "part of the Famine Walk. It was where the poor starving devils walked when they were on their way to the famine ships in Kinsale harbor. Maybe that's where some of your people walked."

Doyle said, "I wouldn't know about that. All I know is that they got the hell out of here."

"Mine didn't. Mine stayed. They toughed it out." Hanratty took a final puff on his cigar before grinding it out in the wet sand. "A million and a half people died here back during that terrible time," he said softly, "either of starvation or fever. Families were broken apart forever. Another million got the hell out. But not mine."

They had a nightcap in the library of the big, now mostly dark house, a room with walls lined with shelves of racing books and papers. Other shelves held works of fiction and poetry, some biographies scattered among them. Several pieces of expensive equine art—Jack admired a Stubbs and two Munnings paintings—added color to the large room.

Doyle said, "Do you do much reading, Niall?"

"Sheila's always been the reader. Early on in my life, I was too busy carving out a living. I didn't have much time for schooling. But I've done a good bit of catching up myself in recent years." Hanratty nodded toward the book shelves. "You had a wonderful novelist in your country who wrote about mine.

Thomas Flanagan. I have first editions of all his novels. And there's much of Yeats that I enjoy. Do you know his poem 'At Galway Races'? Some lovely lines.

And we find hearteners among men
That ride upon horses.

"Myself, of course," he added, "I find more 'hearteners' among men who bet on horses."

When the maid brought in their drinks, Irish coffee for each, Doyle took a swallow and, seconds later, felt his scalp tingle and begin to moisten. "Did the maid put four or five shots in here?" he said, placing the cup down on the table next to him and reaching for a water glass.

Hanratty smiled. "They must not provide you with proper proportions over in the states.

"Sheila tells me you're not averse to a bit of local music, Jack. There'll be a session tonight at a pub not far from us. Even with your great interest in jazz, I think you also might have a feeling for some music coming out of our own people."

"Try me, Niall."

Chapter Twenty-One

Hanratty drove the three of them in his BMW some five miles down dark, narrow, tree-lined roads to an intersection that had a closed petrol station on one corner, a one-story building surrounded by cars on another. The lighted sign above the door read Sheridan's Pub. Noting the large number of parked vehicles, Doyle said, "Where do all these people come from? I haven't seen a house for miles."

"Oh, from various places around the area," Sheila said. "The band that's on tonight has quite a following."

"Evening, Mr. Hanratty," the bartender said with a wave as they followed a waitress to the only empty table in the large, jam-packed room. The table sat beneath a poster with black and white photos of Joyce, Yeats, O'Casey, and Shaw, under which someone had scrawled in ballpoint pen The Holy Trinity Plus One. To the right side of the poster was an autographed color photo of a young, grinning, bleary-eyed Brendan Behan, a half-full pint in hand.

The waitress took their drink orders. Doyle looked around the room. Above the long bar, color television sets showed soccer matches from various venues. A half-dozen men surrounded a pool table being used by two silent, very intent players. There was a sizeable cadre of senior citizens at the far end of the room. *Jesus,* Doyle thought, concentrating on one small, male, pipe smoking figure in their center, *it looks like the ghost of Barry Fitzgerald.*

At the front of the tables, wheelchair placed aside one, Doyle saw a young man he thought he recognized. He nudged Niall. "That's your premier customer up there, right? Maurice Banion."

"None other. Poor lad used to be star fiddler before his Parkinson's took over." As if he'd been privy to their conversation, Banion looked back at them and raised his glass, smiling broadly. Hanratty toasted him back. "It's a blessing, you know, that Maurice has his gambling to distract and amuse him." Hanratty took a sip of his pint. "He dropped eight thousand Euros in my Kinsale shop this afternoon."

The band was called The Nolans, its leader Ciaran Nolan, a tall, slim, fortyish man with full black beard that threatened to lay across the strings of his fiddle once he began to play. Ciaran his five colleagues were snugged into a U-shaped corner of the room. The four other men, on guitar, concertina, banjo, and tin whistle, were built like football linemen. In their midst stood a slender girl with long black hair, a fiddle in her hand. "That's Ciaran's sister Blathnaid," Sheila informed Doyle. "Ciaran and Blathnaid are from Listowel. Blathnaid married a lad from near here, Martin Murphy, the fella with the guitar."

Suddenly, without a word of introduction, music leapt off the instruments, a fulsome sound that rippled through the room without need of microphone. Tempos were quick. One melody seemed to Doyle to float effortlessly into another. No one danced, all the listeners leaning forward, some with their eyes fastened on the musicians, others with their eyes closed, heads nodding. Almost all, including Doyle, were tapping feet to the lilting beat. For a moment Jack envisioned Celia in this setting. He pictured her, with graceful legs and long red hair, dancing to the lovely strains of music he knew he'd never heard before, yet somehow recognized.

His reverie ended when Sheila gave him a nudge. She was pleased by his obvious appreciation of the Nolans' music.

"You have a far away look, Jack," Sheila said. "Where are you now?"

"Not far away. I think I'm home."

The band played without break for almost an hour. When they finally laid their instruments down, bowing to their enthusiastic audience, and moved to a table where drinks awaited them, Doyle tapped Hanratty on the arm. "That was fantastic, Niall. Great stuff. But I have a question. Why doesn't the leader, Ciaran, ever announce the titles of the songs? I'd like to know what they were. But the band just seems to glide from one number into the next. Am I right?"

"That's the way they do it, right," Hanratty smiled. "It's a tradition around here. The assumption is that everyone already knows the songs. With the exception of the occasional visitor from America, of course, that is the case."

Hanratty downed his pint, signaling the waitress to refill the glasses on his table and those on the table where the band sat. "All right, then," Hanratty said, "they started off with three jigs, 'Petticoat Loose,' 'The Geese in the Bog,' then 'O'Sullivan's March.' Next, they slid in one of the slow, sad, old rebel songs, 'The Wind That Shakes the Barley.' You might have noticed how quiet it got in here during that number. A meaningful song. They followed with some reels, 'Lucy Campbell' and 'Tarboltin' and 'The Repeal of the Union.'

"Finally, at my request," Niall said, leaning closer and whispering, "the lad on the flute finished up the set with 'The Piper Remembered.' It's one of Sheila's old favorites." Doyle had glanced at the Hanrattys during the playing of that song, seeing Sheila listening with her eyes closed, nodding along to the slow rhythm of the sweet melody, Niall's large hand clasping hers.

Two music-packed hours later Sheila, who had been drinking only sparkling water throughout their stay at Sheridan's Pub, drove them home. "They've cracked down something fierce on drinking drivers in Ireland, even out here in the country," Niall said, "Garda lying in wait outside pubs at night." He sighed. "I suppose it's just as well. Before all the money rolled in, and the cars, we just staggered home at night like proper upright citizens. Or weaved our way in cars not going fast enough to make a decent dent in anything. It's all changed now."

Two miles down the road from the pub Niall said, "Sheila, pull over there to the side for a bit." When she'd done so, Niall rolled down his window. He reached out to wave at the Garda car that was half-hidden alongside a tall, thick hedge. The Garda driver flashed his headlights in response. "Nice fellas, those two," Niall said as Sheila put the BMW in gear. "They bet a lot of hurling with me."

Doyle said, "Have you ever gotten a speeding ticket from those fellows, Niall?"

"I received a speeding ticket the first month I ever owned a car. Up in Dun Laoghaire it was. I was on my way to collect Sheila for a movie. That was more than twenty years ago. I've not got one since. I don't believe in them. A completely unnecessary expense."

There were hurried good nights once they arrived at the Hanratty home. Sheila gave Doyle a hug, Niall a strong handshake before they went upstairs. In the guest room Doyle undressed quickly, brushed his teeth, and fell gratefully, happily into bed. "I'm starting to get a good feeling about Niall," he murmured before easing into sleep.

Chapter Twenty-Two

The next day dawned as beautiful as its predecessor. Jack, Sheila, and Niall breakfasted early and well, Jack hoping that Niall would be forthcoming with his decision about Monee Park. But that was not the case. Realizing this, Doyle concentrated on the food. His appetite had never betrayed him, and it didn't now. He worked his way through two servings of rashers, scrambled eggs, bangers, black pudding, baked tomato halves, three slices of wheat toast with blackberry jam, and half a pot of coffee before offering "my compliments to the cook. That was great." Sheila had watched him with wonder, then appreciation, as he ate. "Sure, it's a marvel you don't weigh fifteen stone the way you put it away," she said with a laugh. "I have a formidable metabolism," Doyle responded, reaching for another scone.

An hour later, driving northeast out of Kinsale, Hanratty pointed out the car window at a run-down property. The old house looked as if it hadn't been inhabited in many years. The acre plot was overgrown with weeds, its few trees holding straggly, nearly leafless limbs. Hanratty said, "A place like that was considered to be worthless until a few years back. There were dozens of such places in this area. Now, most have been sold, knocked down, and replaced with homes worth a half-million Euros and upward. The old folks around here can hardly believe it. Neither can I, for that matter."

Hoy sped over the bypass at Cork City, the one leading to Dublin. Doyle said, "I've read quite a bit about the economic boom here. One article said net worth had grown more than three-hundred and fifty percent in the past ten years. And a great deal of that new money has gone into property investment."

"I'm sure that's accurate. The last report I read said the average house in Dublin now goes for more than 600,000 Euros. It's amazing, it is," Hanratty said with a laugh.

As they continued on their ride, Hanratty spent much of the time on the phone, discussing business with various of his employees around the country. Doyle stifled his urge to bring up his own business, not wanting to appear overly eager. Between phone calls, they spent most of the time talking horses.

Doyle leafed through the numerous pages of the *Racing Post* that were devoted to Irish racing. He was envious of the extensive newspaper coverage the sport received not only in the trade papers but in the national dailies. After looking at the schedule of upcoming Irish racing meetings, he turned to his host, who had completed his most recent phone conversation. "Niall, how is it that these Irish meetings are so short? Some of them, I see, are only one or two days per year. I know the Curragh is open a few weeks a year, although not in a row. But how do these other, abbreviated meets make it?"

"How do you mean, Jack?"

Doyle shrugged. "I guess I don't understand how they are open for so few days and make it financially. In the States, there's hardly a track that isn't open a minimum of thirty days. Monee Park runs all summer and part of the fall. We've got more than a thousand horses on the grounds, housed in barns that also include living quarters for some of the backstretch workers. Heartland Downs, the big Chicago track, races ninety-five days. They've got more than two thousand horses on their grounds throughout that period."

He pointed down at the *Racing Post* in his lap. "I'm looking here at the Irish racing schedule. There's just four days at Killarney. Four days at Punchestown. Only one day at Tipperary.

How do they staff these places with maintenance workers, mutuel clerks, concession people, and so on?"

"It's an entirely different situation here, Jack. The only horses on the grounds of any of our tracks are the ones that are to race that day, maybe one-hundred thirty or so at the big tracks, eighty to a hundred at the smaller ones. They are vanned in from their trainers' yards, or farms. So, there's no huge capital investment in barns or dormitories as in the States. As a result, permanent staff is kept small. The totalisator system is owned by a semi-State organization called Horse Racing Ireland and moves with its own staff from track to track."

Doyle said, "Is this setup profitable?"

"Not really. I doubt there's a handful of tracks in Ireland that are making an adequate return on capital investment. However, for the most part, the tracks are owned by groups who have the interests of the sport at heart. Essentially, all profits are re-invested. Prize money, or purse money as you call it, is funded entirely by owners, commercial sponsors, and Horse Racing Ireland. Some sixty million Euros of government funds was channeled into the industry last year."

"Government subsidies," Doyle said wistfully. "What our tracks, especially a struggling enterprise like Monee Park, wouldn't give for something like that."

"Remember, most people in Ireland are still only one or two generations removed from rural communities. There is a great, continuing affinity among the people for the horse and all that goes with it. We love our racing.

"But," Hanratty continued, "most of our racecourses were built by wealthy owners many years ago. Some of the current generation of owners may not have the same interest in the sport as their forebearers. They're now facing the option of keeping the courses open without enjoying any real financial return, or selling out to real estate developers for big bucks."

"That sounds familiar," Doyle grunted.

"I thought it would. It probably would to Cousin Celia now, wouldn't it."

Doyle thought Hanratty's last remark would segue into a declaration of his intentions regarding Monee Park. Instead, the bookmaker made another call on his cell phone, then said, "Are you a bettor, Jack?"

"On occasion."

"Then I suggest you make one of those occasions the third race this afternoon. All the smart lads are pounding in bets on a two-year-old named Long Kinch, a first-time starter from one of our top stud farms. The word is that he's a proper flier."

"Thanks for the tip," Doyle said.

Their destination, the Curragh, one of the world's famous racetracks and site each year of the Irish Derby, was located some thirty miles southwest of Dublin. "They started racing horses at the Curragh in 1741," Hanratty said. "It sits on a limestone plain near many breeding farms. The belief is that the land is the best bone-making land for raising thoroughbreds."

"Curragh, what does the name mean?"

Hanratty said, "It means 'place of the running horse' in Gaelic."

Doyle looked with interest at the massive stands so visible in this rural setting. White rails swept around the huge, grass-covered oval. Cars were streaming into the parking lots. There was no wind, and huge white clouds sat like dumplings in the summer air.

Hoy pulled up to the main entrance, letting the two of them out, then driving away to park after Hanratty had said, "Five sharp, here, Barry."

Hanratty was waved through the entrance after being enthusiastically greeted by its attendant. "Let me show you a bit of the place," he said to Doyle, steering him toward the large paddock, which was now filling up with horses for the first race.

Hundreds of people surrounded the paddock, looking over the horses, at their track programs, some calling out greetings to the grooms as they walked their horses past. The feeling of enthusiasm was palpable. Doyle couldn't help but be struck by the lively interest shown by these fans of all ages. At Monee Park, he'd noticed, many of the regular patrons never seemed nearly that engaged as they went about their gambling, rarely venturing outside the building to see a live horse, or race, concentrating entirely on televised racing action. This Curragh crowd, their attention riveted on horses walking within feet of them, was in marked contrast to their Monee Park counterparts.

Hanratty led Doyle down the front of the stands, where the licensed bookmakers had set up shop. Changes in the odds were posted by one man, another man recorded wagers. "Yes, they still offer this archaic form of bookmaking here out in the open air. The pari-mutuel machines are inside," Hanratty said. "Many of the older fellas have never, and will never, bet with anybody except a live bookmaker."

Hanratty paused just outside the Curragh's winner's enclosure. He shielded his eyes from the bright sun as he looked at it. "That, Jack," he said, "is where Ireland's Derby winner gets his photo taken every year. You could rightly call that the most expensive little piece of land in the country. There are many men and women who have spent countless millions trying to buy a horse that will turn up in there."

They strolled into the interior of the grandstand. "That is one of the longest bars in the world," Hanratty said, pointing ahead of them toward a busy section where hustling bartenders worked behind a stretch of mahogany that ran for hundreds of feet. The huge area was abuzz with racing talk, arguments over various horses' merits, voices being raised and then briefly stilled as their owners lifted glasses to their mouths. As Doyle took in the scene, he felt a tug at his elbow. He looked down at a dapper, older man, ex-jockey size, whose wide grin ran under a large, red nose. The little man lifted a thumb in the direction of the long bar. "Sure," he said, "there's no finer sight in the world than a furlong of bent elbows. Am I right, now?"

"You are indeed," Doyle said, laughing as he followed Hanratty to a nearby elevator.

◇◇◇

They stood on the balcony outside Hanratty's suite that over-looked the Curragh's finish marker, watching the running of the third race. As the winning two-year-old flashed across the line below them, many lengths the best, Hanratty smiled. "Long Kinch won like a thief in the night," he said with satisfaction.

"Like the 'good thing' he was, as we say in America about a touted horse that lives up to his billing," Doyle replied.

Back inside the suite, Hanratty pointed Doyle to a seat at the dining table. The large room was comfortably furnished and contained a small kitchen area, refrigerator, bar, and a sound system out of which poured American jazz. Doyle had pronounced himself surprised by Hanratty's interest in what was Doyle's favorite music. "A friend of mine in the States sends me CDs of Marian McPartland's 'Piano Jazz' programs," Hanratty explained. "What a lovely woman she is," he continued. "It's because of her that I began collecting CDs of your great piano players. Oscar Peterson. Bill Evans. Gene Harris and Dave McKenna and Dave Brubeck, to name just a few.

"But," he said, "we're not here today to discuss my tastes in music, are we Jack?"

"Go on."

Hanratty leaned forward, forearms on the table, his large hands clasped. "I'll get right to the point, Jack. My answer to you, and to cousin Celia, is that I'm going to press forward trying to effect a sale of the Monee Park land. I've retained an attorney in Chicago. I won't be changing my mind," he said. He sat back in his chair, grim and determined.

"Why am I not surprised?" Doyle said. He got to his feet and walked over to the window that overlooked the racetrack. "What a damn waste of time this trip was." Turning back to his host he said, "Can you tell me your reasoning? I'd like to be able to report at least something I've learned here."

Hanratty said, "It's as I've indicated earlier. I want to cash out that money now. I have an immediate use for those funds. I don't want to wait a year, or two years, for those video slot machines to become a reality. If they even do. If I'm getting the proper information from the states, those machines are no sure thing at all."

He rang the bell on the table and a tuxedoed waiter promptly came through the door. "Whiskey, Miles," Hanratty said. The man hurried away.

"Who's providing you with your information?" Doyle asked.

"That's not really any of your business."

"Well, if it's that shyster Art Riley, as I've been led to believe, you may not be getting the real thing."

Hanratty's handsome face flushed. "I always get the real thing, Jack. That's how I've gotten to where I am."

The waiter politely knocked, then entered with a tray bearing a bottle of Bushmills, an ice bucket, two glasses, and a small Waterford crystal pitcher of water. He set the contents of the tray on the table and left. Hanratty poured himself a glass of whiskey, neat, then pushed the bottle across the table to Doyle. "Not just yet, Niall," Doyle said.

Hanratty downed his drink in one gulp, poured another of similar size, and sat back in his chair. "It's too bad you had to come all this way for nothing," he said. "If Celia had taken me at my word, you wouldn't have." He sipped his whiskey. "Can I ask you something?" he said.

Doyle nodded, and Hanratty said, "I've never laid eyes on cousin Celia, but I've seen a photo or two of her, courtesy of Uncle Jim. Is she the beautiful creature she appears to be?"

"She's all of that," said Doyle, not liking the direction this conversation was taking. He shifted slightly in his chair as Hanratty looked at him over the rim of his half-full glass. Through a half smile Hanratty inquired, "And how do the two of you get on?"

Doyle's hands tightened on the arms of the chair. He made an effort to relax. "You know, Niall, I not only don't like your answer about the Monee Park business, I don't like the tone of that last question. How I get along with your cousin is none of your business."

Hanratty polished off his second drink and quickly poured another. The liquor seemed to have absolutely no effect on him.

"Now, Jack," he said, "don't take me wrong. I was just curious. I know little about my cousin. What I do know makes me sympathize with her situation. A failing racetrack. A husband doomed to die in the fairly predictable future. The pressures on her must be enormous."

Voice rising now, Hanratty said, "Why doesn't the woman just sell the damn place? Take the money? Then I could take mine, and we could get on with our lives."

"You forget something here, Niall," Doyle said. "Celia feels she is honoring your Uncle Jim's memory by keeping Monee Park in operation. She feels a powerful obligation to the memory of the man who raised her, schooled her, loved her. She's not about to turn her back on that," Doyle said forcefully. "It is," he added more softly, "just the way she is."

Hanratty pounded the table with his right fist, his face reddening. "Can't this woman see the reality of the situation? There's not a thin line between tradition and stagnation, there's a crevasse. What she feels for Uncle Jim shouldn't be a factor in what is a business decision. Going the way she is, Celia will run that track into the ground. It might take a year or two, but she'll wind up costing us both."

He got to his feet, hands on the table, glowering, shoulders bunched beneath his suit coat. "I won't put up with it," Hanratty said.

Doyle said, "You're quite the fellow, Niall. I can recognize that. But what you'll put up with, and what you'll get away with, are two very different things."

The bookmaker took a deep breath before walking over the balcony window. He looked out, hands on his hips. Without turning his head, he said, "I don't suppose you'd consider joining my team on this project. See it my way, and go back to Chicago and persuade Celia to sell. I'd make it very much worth your while."

Doyle snorted. "You've got plenty of nerve, Niall. But not much fucking class."

He got out of his chair. He poured himself a finger of Bushmills and quickly drank it down.

"Don't call the faithful Hoy for me," Doyle said, walking to the door of the suite. "I'll find my own way to the airport."

It was early evening when Hanratty reached his Dun Laoghaire headquarters. He phoned Riley in Chicago. The lawyer had returned from court and was preparing to walk across LaSalle Street to lunch. A breaking and entering charge against one of his regular clients had been dismissed and Riley was in a jubilant mood. It evaporated when he heard Hanratty's bitter tone.

"This campaign of yours, Mr. Riley," Hanratty said, "it's not working. Celia McCann isn't budging from her position. That's just recently been made very clear to me by her employee Jack Doyle. What the hell are you planning to do about this?"

Riley took a deep breath. "Mr. Hanratty, I'll be doing better very soon, I assure you. My, er, associates have actually done what I've instructed. But perhaps I've set our sights too low. Give me a couple of days to rethink this matter. I'm sure more pleasing prospects are in store." He wiped his sweaty brow.

There was a brief silence. Then Riley heard Hanratty say, before he hung up, "I didn't take you for a fella to be satisfied with ten percent of nothing."

Chapter Twenty-Three

The Aer Lingus flight landed on time at O'Hare. But at this extremely busy international airport, more than forty-five minutes went by until a gate became available. Doyle took deep breaths as he tried to relax amid the increasingly impatient passengers, both on the plane as it sat on the tarmac, then in the lengthy customs line. The only break in the tedium came when one of Airport Security's drug dogs, an active and inquisitive beagle, discovered several rashers of Irish bacon in the carry-on of one embarrased returnee. It was nearly seven o'clock before Doyle could retrieve his Accord and begin the seventy-minute drive south and east to Monee Park. He called Celia on his cell phone as he drove. They agreed to meet in the Turf Club once he'd arrived at the track.

Doyle got there first. Marilyn, the Turf Club hostess, said, "Celia will be down in about fifteen minutes." She walked him to a window table overlooking the racing strip. Three tables away there was a lively party of six people, among them a man who was the oldest of them by several decades. He was wearing expensive looking sport clothes and a blue tie on a glistening white shirt. Doyle said softly to Marilyn before she turned to go back to her post, "Who's that old guy? I've noticed him here before. But I don't know his name." Marilyn smiled, then pulled out a chair next to Jack's.

"That's Izzy Kreinberg."

"Never heard of him."

"Well," Marilyn responded, "you should get to know him. Mr. Kreinberg owns a lot of horses that run here, including some pretty good ones. He's quite the character. Made his money in the commercial glass business. He's owned racehorses for, oh, gosh, I couldn't even tell you, but I know it's a long time. I can tell you his age, though," Marilyn added, smiling again. "Mr. Kreinberg will celebrate his ninety-ninth birthday this summer. There's going to be a party here for him."

Doyle turned to take another look at Kreinberg. "Nearing ninety-nine! He doesn't look a day over eighty."

"Doesn't act it either," Marilyn said. "And talk about a positive view of life! Mr. Kreinberg is still buying yearlings at the sales. He's a wonderful old gentleman, usually very good natured, famous for his philanthropy. He's a long time widower who has quite a lively eye for the ladies. But," she added, frowning, "he can be irritable at times. I think this is one of them."

They saw Kreinberg glowering as Hugo the waiter placed a bottle of Beck's beer down in front of him.

"I wonder what's bothering him," Doyle said.

Marilyn tried to hide a laugh with her hand. Leaning close, she said, "I know *exactly* what's bothering Mr. Kreinberg. I saw the same scene when he was here last weekend. He looked so unhappy that I went over to inquire if there was something wrong with the service. After all, he's one of our best customers.

"Anyway, he told me all about his problem. It seems that when he had his annual physical last month, his doctor told Mr. Kreinberg that his triglyceride count was a bit too high."

Doyle laughed, then apologized to Marilyn for interrupting her. "Excuse me, but I couldn't help but think that Kreinberg has probably had more physical exams than all the cars I've owned over the years have had oil changes. If I ever get to be Kreinberg's age, I'd be happy just *having* triglycerides. But, go on with what you were saying."

"The doctor advised Mr. Kreinberg to change his drinking habits. No more of his favorite gin martinis that he's been enjoying all these years. If he had to have alcohol, the doctor said, Mr. Kreinberg was to limit himself to an occasional beer."

Doyle shrugged. "So? I mean, I guess that's kind of a sacrifice on the old guy's part. But he hasn't been forced into becoming a teetotaler. What's his big problem?"

Marilyn looked over her shoulder to make sure she was not being overheard. "Mr. Kreinberg's complaint, and this is exactly how he put it to me, was, 'The damn beers make me go to the bathroom too often. And when I'm gone, some of these young fellows try to steal my dates.'"

Marilyn and Jack looked on in amusement as Kreinberg spoke earnestly to the tanned, blond woman to his left, a woman probably a half-century his junior, his hand on her arm. Kreinberg said something that made her laugh loudly, and the old man beamed.

"Well, bless his jolly, old horny soul," Doyle said admiringly.

A few minutes later Jack got to his feet and held the chair for Celia. "I'm sorry I'm late," she said, eyeing him expectantly. He grimaced. "I wish I had better news. But your cousin Niall has a head as hard as the Blarney Stone. I'm afraid I didn't get anywhere with him."

He went on to recount his conversations with Hanratty. Celia listened glumly, occasionally sipping her coffee. Finally she sat back, resigned but determined. "I'll just go ahead without any help or understanding from Niall," she said. "It would make it a lot easier if I had his support on the video slots project, just so we could present a united front to the legislators. I've been told by Lew Langmeyer that that's desirable. But, if it's not to be, it's not to be. I'll go it alone."

She reached across the table and patted Doyle's hand. "I should have said earlier, thanks for your efforts over there. I really appreciate it, Jack. I know you tried your best."

"My best was a long way from good enough," Doyle said, adding, "There's something else I've been thinking about. Cousin

Niall made it known to me that he was aware of what he termed your 'recent Monee Park troubles,' the robbery and then the electrical failure."

"Well, both of those were covered in all the papers here, and on the horse racing websites. I would imagine that Niall keeps up with the internet racing news. I've been sort of keeping track of him lately, myself," she admitted. "I Googled his OTB chain and even found a short biography of him, along with a photo of him. He's got a stubborn kind of look about him even in that picture."

Doyle momentarily shifted his attention to the nearby table where Izzy Kreinberg was excusing himself from his party, about to hurry off to the men's room. When he turned back to Celia, Doyle said, "Seems to me, and my naturally suspicious nature, that these occurrences are not random, unconnected. That first the robbery, then the electrical failure were acts aimed at harming this track financially. And making its owners more likely to sell it and get the hell out."

Celia's pretty mouth tightened. "Not *this* owner," she said sharply.

Doyle smiled, looking at her with her Irish up, green eyes ablaze. "Hold on," he said, "I didn't mean to get you riled up." He thought how even more appealing this tall, elegant, caring woman was when she permitted herself to reveal how she really felt, when she let down her barrier of cool reserve.

Celia said, "What is Niall like?"

"I spent less than three days with him. But I saw enough of him to realize he's a very formidable rival, or opponent, or whatever you want to call him in this fight over use of the track. He's smart, very sure of himself. He's not gotten to where he is without edging a few bodies toward the cliffs. And he's got a guy working for him, named Hoy, who looks like he might have taken a pass on the Provos because they were too tame for him."

Celia sat back in her chair, composed now. "I still don't know enough about Niall to say he'd resort to criminal acts being carried out here in order to get his way. How could he orchestrate anything like that from so far away even if he wanted to? No, Jack, I just can't see him being behind some long range conspiracy against me."

"I hope you're right," Doyle said.

◇◇◇

Minutes later Doyle climbed the iron stairs to the press box, two at a time. Spending time with Celia seemed to energize him. Before he'd reached the phone outside the door, the door was jerked open from the inside. Morty burst through it, head down, swearing. His shoulder banged into Doyle's. Morty, startled, looked up, wild eyed, prepared to continue his descent down the stairs. Doyle grabbed Morty's left arm. "What the hell's the matter with you? Where are you going? We're not done working tonight."

The little man's answer was almost indiscernible, delivered as it was in a torrent of speech at an increasingly high pitched level. *I've read about people spluttering*, Doyle thought, *but I've never seen or heard anyone do it. Until now.* He grabbed Morty by the lapels of his sport coat and shook him. "God damn it," Doyle said, "settle down. Tell me what's going on with you. Hear me?"

Morty slumped against the staircase railing, head lowered. "I bet the five horse in the last race $100 across the board. He's coming from behind like a runaway freight train in the stretch, about to run right past them all. He's going right over the top of them, Jack! Then some tiring pig in front of him veers out right in his path. My jock, Jason Lebeau, has to take up. When Jason gets the five horse going again, it's too late. He finishes fourth."

Doyle said, "Morty, you've got no business betting that kind of money. Not on your salary." The anguished look on Morty's face made Doyle restrain any more reprimanding. This was a subject for another day.

Morty looked upward as if trying to peer through the grandstand ceiling for guidance. He inhaled a great gulp of air. Then he bellowed, "Fuck horse racing! And everybody who likes it!"

He glared at Doyle as he brushed past him and ran down the stairs.

"Jesus," Doyle said to himself, "this man needs help. He's got to stop betting before he works himself into bankruptcy or a heart attack. Or a parlay of the two." Morty was the sole support of his aged mother and lived with her in a bungalow only a mile or so from Monee Park. That arrangement would serve to reduce Morty's expenses, but $300 bets going into the dumper surely wouldn't.

An hour later, Doyle looked up from his computer screen to see his chagrined assistant. Doyle said, "You look sheepish in loser's clothing, you know that?"

Morty blushed. "I'm more embarrassed than anything, Jack. I'm sorry I acted like such an asshole before. I've just been on kind of a cold streak lately, and that last race really got to me. I mean, I was on the verge of a major win, you know? But again, I apologize."

"Have you thought about laying off betting for awhile? Especially now, when you're going so bad?"

"I guess I'll have to," Morty said.

Driving to his condo later, Doyle put Morty and his betting travils out of his mind, at least for now. Instead, he reviewed his debriefing session with Celia, feeling alternately exhilarated at having earned her trust, if not admiration, then depressed because he'd failed her in his mission to Ireland. Traces of her perfume seemed to linger in the air. He could still feel the touch of her cool hand on his. "What a schmuck you are, Doyle," he said aloud as he zoomed around a crawling semi on the Ryan near Ninety-fifth Street. "Get your mind off that woman."

He turned on the radio to WDCB and listened as Billie Holiday worked her slow and lustrous way through "I Fall in Love Too Easily." He grinned ruefully when the beautiful old ballad was over, saying to himself, "Watch out, Doyle."

Chapter Twenty-Four

SPRINGFIELD—A bill that would expand casino gambling and legalize video slot machines at horse racing tracks cleared its first hurdle here today when approved by the Illinois House Committee on Gaming by a vote of five to two. The bill now moves on for consideration by the full House.

The proposed measure, sponsored by Representative Lew Langmeyer (D-Palatine), would create a casino license to be used in the city of Chicago and would also enable the state's six race tracks to offer video slots betting not only during the racing season but throughout the year. Illinois currently has nine riverboat casinos. Backers of the bill contend that these casinos have seriously harmed the horse racing industry since their legalization twenty years ago.

Representative Langmeyer maintains that "the agribusiness involving racetracks, horse breeding farms, feed suppliers, and track workers is responsible for some 40,000 jobs. It's a billion dollar business of vital importance to the Illinois economy. I feel it is incumbent upon the legislature to help level the playing field in competition for the gambling dollar. This bill sets out to do just that."

Opposition to the bill has come from the existing casino interests as well as from Reverend Wardell Simpkins, who founded and continues to head the anti-gambling organization CAB (Christians Against Betting). "Passage of the Langmeyer bill would greatly expand the evil presence of gambling in our midst," Reverend Simpkins said in a statement released to the press today.

The bill now goes to the full floor of the House, where it is expected to be considered some time in the next few weeks. It is opposed by House minority leader Ralph Muncell (R-Rockford). House majority leader William "Willy" Wilgis (D-Kankakee) has not taken a public position on this matter.

Senate President Stella Jackson (D-Chicago) has come out in support of the Langmeyer bill, as has Democratic Governor Otto Walker.

Chapter Twenty-Five

Through a bedroom window of the apartment on the top floor of the Monee Park clubhouse, Bob Zaslow watched the racing action before him from his wheelchair, his attending nurse Fidelia Rizal reading a book while seated nearby. As Rambling Rosie pranced back toward the finish line she'd just flashed across, Zaslow's face lit up. It was nine straight wins now for the increasingly popular Rambling Rosie. Fidelia leaned forward. She could see Bob was about to say something. Slowly, through an expression that was part smile, part grimace, the words seeped out. "Good for old Tom Eckrosh. One of the nicest guys around here."

Fidelia nodded in agreement. Her look of concern was not evident to Bob, who was still staring out the window. Fidelia had been Bob's nurse for the past year and a half. The decline in his condition had accelerated in the past three months, so much that it pained her deeply even though she was a veteran observer of anguish after more than two decades in the nursing profession. Fidelia had come to know Bob and Celia as intimately as an employee can. She was extremely fond of them both. The shield of indifference most caretakers have to cultivate in order to survive was weakening for her. She knew it, but could do nothing about it. They had become family to her.

She and Bob watched together as groom Maria Martinez led the lively filly into the winner's circle. In profile, as Fidelia observed Bob's face, there was little evidence of his illness. He had lost strength in his neck but his face, which she or Celia shaved every other day, reflected both an inner strength and a basic kindness, she thought. Fidelia, a forty-eight year old single woman, was a born care giver, one whose parents and lone sibling were long deceased, victims of a horrible social upheaval in the Phillipine village where she'd been born. The loss of her family had convinced her years ago not to make an emotional investment in one of her own. Her patients were the focal point of her life. She did the best she could for them, then moved on. Looking at Bob, she chided herself for speculating how soon her next move would come. She reached forward and straightened the collar of his robe. He didn't seem to notice. After glancing at her watch, she sat back in her chair and resumed reading. It was still another half-hour or so before Celia would return.

The view from the apartment window was vivid on this clear night. Light stanchions rimming the racing strip were surrounded by clouds of small, flying insects. To the south, where the broad corn fields lay beyond the boundaries of the old track, the night was pitch black. Fidelia thought she'd never seen a summer moon as bright as this one.

Fidelia closed her book, leaning back in her chair. Bob was still intent on the scene before him. She marveled at his ability to look beyond his illness, to cheer up friends who struggled to repress their emotions when they visited him, at his ability to frequently laugh in the face of the physical decimation he was suffering.

Her thoughts turned back to late the previous afternoon when she and Bob and Celia had relaxed in the apartment living room before it was time for Celia to leave for a fund raising dinner in downtown Chicago. The organization involved had been one of Uncle Jim Joyce's favorite charities. Celia and Bob had never missed one these events, until this year. This year, Bob would be absent. He had not been able to accompany Celia anywhere for the past several months. But he encouraged Celia to go.

As the three of them chatted, the women sipping tea, Bob had raised his chin, then begun talking. "You know, Celia," he'd said, "I've thought of something practical. Regarding me.

Regarding us." There were long pauses between his sentences as he struggled to speak audibly.

The women leaned forward to hear him better. The hint of a grin preceded what he said next.

"When I'm gone, I want you to have me cremated," Bob said. Celia cut him off sharply. "Bob, please I won't listen to this. No." Her face was flushed.

Stubbornly, her husband pressed on. Fidelia touched Celia on the wrist, indicating that she should let Bob continue. "Once I'm cremated," he said, "I want you take that gold locket I gave you last year, the one on Valentine's Day. I want you to put some of my ashes in it."

He was speaking so slowly now, fighting to get the words out, that Celia had to look away, hiding the tears that had formed in her eyes. His eyes, however, were bright. When she turned to look at him, she said, "And why would I do something like that?"

Bob inhaled, accumulating the breath he needed in order to respond. "Because," he said, "then you could finally go places and tell people, 'Bob came out with me tonight.'"

Celia wiped at her eyes. "Oh, Bobby," she said, "you're cut from a strong bolt of cloth, you are." She reached over and kissed him on the lips. To Fidelia she said, "I've got to go down and make the winner's circle presentation before I leave for the city. Call me on my cell phone if this humorous man here needs me in the next two hours. I'll try to be back earlier than that," she added. She walked quickly to the door. Fidelia watched as Celia wiped again at new tears. It was a scene Fidelia would never forget.

Minutes later Bob struggled to lean forward in his wheelchair as he looked down at the Monee Park winner's circle. "Let me get you closer, Bob," Fidelia said. She eased his chair a foot or so nearer the wide window. "There," she said. "Better?" He made a sound that she knew meant "yes."

They watched Celia as she laughed, her head back, red hair flashing in the winner's circle lights, as she presented the small trophy to Tom Eckrosh. He accepted it as if he'd just been handed an eviction notice, then quickly passed it off to an attendant. Eckrosh had never been much for ceremony. Fidelia heard a wheezing sort of chuckle from Bob.

With her jockey and his saddle off her back, Rambling Rosie waited calmly for Maria Martinez to lead her back to the barn. It was as if Rosie knew that night's proud moment was over, that it was time to leave the spotlight.

Fidelia heard Bob grunt something as he activated his wheelchair. He turned it away from the window. His face was suddenly somber.

She glanced back down at the winner's circle. Fidelia saw Celia, laughing again, one hand on the arm of Jack Doyle. He was as animated as Celia, regarding her with the kind of connective look whose strength could stretch up five stories, to this apartment, where Bob Zaslow now waited to be helped into bed.

Chapter Twenty-Six

Morty's voice coming over the in-house phone on Doyle's desk was hushed, urgent. "Jack, meet me at the jocks' room kitchen right away. Bring money."

"What, has Clarence Meaux raised his prices?" Doyle said with a laugh.

Morty said, "This is serious business, boss. Get down here." The phone clicked off.

Doyle completed his morning tasks before heading downstairs and into the jockeys' sanctuary. He nodded hello to several riders he'd gotten to know as he walked over to the table where Morty and Clarence Meaux appeared to be in the middle of a dispute. They were talking in low, serious tones. Doyle pulled up a chair.

Morty leaned toward Jack. He whispered, "I've got a steamer for us. First-time starter. Big odds, nobody knows about him. Second race today. I'm going to bet this horse good to win and back wheel him in the double. Want to go in with me?"

Doyle's gaze shifted to Clarence, who was shaking his head from side to side. Doyle said, "Morty, where'd you get this hot horse?" Morty nodded in the direction of the lunch counter, at the end of which sat Monee Park's current young riding star Jason LeBeau. "Jason there," Morty said. "He's been working the horse in the mornings for trainer Buddy Bowman. Jason says this colt can run a hole in the wind. The whole stable is betting. Horse's name is Comet Colin. He's Number Five. His breeding isn't much, but Jason says don't pay any attention to that," Morty said earnestly.

Clarence snorted. "Hole in the wind? You've got to have a hole in your head to believe that, Mr. Morty."

"Why's that, Clarence?" Doyle said.

"Look," Clarence replied, "I like young Jason down there. Nice boy, not a bad little rider. But," he continued, leaning forward and tapping the table with a finger for emphasis, "you got to keep in mind that these jocks are the worst damn handicappers in the world. The whole wide world, I'm saying."

Doyle was puzzled, and looked it. Clarence said to him, "Like I've been tryin' to tell Mr. Morty, they know how to *ride* the damn horses, but not how to bet on them. Eddie Arcaro, remember him? Maybe the greatest jockey ever. Mr. Eddie said one time that if he could book bets in the jocks' room for a year, he'd make so much money he wouldn't have to go out there every afternoon, risking his life in races.

"These boys get enthusiastic, they want to share their hot tip with people they like so that they'll look smart. They wind up burning up everybody's money. Not *every* time, mind you. Once in a red moon they'll be right."

Doyle sat back, bemused. Was Clarence arguing that you couldn't get a tip from these obvious sources of inside info, the people most closely involved with the horses? As if reading his mind, Clarence said, "Mr. Jack, you got to remember this whole business is crowded with dreamers, people full of more hope than sense. They get to the point they *make* themselves believe they're going to win. A smart man shouldn't pay any attention to them. You bet on horses, Mr. Jack?"

"Sometimes."

"Then stick with whatever method you're using—cold, hard facts, speed figures, Madame Fran's predictions, whatever. Don't let yourself get buried under this kind of 'inside info.'"

Morty looked disgusted as he got to his feet. "I don't care what you say, Clarence, I'm going to lay my money down on Comet Colin. See you upstairs, Jack."

Watching Morty stalk off, Clarence sighed. He said, "You going to bet that horse, Mr. Jack?"

"Not me. I'll take your advice on this, Clarence."

Meaux nodded in approval. "You're doing the right thing. Besides, Mr. Morty, he's a Jonah. I found out that about him years back."

Doyle said, "He's a *what?*"

"A Jonah. Like from the Bible. Round any racetrack, you've got to know who's a Jonah, and Mr. Morty, he sure qualifies."

"Oh, I get you," Doyle said. "Jonah and the whale. 'He made his home in that fish's abdomen, it ain't necessarily so,'" he recited. "Remember that song, from 'Porgy and Bess'?"

"I don't know about any song. I just know the Bible story. The Lord tells Jonah, get yourself over to Nineveh, and lay into them people about their sinful ways. But Jonah, no, he doesn't do what the Lord says. He cuts out and goes the other way on a ship, the fool, trying to get away from the Lord. Well, old Jonah, he paid for that. The Lord sends down a mighty wind that stirs up the sea. The sailors on Jonah's ship, they're scared to death, they start throwing cargo off to lighten the load. And then there's Jonah, down below the deck of that tossing ship, sleeping like a baby."

Clarence paused, leaned back in his chair and, as some portly people occasionally do, gave his belly a pat, as if to reassure himself it was still there. Apparently satisfied, he resumed talking.

"These sailors now, they figure out somebody has made the Lord mighty mad and put them in this trouble. They decide to roll some dice, trying to figure out who that man is. Turns out, it's old Jonah. And to Jonah's credit, he owns up, tells them, 'Okay, fellas, toss me over the side, maybe things'll calm down then.' So they did. And things calmed down, for those boys on the ship.

"Down there in that sea, of course, where the Lord has put him to wait, was the great whale. He spots Jonah and swallows him right up. Jonah's down there in that big fish's belly, praying his heart out now, promising the Lord he'll never turn his back on him again. Good idea. The whale spits Jonah out on the shore.

"Old Jonah gets his life going the right away from then on. But," Clarence said, tapping Jack's arm for emphasis, "ever since I been around the racetrack and gamblers, there's always a guy or two who's got trouble seeping out of him like Jonah. There was a guy at the Fair Grounds down home, Alan LaCombe, they called him the Black Cat because not only was he unlucky, he *spread* unluckiness. He'd bet on a horse that looked like a mortal lock, and the horse would fall down. A rider'd get a winning streak going, Black Cat starts betting on him, boom, the streak's over.

"Some guys are just made that way. That's why they're called Jonahs. And," Clarence concluded, "Mr. Morty, he's the biggest Jonah I know around this here racetrack."

That night, watching as the first four furlongs of the second race unfolded, Doyle began to believe that Morty, who was standing next to him on the press box balcony and rooting loudly, had been given a very bad rap by Clarence Meaux. Down on the track, Comet Colin was rolling along, seven lengths in front of his nearest pursuer, Jason LeBeau sitting chilly on him. The tote board showed the odds on Comet Colin to be 31-to-1. This fleet first-time starter, Morty's "steamer," was apparently going to "win laughing" as the old racetrack expression put it. Morty was pounding the porch railing with both hands, shouting, "This is the one that gets me even for the meeting. Maybe for life! C'mon, baby, c'mon home!"

Then, just inside the sixteenth pole where one of the light stanchions cast a shadow across the track beneath it, Comet Colin suddenly spooked. He jumped to avoid the broad shadow. Then he took an abrupt left turn and leaped over the infield fence. Jason LeBeau was, amazingly, able to bail out as the colt made this startling move. LeBeau landed on his back on the infield grass, bounced, and lay there, still as stone but with only the wind knocked out of him. Out of the corner of his eye Jack saw Morty fall to his knees and begin to unleash a steady stream of curses.

Once he'd cleared the fence, Comet Colin kept going over the infield grass, eyes wild, tossing his head. He ran full speed into the infield lake, where he churned the water in his fear and panic. As track workers started to rush to his rescue, Comet Colin revealed himself to be no Black Stallion. Before the men could swim out to him and attach a rope to his bridle, Comet Colin drowned.

◇◇◇

Doyle went back to his desk in the press box. He avoided looking at the stricken Morty, who had his head down on his desk and obviously didn't want to be disturbed. Doyle made a mental note to order Morty never to bet on Rambling Rosie. Then he began writing a news release about the incident he'd just witnessed. "If this doesn't make all the papers," he muttered, "nothing from Monee Park ever will."

Doyle's report of this bizarre event was indeed picked up by the next day's Chicago area papers as well as two wire services. The story lamented the loss of "this obviously talented but unfortunate young horse," mentioned the "great good luck of his rider, Jason LeBeau, who miraculously escaped injury," and concluded with a quote from Comet Colin's trainer, Buddy Bowman.

"I thought I'd seen it all in this game," said the stunned horseman, adding, "It's bad enough when you have to call an owner and tell him his horse lost. But how in the hell do I tell Comet Colin's owner that his horse didn't just lose, he drowned?"

The next morning Doyle got a call from Moe Kellman. "Congratulations," Kellman said, "Monee Park is all over the news today."

"Yeah," Doyle said, "but it took a disaster to do it. Poor Comet Colin. And poor Morty 'Kiss of Death' Dubinski." He went on to describe his assistant's amazing record of lousy luck. "It's incredible," Doyle said. "If Morty bets to win, his horse runs second. If he bets to place, his horse finishes third. His exactas almost always come back first-third. When he bets a trifecta, his picks run one-two-four. He's also lost thirteen photo finishes in the last month. I've never seen anything like it. The man is cursed."

Kellman said, "It might be time for him to try prayer."

"I don't know about that," Doyle said. "I don't think Morty is religious."

"Well, the way he's going, it couldn't hurt," Kellman said. "Did I ever tell you about two of my old friends, Al Brody and Arnie Rosen? This was years ago, when they both used to go to the track every weekend during their winters in Florida. Hialeah Park, before they closed it up for lack of business. Beautiful old place.

"Anyway, one winter, Brody gets on a tremendous hot streak. He's betting winner after winner. Rosen, on the other hand, is colder than a Duluth December. He's going nuts watching Brody cash while he's tearing up losing ticket after losing ticket, race after race.

"One evening when they're driving home after the races, Rosen says, 'Al, I don't get it. You and I have been playing the horses together for years. Usually, we come out about the same. But not lately. How come you're going so great all of a sudden while I'm bombing out?'

"Brody shrugs. He says, 'Arnie, maybe you should go to temple more often.'

"Rosen hasn't been to services since his bar mitzvah. He is not what you call a practicing Jew. But he's so desperate, he starts thinking this over. And, the next Saturday, he goes to temple before he meets Brody at Hialeah. However, nothing changes. It's the same old story. Brody's knocking them dead at the windows, Rosen is getting killed. After the last race, Rosen throws down his *Racing Daily* on the clubhouse floor and starts stomping on it, hollering 'I can't take it anymore.'

"Brody does his best to try and calm down his old pal. He says, 'Arnie, didn't I tell you to try going to temple? Why didn't you listen to me?'

"Rosen is in agony, all red in the face, sweating. He says, 'Al, I went. I *went*. I went to Beth Shalom this morning and I prayed my heart out for a change in my luck at the track. And what happened? *Bupkus.*'

"Brody steps back, gives Rosen a sympathetic look. 'Beth Shalom?' he says. 'No wonder it didn't work, you shmuck. That's for *basketball*, not racing.'"

As he laughed, Doyle pictured Kellman on the other end of the phone, eyes twinkling as he gazed out a window of his John Hancock Building office suite toward Lake Michigan. "Maybe I can cheer up poor Morty telling him that story," Jack said.

"It's worth a try."

Chapter Twenty-Seven

Aiden Lucarelli and Denny Shannon were heading home from work, a small construction job in Berwyn, when Lucarelli's cell phone rang. Shannon winced. The phone's signal for incoming calls was the first two bars of "The Godfather" theme. He hated the sound and had said so. Once. Aiden's response was such that Denny never again brought up the subject. He brushed his forearm over his forehead. It was a sweltering Chicago summer afternoon. The Taurus' air conditioning was laboring. Sweat dripped from Lucarelli's forehead as he answered the phone.

"Aiden, it's Art Riley. We need a meeting. Right away."

"Where?"

"I'll see you at Haller's at 5:30. I'll buy the beer for you boys."

"Deal," Lucarelli said. He closed the phone and took another swipe at his forehead with his sodden handkerchief.

Shannon said, "Wazzup?"

"A meet with Riley. At Haller's. We'll head over there now."

"Did he sound pissed off?"

Lucarelli shot him a look before saying, "Why should he sound pissed off? We robbed the fucking racetrack. Then we got its lights turned off, just like he wanted. If he's pissed off, it can't be at us. We did our part." Lucarelli spat out the car window before adding, "Maybe smartass lawyer Riley hasn't been doing such great planning. Maybe that's why he needs us again."

Shannon reached into the cooler on the floor in front of him. He popped open a Bud Light. "As long as Riley's buyin', we'll listen. Right, Aiden?"

"Fuck'n A."

◇◇◇

Riley was alone at a table near the rear of Haller's, reading the *Tribune,* drinking an Old Fashioned. Though Riley had helped extricate him from several legal jams, Lucarelli had never liked the attorney. He found himself now filled to an even new level of disgust as he looked Riley over, from his wrinkled suit, rumpled dress shirt, twisted tie, to his doughy face with its small, mean mouth and eyes that flickered about, never holding a gaze in one place for more than a second or two. But "liking" was not a factor in their relationship.

For nearly a quarter hour Lucarelli sat back in his chair, nonchalant, as Riley described their next assignment. Shannon leaned close to the attorney, frowning, paying close attention. Riley's eyes darted from one to the other as he talked quietly, pausing only to signal Marge Duffy, behind the bar, for "one of the same for me, and the same for the lads here."

At 6:45 Riley drained the last of his drink and got to his feet. "Got to leave you. I've got great tickets for tonight's Sox game. Meeting my son and his boys." He concentrated on Aiden when he asked, "Are we clear on this?"

Lucarelli finished his Bud Light before answering. "It'll get done. Don't worry about that."

Shannon, still frowning, looked up at Riley. He said, "I don't understand, like, what they are, these fool papers you're talking about."

Lucarelli broke up, laughing so hard and loud that Riley looked at him with alarm. Shannon knew what this was about. He'd seen Aiden snort crystal meth before they'd entered Haller's, knew the effect it had on his cousin.

"Not fool papers," Aiden said, face flushed, reaching to grab Denny's wrist. "Foal papers. Foal fucking papers." He was laughing uncontrollably now, the drug and alcohol ripping through him. "Foal," he repeated, "not fool. You fool." He pounded the table in appreciation of his wit. Shannon still didn't understand, but he shrugged. He knew a long, uproarious night lay ahead of them, Aiden riding his high and in a soaring mood with the promise of more Riley money. Maybe they'd hit Rush Street, have some fun, bust some balls up there in yuppie land.

Riley scuttled out the door. For a few minutes he sat behind the wheel of his new Cadillac DTS, the finest car he'd ever owned, in the sun-baked parking lot of Haller's, motor going, air conditioning blasting, a sheen of perspiration still lingering on his brow. He checked his suit coat pocket, making sure he had the Sox tickets. He looked forward to seeing his excited grandsons at the ball park, to spending at least the next few hours with his mind off of the unsettling duo he had just left. "If it weren't for the big fee I'll get from Hanratty," he said to himself, pulling out onto Halsted, "I'd wash my hands of those two."

Chapter Twenty-Eight

Late July had rustled up one of those all-night, all-day rain productions that marked portions of every Chicago summer. The previous night's thunder storms had dumped more than an inch of rain on the Monee Park barn area whose dirt roads were ill-equipped to handle it. Early on this Friday morning, Doyle stepped carefully around large pools of standing water, over mud-slicked surfaces, as he made his way toward Tom Eckrosh's barn. He had an eight o'clock appointment with the crusty old trainer to talk about plans for Rambling Rosie. Doyle hoped the resulting press release would find space in the area's weekend newspapers, thus generating some much needed publicity for the struggling racetrack.

Around 7:45 the rain suddenly resumed, really hard. With time to spare before his meeting with Eckrosh, Doyle quickly ducked beneath the tin roof overhang of an equipment shed. He was wearing a rain slicker, boots, and rain hat, but none of this gear was a match for the latest deluge.

Doyle was leaning against the open doorway of the shed when he spotted a solitary figure across the road. Peering through the sheets of rain, he saw a man, hatless, wearing only a light jacket, pacing back and forth in front of Barn C. When the man turned around at the end of the shed row and began walking back his way, Doyle recognized the tall, gaunt figure, hair plastered to his head, of Reverend Dave Livingston, Monee Park's backstretch chaplain. Livingston, thirty-eight, was a former horse trainer, reformed gambler, and recovering alcoholic who eleven years earlier had undergone a notable transformation. Besides giving up his destructive life style, he became a born again Christian, graduated from a small, southern West Virginia bible college, then returned to the racetrack to establish a ministry. Reverend Livingston was very popular on the backstretch, especially among the Hispanic workers for whom he conducted a Spanish-speaking service each Saturday night.

Watching Reverend Livingston pivot at the far end of the barn and turn back his way, Doyle thought, not for the first time, how much the minister reminded him of the long-jawed country singer who had been briefly married to one of the nation's favorite movie actresses. Reverend Livingston sloshed toward him through a wide puddle as Doyle called out, "Hey, Reverend." Doyle darted out from the shed and sprinted across the road to where Livingston had stopped to look quizzically at him. "Is that you, Mr. Doyle?" the minister said as Jack jumped a final puddle and made it to the shelter of the Barn C overhang. "It is," Doyle replied, "please make it Jack. And why don't you step over here, get out of the rain?" Reverend Livingston brushed his long, black hair off his rain-beaded forehead. "Why yes," he said, as if the thought had never occurred to him, "I think I will."

The two men stood silently for a few moments, listening to the percussive sound of water on the old tin roof above them. Doyle said, "You're drenched. Do you mind if I ask you why you kept walking out there through the rain? Why," he added with a smile, "you didn't stay under the roof if you were determined to get your exercise miles in during this downpour?"

Reverend Livingston responded with a blank look. He looked down at his mud-caked boots. "Well, of course I was walking in the rain, wasn't I? Why? Oh, I guess I wasn't really noticing the rain, Mr. Doyle, er, Jack. I've got a great deal on my mind these days."

"Hard to ignore a rain like this," Doyle shrugged. They both stepped back as a manure hauling truck barreled down the path between barns, spraying sheets of water from all its wheels. Doyle started to swear as the truck sped past, then remembered whose company he was in.

The rain increased in intensity for a minute or two before resuming its quieter, steady beat. Doyle glanced at his grim-faced companion. The frown lines on Livingston's broad forehead looked as if they'd been carved there. "How's the chaplaincy fund drive coming?" Doyle said, not really caring, just making conversation. Doyle for years had devoted his charitable spending to non-sectarian groups, operating under his theory that "God couldn't possibly have that many legit mouthpieces competing for my money."

Reverend Livingston shook his head sadly. "The fund drive is far, far from meeting its goal, Jack," he said with a sigh. "Our needs are greater than ever. There are so many of our racetrackers coming to us now needing day care for their children, English language instruction, advice on how to get green cards, apply for citizenship. This is all on top of our ongoing counseling on drug and alcohol abuse. The demands keep increasing. We badly need to expand staff, but we can't, not with the way our level of funding is lagging behind."

Doyle glanced at his watch. It was nearly time for him to meet Eckrosh. He took another look at Reverend Livingston's long, sad, wet face. He decided to break his own rule. "Look, Reverend," Doyle said, "I've got to get going." He took out his wallet and pressed a pair of $50 bills into Livingston's damp hands. The chaplain's face brightened as Doyle said, "Put these in your kitty. I admire the good work you do here."

"Well, thanks be to Jesus," Reverend Livingston exclaimed. "And may he bless you, Jack."

As if a celestial spigot had been turned off, the rain abruptly stopped. "Perfect timing for once," Doyle said. "I can be on time at old man Eckrosh's barn."

"Say hello to Tom for me," Livingston said. "And thank you again."

Doyle walked away a few steps, then stopped. Turning to face Livingston he said, "I'm curious. Why were you tramping around in this storm on this lousy morning when your nice, dry office is only a block or so away?"

Reverend Livingston smiled sweetly. "What was I doing out in weather like this? Why, waiting for somebody like you, Jack Doyle."

Doyle gave the reverend a mock salute before he started to walk away, laughing as he said to himself, "I've just seen another form of racetrack hustle."

Chapter Twenty-Nine

After Rambling Rosie's tenth straight resounding victory, even grouchy old Tom Eckrosh permitted himself a proud smile in the Monee Park winner's circle. Patting the preening filly on her neck as the photo was being taken, Eckrosh accepted Doyle's congratulations. Eckrosh said, somewhat reluctantly, "I guess it's time we moved her up."

Doyle was surprised at this volunteered information from the man whom he had recently described to Morty as being "so closed mouth he wouldn't tell you if he saw a tarantula crawling up your tie." He looked closely at the trainer. "What have you got in mind, Tom?"

Eckrosh reached into his a pocket of his sport coat and extracted a well thumbed copy of the Heartland Downs stakes schedule. "They've got a race she could go in over at the big track in a week," the old man said. "A $50,000 race, the Miss Amara Stakes. For three-year-old fillies going six furlongs."

Doyle felt himself getting excited at this possibility. Win or lose, he could get a lot of publicity mileage out of blue collar Rambling Rosie taking on the expensively bred competition she would meet at Chicago area's major racetrack. "The Odd Couple and Their Underdog"—he could almost hear popular Chicago television sports anchor Max Suppelsa leading off his show with those very words to describe Eckrosh, Maria Martinez, and Rosie.

He clapped Eckrosh on the back and was rewarded with a scowl. "Sorry," Doyle said. "It's just that I think it's a great idea."

The old man looked up at Doyle. A hint of a grin came and went before he said, "Well, son, so do I."

The morning of the Miss Amara Stakes, Doyle arrived at Monee Park just before six o'clock. Birds were vocal in the old elm trees that lined the barn area, a few of them zipping down to poke their bills into the mound of horse manure that wouldn't be picked up until later in the morning. He walked toward Tom Eckrosh's little office. He'd already seen Maria Martinez outside of the barn, preparing to load Rambling Rosie into the one-horse trailer attached to Eckrosh's white Ford pickup truck. The filly walked calmly up the ramp and settled in nicely. "Rosie's a good little traveler," Eckrosh said, coming through the office door, "always has been. After I bought her and brought her up here, she walked right off the van and won her first race."

"You think the traveling did it for her?" Doyle said, half-kidding. "She hadn't won anything before that."

Eckrosh gave him a sharp look. "I didn't have her before that. After I got her, I changed her shoeing, and her diet, and her training patterns, and turned her over to a good groom, Maria. Did the vanning have anything to do with it? I don't know. But it seemed to help at first, so I've kept doing it. Even though she's been running all of her races here at Monee, before every one of them I put her in my trailer about four hours before race time and drive her around for a few miles. She likes it."

Minutes later Eckrosh climbed into the truck's cab behind the wheel, Maria moved to the middle of the bench seat, Doyle got in and closed the passenger door. The truck lurched violently toward the exit gate. Doyle tried to get a grip on the dashboard, muttering "Jesus!" Maria's eyes were closed, hands clasped together as if she were praying. She was evidently familiar with Eckrosh's driving.

After some two miles of erratic progress, Doyle said loudly, "Tom, pull over." Doyle had seen the old man peering through the windshield as if he were searching for a route through a blinding snowstorm. Doyle had heard stories about Eckrosh's short, thrilling drives to and from the Monee Park track kitchen, scattering autos and pedestrians in his wake. Now he believed them. Doyle shuddered at the thought of Eckrosh motoring around with his sensational filly and her faithful groom. He said, "Tom, I'll drive."

Surprisingly, the ordinarily stubborn old man didn't argue. Maria gave Doyle a grateful smile as he slipped behind the wheel, him thinking, *If this filly runs good after being driven around by this old man, he should prep her the next time on a roller coaster at Great America. She'd break all the damn records.*

The trip took nearly an hour, through the early morning traffic leading north and then west to Heartland Downs. As usual, the expressways were clogged, some portions of them under construction, a Chicago auto commuter's nightmare. Many of the work crews were manning trucks and spreaders marked Bonadio Construction. Doyle had heard of this politically connected company, owned by Moe Kellman's boyhood chum.

Eckrosh and Doyle chatted about the quality of the rivals Rambling Rosie would be facing that afternoon. The trainer said, "It's the saltiest bunch she's seen yet." He looked concerned. Maria spoke to reassure him. "Mister Tom," she smiled, "these feelies have not seen one *muy rapido* like our Rosie, either." Doyle, himself not completely convinced, nevertheless nodded as if in agreement with this optimistic assessment.

They were questioned at the Heartland Downs stable gate by a security officer wearing the sort of uniform often seen on bodyguards of South American dictators. The guard examined Eckrosh's training license for several minutes before waving them forward. "How'd they miss getting this guy into Homeland Security?" Doyle said.

Doyle parked the truck at the entrance to the stakes barn where Rambling Rosie would remain until her race that afternoon. He got out of the truck and helped Eckrosh open the trailer doors. Maria said, "Come to me, Mama," and Rambling Rosie carefully backed her way down the ramp, her four white feet flashing in the sunlight.

That afternoon, Eckrosh and Maria definitely were the "odd couple" in the Heartland Downs paddock prior to the Miss Amara Stakes. The trainers of the other horses wore sport coats, khakis, shining boots. A couple of them sported big, beige Western hats. All but one besides Eckrosh had on dark sun glasses. The owners of the horses were expensively dressed, their wives or girlfriends equally so. Even the grooms employed by these people, who were taking their horses around the rubber-padded walking ring prior to saddling, were turned out neatly.

Tom Eckrosh stood outside Rambling Rosie's stall. In his unpressed gray slacks, worn black sport coat, and battered fedora, Doyle thought, the old trainer might be taken for a panhandler who had somehow sidled past the Heartland Downs gate guard. Maria wore her regular working outfit of gray sweatshirt with the sleeves rolled up, jeans, worn running shoes. She had tied her thick, black hair into a long braid at the back of her head. Her clothes were clean and pressed. It was obvious to Doyle that her earlier level of confidence had taken a couple of hits in the midst of this comparatively upscale milieu. Worry lines were evident on her forehead.

By far the most comfortable and confident looking member of this close-knit trio was Rambling Rosie. She gazed around the paddock like a diva eager for the downbeat. After checking out the horses that would be running against her, she nuzzled Maria's neck as a serious looking Ramon Garcia strode across the gleaming grass like a miniature conquistador about to go to work. Garcia looked neither right or left. He tapped his whip against his right riding boot as he advanced. Rosie nickered when Garcia walked up to her, ready to be boosted aboard.

Paddock judge Keith Polzin gave the call of "riders up." Eckrosh boosted Garcia into the saddle, grunting slightly as he did so. "Say there, old timer," came a voice from across the way. Advancing toward them was Frank Lester, Heartland Downs' leading trainer. He also had a filly in the Miss Amara. With his dark glasses, gleaming smile, expensive suit and moussed black hair, Lester looked more like a visiting movie star than a working horseman. He walked up to Eckrosh, his hand extended. Eckrosh nodded curtly and turned away. Lester shrugged and walked off without another word.

Doyle remembered reading that Lester had apprenticed under Eckrosh years earlier. The two had had a major falling out when Lester suddenly went out on his own, taking several of Eckrosh's major clients with him. He'd gone on to gain national prominence as the buyer and trainer of very expensive stock.

Walking through the tunnel toward the track, Doyle couldn't restrain himself. "You and Lester still friendly?" he asked, knowing full well that was not the case, but looking to get a rise out of the old man, maybe get his mind a little bit off of the important upcoming race.

Eckrosh stopped to glare at Doyle as he answered. "Don't ask me nothing about that smart ass, conniving, son of a bitch. I've been finished with him for years. Wouldn't trust him as far as I could throw his big, fat stable pony. And you can quote me."

Doyle said, "Well, I don't think I'll be doing that. Celia is hoping to get Lester to send over a few of his horses to Monee."

Eckrosh shrugged. "Celia's got to do what she's got to do. I give that girl credit for keeping Monee Park going."

They took their places at the rail near the finish line, just outside the winner's circle. Lester already stood in that enclosure, as if confident his filly would be arriving to join him minutes later.

Eckrosh nodded toward his one-time protégé. "Only horse he's going to see in there in a couple of minutes will be mine," he growled.

Doyle smiled. "You're pretty sure you're going to beat him today with Rosie, aren't you?"

"Damn right," Eckrosh replied. He placed his elbows on the fence, still looking out the corner of his eye at Lester, who was now being interviewed by Christine Davis, Heartland Downs' in-house television personality.

"Keep in mind, son," Eckrosh said, "that I taught Frankie Lester everything he knows." He paused before adding, "Not everything *I* know."

They looked across the infield at the horses approaching the starting gate. Rambling Rosie was bouncing around, nuzzling the accompanying outrider's pony, swishing her tail energetically. Doyle grinned as he watched her through his binoculars. All of her body language seemed to be saying to one and all, "Damn, I'm glad to be here. And I'm gonna kick some butts."

That she did. It was almost as if Rambling Rosie understood the jibe aimed at her jockey, Ramon Garcia, by Heartland Downs' foremost rider Larry Porter. Looking over at Garcia in the starting gate Porter said, loud enough to make some of the gate crew members snicker, "Welcome to the big leagues, *amigo*. Things are going to be different here."

But they weren't, not after the starter had sprung the latch and Rosie exploded out of the gate, a copper colored blur on this bright blue afternoon. Garcia tucked his chin down near her neck and let her roll, his hands still on the reins. She'd begun to noticeably detach herself from the field after the first quarter mile. By the time she'd reached mid-stretch, she was six lengths clear of her nearest rival. Uncharacteristically, Garcia gave her a whack on the shoulder with his whip about seventy yards from the finish. She was seven on top at that point. Irritated, Rosie swished her tail and turned her head to the side as if to give Garcia a chiding look. After they'd flashed under the wire, the normally stoic Garcia stood in the irons, grinning, and patted Rambling Rosie's neck. The crowd erupted in applause when track announcer Calvin Gemmer announced Rambling Rosie's winning time of 1:08 3-5 and said, "And that, ladies and gentlemen, is a new track record."

Doyle was antsy in the winner's circle, pumped up, looking for someone to high five, or hug. Eckrosh, a picture of contained jubilance, didn't appear to be receptive to either gesture. The old man was busy anyway, gripping Maria's hand tightly. She held on to Rambling Rosie's shank with the other hand. Tears streamed down Maria's brown cheeks. After the photo was taken, Garcia dismounted with a leaping, trampoline-like flourish. Smiling broadly, he shook hands with Eckrosh, then patted Maria on the back. He delivered another pat to Rambling Rosie before going to the official scales to weigh out.

Doyle stood to the side, not wanting to intrude on this scene. This horse, this victory, meant so much to these people, it made him envious of their passionate involvement. He thought fleetingly of Celia, imagined her being there to share the moment with him. Ah, well....

Chapter Thirty

"Hey, this is a good idea. I know it is. Even if it isn't mine."

Doyle stopped speaking and looked around the conference table. Celia sat at its head, leaning forward, obviously interested. Shontanette was next to her, non-committal. Bob Zaslow was in his wheelchair, which was placed midway of the table, his nurse Fidelia to his left. Bob looked dubious at what he'd heard. Fidelia, among the dwindling few young U. S.-based women who crocheted, concentrated on the intricately patterned scarf she was making for her youngest niece's birthday.

"Well?" Doyle said. "What do you think?"

Celia said, "Inviting Willy Wilgis here is, well, kind of a stretch, don't you think? I don't know the man. The only state legislator I really know at all is Lew Langmeyer. Why do you think Wilgis would like to make an appearance at Monee Park?"

"Glad you asked," Doyle responded. "Here's the deal. Representative Wilgis' secretary, aka mistress, is a woman named Evelyn Stortz. She happens to be a customer of our good friend Moe Kellman. When she was visiting Moe's fur salon recently, she mentioned that Wilgis has a birthday coming up. He's going to be seventy-nine. She wants to surprise him with something special, and she asked Moe if he had any ideas. They chewed this over, Moe probably leading the patter. Then, God love him, Moe suggested that Evelyn bring Wilgis out here for dinner and a night at the races. We'd name a special race for him in honor of his birthday. We'd have the old boy present the trophy to the winner of that race. According to Evelyn that would be a first for Wilgis, who apparently has been feted, honored, fawned over, and had his ass smooched in numerous ways all over the state. But not like this.

"Anyway, that's what Moe suggested, and he said Evelyn bought right into it. Moe called me, and I said 'great idea.' We need Wilgis' support in the legislature with the slot machines bill. Why not take a shot with something like this? At least we'll get to know the old rascal a little bit. And he'll get to know us, and Monee Park."

He looked around the table. Silence. Then there was a vocal rumble from next to Fidelia. Haltingly, painfully, Bob Zaslow managed to say, "That's a great idea, Jack."

It was as pleasant an early September night as the Chicago area can produce: temperature in the high 60s, stars looking ripe to pop right out of their deep black background. The row of old elm trees bordering the far side of the racing strip was beginning to hint at fall colors to soon follow.

Willy Wilgis pushed his chair away from the dining room table in the Monee Park's Turf Club. He patted his lips with the napkin he'd removed from his shirt front. Evelyn Stortz leaned over from her seat beside him and dabbed at a gravy spot that had somehow found its way onto his white tie. Wilgis burped gently. Addressing his hostess he said, "Celia, that's about as good a beef Wellington I've ever had in my life. Which, as you know, is getting long." He winked at her as he reached for another dinner roll.

"Thank you, Willy," Celia said. "Beef Wellington is one of the specialties of our Turf Club chef. He would like to come out and say hello. He kind of keeps a record of the important people he's prepared meals for, and he'd like to add you to it. That's if you don't mind, of course," she said, giving Wilgis one of her thousand watt smiles.

Doyle was thinking, *Let's not lay it on too thick here, Celia,* when he heard Wilgis announce, "Delighted to meet the man, darling," at the same time starting to reach forward with a hand to touch Celia's until Evelyn politely intervened.

Doyle, on the opposite side of the table from Celia, smiled and leaned back in his chair. He signaled Hugo the waiter to call the busboy for clearing his plates. He'd been too jumpy to eat much, wondering how this caper would turn out. So far, so good. Celia had engaged Wilgis in intelligent conversation about Illinois politics, they'd all laughed at the veteran legislator's jokes, and Doyle had flirted with Evelyn Stortz, much to her delight. The night was going great.

Celia glanced over her shoulder, smiling, as Horace Tate approached. The Turf Club chef's white shirt, pants, tall hat, and smile contrasted with his handsome black face. Tate and Wilgis were about the same medium height, Wilgis outweighing the chef by fifty or sixty pounds. Wilgis got to his feet and stuck out his hand as Tate neared. Celia made the introductions.

Celia had known Horace Tate since they were children, running around Monee Park in their summers off from grade school. Horace's father Ralph was the long time personal driver of Uncle Jim Joyce. It was Uncle Jim who had paid for Horace's later education and training at Kendall College in suburban Evanston, a premier culinary school.

The old pol said, "Mr. Tate, I've eaten beef Wellington all over the English speaking world, and in some precincts I shouldn't have. Yours is, by far, the most wonderful version I've ever encountered." Wilgis plumped back down into his chair, smiling up at the chef.

Tate looked bemused. He was a man accustomed to praise for his handiwork. Always happy to receive such praise, he smiled back at Wilgis and bowed slightly. "Thank you, Representative Wilgis. I appreciate that." He started to leave, then turned back to the table. "Representative Wilgis, do you have any interest in a slice of apple-cherry cobbler, a specialty of mine? Accompanied, of course, by a scoop of the vanilla ice cream I make myself in the kitchen here? Followed, perhaps, by a pony of armangac?"

"Let the ponies run, and full steam ahead in the kitchen, Mr. Tate," Wilgis said. He planted a kiss on Evelyn's cheek, his right hand massaging her left thigh. "This is some kind of a blue ribbon night, now, isn't it darling?" he said.

Celia's look of relief, if not triumph, locked with Doyle's.

The Representative Willy Wilgis Purse was the eighth race on that night's card. Doyle had drummed up a decent attraction to immediately precede it: a public workout by Rambling Rosie, rapidly becoming one of the Chicago area's more popular athletes.

Celia led her guests to the elevator, then down to the railing near the winner's circle. They watched as Rambling Rosie cantered past, jockey Ramon Garcia standing up in the irons like a circus trick rider, both he and the horse just loosening up. Doyle kept a discreet eye on Wilgis, who was watching the horse and rider with keen interest.

Rosie kept running easily around the far turn and into the backstretch. As she approached the five-furlong pole, Garcia dropped down into her saddle. The filly, legs extending, all business now, went from a canter to a dead run in the matter of a few strides. She zoomed around the far turn and then flew down the stretch, Garcia doing nothing to encourage her progress. Tom Eckrosh had instructed Garcia not "to ask her for anything" tonight, and Garcia followed orders. Still, when the time of the workout flashed up on the infield board, a roar went up from the crowd. Fifty-seven seconds flat, a sensational workout time for the distance any day or night. Doyle heard Eckrosh say with satisfaction, "And she did it easy as pie."

As Rosie galloped out, Doyle introduced Wilgis to Eckrosh. The old trainer looked warily at the legislator until Wilgis said, "Well, I've never seen anything like that down in the country, where I hail from." Eckrosh beamed with pride. The two rural-raised senior citizens continued to converse while Rosie stopped, turned around, then cantered back toward them. Garcia brought the lively filly to a halt in front of the two men. Eckrosh reached out to rub her neck. Rosie nickered and thrust her nose toward Wilgis. The politician stepped back for a moment, then leaned forward and tentatively placed a hand on the horse's nose. Again, Rosie made an appreciative sound. Doyle whispered to Celia, "This horse can not only run fast, she must be reading our minds. She's coming on to Wilgis like an equine gold digger." Celia, giggling, nudged Doyle with her elbow. "Hush," she said.

Wilgis' initial apprehension about his proximity to a friendly horse had vanished. Rosie gently nuzzled Wilgis' shoulder, nickering at him. The old pol was obviously lapping up her attentions now.

Doyle said admiringly, "Rosie, you little equine tart."

Celia said, "What did you say?"

"Never mind," he grinned.

Doyle moved next to Wilgis. He said, "Tell me, Mr. Wilgis, have you ever had the desire to own a racehorse?"

"Son, just call me Willy," he said, hand now smoothing Rosie's neck. "The answer has been No. I've gone along with what a real smart man once said to me: 'I don't ever want to own anything that can be eating while I'm sleeping.' But," Wilgis added, giving Rosie a final pat, "a grand little animal like this could sure tempt me to change my mind."

Thirty minutes later, Wilgis had presented the small trophy to Buck Norman, owner and trainer of Letter to Lee, winner of the Willy Wilgis Purse. Wilgis shook hands with Norman, patted him on the back and his horse on the neck, then took the cordless microphone from Doyle. Turning to address the crowd, he was smiling broadly. Wilgis thanked Celia and her "wonderful staff for this very, very special night in my life." A half-drunk bettor in the first row of the grandstand tried unsuccessfully to inspire the crowd to sing "Happy Birthday," but Wilgis ignored him and continued to talk.

"This great filly we saw here tonight, Rambling Rosie, well, I can't tell you how proud I am that she will represent the great state of Illinois in the Breeders' Cup Sprint a few weeks from now. Her great trainer, my good friend Tom Eckrosh, just broke that news to me. I'm confident Tom will have her sharper than grandpa's apple cider."

Doyle said to Celia, "Well, I'll be damned. Eckrosh never told me he was considering the Breeders' Cup. That's fantastic news! For you, for Monee Park." He stopped himself from talking any more about Eckrosh's unexpected decision as he began to fear that Wilgis might ramble on until the next race was over. Doyle started to move toward the microphone. But Wilgis' sense of timing kicked in. "In conclusion," he said, "I want to thank you all for coming tonight, be ye Democrats or otherwise." He paused for the expected ripple of chuckles mixed with boos. He raised his hand to quiet the crowd.

"I know there's one thing we can all agree on," he said, voice volume increasing word by word. "We'll all be rooting for our Rambling Rosie in the Breeders' Cup. She'll show those hot shots from the Blue Grass, and New York, and the great West, what a little gal from Illinois can do!"

The cheers resounded. Wilgis paused, reveling in the sound, before adding, "Rosie will leave those so-called heavy heads with their tongues hanging out and dust all over their windshields." This brought forth another roar from the crowd. Wilgis mopped his face with a blue bandana he'd extracted with a flourish from his trousers pocket. He waved it at the crowd as Doyle began ushering him out of the winner's circle and toward the exit.

With one race yet to be run, the Monee parking lot was relatively quiet. Wilgis' limousine pulled up to the Preferred Parking entrance and its driver jumped out and came around to open the door for Evelyn. Tom Eckrosh had walked along with Wilgis. The two old men stood under the canopied entrance, deep in conversation, until Evelyn called from the car, "Willy, it's time we left these nice people."

Wilgis shook hands with Eckrosh and Doyle. He extended his arms to Celia who, after a brief hesitation, walked warily into the old lecher's embrace. He tried to kiss her on the lips, but she turned away just in time and received a murmured utterance in her ear instead. For a moment, she looked startled. Then Celia said something that made Wilgis bow to her before entering the limo. He waved as his driver closed the door.

Celia and Doyle said goodnight to Eckrosh before they began walking back into the building. Doyle said, "What did the old rascal say there at the end?"

Celia frowned. "He said he'd had a wonderful evening. That he'd gained an appreciation of horse racing, emphasis on Rambling Rosie. He said we should keep fighting for the slots bill, to 'keep our dobbers up.' Then right away, I think he was blushing, he said, 'No, please forget that last suggestion, Ms. Celia. That was inadvertent. I believe that high-priced brandy I had at dinner has created some crevices in my mind.' That's not word for word, but pretty close to what he said. What do you suppose he was apologizing for?"

They were in the elevator now, riding up to Celia's apartment. Doyle's head was back against the padded elevator back wall as he laughed, thinking of Willy Wilgis' advice. Celia appeared irritated by his failure to answer her question.

Finally, he stopped laughing. "Okay, my dear, what old Willy was advising you to do was 'keep on keeping on.' Or words to that effect."

"'Words to that effect'? What do you mean by that?"

"The literal definition of dobber is the float on a fishing line, okay? But, it's also an old locker room expression. Male locker rooms, I mean. When I was playing football in high school, before I took up boxing, our old coach, Boomer Kincheski, would exhort us before every game, 'Boys, no matter how bad you hurt, or how tired you get, keep your dobbers up. Show those punks what kind of men you are.' It was a legendary call to arms for all Coach Kincheski's teams. Then he'd give, well, kind of an obscene gesture. Relating to his private parts." Doyle was stumbling along now. "Part, I mean." He stopped himself from adding "The thrust of it," because Celia's face had turned red. "Oh, hell," he finally said, "you get the idea?"

The elevator stopped and its doors opened. Celia could restrain herself no longer. She let out a whoop of laughter, her eyes on his. He realized that his discomfort was the cause of her mirth. That this bright, worldy woman had been pulling his leg about as far as it could go.

They were out of the elevator now, walking down the corridor toward their offices, Celia leaning against his shoulder, still shaking with laughter.

Doyle said, "So, you know from dobber."

"Uncle Jim was a great Chicago Bears fan," Celia said. "In the years when the Bears were awful, when I was a kid, Uncle Jim would always invite some of the players and coaches to Monee Park in their off season. Give them dinner. Give them drinks. And he'd always tell them, at the end of the evening, 'Fellas, keep your dobbers up. There are better days ahead.' I asked him for an explanation one time, and Uncle Jim, embarrassed but honest, gave it to me."

They'd reached the door to Celia's apartment. "So, Jack Doyle," she said, "I admit to knowing that dobber is a synonym for a male appendage. And, I suspect, a synonym for the male ego, in the way that the expression is used in your locker rooms.

"But then," she said, smiling back over her shoulder, "those are corresponding entities, are they not?"

She said goodnight and eased the door closed, so as not to awaken Bob.

Chapter Thirty-One

SPRINGFIELD—Two busloads of demonstrators descended on the state capitol Monday to march and picket for nearly three hours in opposition to House Bill 134, which would expand legalized gambling in Illinois. Most of the participants were senior citizens, some of whom were under the erroneous impression they were scheduled to attend a private luncheon with the governor.

The demonstrators were led by Reverend Wardell Simpkins, president and founder of CAB (Christians Against Gambling). Reverend Simpkins, of Glen Ellyn, Illinois, has long been a vocal opponent of gambling. In a statement read from the capitol steps, Reverend Simpkins charged that "Insidious interests of the devil are attempting to broaden even further the presence of harmful gaming in our already casino-plagued state. To add another casino, in Chicago, one of the great cities of the world, would be added proof of how widely this moral cancer has spread, how far public morality has sunk.

"I call upon Christians all over the state, and other people of good will and high morals, to join with CAB in fighting the passage of this corrupt and corrupting piece of diabolical legislation."

Asked about the misinformation involving a luncheon meeting of his group and Governor Otto Walker, Reverend Simpkins smiled. "I can't imagine where our people got that idea," he said. "Some of our more elderly CAB members tend to become a bit confused at times."

In addition to legalizing a casino in Chicago, the proposed measure would also permit the state's six pari-mutuel racetracks to offer slot machine betting. The tracks, particularly struggling Monee Park, claim that the introduction of slots is vital to their financial survival.

Jack Doyle, a Monee Park spokesman, told reporters here Monday that "The advent of casinos cut drastically into horse racing's base audience both here and in other states. But other states have responded by enabling their tracks to compete via the legalization of slots. All we are asking is to be able to offer some of the same kind of gambling as the casinos, to be able to compete with them on a level playing field. Revenues from slots would not only contribute significantly to the state treasury, they would also allow us to improve purses and therefore attract better quality horses to Illinois tracks.

"Pari-mutuel horse racing has been legal in Illinois for more than eighty years," Doyle added. "We want it to continue, and passage of House Bill 134 is vital if that is to happen."

Under provisions of Bill 134 Monee Park, located south of Chicago, would be permitted to install 1,000 video slot machines, as would downstate Devon Downs. The four larger Chicago area tracks each would be authorized to operate a maximum of 2,000 slot machines on their properties.

Near the end of Monday's CAB demonstration, Doyle and Reverend Simpkins engaged in a heated exchange of words on the capitol steps. Doyle accused Reverend Simpkins of being a "willing ally of the current casino owners, who don't want any competition from the racetracks. I'd like to review your CAB books and find out who your major contributors are," Doyle said to the clergyman. Reverend Simpkins retorted that Doyle's "statements are not surprising, emanating as they do from a paid lackey of a struggling business enterprise."

Reverend Simpkins is an ordained minister presently "without a church or congregation," he said, adding that "I am devoting my life efforts to the great cause of combating gambling's expansion."

Doyle was a key figure in the case against media mogul Harvey Rexroth two years ago. Rexroth was convicted on a number of *charges involving the killing of thoroughbred horses for their insurance values. He is currently serving a twelve-year sentence in federal prison in Minnesota.*

House Bill 134, sponsored by Representative Lew Langmeyer (D-Palatine), was passed by the House Gaming Committee late last month. It is expected to come up for a vote before the entire House some time in the next several weeks. Influential House majority leader William "Willy" Wilgis is reported to now be leaning toward favoring its passage.

Chapter Thirty-Two

Niall Hanratty rapidly read the previous day's summary report from his burgeoning betting empire. Business was as strong as it had ever been. He put the computer printouts down on his desk, swiveled his chair to look out of his office headquarters at the sun-drenched buildings across the way. Another beautiful day. It was one of the driest stretches of weather in the Kinsale area in recent history. Why was it that these impressive business figures, normally guaranteed to produce a flood of satisfaction, meant so little to him this lovely morning?

He rose from behind the desk and walked to the window overlooking Kinsale's crowded downtown summer streets and the harbor beyond. Tourists were bumping into each other as they walked from shop to shop. The harbor was replete with various craft, including a couple of luxury yachts that had evidently arrived late last night or early in the morning. The sun bounced off their gleaming brass fittings. He could see his driver, Barry Hoy, cell phone attached to his belt, leaning on the metal railing above the gently moving waters, apparently admiring the nearest of the moored yachts.

Despite the heartening business summary, the beauty of this summer morning, Hanratty's mood was decidedly mixed. That was because of the e-mailed newspaper report he'd received from Art Riley, describing the previous day's developments in Springfield, IL. It should have elevated his spirits, for the campaign to thwart Monee Park's quest for slot machines seemed to be on track, thanks to Reverend Simpkins. Riley had pointed this out in the note he attached to the news story. "Things are looking good," Riley wrote. "If your cousin doesn't see this handwriting on the wall, she must be blind. I would expect her to buckle under and agree to sell the track property in the next week or so."

"Maybe she will," Hanratty muttered as he deleted the e-mail, "and maybe she won't." The fact that Celia had heretofore held firm in her resolve to save the track both impressed and depressed Hanratty. He resented but respected her refusal to give in, recognizing in her the kind of fighter he admired, one much like himself. This occasionally gave him pause, as was the case today. He couldn't help but feel some sympathy for Celia, burdened by a seriously ill husband and an ailing business. This was the kind of matter that, ordinarily, he would discuss with his wife. Throughout his rising career, Sheila had served as his sounding board. Niall had kept very little back from her, primarily details of some rough work involving reluctant owners of off-track shops he'd wanted to acquire. No need for her to know about those few incidents, the methods of persuasion employed by himself and Barry Hoy and, on one occasion, a few of Hoy's cohorts.

And no need, or desire, on his part to let Sheila in on the campaign against Cousin Celia. He realized that the longer this effort went on, as reported by Riley, the more distasteful he found it. Had either of the attacks served to convince Celia to sell, he could have lived with that all right. The robbery, the electrical sabotage, those sort of things he'd believed would get the job done. But they hadn't. Now, the pressure would have to be intensified, in ways Hanratty preferred not to know about in advance.

Hanratty sighed and went back to sit at his desk. He was truly starting to regret ever having listened to Riley, having become involved with him. But he couldn't turn back now. The stakes were too high.

Chapter Thirty-Three

Shontanette was sitting at a window table in the Turf Club when Doyle came in planning to grab a quick lunch. She waved him over to her table, looking very serious, no smile. "I hate to eat alone," she said. "Would you mind sitting down with me?" Doyle was surprised to see this normally forthright, self-assured young woman evade his gaze as she fiddled with her silverware.

Doyle eyed her warily. Shontanette pretended to concentrate on a menu that, after all her years at Monee Park, she must have known backward. He said, "I'm getting the feeling that we've not met here today by accident. Could I be right?"

Without waiting for an answer, he said to Hugo the waiter, "A Bushmills on the rocks for me. A cup of truth serum for my companion."

"Make it a Merlot, Hugo," Shontanette snapped. She waited until the old waiter had shuffled away before she said, "I want to talk to you about Celia. About you and Celia."

"I can see you're serious," Doyle said, "but it's hard for me to take you seriously. What about Celia and me? What are you talking about."

Shontanette shrugged and began nervously tapping her spoon on the tablecloth. "This is hard for me to talk about. It's just that I'm worried that you and Celia, are, well, getting too close. Together. I see the way you look at each other. It's obvious there's an attraction there between you two." She took a sip of her wine. "It's not a good thing. It could be disastrous, because I know how that girl thinks. If she doesn't stay faithful to Bob, she would never, ever, forgive herself.

"Celia's my best friend. I hate to see her hurting with all of her worries about Bob and about the track's future. I realize that you've become a presence here that seems to lessen those hurts. You've made her laugh and act more lively in the past couple of months than I've seen her since Bob got sick."

She took another sip of wine before saying, "This is very uncomfortable for me, Jack. I'm not one to serve as someone else's conscience. I'm just saying that Celia is very vulnerable at this stage of her life. I don't want her to be, well, preyed upon."

Doyle's disbelief at Shontanette's last statement was quickly followed by a wave of anger that turned his face crimson. "Well, I'll be goddamned," he said. "I'm a lot of things to be sure, but predator has never been among them. I can't believe you think that of me."

She didn't back down. "You can't fault me for bringing this up. I want to make sure you know what you're doing in regard to Celia."

"I'm not doing anything," Doyle shot back. "I recognize the futility of me envisioning any kind of romance with her, no matter how much I might like to have it happen. It's not in the cards."

Shontanette sat back in her chair. "Maybe I've mis-read the situation. And you. I love Celia like a sister. It kills me to see what she's been going through. I, just, wanted to try to head off any further trouble for her if I could."

"Trouble. In the form of me," Doyle said bitterly. "Me, who's been working marathon hours here? Who's been busting his butt tramping around the backstretch of this broken down old joint, trying to find ways to put a positive spin on the whole struggling scene? You're accusing *me* of being trouble?"

Hugo shuffled up to the table with their lunch orders. "Another Bushmills, please," Doyle said. "Give the lady what she wants."

Shontanette waved away the old waiter. "Oh, c'mon Jack, don't get on your self righteous high horse with me. I felt I had to get my concerns on the table and I did. Maybe I'm being presumptuous, or over protective. But that's the way I feel."

"All right, I accept that," Doyle said.

Shontanette started on her chicken salad. Doyle ignored his turkey club. He said, "As long as we're being forthright with each other, I have something to ask you. I want your opinion. You've known the person involved for a long time."

She put her fork down. "Go on."

Doyle leaned forward, talking softly. "The stuff that's been going on around here, the attacks on the track, I'm thinking there's maybe somebody on the inside here helping to create these potential disasters by providing needed information. The electrical failure, the money room robbery, the attackers would have needed details about our operation here in order to carry those out. We might well have an informer in our midst."

"Well, yes, I guess that's a possibility," Shontanette said.

"Here's another one. Maybe the so-called Inside Man is Morty."

Shontanette leaned back in her chair. The querulous look on her face was replaced by one of astonishment. "Morty Dubinksi?" she hooted. "You have *got* to be kidding. That little, old, inoffensive creature who's worked here since I was a kid? He'd no more do harm to this place than I would. Where'd you get that crazy ass idea?"

"Hey," Doyle said, "I'm not accusing Morty, I'm just thinking about possible allies on the inside here that those thugs might have. He's one of them."

"Why do you say that?"

"I've become very aware of his gambling habits in the last few weeks. He's a terrible bettor, or maybe just one of the unluckiest ones in history. He's what Clarence Meaux down in the jocks' room calls a Jonah. Somebody like that, well, hell, they're vulnerable to be coerced, or bribed, or threatened. And Morty pretty much knows everything there is to know about Monee Park."

"Oh, Jack," Shontantette said, "I've known Morty for years. There is no way he'd be capable of doing what you're suggesting. No way."

"Nobody ever really knows everything about anybody," Doyle said. "Probably not even about themselves. I guarantee you, I'm going to keep an eye on little Morty."

"You're not just barking up the wrong tree, Jack, you've wandered into the wrong forest with Morty the Mole. It's almost comical," she said, before adding softly, "At least I think so."

"I hope you're right," Doyle said.

A busboy cleared their plates. They both declined coffee, or dessert. Shontanette looked at Doyle appraisingly. "Sometimes you remind me of my Uncle Arthur. He thought he pretty much knew everything, too. He'd tell you who was buried in the Tomb of the Unknown Soldier. Who was going to win the feature at Oaklawn Park on Saturday. How many calories were in the bowl of cheese grits you'd just eaten. When it came to confident, expert, pains in the ass, the man was royalty."

"Sounds like my kind of guy," Doyle said. "And I remind you of him? I'm flattered."

"Yes, you do. You're always so confident in your opinions at every staff meeting, in all your dealings with the media, with the trainers, and the jocks. Everybody around here has picked up on that about you. People talk about it. 'So cool.' Oh, that 'Cool Jack Doyle.'"

Doyle said, "Woman, if you only knew how wrong they are on that count." He drained his Bushmills and pushed his chair back from the table. "You ever hear of Mose Allison?"

Shontanette said, "That white cat who sounds black? Jazz singer and piano player? Sure. Uncle Arthur is a big fan of his."

"I heard Mose interviewed one time on the radio," Doyle said, "talking about how fans of his always thought *he* was so cool. Know what he said?"

"I know you're going to tell me, Jack."

"Mose Allison said, and I know damn well where he was coming from, he said to the interviewer, 'I am not cool. I spend my whole life gravitating between boredom and hysteria, just like you.'"

Chapter Thirty-Four

It was well after the night's final race and Jack was just finishing his wrap-up story when the door to the otherwise deserted press box opened. Still looking at his computer screen, he muttered, "Who the hell is coming in here now?" He was tired, both physically and mentally, from another twelve-hour day, so many in a row now. An hour or so before, he'd asked himself, not for the first time, "Why did I take this damn job?" The answers always were, "I need the money...Moe asked me to...I feel obliged to help Celia."

He heard the water cooler burble. When he looked up he saw Celia's tall form bent over the spout handle. She drank thirstily from a small paper cup, then refilled it. Finally, she turned to wave to him, one hand extended, before going over to sit on the long couch at the far end of the darkened press box. It was an area containing three armchairs, a coffee table, and a couple of floor lamps. Celia reached up and turned off the only lamp that was on. She leaned forward and put her head in her hands. From where he stood, he saw her shoulders begin to shake and heard muffled sobs. He walked rapidly over to stand in front of her, saying softly, "Celia...Celia." She raised her tear-streaked face. "There are just times, Jack, that it all gets to me. Bob—he's had a terrible day. Fidelia and I put him to bed an hour ago. He looked desperately unhappy before he finally dropped off to sleep.

"That was the worst piece of a very, very bad day," Celia continued. "There are the track finances. Al Hannan, our comptroller, told me this morning that we're barely meeting the weekly payroll. We'll be lucky if we can hang on until the end of the meeting. I don't know," she whispered, "it just gets to be too much some days. This is one of them."

Doyle knelt before her. Looking at this beautiful embodiment of sadness, he felt a catch in his throat. He reached forward and lifted her chin up. He said, "I wish like hell there was something I could do to help."

Celia suddenly rose to her feet. He was surprised by the speed of her movement and he got up quickly. She looked directly at him, eyelids still wet, her mouth drawn down. Hers was a look both imploring and determined before she stepped close to him, pressed her moist lips on his, arms tightly around his neck. He took an involuntary step backward.

Celia clutched him more tightly. Jack felt himself begin to harden as she pressed against him, her mouth all over his now, her breath coming in short gasps. "Hold me, Jack. Please, hold me," she said urgently. "I've no one to do that for me anymore. No one. Not anymore." He kissed her deeply, cupping a breast in one hand, running his other hand down her trembling back. Her moan carried a hint of desperation.

As they kissed and held each other, Doyle's thoughts, in quickly dismissed flashes, were of the unlocked press box door. Of Bob Zaslow, asleep in his apartment bed one floor above. His own recent statements to Shontanette. A couple of Commandments whose numbers he could not readily recall at the moment. Hemingway's description of a moral act as something you felt good after.

All such speculation ended when Celia moved her mouth away from Jack's and looked up at him, eyes locked on his. She took his hand and led him to the couch, sat down, and lay back on it, beginning to unbutton and wriggle out of her green skirt, never taking her eyes off of his face.

Jack knelt beside the couch and hurriedly but gently began to open the buttons on her white blouse. When, moments later, Celia was naked, Jack's eyes riveted on the lovely length of her. She watched hungrily as he rapidly discarded his clothes in random piles. When he was done and stood before her, Celia arched her back and reached one arm to the floor lamp above and behind her, and the room went dark. And she reached for him.

Some ninety minutes later Doyle walked with Celia down the long corridor leading to the entrance to her apartment. Celia stopped at the door, turned to him, and gave him a soft, brief kiss, and a flash of her great wide smile. It was followed by a long, silent look before she turned the key and slipped through the doorway. He remained there, staring at the closed door, hoping it would open and she would come out to him having changed her mind. But he knew she wouldn't. He knew she meant it when she'd whispered to him, only minutes before, still in his arms, "Thank you, Jack. That was, well, what I thought it would be. What I wanted, what I needed...Had we met in a different time...." Her voice trailed off before she added, "What we did will never happen again."

"So this is how you define bittersweet," Doyle said to himself as he slowly walked to the elevator. He kept recreating in his mind Celia's hungry touch, the feel of her, their love making which had evolved from a frantic pace to a gentle rhythm. Those memories would haunt him, that he knew.

In his Accord, Doyle sat back and took a deep breath before leaning forward and laying his arms and head on the steering wheel. A wave of shame swept over him as he thought of Bob Zaslow, imprisoned in his wasting body, sleeping, or perhaps awake and wondering where his wife had been. Doyle knew he had no business falling for Celia McCann. Knew that he had, and that it loomed as another bold faced entry in the Doyle Dossier of Poor Decisions.

He finally started the car and eased it through the dark, quiet night toward Monee Park's west entrance. Driving past the old wooden building that contained the office of racing secretary Gary Gabriel, Doyle thought he saw a light flash on, then off. Probably his imagination. There'd be no one in that office at this hour. He drove another half-block, eyes flicking toward his rear view mirror, before he suddenly braked. He'd seen a light back there again, where it shouldn't be. He was sure of it.

After turning off his car lights, he made a quick U-turn. He drove up next to the racing secretary's building and parked in the shadows, several car lengths from where he knew the entrance to be. He eased his car door shut before slipping to the doorway of Gabriel's office. This was an area he was very familiar with. Doyle often stopped here in the mornings to ask Gabriel about possible entrants into the weekend's best races, horses he could publicize in advance. This was where trainers came to enter their horses in races, where jockeys' agents hung out seeking assignments for their clients. Most important, it was the repository of foal papers, or registration records, of every horse stabled at Monee Park. No horse could race at Monee, or any other track in the United States, without these identification papers being on file with the racing secretary.

Doyle ducked low as he approached the windows to the office. He cautiously raised his head to peer into the dark interior. He could make out two figures, both wearing dark, hooded sweatshirts. One held a shielded flashlight aimed at the rows of opened filing cabinets that held the foal papers. From the street light coming over his shoulder, Doyle could see something silver in the man's other hand. Then the man flicked it open. It was a cigarette lighter. The other short, hooded figure began removing the cap from a large red gas can.

Doyle quickly took off his sport coat and bunched it around his left hand. He leveled a hook, always his best punch, through the lower window panel. The shattered class clattered to the office floor. Doyle dropped down below the window level, muttering,

"I hope these bastards don't have guns. Which I should have thought of before."

The sudden quiet was broken by the muffled sounds of panicky voices, then shoes scraping over glass. The door burst open and the two hooded figures dashed out. Startled, Doyle was able only to make a lunge at the second figure, and he missed him. Doyle skidded across the sidewalk on his chest before jumping to his feet and sprinting after them.

The hooded men never looked back as they sped toward the chain link fence bordering the wide parking lot. They went over the fence like Marines on a Parris Island obstacle course. On the other side they jumped into a dark blue sedan and sped down the alley toward Crain Avenue. Doyle crashed the backs of his fists against the fence in frustration. Their car was moving so fast, its lights off, that he never got a look at their faces. There was no license plate on the car, which careened around the corner on Crain and was soon out of sight.

Doyle limped back to the racing secretary's office. He'd badly scraped his right knee during his pavement slide, tearing a wide hole in his slacks. He found his cell phone, which had fallen out of his sport coat, on the edge of the pavement and called Track Security. Though the night was warm, and he had run hard, his breathing was easy. *My days in the gym are still doing me good,* he thought as he pressed in the security office number. *But those bastards were fast.*

The main night shift security guard telephoned Monee Park security director Karl Mortenson at home. Mortenson lived nearby and arrived at the racing secretary's office eighteen minutes later. Doyle watched Mortenson examine the broken lock on the outer door, the open cabinets, the discarded gas can still full, a look of disgust on his face. The locked file drawers had been crudely pried open, either with a crow bar or a jack handle.

"Well, these guys are no locksmiths," Mortenson said. "Did you get any kind of look at them, Jack?"

"No. When I looked in through the window, they had their backs to me. As I said, they were on the short side, stockily built. When they ran to the fence, all I could see was their legs pumping. And they were moving. They scaled that fence like monkeys. I never saw their faces because of the hoods. But these have got to be young guys. In good shape."

Mortenson looked around the large room, then up at its aged ceiling beams. "Jesus," he said, "a fire started here would rip through this whole building within minutes."

"Looks to me like those guys were aiming at the foal papers," Doyle said.

"But any blaze started in those papers would spread instantly," Mortenson responded. "The sprinkler system in here looks so old I doubt it could douse a bonfire."

He shook his head. "This whole plant needs serious upgrading," Mortenson said.

The security chief stationed two guards at the door to Gabriel's office, telling them, "Stay there until we get a locksmith over here first thing in the morning." He walked with Doyle toward Doyle's car. Doyle said, "The two guys that robbed the money room. Their descriptions were 'short, stocky.' Nobody saw faces that night, either." Mortenson paused, then reached into his jacket for a cigarette. "Maybe it's the same two guys," Mortenson said. "But why?"

After Doyle had grabbed four hours of sleep, a twenty-ounce container of black coffee, and had reached his desk in the press box, he picked up the phone and heard a familiar voice say, "I heard what happened last night."

Tired, irritable, Doyle barked at Moe Kellman, "How did you find out about this already?"

There was a prolonged silence on the other end of the phone. Doyle could picture Kellman, probably at his Hancock Building office suite, sipping tea after his early morning workout at Fit City, flush with good health and curiosity.

Kellman said, "Jack, Jack, try to harness your deep seated aversion to normal human interaction. We're just having a conversation here. Relax. I found out about the break-in at Monee Park because I hear things. I understand that you, or Celia I should say, are not making this public. Good idea. Why make the track look like it's under attack. Which I think it is, by the way."

Doyle sat back in his chair and put his feet up on his desk, trying to relax. "That was a disaster averted last night," he said. "If those guys had managed to set fire to the horses' registration papers, our racing meet is over. They, or whoever sent them, were striking right at the heart of our operation. When the money was stolen, we survived, thanks to you. When the electricity went out on the Fourth of July, we survived. We lost a lot of money, but we survived."

"But," Doyle said, sitting up in his chair, feeling anger rise within him, "if those bastards had burned down that office, the 2006 Monee Park racing meet would have been history. And so, in the long run, probably Monee Park itself."

He took a deep breath, sat back, put his feet upon the desk again. "But of course, Moe, you know that. Like you seem to know everything else."

Kellman didn't respond to the jibe. He said, "I spoke to Celia before I called you. She agrees with me that there's nothing random about what's going on out there. That there's a concerted campaign to shut down Monee Park."

"Looks that way," Doyle said.

Kellman said, "Are you thinking, along with me and Celia, that Niall Hanratty could be behind this?"

Doyle said, "Hanratty's got motive, all right."

"Yes, he does. What you've got to find out is who the locals are that have been hired to do his dirty work."

"Me? Finding out is a specialty of yours, as I recall," Doyle said. "Go to it. I've got my hands full trying to keep this joint afloat as it is."

There was another silence. Kellman was probably putting down his tea mug and reaching toward the large platter of fresh fruit that was constantly replenished throughout the working day in the Hancock suite.

Finally, Kellman said, "I intend to go to it, Jack. I've got Celia's best interests in mind. And the track's. And even, believe it or not, yours."

"I'm touched, and encouraged," Doyle said. "Really, I mean it. Thanks, Moe."

"One other thing. A final question, if I might ask. What were you doing at Monee Park after one o'clock in the morning, long after the races were over? I've never figured you for an overtime type guy."

Doyle fought off the almost tensile memory of Celia's mouth on his, her warm loveliness beneath him, concentrating on his answer. "Moe, sometimes I surprise myself," he said lightly. "You remember Julius Erving? The great basketball player?"

"Who could forget? What about him?"

"Dr. J. said one time that 'being a professional is doing things you love to do on nights when you don't feel like doing them.' That's me, sometimes."

Moe sighed. "Jack, you are sometimes so full of shit it defies the borders of imagination."

"So long, Moe," Doyle said.

Chapter Thirty-Five

The attempted arson was the raging talk of the racetrack the next morning. When Doyle drove through the stable gate a little after eight Bernice Webb, the woman security guard on that shift, smiled at him for the first time. Usually Bernice treated his arrival, despite the official sticker on his windshield and the identification tag hanging from his rear view mirror, as if she strongly suspected him of an Al Qaeda affiliation. Stopped him every morning, visually checked his car. Not this time. "Heard you did some good here last night, preventing an arson and all," Bernice said. "Have a great day."

Doyle groaned. "If you only knew what else I did last night," he said to himself as the memory of Celia's touch swept over him, accompanied by a wave of guilt.

The staff meeting was held in Celia's office. Security Chief Mortenson conducted it, noting Doyle's luck in being "in the right place at the right time to prevent a potential disaster," also praising the quick response of his men, though lamenting their inability to apprehend the fleeing culprits. He laid out plans for beefing up security throughout the plant.

Celia and Jack avoided looking at each other. Jack imagined he could feel Bob Zaslow's eyes boring into the back of his neck. Zaslow, as always attended by Fidelia, sat in his wheelchair at the side of the conference table.

Gary Gabriel, the racing secretary, pushed his glasses up on his nose. He wore a worried look. "Will there be a guard at my office every night?"

"Every night from now until the end of the meeting," Mortenson assured him. He looked around the table, eyes going from Celia to Jack to Gabriel to Bob to Shontanette, who was taking notes on her laptop computer. "I hope I'm wrong, but I think we've got to assume that whoever is doing this stuff will try again," he said. "I only have so many personnel to work with, and they can't cover everything. We're all going to have to be as vigilant as possible."

Shontanette looked up from her computer. "Okay, they've robbed the track, sabotaged the tote board, and tried to burn down Gary's office. What could they do next?"

"I don't believe whoever it is will try a repeat of any of those efforts," Mortenson answered. "If they're paying attention, and getting the right information, they'll know we've pretty much locked down those doors." He shrugged. "What they have in mind next is anybody's guess."

The meeting broke up on that disheartening note. Doyle lingered, watching Celia shuffling her papers on the table. When she glanced up at him, she blushed a vivid shade of pink. She didn't speak until Fidelia had finished wheeling Bob out of the room. Then Celia said softly, "I meant what I said last night, Jack. Or, rather, this morning." Flustered, she continued to shuffle the papers in front of her. He resisted the impulse to move to her, cup her sad face in his hands, hold her again. He said, "I know you did, Celia." He walked out of the office, closing the door gently behind him.

Shontanette started to say something to Doyle as he passed her desk in the reception area. When she saw the look on his face, she kept quiet.

Doyle took the press box stairs two at a time. Morty looked up from reading *Racing Daily*, startled, when the door banged open. Doyle went to his desk and picked up his briefcase. His face was grim. "I'm taking the rest of the day off, Morty. You're in charge." Then he was out the door.

◇◇◇

Doyle snatched his hand back from the hot steering wheel of the Accord. He'd parked it carelessly that morning, windshield facing the unusually hot September sun. The temperature had already climbed to ninety-two. Wrapping his left palm in a handkerchief, he placed it on the wheel, starting the car with his other hand. He drove out of the Monee Park parking lot. It would be several minutes before the Accord's air conditioner won its fight with the fierce temperature.

At Seventy-ninth Street, Jack glanced at the speedometer. It read seventy-five mph, or twenty over the posted limit. He had to get his mind off Celia. He adjusted his speed and punched Moe Kellman's private number into his cell phone. Moe answered on the second ring, saying, "Hello, Jack."

Doyle said, "How about I buy you lunch at Dino's?"

"Ah, Jack, I'd like to. But I can't."

Doyle realized he sounded almost petulant when he heard himself say, "Why not?"

Moe said, "I didn't mention it when we talked earlier today, but I've got a lot of work to catch up on. Remember, Leah and I only got back from Cuba two days ago. That's why."

Moe's visit to Cuba had completely slipped Doyle's mind. With U. S. citizens prohibited from traveling from their homeland to Cuba except on humanitarian or cultural missions, Moe and his wife had months before joined a group at a Chicago synagogue that had been granted permission to bring medical and school supplies to Havana.

"So how was your trip?" Doyle said.

"Excellent. We stayed in a five star hotel owned by a Spanish chain. Went all around Havana for a week, distributing what we brought. We also visited galleries and markets and a lot of historic sites. The people there were great to us. As I think I told you before, I hadn't been to Havana since before Castro. It was great to see it again, even in the shape it's in today."

Doyle said, "I don't suppose I should ask what your business was in Havana in the fifties."

"Correct."

Now, caught up in the Dan Ryan Expressway construction traffic slow up, Doyle said, "What's Havana like today?" He couldn't believe he was asking these questions. Anything to get his mind off last night, off Celia.

"Havana today?" Moe said. "It's impressive, like it always was, but very sad now, too." He paused. "Like a beautiful woman you were in love with years ago. You see her today, you can still recognize the great bone structure, but the rest is in decay.

"It's a very, very poor country," Moe continued. "The doctors are paid about $30 a month, and they're among the top earners. Castro's government has no money for maintaining the Spanish colonial buildings in old Havana. It's a shame. Jack, you should have seen Havana before Castro, when it was wide open. Casinos, night-clubs, music, women like you've never seen. It was a world apart, especially for young guys like me then, down from Chicago."

"Yeah," Doyle said, the 'good old days.' Widespread poverty. And illiteracy. And disease. I've read a lot about the good old days. United Fruit and other American enterprises, including the Outfit, cutting up the pie."

Moe sighed. He said, "In truth, I can't disagree with you. But I miss it. It's a fascinating little country. It'll be interesting to see what happens when The Goat goes."

"Who?"

"Fidel. A lot of the Cubans we met wouldn't mention him by name. When they wanted to talk about him, they pretended to pull at an imaginary beard. So, The Goat."

Doyle laughed. He could feel the tension in his shoulders begin to ease as he passed Cellular Field, home of the White Sox. Moe could have that effect on him. Doyle said, "Did you go to that synagogue you said you were going to visit? The one you told me Meyer Lansky helped finance years ago?"

"You mean the one that putz Silverstein came from? Yeah, we visited there," Moe said. "The congregation is doing fine, even without a rabbi."

Doyle knew that this was a very sore subject with Kellman. Ten years earlier, Moe and some of his friends learned about the 1,500-member Havana synagogue that had long been without a rabbi because of a death and no ready replacement. They wrote to the leader of the congregation and eventually arranged for Raul Silverstein, a bright, promising, Havana-born young Jew, to obtain a student visa, enter the U. S., and enroll at Yeshiva University in New York City. Moe and his fellow Chicagoans agreed to pay for Raul to complete rabbinical studies before he returned to lead the Havana congregation.

Instead, Silverstein had graduated, been ordained, and immediately married the daughter of a prominent New Jersey builder, taking over a congregation in Princeton. Raul Silverstein's Chicago sponsors remained extremely bitter about this, Moe in particular.

Doyle was approaching Hubbard's Cave when he heard Moe say, "Don't remind me anymore of Silverstein."

Moe changed the subject as Doyle changed lanes passing Ohio Street. "I've only got a minute or two here, Jack. We'll get together in a day or two, once I've caught up. But let me tell you what one native Cuban, guy about your age, told me when we there."

"Who was this?"

"One of our tour guides, Rivelio Hernandez. Very sharp, well educated, spoke three or four languages. He showed us where Pope John Paul said Mass on his visit to Havana in 1998. The Cubans still talk about that. It was a huge deal for them.

"Anyway, Rivelio's story goes that Castro took the Pope for a boat tour of Havana harbor. They go out a little ways and suddenly a huge storm comes up. The boat capsizes. Both men are thrown overboard. But, somehow, they rise up and walk together on the water back to shore.

"Next morning, the headline in the Vatican newspaper says Holy Father and Castro Saved by Miracle.

"The headline in *Granm*a, the Cuban government's official newspaper, reads Fidel Saves Pope's Life.

"In Miami, the major Cuban-American paper's top headline is Castro Can't Swim."

Moe laughed and Jack did, too. He said, "Moesy, thanks, I needed that." As he pulled into the underground parking garage of his condo building he heard Kellman say, "You take care of yourself, kid." Then the phone went dead.

Chapter Thirty-Six

SPRINGFIELD—*A bill that its sponsor claims is needed to "save Illinois horse racing" stalled in committee after a contentious legislative hearing here Thursday. House Bill 134 would open the way for a casino to be introduced in Chicago and also place video slot machines at the state's six racetracks, one of which, Monee Park, "is foundering financially" according to its president and CEO Celia McCann.*

Ms. McCann was one of several witnesses heard by the House Gaming Committee, whose chairman, Representative Lew Langmeyer (D-Palatine), is the chief sponsor of HB134. Langmeyer had originally intended to bring the bill to the House floor for a vote this week. But, reportedly acting at the suggestion of House Majority Leader William "Willy" Wilgis (D-Kankakee), he called for another hearing on the matter.

At the end of Thursday's five-hour session, the eight Gaming Committee members split down the middle on whether to vote the bill out of committee: four Democrats in favor, four Republicans against. The ninth member of the committee, Representative Sam DiCola (D-Glenview), was out of the country. Langmeyer said he would schedule another hearing on the bill "in the weeks ahead," adamantly refusing to be more specific. Langmeyer was visibly upset over Thursday's vote.

Ms. McCann testified that "competition from the state's nine casinos has horrifically impacted the Illinois horse racing industry in general and Monee Park in particular. We are struggling to survive.

We have a sixty-year-old track that has contributed significantly to the state's economy. We need to be able to offer slot machine gambling in order to remain in business and continue to contribute."

Opposing the bill was a series of casino owner/operators. Harrison Millard, owner of the Show Place casino group whose Illinois riverboat is one of nation's most profitable, argued that *"We entered the Illinois casino picture with high hopes, most of which have been realized. Why should we be now be forced to face competition from racetracks?"*

Also speaking against HB134 was Reverend Wardell Simpkins, founder of CAB (Christians Against Gambling). In reading from a lengthy statement, Reverend Simpkins traced the *"life of my late brother Roger, a gambling addict who lost everything at racetracks—his savings, followed by his wife and children, who were forced to abandon him. Allowing these iniquitous dens to expand their reach even further into the pockets of the deceived would further lower our steeply declining moral standards."*

Committee member Ray McGrath (D-Chicago) remarked after Simpkins' testimony that he was *"surprised the good reverend was unable to lead his unfortunate sibling to the path of righteousness."* This comment drew a torrent of boos from CAB members in the audience.

Chairman Langmeyer expressed sympathy *"for your brother's plight, Reverend Simpkins. But, with all due respect,"* he added, *"I don't see how his fall from grace should justify you trying to prohibit gambling for the hundreds of thousands of our state's citizens who enjoy betting on horses in a responsible, recreational manner."*

Chapter Thirty-Seven

That evening at Monee Park, Celia and Shontanette sat on the balcony overlooking the racetrack. Celia had just returned from her depressing day in Springfield. She was exhausted. When her oldest friend saw her walk into the office, she said, "C'mon, girl, let's have a drink. We can sit outside. It's a nice night."

Shontanette made the drinks at the small office bar, an Absolut Citron over ice for Celia, a glass of sherry for herself, and brought them to the nearby balcony that ran the length of this part of the top floor, outside Celia's office and Celia and Bob's apartment. Placing the glasses on the round, glass table between their chairs, she reached over and took Celia's cell phone out of her hand and turned it off. "You look worn out, girl. Let's just forget business for a few minutes and relax, all right?"

Celia put her head back on the chair, stretching her long legs in front of her. A wisp of a breeze blew strands of dark red hair across her cheek. She took a long drink from her glass. "Great idea, Shontanette," she said. "I feel like I've been through the ringer and back, as Uncle Jim used to say. This is nice out here tonight." She described that day's Springfield hearing before finally saying, "I'm far less confident than I was. Lew Langmeyer is doing everything that he can for the bill, but it may not be enough. If only Willy Wilgis would get behind it more strongly…."

The two friends sat quietly for a few minutes until Shontanette said, "God, Celia, I'd hate to think Monee Park would have to be sold and turned into some damn subdivision. Some of the best times of my life were those summers when we worked here as kids. And being able to come back and work here for you, well, that's the greatest break I could have gotten. I love this place. And I know how you feel about it."

Celia felt tears come to her eyes. They blurred her view of the track infield with the maple trees she and Shontanette used to eagerly climb. Of the backstretch, where they both worked one summer as hot walkers for trainer Marty Morrison, a great friend of Uncle Jim's. She thought of the high school summers when they had jobs inside the building, and of the nights after work when they played in the Monee Park coed softball league. Celia's first boyfriend was a young jockey. Shontanette met her future husband, Cecil, son of Monee's Turf Club chef Horace Tate, the summer she apprenticed as the restaurant's hostess.

"Remember when Uncle Jim gave us Smokey?" Celia said. "How nervous we were?" Shontanette smiled at the memory of when they were put in charge of a gentle, brown stable pony, which they rode every single day before and after work, gaining confidence in themselves and their ability to tack up, feed, water, and care for a thousand pound pet.

"Old Smokey," Shontanette said. "I've still got pictures of both of us with him. When he got colic and died that year we started college, I was miserable for months. I still think that lazy groom we gave him to, Hector, didn't take the right care of him," she said bitterly.

Celia went inside to refill their drinks. When she returned, Shontanette said, "Well, the news today isn't all bad. I had a look at last week's business figures. They were up considerably from the same period a year ago. In fact, most of the month has been good."

Celia said, "Rambling Rosie has had a lot to do with that. She's a draw. And Jack has done a great job publicizing her. A great job, as a matter of fact, in publicizing the track. We've gotten more media coverage this year than in many years. Of course," she said, "not all of it was what we wanted. News of the tote board sabotage couldn't be suppressed. But Jack managed to keep the attempted arson out of the media."

Shontanette's eyes narrowed at Celia's mention of Doyle. "He's got a lot of rascal in him, that's for sure," Shontanette said with a short laugh. "But he sure knows his job. And I've got to admit, I can't help liking the guy."

Celia said softly, "I know what you mean." Shontanette cast an appraising eye on her friend before glancing at her watch. "Got to go, honey," she said. "Cecil's picking me up downstairs in fifteen minutes." She patted Celia's hand before leaving.

The breeze picked up a few minutes later and Celia, still in her chair, her second drink untouched before her, shivered slightly. She knew it was nearly time for her to help Fidelia put Bob into his bed. She would then recount for him what happened today, what the track's prospects were, trying to put the best possible spin to it that she could. For a moment she pictured her husband on their wedding day, a tall, vibrant, confident man with a face and personality that had drawn her to him like a super magnet.

Celia went inside the apartment and emptied her untouched drink into the sink. She leaned her hands on the sink rim for a moment before shaking her head and turning around. Her eyes filled briefly again as she looked at the door to Bob's bedroom. She dried them, straightened her back and smile, and walked toward it.

Chapter Thirty-Eight

"Call for you, Jack," Morty said. Doyle finished pouring himself a cup of coffee at the press box kitchenette counter and went back to his desk. It was Moe Kellman, who said, "I'm sending the check out with Pete Dunleavy. Can you meet him at the clubhouse entrance at four o'clock?"

"Sure," Doyle said, before adding, "This is kind of getting to be a habit with you, isn't it? Sending badly needed money to Monee Park?"

There was a grunt on the other end of the line. "The money I loaned to Celia after the track was robbed I fully expect to get back, either if Monee gets slots or the property is sold. That gesture was because Celia is the niece of one of my dear departed friends.

"This bet I'm making on Eckrosh's horse is another matter," Moe contined. "Occasionally, at Leah's urging, I do question my own sanity. This is one of those occasions. Let's hope for the best. Make sure Tom Eckrosh deposits it right away. I don't want to worry about him misplacing it or something."

"I'll take the check right over to Eckrosh's barn, then drive him to his bank," Doyle said.

The check made out to Tom Eckrosh was for $50,000. Once the old trainer deposited it in his account, he'd be able to write a check of his own, in that amount, to Breeders' Cup Ltd., thus making Rambling Rosie eligible to run in the $2 million Breeders' Cup Sprint at Churchill Downs in two weeks.

This plan began to take shape two days earlier. Doyle had nearly finished reading the current issue of *The Blood-Horse*, thoroughbred racing's foremost weekly magazine, when he turned back to a page that listed the Best Times of the leading horses in each of eight divisions. In the Sprint column, he spotted Rambling Rosie's name. She was rated the fifth fastest sprinter in the country based on her winning times from the current season.

Doyle called Eckrosh at his barn. "Tom," he said, "have you given any thought to running Rosie in the Breeders' Cup Sprint?"

There was a hoot of derisive laughter from the old man. "Son, you've got a mean sense of humor. 'Course I *thought* about the Sprint and Rosie. Then I reminded myself about the size of the entry fee. All my savings don't add up to that. So, that was the end of my Breeders' Cup thinking."

Doyle said, "Let me ask you a question. If she could get in, how do you think Rosie would do in the Sprint?"

"She'd be one, two, or three," Eckrosh said confidently. "No doubt about that in my mind. She's the fastest filly in America."

"Even going up against colts? You think she'd do that well?"

"Take an honest old man's word for it."

"Let me get back to you on this," Doyle said.

Doyle met Moe for lunch at Dino's that noon, figuring business such as this would be best conducted in person. As Doyle laid out his plan, ignoring his order of shrimp orzo, Moe listened without talking, spooling up a steaming platter of linguini smothered in roasted garlic slices, mushrooms, artichoke hearts, and hot roasted peppers.

When he'd cleaned his plate, Kellman picked up his cell phone. "I need to make a call, Jack." The muffled conversation that followed took less than five minutes. Doyle heard the words "Rambling Rosie... Breeders' Cup...the numbers" and "thanks, Dave." Moe closed the phone and looked at Jack.

"I can see where you're coming from," he said. "Getting Rambling Rosie into the Breeders' Cup Sprint, on national television, all the publicity would be a bonanza for Monee Park. Win or lose, she's a great story. Broken down old trainer, obscure breeding, coming out of the claiming ranks at a small track like Monee Park to challenge the best sprinters in the world. It's a natural."

"You'll do it then? Front Tom Eckrosh the entrance fee?"

Moe signaled for coffee before answering. "I checked with a Vegas guy who is very, very sharp with the numbers on racehorses. Dave Zimmer. He compares numbers from all over the country. Makes a great living doing it, betting horses, selling his numbers to a handful of high rollers at a premium, and advising owners what horses they should buy. Tremendously successful young guy."

Moe sipped his coffee. "Dave says your Rosie is legit. That she's got a real shot in the Sprint if she runs in it, even though only two fillies have won the race in almost twenty-five years."

Doyle grinned. "Didn't I tell you?"

"Whatever you tell me, Jack, I still like to check out. No offense intended. It's just my nature."

"So you'll give Eckrosh the money for the entrance fee?"

Moe said, "Jack, remember, I'm in business. My charity work doesn't involve horse racing. Yes, I'll provide the money for the entrance fee. Here's my terms: If Rosie gets any part of the purse, first, second, third, fourth, or fifth, I get the entrance fee money back plus fifteen percent of her winnings."

Doyle whistled softly. He said, "Fifteen percent. That seems kind of steep. About as high as some of the Outfit's street rates." He saw Moe's mouth tighten, so he hastened to add, "But I get it. It's not a loan, is it? You're making a bet."

Moe smiled. "Exactly. If Rosie runs up the track, I'll eat my loss. Tom Eckrosh can't lose anything. If she wins, or finishes in the top three, I'll come out pretty good and so will Eckrosh. If she runs fourth or fifth, we each still make a little money. Either way, Jack, Eckrosh gets an opportunity he'd never have otherwise. And you've got a chance to put Celia's track on the national map, thanks to me."

"Modesty occasionally becomes you, Moe," Doyle said, reaching across the table to shake Kellman's hand.

"That's what Leah occasionally tells me," Moe said.

Doyle parked his Accord next to Barn D just after 4:15, but he didn't have to get out of the car. Tom Eckrosh hurried out of his office and up to the driver's side window, looking both anxious and hopeful.

"Did the man come through, Jack?"

"Tom, the man came through. Let's go to the bank."

Forty-five minutes later, they returned to Barn D. After the bank, they'd gone to the post office. Their Breeders' Cup adventure had begun. Eckrosh said, "I want to check on 'Rosie.'"

"I don't blame you," Doyle said. "With the money riding on her, she should be stabled in a bank vault."

They said hello to Maria, who was sitting on a stool outside Rosie's stall. "Bring her out for a few minutes, will you, Maria?" Eckrosh said.

The lively filly with the four white stockings grazed on a nearby patch of grass, Maria holding the shank attached to her halter. The late afternoon sun highlighted Rosie's chestnut coat. Doyle said, "Tom, what is it about Rosie that makes her so special? I mean, no offense intended, but except for her beautiful color she doesn't look much different than all kinds of run of the mill horses I've seen." He shrugged. "Maybe I don't know that much about how good horses are supposed to look."

Eckrosh said gently, "Maybe you don't, Jack." His gaze swept over his prize filly. " Rosie's pretty muscular for a filly, but she's no amazon. She's smart, and keen to run, she's got about as much personality as any animal I've ever been around. And she's got one other thing that's mighty, mighty rare," he said admiringly. "She's got a big engine."

Doyle laughed, but he could see the trainer was serious. "Listen," the old man said, "I've seen dozens of beautifully bred and conformed million dollar horses who couldn't earn what it cost to feed them. The will to win—that's what Rosie has. A lot of horses are what we call 'cheap.' They're real brave when everything's going their way, but they fold up when they're challenged. Rosie's not like that. She's a fighter. She's got a big engine."

It was twilight now, nearly time for the first race, when Jack got to the press box. Morty said, "You're looking pretty pleased with yourself boss."

"I've put in a good day's work," Doyle said. Morty's excitement grew as Doyle recounted the happenings leading to Rambling Rosie becoming a Breeders' Cup Sprint starter. "Fantastic, Jack," he said. "That's fantastic."

"Yeah," Doyle said. "Now, I'm going to go upstairs and personally deliver the good news to Celia and Bob."

As he neared the press box door, he heard Morty say, "Before you go, Jack, let me ask you something." Morty was beaming. Jack groaned, aware of what was coming. He said, "Morty, I'm not sure that sly look becomes you. But go ahead."

"Roy Rogers," Morty said. "What was his horse's name?"

"Well, I've got you there," Doyle replied. "That one I know. Trigger. I read one time that he's stuffed and in some kind of Roy Rogers museum in California. Am I right?"

There was a short silence. Then Morty said, "What about Dale Evans' horse?

Doyle was stumped, and he admitted it. "Buttermilk," Morty said triumphantly.

Chapter Thirty-Nine

As promised, they found that the fire escape on the dark east side of the Monee Park clubhouse had been lowered for them. They climbed up it wearing dark blue sweats, black ski masks, and cross trainers. For squat, solidly-packed men they moved silently and well across the roof to the door of the penthouse apartment belonging to Celia and Bob. Lucarelli was in the lead. He slowed his approach as he neared the glass door whose interior was obscured by dark drapes. "Gimmee the flashlight," he said to Shannon. He put his blackjack into the side pocket of his sweat shirt.

This nocturnal venture had been planned two nights earlier. It was the idea of the increasingly desperate Art Riley. The attorney had summoned them to his downtown Chicago office and read them the riot act.

"Nothing you two have done has worked," Riley said angrily. Seeing Lucarelli's face darken, he quickly added, "Now, I know some of that isn't your fault. You couldn't have known the tote board failure wouldn't bring Celia to her knees. Or that Moe Kellman would come up with the money to keep Monee Park operating after your robbery.

"But," Riley continued, regaining some confidence, "you screwed up big time when you didn't get the racing secretary's office to go up in flames. That would have ended the Monee Park meeting. That would have done the job. But you two," he sneered, feeling himself completely back in command of these two bozos now, "got run out of there by a goddam publicity man. You should be ashamed."

Shannon looked down at his feet while rubbing his hands together nervously. He wanted to ask who Moe Kellman was, and what publicity man Riley meant, but he figured he had best be quiet. Lucarelli, however, shot Riley a defiant look.

"We screwed up with the fire," he admitted. "But the other things you laid out for us to do, we goddam well *did* do. Maybe your choice of targets wasn't so cool. You were the one that picked them out. We didn't think them up ourselves, you know," he said, jabbing Shannon with his elbow, seeking some props for this defensive thrust.

Riley was about to lash back, but thought better of it. No sense getting into a pissing match with these imbeciles. Time was running out. The casino/slots bill was still alive in Springfield. If Celia was going to be convinced to sell the property, that convincing would have to take place soon.

"Fellas," Riley said, leaning back in his creaky chair, conciliatory now, "I don't think Ms. McCann has taken us seriously. I guess I shouldn't say 'us,' because she doesn't know it's 'us' aligned against her." He gazed out the dusty window of his south LaSalle Street office. Plucking a cigar from the middle drawer of his desk, he lighted it and began to puff thoughtfully. Shannon's head was still down. Lucarelli shifted impatiently in his chair.

"All right," Riley finally said, "this is what I want you to do."

When he was finished, Denny finally looked up. "How do we get in there? We're not fucking cat burglars you know."

"This is what the setup out there is," Riley said, beginning to explain it. "You can count on this being the way it is. Don't ask me how I know, just know that I do."

On their drive to Monee Park two nights later, Lucarelli said, "You've got to give the old man credit. Riley knows what we do best. Terrorize!" He cackled, pounding the steering wheel of the

Taurus with the hand not holding the spliff. He was high on crystal meth again, using a few hits of pot to balance things out, liking the whole feeling, thinking about their assignment: break into the McCann rooftop apartment, rough up the residents, "scare the shit out of that stubborn woman," as Riley put it, "so she'll finally see what's good for her."

Lucarelli was raring to go. Shannon sucked on a Bud Light twenty-four ouncer, looking solemnly out the window as they drove south on the Dan Ryan. "You're going to like this, Denny," his buddy assured him. "I've seen this McCann broad's picture in the paper. She one of those haughty looking bitches that're stuck way up on themselves." He took a deep hit on the joint, held it in for a couple of blocks, then gasped, "She's never seen the likes of us." He got his breath back. "I might just give her an introductory-to-real-life fuck while we're up there." He cackled again and began to again pound the steering wheel as they picked up speed in the express lane. Shannon finished off his beer and reached into the cooler for another. He was starting to feel a little click of enthusiasm for the task at hand, his cousin's mood becoming contagious as they got closer to Monee Park.

Doyle followed Celia up the back stairs from the clubhouse to her apartment, trying to keep his eyes off the entrancing hip swing she produced in high heels while ascending. They each had their arms full, carrying items from the just concluded Turf Club birthday party for Izzy Kreinberg. It was number ninety-nine for the lively, wealthy businessman and horse owner whose zest for fast horses, beautiful women, and gin martinis apparently never abated.

The honoree on Izzy Kreinberg Night had horses he owned compete in four different races and heavily bet each one. Three of them won. The sparkling-eyed nonagenarian went down to the winner's circle after each victory. Following the last one, he returned to the Turf Club for the cutting of the huge birthday cake and opening of gifts, saying to Celia, "This is the most glorious night of my life."

Kreinberg had received dozens of gifts from the fifty guests at the Turf Club party. When the affair was winding down, Kreinberg again thanked Celia for her efforts in hosting it, then asked if she would "please keep them for me overnight, honey, the valuable stuff. I don't want to worry about getting it all home tonight," he'd said as he gazed fondly at a striking brunette on his arm, one of several young women he'd introduced earlier as "my niece."

The gifts included plaques, two humorous videos of Kreinberg's life, a scrapbook, telegrams from Chicago's mayor and the governor of Illinois. Celia toted two packed shopping bags up the steps. Doyle had in one hand the new laptop that Kreinberg intended to use to store his betting records. In the other he had the huge floral arrangement with its banner reading IZZIE IS OR IS HE AIN'T THE BEST?

Riley had assured them that "there's not much of a lock on the penthouse door," and he was right. Lucarelli forced it open with his switchblade in twenty seconds. The yellow early autumn moon slipped out from behind cloud cover, momentarily allowing light to reach the rooftop. Lucarelli stepped quickly into the dark living room, Shannon at his heels.

They stood still for a minute or so, getting accustomed to the surroundings. Lucarelli briefly swept the large room with his flashlight. There was a dining area to their right, a door perhaps leading to the kitchen at the far end of it. The door they had been told led to the corridor outside the apartment was in the center of the room. Lucarelli moved around from behind the couch that backed up to the sliding glass door.

Bob Zaslow, seated in his wheelchair in his bedroom at the window overlooking the darkened racetrack, started. From the corner of his eye he saw a brief flash of light under the bedroom door. He slowly began to turn the chair away from the window.

Lucarelli walked softly across the carpeted floor to one of the bedroom doors. Just as he neared it, the door began to open. He jumped back a yard, banging into the equally startled Shannon.

Bob drove his electric wheelchair through the doorway. He looked up at them in astonishment, his jaw laid awkwardly on the left side of his chest, mouth in a frozen twist.

"Where's your wife?" Lucarelli said. He leaned forward, his breath hot on Zaslow's face. "So you can't move," Lucarelli snarled, "you can still talk. Where the fuck is your wife?"

Outside the apartment's kitchen door, Celia stopped and put her bags down. She unlocked the door and went in, flicking on the small light over the sink. Doyle placed the floral arrangement on the counter, the laptop next to it. Celia whispered, "Bob said he'd wait up for me. I'll take care of all of Izzie's gifts tomorrow. What a great night for that old fellow. Thanks for all the help, Jack." She looked at him directly for only an instant before turning away.

Doyle, frowning, said, "What's that?" Celia gave him a puzzled look. "I thought I heard a guy talking in there," he said. "Not Bob." Doyle put a finger to her lips and reached to turn off the light.

Shannon, shocked at Zaslow's condition, put a hand on his cousin's arm. He said, "Let me look in the next room, man. Cool it. Maybe that's where the broad is."

Lucarelli yanked at his ski mask, pulling it down more tightly. "Check it out then." Within seconds Shannon was back, shaking his head no. "God dammit," Lucarelli said, "she probably don't sleep with this crip. Where the fuck is she?"

The chemical ride was taking over Aiden now, a vicious combination of drugs, anxiety, and frustration. He leaned in close to Zaslow's frozen face. "What a mess you are," he said, waving the heavy black flashlight in front of Zaslow. "I'm going to beat your fucking head in if you don't start to answer me." There was no response, just Zaslow looking up impassively. *"Do you fucking hear me?"* Lucarelli shouted.

Doyle grabbed Celia's wrist. "Go to the elevator down the hall," he said, "use the emergency phone in there and call Security. Tell them to jump up here. Hurry. Do it."

She tensed and began instead to move toward the door leading to the dining room. "*No*," Doyle said, grabbing her arm and spinning her toward the door to the corridor. "I'm going in there. You stay out of there. *Go.*"

Celia ran out the kitchen. Doyle again heard the angry male voice from the other side of the kitchen door. He took off his sport coat, ripped off his tie, and took a deep breath before he burst through the kitchen door into the dark living room.

Doyle charged toward where Bob sat in his wheelchair. The hooded figure in front of Bob turned and shone the flashlight in his face. Doyle straightened up for an instant, blinded by the light, arm shielding his eyes. Denny Shannon, coming at him in a rush from behind, delivered a crushing karate kick to the middle of Doyle's back. He fell face forward onto the carpet, the breath knocked almost completely out of him, pain ripping through him. He tried to move but couldn't. "Who the fuck is that?" Lucarelli said. Shannon laughed. "That's a fucking failed rescuer." He stepped back to get his balance set, then kicked Doyle in the ribs.

Suddenly all of the ceiling lights in the living room went on. Lucarelli and Shannon saw standing at the far end of the room, next to the light panel, pink housecoat pulled tightly around her small frame, an outraged Fidelia Rizal. "You, you men," she spat, "get away from Mr. Zaslow." What about me, Doyle wanted to say, but he still hadn't gotten enough air in his lungs to produce a syllable.

Lucarelli started moving toward the little nurse when she reached for a button next to the light panel. She pressed it and immediately a loud alarm buzzer began blasting through the building. Shannon, panicked, stumbled toward the door to the roof. He said to Lucarelli, "I'm fucking out of here, man." Lucarelli looked wildly around the living room, pounding the flashlight into his left palm. His face was flushed, his breathing harsh. The meth rode through him like an electric current. Then he pivoted and ran for the doorway to the rooftop, Shannon hustling away in front of him. Still immobilized on the carpet, Doyle heard pounding footsteps from the interior of the building, Celia's voice above them, urging the security guards to "*Hurry. Please hurry.*"

Wally Farnsworth, the first security guard into the apartment, was heading for the open rooftop door when he tripped over Doyle. Farnsworth, at two-hundred thirty pounds, some forty overweight, fell heavily onto the glass coffee table, shattering it. His partner, Kurt Borchers, stopped his pursuit to help Farnsworth to his feet. On all fours now, Doyle groaned audibly watching this scene.

Going down the fire escape much faster than they had ascended it, Lucarelli and Shannon reached the ground before the guard Borchers leaned over the edge of the roof above them, shouting, "Stop you two. Stop there." Within seconds they had made it to the Taurus, were in it and moving, lights off, through the darkness of the large parking lot and toward the north exit of Monee Park.

Lucarelli drove fast and erratically, zooming around slower cars on the Dan Ryan, then tucking in between trucks heading to the city. His eyes flickered between the road and the car mirror for miles, until he was satisfied there was no pursuit. Shannon said, "Aiden, for chrissakes settle down. We don't want to get stopped by no cop."

There was no reply from Lucarelli until he had sped up the east bound ramp at Forty-seventh Street. Two blocks later he abruptly pulled over to the curb and shut off the motor. He said, "Hand me a Bud."

Lucarelli gulped half the beer. "Riley's not going to pay us a dime for tonight. Goddamit." He finished the beer and crushed the can into a tight ball.

His cell phone rang. He looked at the caller ID before saying to Riley, "She wasn't even fucking there."

Riley said, "I tried to call and tell you that. Called an hour ago. I'd just found out Celia was at a big birthday party down in the Turf Club. I was going to tell you to hold off for an hour or so. What the hell happened?"

"We broke into her apartment. Some gook nurse finds us trying to get word from the cripple where his wife is, turns on an alarm you could hear in Joliet. Some other dude comes charging at us out of the kitchen. Denny put him down good. But it was a fucking circus. Security guys chasing us over the roof. Where do get your so-called inside info from? We barely got out of there," Lucarelli said, almost shouting now.

Riley said, "Well, it's not my fault. I tried to call you. You didn't answer."

"No shit. You think I keep my cell phone on while we're breaking and entering in the middle of the night?"

That silenced Riley for a few moments. He said, "I'll get back to you in a day or two. We'll have to try something else. You'll never get close to Celia McCann after what happened tonight." He hung up.

The two men sat quietly before Lucarelli, still fuming, could bring himself to tell Shannon what Riley had said. He reached for another beer. "You know what's the fucking craziest part about what went on up there in that apartment?"

"What?"

Lucarelli said, "When I got pissed off up there and felt like smashing that crip's face in, he gave me this weird look. It took me back. It was a look, like, well he wouldn't *mind* me smashing in his head."

Chapter Forty

Celia, Jack, Shontanette, and several dozen trainers, jockeys, and grooms were waiting outside Barn D when the Botzau Van Service vehicle arrived. It was right on time, but Tom Eckrosh looked impatiently at his watch as the van's driver-owner, Norm Botzau, jumped down from the cab. "Sorry, Mr. Eckrosh," he said, "that traffic over there on the Ryan was...." Eckrosh cut him short. "You're only a minute late, son. It's all right."

Doyle glanced at his watch, 8:31. Not enough hours for him after last night's excitement. He had forced himself out of bed and into a hot shower before he felt even comfortable enough to get dressed. The area of his back where he'd been kicked by one of the two assailants felt as if it had been hit by a sledge hammer. His bruised ribs were painful, though not as bad as his back. He grimaced as he thought of the thwarted attack, how close the two men had come to doing serious damage to Bob, Celia, and Fidelia.

The long blue and white Botzau van contained stalls for eight horses. Seven were already inside, some pawing with their feet, shuffling about, others peering out curiously from the screened windows. All seven heads turned when Maria Martinez led Rambling Rosie out of the barn to the back of the van. Botzau quickly lowered the ramp. The little chestnut filly walked up it sure footedly, her head high, as if she were ascending a familiar staircase. Maria settled Rosie in the only empty stall and remained at her head, patting her and talking softly and soothingly in Spanish. Rosie laid her head on Maria's shoulder.

Tom Eckrosh said, "You got a full load in there?"

"Yes, sir," Botzau replied. "The other seven all belong to that Calabrese fella who races over at Heartland Downs. That good filly of his, Satin Maiden, runs in the Juvenile Fillies' on Breeders' Cup Day. Mr. Calabrese plans to run the others at Churchill the day before the Cup."

Botzau nimbly jumped up into the driver's seat and closed the cab door. Squinting up at Botzau in the morning sunlight, Eckrosh said, "Well, I hope you know who your number one passenger is. You take good care of my filly."

Botzau was insulted. "That's the second time today I've gotten that advice," he said. "First, my wife Nan says to me early this morning before I left home, 'Norm, take good care of Rambling Rosie. She's a real favorite of mine.' As if I'm not careful of *all* the horses I van," he huffed. He settled behind the wheel, muttering, "I've been getting them back and forth, safe and sound, for twenty-two years."

Celia stepped forward and gave Eckrosh a peck on the cheek. "Enjoy every minute of it, Tom," she said. "You deserve it."

The old trainer blushed. He looked at Doyle, who gave him a thumbs up, and at Shontanette, who was waving her goodbye. Botzau called down from the cab, "You riding up here with me, Mr. Eckrosh?"

"Sure am," Eckrosh said. "My groom Maria will stay back there with Rosie." He carried his battered suitcase around to the passenger's side and pulled himself up into the seat.

Walking back to the offices, Celia said, "A horsemen's representative will be waiting for Tom at Churchill. Tom's all set up with a motel room near the track. Maria insisted on staying in the barn, near Rosie. Tom said there was no talking her out of it."

Doyle said, "I'm sure they'll all be fine. From all I've heard, the Churchill Downs people know what they're doing. And, Rosie's getting to be kind of a big name."

"Partly thanks to you, Jack," Celia said. "Amen," added Shontanette, "mainly thanks to you." The women were walking on each side of him. Doyle glanced from the grinning Celia to the trying-to-look serious Shontanette, recognizing they were watching for his reaction, like conspiring school girls teasing a callow male friend.

"You two should be ashamed of yourselves," Doyle said, "trying to yank the chain of a man trained to yank chains."

The three were laughing as they approached the Monee Park clubhouse entrance. When Jack saw Karl Mortenson waiting for them, the smile froze on his face. Mortenson greeted Celia and Shontanette before Doyle took the Security chief by the elbow and said, "I need to ask you something. Those clowns that supposedly came to our rescue last night, where did you get them?"

Mortenson's expression darkened. "Those are two of my veteran guards. I know they didn't handle things right last night, but, hell, it was *you* that Farnsworth stumbled over. He's not the nimblest guy, you know. But what do you expect for minimum wage? James Bond? Jackie Chan?"

"I'd expect somebody who could pick up his damn feet," Doyle shot back. Mortenson, glowering, nodded to the women, then stalked off. Celia said, "That was kind of harsh, Jack." Shontanette, frowning, murmured something about minimum wage, but Doyle didn't take notice as they continued walking. He was still steamed, his back hurt, and his ribs pained him every time he took a deep breath.

In his office minutes later, Doyle again found himself regretting his decision not to accompany Eckrosh to Louisville. As he'd said to Celia, "That old guy hasn't raced outside of Illinois since his boyhood. I worry about him handling himself down there with those hardboots."

"I wouldn't worry, Jack," Celia had replied. "Tom has seen about everything there is to see in racing. And remembered all of it."

Doyle had reluctantly reasoned that it was his primary duty to remain at Monee Park and do everything he could to make its Breeders' Cup Day program—four live races, eight with simulcast coverage from Churchill Downs—the biggest of the year. He had designated almost all of his remaining advertising budget to the process. Some of the buzz he was trying to create actually had carried over to him. Doyle was excited about Rambling Rosie's chances, pumped up about what he was sure would be a big Breeders' Cup day at Monee. After assigning Morty his morning tasks, Doyle poured himself a cup of coffee and called Moe Kellman.

"Any chance we could have dinner tonight, Moe?"

"Sorry, Jack. I've got some out of towners coming in for a look at our fall line of furs. They're big hitters. I've got to be here for them."

Doyle was disappointed but didn't say so. He perked up when Kellman said, "Your publicity campaign seems to be going great. I've heard Monee Park mentioned more in the last few weeks than in the previous five years combined."

"Yeah, well, when you've got a great story like Rambling Rosie, it makes it a lot easier to get coverage. Are you going to bet her, Moe? I think she's a cinch to upset that field. She's been training like a wild horse. Believe me, old Tom Eckrosh has got her sitting on ready."

There was a brief silence before Kellman said, "Jack, be careful you don't get carried away. You're real close to this story. I know you like that horse and her people. Your judgment may be a bit influenced by that."

Doyle said, "Hell, it's not just my judgment. All the sharpies, the speed boys, have got Rosie near the top of their lists. She's the wiseguy horse of this Breeders' Cup. I'm telling you, Moesy, we pound it in on Rosie, we'll be farting through silk."

Kellman said, "Some of us already are." There was a pause before he said, "Did I ever tell you about my brother-in-law Barney, the tailor?"

"No. You told me about Pincus the tailor, the guy who hustled the twins who were rabbis. Same guy?"

"No relation. That was Itzak Pincus, a real *shmuck*. I'm talking about Barney Passman, my sister Sarah's husband."

"Okay. What about Barney the tailor?"

"Barney had a shop on the west side, out near old Harthorne Park. One fall years ago, about a week before the big Harthorne Derby, a bunch of jockeys come in to his shop. They've all decided they want to get measured for new tuxedos to wear to the big dinner-dance the night of the Derby, a strictly black tie affair. There were seven, eight of them. Barney takes all their measurements, tells them their orders will be ready the day before the dinner-dance. Then he tells them how much each one owes him, saying they've got to pay in advance.

"Seven of the eight reach into their pockets and pull out a couple of hundred bucks each and pay him on the spot. The eighth is a guy named Sandy McCreary, who was Harthorne's leading jockey at the time. He's just made a whopping alimony payment and he's nearly out of cash. He says to Barney, 'I'll pay you the day after the Harthorne Derby.'

"Barney looks at McCreary, shaking his head 'no.' McCreary says, 'But listen, I'm riding the huge favorite in the Derby. The horse can't lose. I'll have the money for you the next day.'

"Barney just looks at him. 'Can't lose?' he says to McCreary. 'They gotta run around, don't they?'

"Guess what? McCreary's horse runs fourth. He went to the dinner-dance in a sport coat and slacks and tried to crash the door. They threw him out.

"They gotta run around, Jack. Remember that," Kellman said.

Chapter Forty-One

Looking up at one of the dozens of television screens on Monee Park's jam-packed first floor, Doyle grinned as he saw Rambling Rosie being walked around the expansive Churchill Downs paddock by Maria Martinez. Fans crowded against the paddock fence at the Louisville track, eager to see up close the starters in the Breeders' Cup Sprint. The paddock was crowded with owners, trainers, members of the press, breeders, and racing officials. In the middle of them stood Tom Eckrosh. He was the oldest person in the assemblage and the only man not wearing a sport coat, or suit and tie. To Doyle's delight, the old trainer had on pressed khakis and a blue windbreaker whose large white lettering on the back read Monee Park. His familiar gray fedora was pulled down low on his forehead.

"Loyalty can be a beautiful thing," Doyle said. A man standing to his right gave him a startled look, then returned his attention to the *Racing Daily*, the margins of which he had filled with enough mysterious looking hieroglyphics, notations, and markings to qualify it for the wall of a pharaoh's tomb.

Twelve minutes remained before the start of the Breeders' Cup Sprint, one of the most eagerly awaited events on American racing's biggest annual afternoon, one that saw purses for the eight races exceed a total of $12 million. The six-furlong, $2 million Sprint was almost invariably exciting, competitive, and extremely difficult to handicap, thus making it one of the most attractive betting races on the program. It frequently produced longshot winners. That made Doyle feel good.

Rambling Rosie was one of twelve horses entered in the event and the only filly or mare. Her current odds were 45-1. Most bettors obviously didn't have much faith in female sprinters, especially one hailing from Monee Park. As Maria continued to lead her around the circular paddock path, Doyle saw that Rosie was easily the smallest of the entrants. This didn't seem to deter her, however. Rosie had her ears pricked and she was looking with interest at her larger male rivals, occasionally buck jumping for a stride or two, as if to say, "Check me out, boys, I'm ready to roll."

Doyle neared Madame Fran's booth on his way to the betting window. He smiled at her, pointing with appreciation toward the long line of customers who awaited her wisdom. Fran motioned him over. She whispered, "Rosie? Bet her to place." Doyle was affronted. "I only bet to win," he said. Madame Fran leaned closer to him, her plump forearms on the table. She paused to give her turban a quick adjustment before saying, with new emphasis, "Jack, Rosie's a huge price. Every vibe coming to me screams out 'bet her to place.'"

"Easy, easy, *mi pequeno*," Ramon Garcia said. He wasn't the only man talking to a horse behind the Churchill Downs starting gate. Many of the other eleven riders were muttering to their mounts as the gate crew members began ushering them into the iron stalls that were barely large enough to contain these thousand pound creatures. Garcia could feel Rosie tense up beneath him. He knew that feeling. She was marshalling all the strength she possessed in order to propel herself forward once the bell rang. The first couple of times he'd ridden her in races, Ramon had nearly been thrown off when caught unawares by her explosiveness. Now, he knew to be prepared.

In the gate, Garcia looked to his right. He saw Larry Porter, still the leading rider at Heartland Downs who'd been brought in today to ride Moseby's Man in the Sprint. Garcia nodded at Porter, and Porter nodded back. There was no "welcome to the big leagues" from Porter this time. Porter knew what Rambling Rosie could do. He eyed her respectfully before dropping his goggles down over his eyes.

Prior to his third ride on Rosie, Garcia had overheard a rival trainer say to his jockey, "Eckrosh's filly comes out of there like she's got a firecracker up her ass." Garcia's command of English at the time was such that he found the statement somewhat baffling. But, the way it was said, he was pretty sure it was a reflection of respect. And now he understood what it meant.

Doyle stuck his head in Shontanette's office doorway. "Let's go upstairs," he said. "It's getting close to post time for the Sprint." They walked up the flight of stairs to join Celia, Bob, and Fidelia in the living room of the penthouse apartment.

Four of them sat. Doyle paced back and forth as the host of the television show said, "And there's the sensational filly Rambling Rosie, winner of ten straight races in the Midwest, one of the bargain buys of recent racing history. Her venerable owner-trainer Tom Eckrosh picked her up at an obscure sale in southern Illinois for $2,700. Since then she's earned more than $350,000 and today tries for a winner's share of $1,000,000 in the prestigious Breeders' Cup Sprint. Young Midwest jockey Ramon Garcia is her rider. For Garcia, a native of Mexico, this is his first appearance in a Breeders' Cup race."

Turning to the show's handicapping expert, the host said, "Bill, I see that Rambling Rosie is 45-1 on the odds board. What kind of chance does Rosie have in here?" Bill could barely conceal a sneer as he replied, "She'll be inhaled and spit out by these major league sprinters in here. Hers has been a nice, heart-warming story all right. But it's going to have a disappointing chapter today," predicted the man who thus far this afternoon had not picked even one horse that had finished in the money.

"What an asshole," Doyle said. "Whoops, excuse me, ladies." The look in Bob Zaslow's eyes indicated he agreed wholeheartedly with Doyle. Celia, concentrating on the television screen, took no notice of either of them. She said, "Gosh, Rosie does look awfully small compared to those other horses. I hope she doesn't get banged around and hurt."

At 3:47 p.m., Churchill Downs' starter Harry Schwartz pressed the button that opened the doors of the massive starting gate. Out of post No. 6 shot a chestnut blur, Ramon Garcia pumping his hands on her neck for a few strides, then settling down in the saddle, head lowered, as Rambling Rosie went to where she loved to be—on the lead. Before she'd run forty yards, Rosie was two lengths in front of her nearest pursuer. It was an explosive beginning that brought gasps from the huge Churchill Downs crowd.

Head down, legs churning, Rosie rocketed on as Garcia guided her five paths over toward the inner rail. Rosie quickly extended her advantage to three lengths as she zipped down the backstretch. She appeared to be running easily, well within herself. "Jesus," Doyle said, hands sweating now, "look at her go. She's running their legs off." Celia watched through fingers spliced over her eyes, her lips moving silently. Shontanette was pounding her fist on the arm of her chair, intoning, "Go, girl. Go." Bob attempted to turn his head to better see the screen. Fidelia quickly positioned his chair to give him a better view.

Some eight lengths behind the flying Rambling Rosie, the race's heavy favorite, Socks in Four, stumbled badly, his shoulder hitting the inside rail. His rider, standing straight up in the stirrups, managed to pull him up. He didn't appear to be seriously injured, but Socks in Four was out of it.

Track announcer Trevor Durkin's excitement was coming through to the Churchill crowd and the large television audience. "Rambling Rosie is running the race of her life," he exclaimed. "She's four lengths in front as she rounds the turn for home."

The crowd erupted as Rosie curved into the long Churchill Downs stretch, Garcia sitting chilly. She flicked her tail once, then again, and came two paths off the rail. Garcia glanced back and then shook the reins at her. He could feel her beginning to tire slightly. "She's now three lengths in front with an eighth of a mile to go," Durkin shouted.

Doyle moved a couple of steps closer to the television. "Hang on, Rosie," he said. "Hang on baby." On the left part of the screen he could see two horses begin to detach themselves from the pack trailing the chestnut leader. "Mike the Dude swings to the outside," Durkin reported, "and that's Loyal Luke coming up the rail." Jack felt his stomach begin to knot. Celia still couldn't bring herself to look directly at the screen.

Inside the sixteenth pole, it was obvious that Rambling Rosie was getting extremely leg weary from her earlier efforts. She again swished her tail, always a sign of fatigue, then bore out slightly toward the center of the track. But she would not quit. Garcia moved his hands on her neck, and the little filly dropped her head, pinned her ears back, and dug in gamely.

It wasn't quite enough. In the shadow of the wire, Mike the Dude swept past her on the outside to win by a half length. To her left, Loyal Luke also closed with a rush, but Rosie held him off by a nose. The remainder of the field trailed in far behind this trio. Mike the Dude's winning time was a new Breeders' Cup Sprint record of 1:08.

Doyle, who had been waving his left hand at the television as if he could somehow push Rosie to the finish line, let out a whoosh of air. He shook his head in dismay. "Damn," he said. "So close. So close." He threw his track program down on the coffee table. "If only Rosie could have hung in for three more strides for that crabby old man. And for Maria."

Celia, on her feet now, her face alight, said, "Jack, what are you talking about? That little filly ran the race of her life. Rosie finished in front of ten of the best sprinters in the world. The one that beat her set a track record." The television camera fastened on Rosie, who had trotted to the path near the winner's circle that led back to the stable area. She was greeted with a kiss on the nose from Maria. As she attached the shank to Rosie's bridle, Maria beamed. Ramon Garcia, his chest puffing almost as hard as his exhausted mount's, grinned down at Maria. Then Tom Eckrosh joined them, his craggy old face split by a wide smile.

"So that's what a curmudgeon looks like when he's happy," Doyle laughed.

"Jack," Celia said, "second money in that race was worth $425,000. That's more than Tom Eckrosh makes in many, many years of training his little stable. This is the biggest score of his life. Look at them," she said, gesturing at the screen, "Tom and Maria and Ramon, they look like they've won three lotteries!"

Doyle concentrated on the television screen that was now displaying the payoffs on the Breeders' Cup Sprint. As the longest shot in the field, Rambling Rosie returned $42.40 to place. Doyle whistled. He patted his right pants pocket, making sure that his $100 place ticket was there.

"Well," he said, "the drinks are on me. And dinner, too. And," he added, "I better go downstairs and invite Madame Fran to join us. I owe her for her good advice about this race."

It was 10:00 p.m. in Ireland when the results of the Breeders' Cup Sprint became official. At the Hanratty's home outside Kinsale, Niall muted the television set. The Hanrattys, along with thousands of others in their horse-loving nation, had watched the race with great interest. Sheila's face was still flushed from the effort she'd made in cheering on Rambling Rosie. "Oh, isn't she the brave little creature," she said to her husband. "I love to see a fine little filly like that do so well."

Her husband's reaction to the Sprint result was decidedly mixed. He'd profited by thousands of Euros bet on Rambling Rosie to win by sentimental, root for the underdog Irish fans. And he couldn't help but admire Rambling Rosie's amazing effort in nearly pulling off a major upset. At the same time, the filly's now internationally known ties to Monee Park would not, he understood, be in his best interests in the least.

"The Mile Turf race is coming up, Niall," Sheila reminded. "Turn the sound back on, please. Who do you fancy in this?"

It was as if he hadn't heard her. Hanratty handed the remote control to his wife. "I'll be taking a little walk down on the beach, now, Sheila," he said. "I've got some thinking to do. Record the next race for me, will you?"

Chapter Forty-Two

One of thoroughbred racing's all-time great trainers, the late Hall of Famer Charlie Whittingham, often remarked of the talented horses he dealt with, "They're like strawberries. They can spoil on you overnight."

That truism hit Tom Eckrosh hard on the Tuesday following the Breeders' Cup Sprint. Back at Monee Park after their van ride from Louisville, he had sent Rambling Rosie out for a mile and a half maintenance gallop under exercise rider Judy Baeza. The filly had left the barn kicking and squealing, feeling and looking great. She returned seventeen minutes later obviously lame in her left fore.

Doyle learned of the injury when he called Eckrosh to ask if he planned to run Rosie any more this season. In the post-Breeders' Cup euphoria, there had been mention of possibly shipping her to Maryland for a sprint stakes to close out her campaign. Eckrosh had told representatives of the eastern track he would "consider it." Now, it was a moot point.

"Rosie's got a hoof abscess," Eckrosh told Doyle. The disappointment in the old trainer's voice was evident. "She's pretty lame. No, it's not life threatening by any means. I've got Doc Jensen working on her. He's the best vet here."

Doyle said, "Well, I better put out a press release. Tell me, what causes something like this?"

"She must have stepped on something sharp that went through the hoof wall. Then something got worked up in there, maybe gravel, a pebble, who knows? It's an abscess in the real sensitive part of her hoof. Doc Jensen cleaned the hoof and drained it. But she's still plenty sore. We've got to watch it close so an infection doesn't come back."

Eckrosh sighed. "You know," he said, "at first I was feeling pretty down when this happened, thinking, hell, Rosie's at the top of her game. Why does this have to happen now? But the more I thought on it, the less I felt that way. She just ran the race of her life and made me a pot load of money. What have I got to complain about, Jack?"

"How long will this take to heal?"

"Doc Jensen thinks he'll get it cleaned up in a few days. It's a good thing it was spotted early. He bandaged her foot and put a pad on it to help protect it. He says the hoof shouldn't develop a crack, even though there's always that possibility. I've seen it happen."

Doyle was relieved. He said, "So, Rosie can race again, right?"

Eckrosh hesitated before saying softly, "She could. But she won't."

"Why not? I mean, you could even give her the rest of the year off, then bring her back in the spring."

"Oh, I could all right," Eckrosh said. "But I won't. I figure Rosie has done all for me that I've got any right to expect. I'm going to retire her. I don't want to take any chances with her getting hurt again. Next spring, I'll have her bred to a good stud down in Kentucky."

"Well, shoot, Tom, I'm sorry to hear that," Doyle said. And he was, not only because he'd become a big fan of the sensational filly, but also because Monee Park's most famous name was about to be removed from the public eye. "I'll get a press release out this morning." Then another thought struck him. "Tom, would Rosie be able to walk down the track some night in a week or two?"

"Sure," the trainer said. "If Doc Jensen is right, and he usually is, she probably could even be ready for some light exercise by then."

"How about having Rosie just parade before the stands between races? Could you do that as a favor to me? And Celia? And Monee Park?"

Eckrosh said, "What have you got in mind, Jack?"

Farewell to Rambling Rosie Night was officially announced at a noon press conference at Monee Park the following day. Lured by the promise of a free lunch and open bar, representatives of all the area's major and minor media outlets showed up in droves to listen to Doyle unveil the plans.

"Rosie has done so much to put Monee Park on the map again that we want to show our appreciation for her, and to her fans," Doyle said, speaking from behind a microphone to the group assembled in the Turf Club. "Our Farewell will feature free admission and parking a week from Saturday afternoon. Along with $1 hot dogs and beers and sodas, and a free color photo of Rosie, autographed by Tom Eckrosh, for every patron.

"In addition, Rosie will make her final racetrack appearance between the seventh and eighth races when she is paraded, under tack and with jockey Ramon Garcia aboard, down our homestretch. We urge all of Rosie's many fans to come out that afternoon, bring their cameras and video recorders, and say goodbye to this amazing filly."

After his statement, Doyle fielded several questions. One came from Buzz Alterhoff, a veteran reporter for a chain of suburban weeklies who never, ever missed an event like this. With a half-eaten sandwich in one hand, third Bloody Mary in the other, Alterhoff said combatively, "Exactly how is Monee Park managing this? The free admission, cut rate prices? I thought the track was in financial trouble. Isn't that why you guys want slots here?"

"Yes, that's why we want slots," Doyle replied. "But sometimes you have to spend money to make money." He dearly wanted to add, "Something you wouldn't know about, Buzz, you freeloading freak," but instead said, "We expect to draw an all-time record crowd on Rosie's Farewell Night. We'll have a complete line of souvenirs for sale. And we're hoping for a record high betting night, too. Does that answer your question, Buzz?"

Buzz, however, had already turned away and was pushing people aside on his way back to the buffet table.

◇◇◇

Clips of the press conference were shown on the WGN-TV nine o'clock news that night, a favorite show of the Haller's crowd, who always perked up at the appearance of the long legged lady who read the winning lottery numbers. Lucarelli interrupted his harangue about the quality of the White Sox pitching staff when he heard the words Monee Park. He nudged Shannon and pointed up at the television screen, where Doyle was shown speaking. "Hey," Shannon said excitedly, "isn't that the sucker I flattened out there that night? Looks like him."

"Cool it, man," Lucarelli said, grabbing Shannon's elbow. "Not so damn loud. Yeah, I think that's him all right." When the Monee Park segment was over, they picked up their beers, grinning at each other.

Fifteen miles to the north, Art Riley sat in the den of his Wilmette home, sipping an Old Fashioned and watching the same newscast. He put his drink down and leaned forward when he saw Doyle on the screen, a huge Monee Park banner behind him. As the sports anchor switched from this horse racing story to hockey scores, Riley shut off the television and picked up his phone. Seconds later, Lucarelli's cell began to ring.

Chapter Forty-Three

Barry Hoy didn't like what he saw when he entered Niall Hanratty's Kinsale office early on the Monday after the Breeders' Cup. The look on his boss' face was one that Hoy, Hanratty's driver and chief bodyguard for more than ten years, had rarely seen. But Hoy remembered it when he saw it. He knew it did not bode well for someone. This feeling was reinforced when Hoy saw Hanratty's business manager, Tony Rourke, busying himself at a computer over in the corner of the office, back turned, striving for invisibility. It was a gloomy morning following a rain-drenched night in Kinsale. The mood in Hanratty's office reflected the day's weather conditions.

Hanrattty twirled a ballpoint pen in one hand while tapping the fingers of the other on his desk. He grunted a greeting for Hoy, motioning for him to take a seat. It was several more tense and silent minutes before Hanratty threw the pen down on the desk. He said, "I've just been talking to your man in the States. Mr. Art 'I'll Take Care of Everything' Riley. Who's turned out to be a sparrow fart of the first order."

"What's gone on?" Hoy said.

"These gobshites Riley has working for him have messed up again. After nearly getting caught trying to set a fire, Riley, without consulting me, dispatched them to scare the bejesus out of cousin Celia. They broke into her home at night, early on the week of the Breeders' Cup. Riley just now got his courage up to tell me about it. His plan was for them to terrorize her and her husband a bit. Didn't happen. His goons got chased out of there by some little Asian nurse who surprised them and set off the alarm. My great friend Mr. Doyle evidently stumbled on the scene and took a larruping. I could hardly believe what Riley was telling me.

"And that's not all. Riley, he says to me, 'Well, we're not done yet. There's another avenue to be explored.'"

"'An avenue to be explored?' I say. 'Sure, and haven't you and your two buffoons fucked up at every turn in the road so far?'

"Well, Riley says, 'I'm thinking we could join forces with this local anti-gambling preacher. I've had exploratory talks with the man, Reverend Wardell Simpkins. A contribution sent to his Christians Against Betting organization could help turn up the heat against the slot machine bill. A sizeable contribution,' Riley says, 'to be funneled through him.'

"It was at that point," Hanratty said, "that I hung up on Attorney Riley. The man must be cracked. Honest to God, how little that idjit must think of us over here."

Hanratty swiveled his chair so he could activate his answering machine. "That isn't all," he said. "This message was waiting for me this morning. From none other than our Mr. Doyle. Listen to this now."

Hoy perched on the edge of Hanratty's desk. O'Rourke, head down and clicking away at his computer keys over in the corner, had evidently already heard it. Hanratty leaned back in his chair, eyes narrowed. They heard Doyle say brightly, "Top of the morning to you, Niall. This is Jack Doyle, calling from Monee Park, where a couple of bozos tried, and failed, to do some nasty damage last week. Some kind of damage designed to encourage Celia to sell the track, I presume."

Doyle's voice grew softer as he continued, taking on an almost reflective tone. "Niall, as you may remember, I'm a serious jazz fan. We discussed jazz during my visit over there. Well, just last Sunday, I was listening to public radio here, the Marian McPartland show, one of the things I look forward to every week. She's in her eighties now, but she still can play and has great guests on her program.

"Here's the part of that show that interested me," Doyle continued. "Marian was about to play 'Jitterbug Waltz,' a Fats Waller tune, when she told a little story about Fats. Seems a friend of hers, another professional musician, years ago had signed up for a lesson from Fats. Her friend was good, but he wanted to get better.

"So, he goes to Fats' house one afternoon, sits down at the piano, and Fats says to him, 'Play something.' The guy plays maybe five, six minutes, one of his best numbers. When he finishes the song, he looks expectantly at Fats. Waller looks at him and says, 'I wouldn't do it that way no more.'

"The guy is puzzled, but he turns back to the keyboard and rips off another one of his favorites, playing his ass off for about ten minutes. He stops, and Fats says, 'I wouldn't do it that way no more.' Then Fats got up and left the room."

There was a pause on the tape. Then they heard Doyle say, "You're probably sitting there now, Niall, thinking, 'What the hell is he telling me this story for?' I can picture you. I wouldn't be surprised if your blood pressure wasn't on the leap."

Another pause, before Doyle, speaking more forcefully, said, "Regarding what's been going on over here at Monee Park, these attempts to disrupt, and frighten, and thwart, well in the words of the great Mr. Waller, 'I wouldn't do it that way no more.' Are ya hearin' me now?" Doyle said loudly, attempting his version of a brogue before banging down the phone.

Hanratty stood up and walked over to the window. Looking out, he said, "How would you like a trip to the States, Barry?"

"Any time, boss. Any time."

Hanratty turned back and placed his hands on the desk. Leaning forward, eyes boring into Hoy's, he said, "I made a mistake using Riley. I believed his crock of bullshit about knowing 'how to handle things.' It was careless on my part. And careless usually has some kind of hefty price tag."

He took his suit coat off the back of the chair. "Bring the car around, will you, Barry?" To O'Rourke he said, "I'll be staying up in Dun Laoghaire until we leave for the States. You'll be in charge of business when I'm gone. Run it like you own it, Tony."

O'Rourke said, "No worries, Niall. Travel well."

Hoy drove rapidly north on the N11 to Dublin. Near the outskirts of the city, he heard Hanratty say, "Barry, go to the passport office, on Molesworth Street. You know it?"

"I do."

"You've got your own, now?"

"Got it last summer. When me and the missus went on holiday to Portugal."

Hanratty would be getting his first passport. Earlier that morning, he'd inquired and been told that it would take a week to obtain and would be good for a stay of up to ninety days in the United States. He wouldn't be there anywhere near that long.

Looking out the window at the Wicklow Mountains, Hanratty said, "Who knew it'd take a crisis like this to get me onto the passport list?"

Chapter Forty-Four

Marge Duffy took a final swipe at the wet bar surface with the sodden towel. It was 4:46 o'clock on Thursday afternoon. Her feet were killing her, her back had tightened up, her calves were aching. Fourteen minutes yet remained in Marge's Haller's Pub shift. She recalled, not for the first time, what her father, a retired printer, had told her years ago. "Anybody who works on their feet for eight hours a day is going to get varicose veins. Like me. Like your mother." Marge thought of her late mother, who had worked behind the perfume counter at Marshall Field's department store for more than thirty years. Just the thought of that made her legs ache even more.

There was a burst of raucous laughter from a corner table. Marge reacted with disgust. Aiden Lucarelli and Denny Shannon had been at the table for nearly three hours, drinking, making fun of most of the other customers, many of whom had reacted by departing early, thereby cutting into Marge's modest tip money. In the mirror she watched Lucarelli pat his jacket pocket, then get to his feet and walk rapidly to the men's room, announcing in a loud voice, "Time to empty the monster." An hour earlier, it had been "Time to drain the snake." Both macho expressions elicited appreciative laughter from Shannon.

Marge figured Lucarelli was lighting himself up with something on these trips to the toilet, for both times he had emerged looking puffed up, face red, eyes blazing. She figured he was on

crystal meth, the current drug of choice among the neighborhood's low lifers. "All it does is make that asshole an even bigger
asshole," she muttered. An hour earlier, when Marge had come
around from behind the bar to deliver Lucarelli's order of buffalo
wings, he'd taken the opportunity to run his hand over her ass
as she bent forward with the platter. She had to place the food
down before she could dodge away from him, see the smirk on
his face. "Ever do that again, I'll cut your fucking hand off," she'd
snarled. Lucarelli threw his head back, roaring with laughter.
Shannon slapped the table with glee. "Oh, ain't you one tough
bitch," Lucarelli gasped as Marge returned to her post behind
the bar. "Hey, Marge," he'd urged, "ease up. You're too cute to
be so mean."

His latest meth infusion had really revved up Lucarelli's
engine. Within minutes he was talking so loudly Marge could
hear him above the drone of the early WGN-TV news. He had
his hand on Shannon's forearm, gripping it tightly. "And Riley
says we've got to do this right. We do, he'll double our money."
Shannon said something Marge could not hear. Lucarelli said,
"What we're going to do? We're going to ruin that fucking
famous horse they got out there. Rambler something. Before
the weekend. Riley's going to get us all set up with…." Lucarelli
suddenly stopped, looked around the bar room, then leaned
toward Shannon and whispered to him for nearly a minute.
Then he sat back in his chair, chest out, empty beer pitcher in
hand. "And that's the fucking plan, my man," he said. Lucarelli
looked over at Marge. "How about some fucking service over
here, Beautiful?"

Marge ignored him. She said, "Hi, Jimmy," to the night bartender who was starting to tie on his white apron. "Jerko over
there needs you," she added. Jimmy knew who she meant.

Minutes later, sitting in her rust-riddled nine-year-old Chevy
Nova in Haller's parking lot, Marge was still seething. She was
so sick of those two, especially Lucarelli. As she reached into her
purse for her keys, there was knock on the driver's side window.
She turned to see the concerned face of old Donal Cochran, a

Haller's fixture and one of her favorite customers. A longtime widower, Cochran appeared at Haller's promptly at one every day and nursed three tap beers through the afternoon, this routine for many years comprising the bulk of his social life. Marge rolled down the window.

"Marge, what's wrong?" Cochran said.

"Ah, Donal, you know how it is. Every once in awhile those two freaks in there really, really get to me. I don't know why I let them, but they do."

"They should have been barred from the place years ago," Cochran said.

"They're a couple of animals," Marge agreed. "Speaking of which," she said, then hesitated before going on to tell Donal what she had overheard Lucarelli saying. The old man's face grew somber as he listened. "I'll be damned," he said. "Is there nothing those young scumbags won't do? You've got to tell somebody about this."

Marge shook her head. "No, sir, Donal. Not me. I don't want to get involved. I'm afraid they'd find out if I did. And you know what happens to people who cross them." She patted the old man's hand and started her engine. "I've got to get home," she said. "My baby sitter's got to leave. See you tomorrow, Donal. Take care."

Cochran watched her drive onto Halsted and turn left. He was disappointed in her, but he understood. Marge was a single mother with obligations and half a lifetime in front of her. He, of course, was not similarly encumbered.

As he began his three block walk home, Donal's shoulders straightened and he started moving briskly. Once in his house, he went directly to the phone and dialed 411, saying, "That racetrack, Monee Park."

Celia immediately called Doyle that night after the first race. "Can you please come up to the apartment? It's important." When he arrived, Celia ushered him into the dining room, where Bob sat in his wheelchair. Karl Mortenson nodded curtly at Doyle, who gave the Security chief an equally cool glance. Shontanette smiled a greeting as Celia began to speak.

"It's hard to believe, considering all that we've gone through already this meeting," Celia said, "but it appears we've got another major challenge facing us. I'm going to let Karl tell you about it."

Mortenson reached forward, hand poised above a tape recorder. "The message I'm going to play came into our office about an hour ago. I didn't receive it, it went to our switchboard operator, who was smart enough to record it and call Celia right away. Unfortunately, our operator didn't check the Caller ID. Celia immediately called me at home, and I came right over. She thought all of you should hear this, too." He turned on the tape. They listened to a man, probably an old man, Doyle thought, speaking rapidly, determinedly.

I don't know you, and you don't know me. Who I am isn't important. What you should know is there is a couple of young toughs from my neighborhood…never mind where…that plan to hurt that famous racehorse you've got out there.

I don't know why. I don't know when, but I think in the next few days. These are two vicious little bastards, that I guarantee you. I know their names, but I can't give them to you. We don't grass, even on people like that, down here…never mind where that is.

Descriptions, yeah, I'll give you those. They're both short, stocky, strong as bulls and mean as snakes. One of them is half crazy half the time. The other one follows his lead. They've done some terrible things…but I won't get into that.

That's the best I can do for you. I've said enough. Except for….

But then the old man stopped. They heard him cough, sigh, and cut the phone connection.

Mortenson played the tape again. They listened even more intently. When it was finished, Celia got to her feet and strode over to the window. Doyle started to speak but held back, watching her face in the window's reflection, her expression to his mind a beautiful combination of shock, anger, and determination.

"This has got to be about Rambling Rosie," Celia said. "But if this is for real, if what's on the tape is true, what's the point? Why would anyone want to hurt her? Unless it's...."

Doyle said, "You've got it. It's got to be those guys who've tried everything else they could to sabotage this race meeting. I've been banging the drums for Rambling Rosie Farewell Night, and we've gotten tremendous media coverage. Annette Ruffalo in group sales tells me we've got the largest list of reservations in years lined up for that day. Which, as you know, is less than forty-eight hours away."

Doyle got to his feet. "Those bastards," he snarled. "This'd be the lowest blow of all, trying to hurt Rosie. Jesus H. Christ." He shook his head. "I've had some experience with stuff like that, people doing damage to horses. One of the men involved is dead, the others are in prison. The old man on the tape, what he's saying is that these must be the same kind of scum. *Dammit.*"

He looked up when Fidelia came into the room carrying Bob's medicine. They waited as Bob struggled to down the pills, his throat contracting. He raised a finger from the arm of his wheelchair, indicating he wanted to say something. Doyle could hardly make himself watch this tortured man as Fidelia angled his wheelchair so that he was facing Mortenson, eyes intense. In his jagged, halting voice Bob asked, "Well, Karl, what do you suggest we do?"

The Security chief squirmed to a position in his chair where he could address both Celia and her husband. He looked directly at them, not Doyle's way.

Mortenson said, "Naturally, I'll increase backstretch security, especially at Tom Eckrosh's barn." He frowned before adding, "You know, Celia, my budget is just about gone for this year and we've got a couple of weeks to go in the meeting. This calls for overtime, additional guards. That'll eat up the rest of the budget."

Doyle could hardly control himself. He said, "You can't be talking about money in a situation like this. For god's sakes, Karl, dig it up somewhere. That horse has got to be protected, as well as this track's reputation. The single most valuable item on the grounds at Monee Park right now is Rambling Rosie. We're looking to have eighteen, twenty thousand people out here Saturday for her farewell day. The revenues from that could keep this place afloat until the slots bill passes. But if somebody gets to that horse, stops that from happening, you can start tacking up the For Sale signs yourself. If you've got any money left for nails, that is."

Mortenson turned an icy gaze Doyle's way. "It's not a question of me pinching pennies. It's that I don't have many left to pinch. That's a fact."

Celia said, "Jack, don't be angry with Karl. He's done a remarkable job on a budget twenty-five percent smaller than last year's. We've had to lay off pari-mutuel clerks, people in concessions, in the restaurants. It's been a nightmare. The security side has suffered, too."

"The so-called security side," Doyle said, "has failed to prevent a track robbery, an attempted arson, and a home invasion. If our defenses get any more 'remarkable,' we'll be having seats stolen out from under the asses of people in the grandstand."

Mortenson's big fists clenched as he got to his feet. "Screw you, Doyle. If I had the money you spent on your failed trip to Ireland, I might have been able to properly secure this track."

Celia rapped her empty coffee cup on the mahogany table. "Gentlemen, that's enough. Enough! We don't have time for that kind of thing. Let's get back to Bob's question."

Doyle took a deep breath before saying, "Celia's right. I apologize, Karl. I guess you've done your best under less than ideal conditions." Mortenson nodded. He said, "All right. And you forget what I said about Ireland, too."

The meeting broke up an hour later with the Rambling Rosie Defense Plan having been hammered out. Mortenson planned to call a general meeting of his security force, emphasizing the need for increased vigilance "at each and every hour," as he put it. He promised to assign his best men to Tom Eckrosh's barn, "twenty-four/seven on a revolving basis." Doyle had suggested Eckrosh's horses be moved to a different barn, but Celia vetoed that idea. "I've known Tom for years," Celia said, "and he's stayed in that barn every one of them, through backstretch floods and wind storms, you name it. He just refuses to move, and that's it."

"Put me down for the eight-p.m.-to-a. m. shifts both tonight and Friday," Doyle said. " I've had some experience protecting horses at night," he added, "down in Kentucky."

Celia said, "I never knew that. What was that about?"

"That's a tale for another time," he said. He got to his feet. "I need to drive home and get a change of clothes for my overnight duties. Celia, please call Eckrosh and tell him to expect me and some guards at his barn each of the next two nights. He'll accept the intrusion if he knows it's coming from you." He said goodbye to Bob and Fidelia and walked out with Shontanette. In the corridor, she tugged at Jack's sleeve and pulled him aside as Mortenson bustled past them, talking softly on his cell phone. Nodding in the direction of the security chief, Shontanette whispered, "Wait till he's gone."

When the elevator doors had closed behind Mortenson, Shontanette said, "This poor mouthing Karl keeps doing about his Security Department budget, it doesn't ring true. I've reviewed the payroll records for the last few months. Something's screwy." She leaned back against the wall and dipped into her purse for a package of Marlboro Lites. "Don't you dare tell Celia you saw this," she said, lighting up. "She's bought me about five packages of those nicotine patches. Honest to God, I've got myself down to a couple of cigarettes a day." She puffed deeply, twice, smiling apologetically at Jack through her exhalations, snubbed out the cigarette, and tucked it into a small plastic zip loc bag that went back in her purse.

Doyle said, "What do you mean about something screwy in the Security payroll?"

Shontanette said, "You remember that day a couple of weeks ago when we were coming back from seeing Rosie off to the Breeders' Cup?"

"Sure."

"Remember Mortenson justifying himself by saying something about what could anybody expect to get for security guards paying only the minimum wage?"

Doyle said, "Yeah, I remember that."

"Here's the puzzler, then," Shontanette said. "I was having lunch with Sandy Doherty last week. She's in the accounting department, in charge of payroll. She's been here for years. We were talking about all the bad stuff that's gone on here this meeting. I mentioned something about how you probably couldn't get topnotch personnel to work security for only the minimum wage. Sandy got real indignant. She said, 'What are you talking about? All those people make more than that. Mr. Joyce *never* had anybody work here who didn't make more than minimum wage. And Ms. Celia has carried on that policy.'

"After lunch, I went with Sandy back to her office. She showed me the payroll records. Every Monee Park security guard is being paid at least $15 an hour, some of them more. This minimum wage claim by Mortenson? It's bogus."

Doyle said, "Have you mentioned this to Celia?"

"No. She was away in Springfield in those hearings for a few days, and when she got back she was super busy." Shonantette paused. "I'm embarrassed to say I then forgot about it, what with everything else that's been going on here."

They walked toward the elevator. Doyle said, "This has got to be looked into. Maybe Mortenson's got some kind of scam working. I wouldn't put it past him. There's always been something off about that guy."

Shontanette smiled. "You mean besides that mothball breath of his? And the alpine after shave, or whatever that shit is he uses?"

"You got it, sister," Doyle laughed. They entered the elevator. As they rode down Shontanette said, "Jack, were you ever a smoker?"

"Naw. I tried cigarettes when I was a kid, but I didn't like them. I guess I was lucky. I've got an idea of what you're going through, how addictive nicotine is. I remember what Mark Twain had to say on the subject. 'It's easy to quit smoking. I've done it many times.'"

Chapter Forty-Five

Doyle got to Barn D shortly before Thursday's sunset. The lower level of the evening sky west of Monee Park was a deep purple bolster holding up a blanket of spreading pink above the tree line. "Nice night," Tom Eckrosh said. "So far," Doyle replied.

They stood on the dirt path outside of Barn D, looking up and then down the quiet shed row, filled with horses at their ease. Doyle saw a Monee Park security guard stationed at each end, a tall, white guy and a short, slim black man, equipped with revolvers and hand radios. The white guy Doyle recognized, Dave Dubinski, a cousin of Morty's. Doyle gave him a wave.

Dusk began to settle on the barn area, wiping the last traces of sunlight off the old, metal barn roofs. A dozen or so children of Mexican backstretch workers kicked up clouds of dust as they engaged in a spirited soccer game on a grassless area between the buildings. It was a peaceful scene. Doyle, a brief acidic flow of apprehension coiling through his gut, hoped the scene would stay that way.

On a nearby surface road, cars were streaming toward the west parking lot. It was thirty-two minutes until race number one of the Thursday night program. A dark blue Buick sedan pulled out of the long line of traffic. It stopped in front of Doyle and Eckrosh. Karl Mortenson rolled down the driver's side window. Ignoring Doyle, he smiled at the old trainer, saying, "Nothing to worry about, Mr. Eckrosh. We've got this place secured." He waved and drove off toward his office. "Huumph," Eckrosh said.

◇◇◇

The old trainer had been a hard sell. Celia had ridden with Doyle to Barn D that afternoon. Doyle watched her out of the corner of his eye as he drove. Her face was drawn, her mouth tight. She looked exhausted.

He said, "How are you holding up?"

"I'm on my feet. That's about it," Celia said, not looking at him but out the car window at some backstretch workers who were lined up to buy freshly made tamales being sold by a woman out of a small stand at the side of the road. Several of the men tipped their straw hats when they saw Celia. She waved at them.

"It's been a tough day," she said. "Bob's condition is worsening. I sat up most of the night with him. He slept a little. I didn't. Now, we've got Tom Eckrosh to contend with. You know how stubborn he can be. He's never tolerated anyone he doesn't know being around his barn, especially at night. When I phoned him to say there was going to be extra security at the barn, he cut me off. 'Ms. Celia,' he said, 'I've got my twelve-gauge with a load of buckshot in each barrel, and a long-term case of insomnia. No sumbitch'll bother me or my horses. Pardon the expression.' That's his stance."

Doyle groaned. "That old man can't see clearly more than ten yards in front of him. Anybody who tries to attack him back there, they'd jump like a pit bull on a tethered rabbit."

"I am well aware of that," Celia said.

Doyle pulled the car up at the north end of Barn D just outside Eckrosh's office. Celia said, "Let me talk to Tom first." She got out of the car.

Doyle waited behind the wheel for a moment, watching Celia's graceful walk toward where the old trainer stood waiting in the doorway of his office, his eyes welcoming her as he doffed his gray fedora. Then Doyle went to join them.

Eckrosh's initial reaction to what Celia told him was disbelief. "Hurt Rosie? What the hell are you talking about, Ms. Celia? Pardon the expression. Who the hell would do that?"

Celia patiently told Eckrosh of the anonymous phone message describing the threat, why Rambling Rosie qualified as a target, why "We need to take protective measures, Tom. This might have been a crank call," she said. "But what if it wasn't? We can't take any chances here."

Maria had appeared, a feed bucket in her hand, soon after Celia began talking. Maria frowned as she listened, bringing her hand to her mouth, saying *"madre de dio."* Eckrosh's face hardened. "You know," Eckrosh said, "I saw some awful things in the war I was in. That's why I went back to the racetrack when I got out of the Army. To forget all that."

The old man scuffed his boot in the dirt, scowling. "I'm too damn old for this. Don't know why in God's name anybody would want to hurt a horse. My horse, or anybody else's. But if we need people coming into my barn to protect my horse, well, bring them in."

He turned to Doyle. "Celia said you'll be with me here tonight?"

"And the next night if need be," Doyle said. "We can't have anyone messing with Rosie and her big day, can we?"

Minutes later, Doyle got his first look at Eckrosh's vaunted twelve-gauge, its finish dulled by time and its stock scarred and worn. He said to the trainer, "Which one left this on the trail? Lewis? Or Clark?"

"Don't be making fun of this shotgun, son. When I went back to the racetrack after the war, on the old Nebraska circuit, it helped discourage a bunch of backstretch thieves. It shoots." Eckrosh sat down in his worn, brown leather armchair, its back to the wall of the office, and laid the shotgun across his lap. Doyle said, "Where's Maria?"

"She's in with Rosie, in the stall right next door. Maria wouldn't have it any other way."

Doyle sat on a hard wooden chair next to the office door, where he could hear any movement outside in the barn. He and the old trainer chatted for the first hour or so, Eckrosh regaling Doyle with stories of his early days in racing. "I rode for a year or so. I wasn't much good at it, but I made some money right after I got out of the service. Then I got too heavy, so I took up training. I bought an old mare named May Kay for $100 at Madison Downs in Nebraska. I paid the man $50 down, $50 on the cuff. First time I ran her, May Kay won a $300 purse. By the time I paid the $50 I owed the man I bought her from, then paid the blacksmith, and the feed man, and the vet, all I had left was my picture in the winner's circle."

Shortly after 10:30, the old man nodded off, shotgun on his lap. He was deeply asleep within minutes. Doyle got up and gently removed the weapon, placing it next to his own chair. He read the next day's issue of *Racing Daily*, two daily newspapers, and a horse breeding magazine before taking a walk around the barn. He spoke to the two security guards, who said they were scheduled to be replaced at 6:00 a.m.

Dawn broke as Maria rattled Rambling Rosie's feed bucket in the next door stall. The filly whinnied an enthusiastic response. Grooms and hot walkers began assembling at Barn D, and the smell of brewing coffee emanated from Eckrosh's office. The old trainer stood in the doorway, smiling at Doyle. "One night down, one to go," he said.

◇◇◇

The early hours of Friday night at Barn D were a repeat of Thursday. Eckrosh, at the end of another fourteen hour work day, dozed off after chatting with Doyle about Rambling Rosie's future as a broodmare. Shortly after ten, Doyle's cell phone rang. He grabbed it quickly, not wanting to disturb Eckrosh, who was again sleeping soundly in his arm chair, shotgun at hand.

"Jack, it's Morty. I can't sleep. Too jumpy about tomorrow, and Rosie, and everything. What about me coming out there tonight, keeping you company for awhile?"

Doyle yawned. "Why not? Bring a couple of large coffees, will you? And a deck of cards. I'll call Greg Stallings at the backstretch gate and tell him you're on your way. He knows you, right?"

"Right. See you soon."

Putting down the phone, Doyle had a feeling of unease as he considered Morty's offer to join him. To Doyle's knowledge, Morty hadn't set foot on the backstretch in years. He was candid about feeling distinctly uncomfortable in the presence of "large, smelly, stupid animals that cost me money." What prompted him to volunteer tonight?

"These pants don't fit worth a shit. And the jacket's too damn tight, Aiden."

A perplexed Denny Shannon was dressing himself in one of the Monee Park security force uniforms that he and Lucarelli had been supplied. The two were in the large men's room of the Lazy Z Truck Stop, eleven miles north of the racetrack. Lucarelli buttoned his tan shirt and brown jacket and straightened his black tie. He grinned at his image in the mirror. An exhausted trucker, shaving at a nearby sink, looked at him bleary eyed. Lucarelli snapped his cap on and turned to his cousin. "Stop your bitching. Get with the fucking program, man. We've got to make tracks."

Shannon gave up trying to button the jacket, a thirty-eight regular, not the forty-two he needed to cover his heavily muscled upper body. His biceps bulged as he put his tie on a collar at least two sizes too small for him. "Fucking blind man must have picked out these threads," he muttered.

The trucker rinsed the last of the lather off his face. "You fellas work around here?" he said.

Lucarelli said, "Once in awhile, old buddy. Over and out." He strutted out the washroom door, Shannon at his heels. Lucarelli whispered, "We'll put on the gun belts once we're inside the track."

Shannon said, "You got our ID badges?"

"Is the Pope a kraut? Do the Cubs suck? Does Pamela Anderson have a prime rack?" Lucarelli laughed. "Are we going to do some *bad* things tonight, my man?"

Oh shit, Shannon thought, *he's really ramped up. Hope he knows what we're doing.*

Lucarelli gunned the old Taurus through the truck stop parking lot toward the highway. Suddenly, he stomped the brake pedal and pulled over. He looked at his cousin. "You all squared away on how we're going to do this horse?" Shannon was affronted. "Damn right! We just fucking talked about it an hour ago."

"So, run it past me."

Shannon sighed. He said, slowly, "After we get to where this horse lives, and we know how we're going to do that, I hold the horse by its rope, or whatever, keep it standing still. You hit the horse in the neck with the needle full of the drug, the intervenial barbee turret, whatever. The big load you give it that means 'bye bye, horsie.' And we're out of there, on our way to get our money. Am I right?"

He waited for a response. Lucarelli delayed a couple of beats, keeping Denny on edge. Then he brought up his right hand. "Five me, man," he said, giving his cousin's palm a resounding slap.

Greg Stallings, the guard on duty at Monee Park's west back-stretch gate, watched the Taurus pull up to the barrier. He put down his coffee cup and walked out of his booth. Lucarelli rolled down his window. He smiled at Stallings. "Hey, buddy, we're a little early for the 1:00 a.m. shift."

Stallings bent down to look into the car, past Lucarelli at Shannon, who nodded at him. "Haven't seen you men before," Stalling said.

"We usually work the day shift," Lucarelli said, presenting his fake ID card. "How do we get to Barn D?"

Lucarelli said, "Denny, I'll take this guy." They had quietly gotten out of the Taurus after Lucarelli parked it in a dark corner of the lot and spotted a security guard seated in a camp chair at the south end of Barn D.

But when Lucarelli approached, he was surprised to see the guard's chair empty. He stopped, listened, heard a noise from a nearby stall. There was a splashing sound. Lucarelli peered into the dark stall. No horse there, just the security guard, Dave Dubinksi, urinating on the stall floor, his back to the door. Dubinski finished, sighed audibly, and yanked up his zipper. Lucarelli hit him in the back of the head with the butt end of his pistol. The guard fell face forward into the spreading pool. Lucarelli holstered his pistol and took a roll of duct tape from his jacket pocket. He bound the guard's hands and feet, working rapidly, like a rodeo bulldogger tying up a downed calf. Finished, he stepped carefully to a spot from which he could tape the man's mouth shut without getting his own feet wet. Then he hurried down the dark back side of the barn to the other end.

Shannon had come around that corner to find a guard seated in a camp chair beneath a seventy-five watt barn light, rocking gently to the music coming through his head phones. Shannon tapped him on the shoulder. The man jumped to his feet. He ripped off the head phones. "Jesus," he said, "you startled me. What's going on? My relief ain't due for another couple hours."

Shannon glanced at the man's name tag. "You're still on duty, Cal. I'm here because they're doubling up the work force on this shift. That's what the office called and told me."

Cal Jackson looked dubious. Shannon said, "C'mon, I've got a copy of the work order in my car. I'll show you." He led Jackson around the corner of the barn. Lucarelli was waiting for them there.

Midnight came and went, unnoticed by Tom Eckrosh, asleep in his armchair. Its passage was marked by Doyle, who walked outside of Eckrosh's office to stretch. It was a cool, frost-promising October night. The only sounds in the barn were of a couple of horses shifting their feet, one whiffling for a few seconds, making Doyle smile. He pictured Maria in the stall with her prized Mama, knowing the faithful groom would have positioned herself somewhere in the twelve-by-twelve foot area that would allow Rosie to lie down when she wanted.

A few minutes later he saw Morty come bustling toward him carrying four containers of coffee in a cardboard holder. Morty said, "Hi, Jack. Here's your coffee. There's one for Tom. I don't know if she drinks coffee, but I brought one for Maria, too. Where is she?"

"In with Rosie, in the stall next door," Doyle said. "Let's put this stuff in the office. Then I'll take Maria her coffee. Be quiet, I think Tom's still sleeping."

Morty said, "I see they've got some different guys working security tonight. I guess my cousin got his shift changed."

"Your cousin Dave? He's working. I talked to him before. He was bitching about having to extend his shift to six in the morning."

"There's a short, stocky guy there now," Morty said, looking back to the guard post. "Or at least there was a minute ago." They both looked to the south end of the barn. The light attached to the barn roof illuminated an empty chair. Doyle turned around to look back up the shed row at the other guard station. No one there, either.

"What the hell?" Doyle said. From the darkness of the parking lot a lone car's headlights blinked rapidly on and off twice. Doyle heard footsteps and instinctively began to brace himself as he turned. A figure charged at him from out of the shadows. Lucarelli wore a ski mask, an incongruity above his Monee Park security uniform. He pointed his pistol at Doyle's middle. Morty dropped the coffees and started to sidle away. "Stay the fuck where you are," Lucarelli barked. With his free hand he signaled the car in the parking lot. It immediately drove off.

Doyle thought that another "What the hell?" was pretty apropos, but he didn't say it, not when he felt a hard metal object being pressed against his spine. "Don't turn around," Shannon ordered him. "Just walk into that office there." Doyle felt himself being pushed forward by the gun in his back. Lucarelli shoved the shaken Morty through the doorway next.

Tom Eckrosh was strapped to his armchair with duct tape, his mouth taped shut. His shotgun lay in the corner, next to his gray fedora. There was a three-inch cut on his forehead, but the old man was conscious. His eyes blazed.

Shannon forced Doyle to face the wall. His hands were taped behind him. Lucarelli pushed Morty down hard on the wooden chair near the door and taped Morty's arms to its sides. As Lucarelli knelt to fasten Morty's ankles to the chair legs, Morty brought his right knee upward, narrowly missing Lucarelli's face. Lucarelli slashed Morty across the face with his pistol barrel, knocking him and the chair over. "Won't need a gag for this mother fucker," he said, kicking Morty in the side of the face. "You son of a bitch," Doyle said. He strained to release his hands from the tape. Lucarelli backhanded him across the face. Doyle moved his head at the last instant, but the glancing blow still dizzied him.

"Show us where that fucking Rosie horse is or we'll leave your two friends' bodies down in that mound of horse manure we saw out there," Lucarelli said.

Eckrosh, mute behind the tape, shook his head from side to side. Doyle saw blood begin to pool on the floor next to Morty's battered face. "Show us which horse it is, we won't hurt these two," Lucarelli said. He was waving his pistol from side to side, his eyes darting from Doyle to Morty.

Doyle sensed the air of desperate determination emanating from the two masked men, guys just about the size of those he'd futilely chased from their failed arson in the racing secretary's office. One of them was impatiently shifting his weight from foot to foot, pistol trained on Eckrosh. The other one moved menacingly closer to the unconscious Morty.

Grudgingly, Doyle said, "This way."

He led them to the door of adjacent stall, almost bumping into Rambling Rosie's outthrust head. The filly backed away as the men pushed Doyle forward. "Open the fucking door," Lucarelli ordered. Shannon's pistol pressed harder into Doyle's back. Doyle said, "Rosie, you've got visitors," loud enough, he hoped, for Maria to hear and then hide herself in the darkness of the stall.

"Shut the fuck up," Lucarelli ordered. "Open the damned door."

Doyle unlatched the broad, wooden half-door and stepped inside. Lucarelli gingerly crossed the threshold. He said, "Turn the flashlight on." When Shannon complied, Lucarelli whistled softly, saying, "God damn, this ain't no little horse." Rosie threw her head up and Lucarelli dodged to the right. He said to his cousin, "Give me that clip to hold her steady."

Shannon barked back at him, "I've got my hands full here, Aiden." Keeping his pistol against Doyle's back, Shannon put the flashlight in his jacket pocket. He handed Lucarelli the halter clip they'd been given. He retrieved the flashlight and pointed it at Rosie, who whinnied loudly and began shuffling her feet.

"Aiden," Shannon said, "I can't hold this guy here and hold the rope and the light at the same time. You take him."

Lucarelli grabbed the collar of Doyle's windbreaker and shoved him down on the floor next to the wall. The smell of straw and horse and fear permeated the stall.

Trying desperately to free his hands, Doyle slid sideways. Underneath Rosie's belly, on the floor on the opposite side of the stall, he could make out the still figure of Maria. He started to say something, but she put a finger to her lips and shook her head no, her long black braid flicking in the shadows.

"Did he say to hit the horse in the neck with the needle?" Lucarelli asked Shannon. "Or in the chest?" Syringe in hand, he waited for an answer.

Maria's breathing became more rapid as she reached to her right side and felt through the straw for the handle of the pitchfork that stood against the wall behind her. Her breathing was almost as it had been when she collapsed that day years ago in the torrid sunshine of the Florida melon field. But this was a cool October night. She took a deep breath, gripped the pitch fork handle with both hands, and scuttled forward on her knees.

"Fuck, I don't remember," Shannon said. "Just hit the horse with it. There's supposed to be enough juice in there to kill a rhino."

Lucarelli said, "I'm going for the neck. Hold the horse's head steady. And can't you remember to stop using fucking names of people?" he said, just before the five prongs of the pitchfork were driven through his thick right calf, the silver colored ends that appeared on the other side of his brown security guard trousers immediately followed by spurts of blood. He let out a scream that awakened every sleeping horse in the barn.

Staggering sideways, Lucarelli dropped the syringe and fought for balance. He leaned both hands against the wall, wounded leg extended before him. Shannon, white faced, let the halter clip slide from his fingers. "Jeez, Aiden, what the fuck…" He stood transfixed at the sight of his cousin. "Help me," Lucarelli managed to say. "Denny, help me get this thing out of my leg. Then shoot the fucking horse and whoever did this to me."

Maria scrambled to her feet and grabbed Rosie's halter, trying to soothe the excited horse. Rosie lashed out with her left rear leg, just missing Shannon.

Shannon hesitantly pulled at the pitchfork handle. Lucarelli screamed as the tines remained lodged in his calf. Desperate now, Shannon said, "I can't do this one-handed." He looked at Doyle, went to him and cut the tape off his hands, keeping his pistol pointed. Shannon aimed the flashlight at his cousin. "Get that thing out of his leg," he ordered.

Doyle gave the handle a nice twist and a sharp yank. The tines emerged, the puncture wounds they'd caused oozing blood onto the straw. Lucarelli collapsed to the floor, his back against the wall, wounded leg extended. He tore off his belt and used it as a tourniquet on his leg. When he'd tightened it, he snarled, "Denny shoot the fucking horse and this guy and the greaser by the horse, then get me the fuck out of here. The other two aren't going to bother us. *Hurry*, man."

Doyle moved to his right, attempting to shield Maria from Shannon. He knew he had to somehow disarm Shannon, who was looking more panicky and dangerous by the second. Then Doyle looked over Shannon's head. Two large figures had appeared behind Shannon in the doorway to the stall. One man stepped inside. He said, "Hello, Jack."

Doyle groaned. "Hello, Niall," he said.

Chapter Forty-Six

There was a momentary silence as Doyle grimaced and the others gawked at Hanratty, who moved quickly toward Shannon. Hanratty was smiling broadly. Hoy followed Hanratty into the stall and stood next to Doyle. The only sound was Rosie tossing her head so hard she nearly pulled Maria off her feet.

Lucarelli glared up at Hanratty. "Who the hell are you?"

Hanratty didn't answer. He concentrated on the stunned Shannon. In his right hand, held behind his back, there was a black object. Doyle couldn't quite see what it was. Shannon raised his pistol. Hanratty brought his hand around and smashed a blackjack down on Shannon's gun hand. His scream was echoed by a loud whinny from Rosie, who lurched sideways against Maria.

Shannon bent over, clutching his shattered wrist with his other hand. Hanratty shoved him toward Hoy. Hoy grinned as he caught the shorter man by the front of his security guard shirt. Bending his knees slightly, Hoy put everything he had into a right uppercut that lifted Shannon inches off the floor before he fell to the stall floor near Lucarelli, out cold.

Shannon's dropped pistol lay on top of the bloody straw near where Lucarelli sat, his back to the wall. Lucarelli suddenly reached out for the pistol. His eyes were wild. "God damn it, I'll kill them myself," he shouted. Twisting onto his left hip, groaning in pain from moving his torn leg, he aimed the weapon up at Rosie's head.

Doyle moved quickly. With one motion, he snatched up the pitchfork and lunged forward. He drove the tines into and through Lucarelli's throat, pinning him to the wall. The pistol fell from his hand.

Maria smothered a scream. The others watched in stunned silence as Lucarelli gurgled once, eyes rolling up in his head, then was quiet. Doyle pulled the tines from the dead thug's shredded neck. "This crazed son of a bitch is done," he growled. He asked Maria for a rub rag, then wiped all the fingerprints off the pitchfork handle before himself gripping it again. "No sense getting you involved in this," he said to Maria.

Doyle turned to Hanratty, who said, "Good work, Jack. You saved some lives."

Doyle gave him a quizzical look. "Surprised are you now, Jack?" Hanratty raised the black object in his hand. "Why, the ould cosh here is a grand sort of weapon for work like this," nodding at Shannon. "Easy to bring into your country, too. You know, back home we don't use guns on each other as often as your people over here. We're more hands on with our violence." He glanced over at Hoy, and they both laughed.

"It's not the weapon I'm surprised at," Doyle said. "I'm surprised you're here. I'm surprised you worked over that bully boy lying there. I was under the impression that he and his late pal were carrying out your orders."

It was Hanratty's turn to look surprised. "You're winding me up, man," he said indignantly. "We've never gone in for killing horses. Where did you get that thought?"

Hanratty reached down and tore the bloodied ski mask off Lucarelli's head, then removed Shannon's mask. "So that's what these gobshites look like," he said.

Doyle said, "We've got to get Morty to the hospital. I suppose that asshole, too," he added with a nod toward Shannon, who was slowly regaining consciousness. Morty rolled slowly over onto his back. His jaw was horribly swollen, left eye blackened and nearly closed by the swelling. "I'll be all right," he whispered. "See about the old man."

"Christ, that's right," Doyle said. He hurried out of the stall to Eckrosh's office. Gently peeling the tape from Eckrosh's mouth, Doyle said, "Everything's under control, Tom. Rosie's safe." He grabbed scissors from a desk drawer and cut through the tape on the old trainer's hands and feet. "I was too slow with the shotgun," Eckrosh said, his hands shaking. "They jumped me from out of the blue. Who are they?"

"I'll fill you in later," Doyle said. "Morty's hurt. I've got to call for paramedics, then the sheriff's office."

Dialing 911, Doyle thought for a moment he sensed the presence of a figure in the shadows outside the office door. Then it was gone. There was no one there when he poked his head out the door, though a familiar pungent odor lingered in the early morning air.

Two ambulances roared up to the barn a dozen minutes later. They were followed by the first patrol cars from the Cook County Sheriff's Department. Doyle led them to Lucarelli's body. He described the nightmarish developments of the last hour. Maria, Morty, and the two Irishmen backed up his account of having acted in self defense.

The paramedics went to work on Morty and Shannon. The latter was now fully conscious and whining. "I want my lawyer. I need to call Art Riley," Shannon kept repeating.

Owen Purcell, the lead detective, frowned. "Are you talking about Art Riley," he said to Shannon. "The downtown lawyer?"

"Damn right," Shannon said defiantly. Doyle recognized the name. So did a concerned Hanratty, who said, "I'd be sorry to learn that's the Riley I retained in regards to Uncle Jim's will."

Doyle muttered, "So that's how Niall's going to play it. Claiming ignorance."

Hanratty, a picture of feigned innocence, said, "Are you talking to me, Jack?" Doyle didn't answer him.

Twenty minutes later, the two Irishmen, Maria, Eckrosh, and Doyle were in the trainer's office when Celia rushed through the door. Doyle had telephoned her as soon as the paramedics left with their patients, and Lucarelli's body, telling her, "You better come to Tom's barn."

"Jack, what's going on? Tom, my God, what happened to you," Celia said. She went to Eckrosh who sat in the armchair, a bandage on his bruised forehead. He struggled to his feet to assure her, "I'll be fine, Celia. Not to worry."

After asking Maria if she was okay, Celia turned to the silent Irishmen. Hanratty and Hoy were standing, arms folded on their chests, backs against the wall. A look of astonishment flashed across Celia's face. "Niall Hanratty?" she said. "Is that you? What in the world are you doing here?"

Hanratty stepped toward her, his hand extended, saying, "Well, cousin, we meet at last." Celia slowly took his hand in hers. "I came over to straighten out a few things, Celia," he added. "Some things had been set in motion that I came to believe had to be stopped."

"And a good thing he did," Doyle said, proceeding to recount the night's events. Celia listened, her face pale, hand to her mouth. "Who were these attackers?" she asked.

"According to a check the deputies ran, a couple of small time hoods from Chicago's south side," Doyle said. "The dead one was a young guy named Aiden Lucarelli, truly a nut case. The other one is Denny Shannon. They both had numerous arrests over the last few years, but no jail time. That's going to change for Shannon."

Hanratty and Hoy were staying at a downtown Chicago hotel, they said. "Will you be back this afternoon for Rambling Rosie's farewell?" Celia asked. "We've got a lot to talk over, Niall."

"Maybe not as much as you think," Hanratty said. "I've given some thought to this situation since I arrived here. I've decided to go along with you and your plans to keep operating Monee Park."

Her surprise evident, Celia said, "Why? What's made you change your mind?"

Hanratty grinned ruefully. "In all honesty, I did not know that cretins the likes of which we dealt with here tonight had been unleashed on you and your track. And," he said, nodding at Eckrosh, "on that man's horse. I am truly sorry. That kind of thing is not what I'm about."

"What about the lawyer, Riley, saying you were planning to contest Uncle Jim's will?"

"That's another non-starter," Hanratty replied. "And my dealings with attorney Riley are a thing of the past."

Celia gave him an appraising look, followed by one of her brilliant smiles. "Well, as long as you're in such a conciliatory state of mind, I don't suppose you'd hesitate in the least to say you'll reimburse me the $127,000 stolen by men apparently under Riley's direction."

Doyle laughed, drawing sharp looks from both Hanratty and Celia. "Is there a Gaelic word for *chutzpah?*" he asked. They ignored him. "I never ordered any robbery," Hanratty said. "That apparently was Riley's idea." He grimaced, then continued, "But, cousin, I'll take responsibility. You can deduct that money from the bonanza coming Monee Park's way when slot machines come on the scene."

"Point, counterpoint," Celia said. "That's what we'll do."

She turned to leave, then paused. "Niall, will you have time to meet my husband Bob before you go back?"

Hanratty said, "Absolutely. But it'll have to be today. Hoy and I are due back home tomorrow."

"Just call Jack when you and Mr. Hoy return this afternoon," Celia said. "He'll show you around and how to find us."

Hanratty and Hoy shook hands with Doyle before he walked them to their rental car, which they'd parked two blocks away, on the other side of the track fence. "Did you two hop the fence on your way in?" he said.

"It seemed the easiest way to do it," Hanratty said. "I didn't think I could convince the gate guard that two visiting Micks had urgent night business on the Monee Park backstretch."

Chapter Forty-Seven

Doyle left the Cook County Sheriff's Department just after dawn. Hours before, he had driven Eckrosh and Maria there and they'd all given their official statements to Detective Purcell. Shannon had been taken to Saint Catherine's, the hospital closest to Monee Park and the one to which Morty had also been admitted. Shannon was treated, then placed under guard there. According to Cook Count Sheriff Jake Poole, Wilmette police had arrested and booked Art Riley.

Eckrosh called a cab to take him and Maria back to Monee Park. "The horses have to be fed and watered and exercised," he said. "That's a nice young fella, that deputy they left there to guard them, but he isn't going to start doing our work for us." Eckrosh thanked Doyle for about the fifteenth time, shook his hand, and held the taxi door for Maria. She smiled and waved as they rode away.

Doyle was so tired he could hardly see straight. He stopped at a 7-11 store for coffee on his way to Saint Catherine's. Neither the caffeine nor the early morning air did much to rejuvenate him. The main reception desk was unmanned at this hour at the small, suburban medical facility. He went back outside and walked around a couple of corners until he came to the Emergency Room. That foyer was empty except for a female receptionist, a heavy set young woman completing a lousy shift who was reading a copy of *Vanity Fair* magazine. She didn't look happy at being interrupted.

"Quiet night?" Doyle said pleasantly.

"All we've had lately is those guys from the racetrack trouble. If it were a Saturday night, you'd have to stand in line to get in here."

"It's a guy from the racetrack I want to see."

"Not the one in the detention area. Nobody's allowed in there except deputies."

Doyle said, "No, the other one."

The receptionist brightened. "The little man with the long head? I took all his information down when they brought him in. He could hardly talk, the shape his jaw was in, but he was very cooperative. A sweetheart. Go down that hallway to the nurse's station," she smiled.

The nurse on duty was a middle-aged woman who looked as tired as Doyle felt. She told him, "Mr. Dubinski is under sedation. They had to anesthetize him to work on his jaw. Fortunately, it doesn't appear that he'll need reconstructive surgery."

"How long will he be out?"

"At least another couple of hours," she said.

"When he wakes up, please tell him Jack Doyle was here, and that I'll be back to see him this evening after the races."

The small Saint Catherine's parking lot was jammed when Doyle drove in that night shortly before eight o'clock. "That receptionist wasn't exaggerating," he said to himself before he was finally able to angle the Accord into a small space at the far end of the lot. He checked with the front desk and was relieved to learn that Morty had been transferred from the Intensive Care Unit to a room on the second floor.

There were three beds in the room. Nearest the window was a young black man, left arm and shoulder heavily bandaged, an IV trailing from his right arm. He was apparently asleep. The bed adjacent to the wall was shielded by a light green curtain that had been pulled around the oblong ceiling track. No sound came from that side, either.

Morty was propped up on pillows in the middle bed. A bandage covered his left eye. His cheek ballooned out beneath the bandage like a small gourd, yellow and black. With his good eye he was reading *Racing Daily*. Hearing Doyle enter the room, Morty put down the newspaper and produced the best version of a smile that he could manage. "Hey, boss," he said, voice husky, "nice to see you."

"I wish I could say the same," Doyle replied. "You look terrible." He went to the side of the bed and put his hand on Morty's shoulder. "I should never have let you come out to the barn last night. I'm sorry I did."

Morty said, "It was my idea, remember? Anyway, we're all alive to tell about it. Sit down, Jack, fill me in on what's happened. All I know is that when I came in here last night, or this morning, or whenever it was, they just told me everything was okay, including Rosie. The drugs put me under before I could get any details. How was Rosie's Farewell Day?"

Doyle pulled a chair up, careful not to brush against the stand with the two arrangements of flowers on it. Morty saw him looking at them. "One's from Celia and Shontanette," he said. "They're coming out to see me tomorrow. The other's from Eckrosh, Maria, and Rosie. Pretty nice, huh? But tell me about today."

Doyle said, "Rosie went out in a blaze of glory. Ramon Garcia cantered her past the stands and she got a tremendous ovation from the crowd, more than 19,000 by the way, the biggest at Monee Park in nearly thirty years. Rosie's foot seemed to be fine. Old man Eckrosh actually smiled in public. Maria cried a little bit, but waved to the crowd as she led Rosie off the track for the last time. The National Racing Channel even had a crew there. Celia had to put people on overtime to count the receipts."

"That's great," Morty said. He paused to carefully insert a plastic straw into the right side of his mouth and take a sip of water. "But what's going on with those two guys who attacked us?"

"One of them, a guy named Shannon, is in a room in this hospital, injured and under arrest and cuffed to his bed. That's what your nurse told me." Doyle paused before adding, "The other's one's dead. His name was Lucarelli. I had to kill him."

Morty let the water glass slip from his hand as he listened to Doyle describe the brutal happenings in Rosie's stall. "Jesus, Jack, that's awful. I mean, I'm sure it had to be done, but damn! Did you ever kill anyone before?"

Doyle looked out the window. "That was my debut. I can't say I enjoyed it. But the bastard would have tried to shoot us all if I hadn't stopped him. The cops agreed."

"What'll happen with the other guy, Shannon?"

"I understand he's plea bargaining as fast as he can," Doyle said, "coming up with all kinds of information about their efforts to damage Monee Park and its people. But he's still going to do time in Joliet. By the way, it turns out he and Lucarelli were cousins, born and bred in Canaryville. Lovely family."

"What does Shannon have to plea bargain with?"

"He served up their lawyer, a scumbag named Art Riley, who apparently directed them in their attacks. Shannon has confessed to all those attacks, including the robbery, swearing that Riley paid them all the way along. The new state's attorney is really after Riley's ass. Riley is going down bigtime."

There was a long, surprisingly loud moan from the bed behind the green curtain. Morty grimaced. "Guy does it all the time. The nurse tells me he's in here for a minor hernia operation. Don't pay any attention."

Doyle said, "It just dawned on me. You'd been knocked out when the Irishmen arrived to help save our asses."

Morty's visible eye narrowed. "What Irishmen?"

"Celia's cousin Niall Hanratty and his bodyguard, a guy named Hoy."

"Well, I'll be damned," Morty said after hearing Doyle describe the Irishmen's actions.

"There was another arrest this afternoon," Doyle said.

"Who?"

"When Shannon was confessing, he mentioned a guy they'd met near Monee Park who'd helped them. Guess who?"

"Boss, if you don't mind, I'm lying here full of pain killers. I don't think I'm up to guessing."

Doyle laughed. "Sorry. You're right." There was an extended moan from the adjacent bed, so Doyle pulled his chair closer to Morty. "After Shannon gave up Riley," he said, "the detective, Purcell, kept pressing him for more. Shannon said he didn't know the guy's name, but that he could describe the man who told them how to go about robbing the money room. Remember? The $127,000 taken?"

"Sure," Morty said.

"Hearing Shannon's description, Purcell makes a connection. He goes on the computer and pulls up a driver's license photo that he shows to Shannon. He identifies the guy. Karl Mortenson."

Morty sat forward a few inches, one eye now widely open. "*Our* Karl Mortenson? The security chief?"

"The one and only. I called Detective Purcell when I was on my way over here. He said they hauled Mortenson in this afternoon. He spilled his guts. Admitted he'd given Lucarelli and Shannon the money room routine and instructions on how to sabotage the electrical system. The car in the parking lot with the blinking lights? That was Mortenson, signaling the thugs that they had fifteen minutes until the next security patrol swung by Barn D. Mortenson confessed to supplying them with the hypodermic needle and drug they were planning to use on Rosie. Said he'd confiscated them from a crooked veterinarian he threw off the track early in the summer. Mortenson also gave the Canaryville cousins their security guard uniforms and fake IDs. And, speaking of security, Mortenson admitted he was taking kickbacks from about half of his Monee Park staff, guys that couldn't get hired elsewhere for that kind of work. They were actually being paid $15 an hour, about a third of which they shoveled back to Mortenson under the table."

Morty said, "I don't get it. Mortenson has worked at Monee Park for years. Why would he do this stuff?"

"He's got a major gambling jones. Evidently nobody at Monee knew, but it had already cost him his wife and his house.

Mortenson met Art Riley when he was a Chicago cop. Riley handled Mortenson's divorce. When Riley decided to launch his anti-Monee Park campaign, he knew Mortenson was desperate for money to feed his habit. He convinced Mortenson to help him. Riley didn't charge Mortenson for his legal work, even gave him cash several times, which he promptly threw away on the riverboats."

Doyle paused, shaking his head. "I should have looked at Mortenson sooner. There had to be somebody on the inside guiding those little gorillas. I should have seen that."

A nurse appeared in the doorway. "Mr. Dubinski should be getting some rest now," she said.

"I was just about to leave," Doyle said. "Morty, I'll come by tomorrow. Hope you're feeling better then. And looking considerably better, too," he grinned. He was at the door when he heard Morty say in a weak but determined voice, "Little Joe Cartwright from Bonanza. His horse?"

Doyle was pretty sure he knew the answer to that one. But he said, "You've got me there, Morty."

"Cochise, Jack," Morty whispered. He couldn't move his mouth much, but Doyle saw the smile in Morty's eyes.

"Go to sleep," Doyle said.

Chapter Forty-Eight

It was the tallest collection of pallbearers Doyle had ever seen, these six Northwestern University alumni carrying their former basketball teammate Bob Zaslow's coffin through the late October sunlight and up the front steps of Saint James Church on Chicago's near west side. The tallest, seven footer Nate Drummond, reflexively ducked his gleaming ebony head as he crossed the threshold. "He probably does that every doorway he walks through," Doyle said to Moe Kellman, who was standing alongside him among the mourners on the church steps.

Moe did not reply as they joined the people walking in behind the coffin and took seats in a pew near the front of the cavernous church, one of the city's oldest, built after recently arrived and subsequently empowered Catholic immigrants used structures such as these to announce that they were, indeed, here. Doyle slid over to make room in the pew as Morty Dubinski, face still slightly discolored but otherwise recovered from his beating, slipped in beside him. They shook hands. Doyle said, "You still look like you got hit by a bus, Morty, but maybe now a smaller bus."

Doyle had arrived at Monee Park three mornings earlier, the final day of the season's racing meeting, to find Shontanette waiting for him just inside the employees' entrance, face drawn, eyes red. She looked exhausted. She said, "Jack, I wanted to catch you when you came in. Bob died about an hour ago. I didn't want to tell you over the phone."

She leaned back against the wall, drained, and Doyle hugged her, feeling her tremble, hearing her strained voice. "I was up all night with them, Celia, and Fidelia, and the hospice nurse. It was…." She stopped, took a deep breath, then said, "It was awful. But it was welcome, too. Father Cavanaugh came, he gave Bob the last rites. Celia held Bob's hand for hours, as if she could hold the life in him." Shontanette looked away again. "And that was that. Bob was with people who loved him dearly. Now his suffering is over."

Shontanette wiped her eyes. "Anyway," she said, "Celia asked if you would write an obituary and send it to the local papers and television stations. A lot of people remember Bob Zaslow."

Doyle hugged her again. He said, "Shontanette, go home. Get some sleep. I'll take care of it."

That people remembered Bob Zaslow was evidenced by the huge turnout at the church. As the service was about to begin, Doyle looked at the crowded pews and the mourners still streaming in. "Full house," he said to Moe. "That's no upset," Moe replied.

Monsignor Francis Flaherty's eulogy made clear why there was such an impressive attendance. Bob Zaslow had been not just a star athlete, but an athlete who truly "gave back to the community, as a Big Brother, as a scout leader, as a youth league basketball commissioner, as a human being," the monsignor said. "And after Bob was stricken with the disease that would eventually take him from us, he became a tremendously effective voice in the efforts to find a cure for ALS."

Three of the six pallbearers also spoke, awkward in their attempts to recount old locker room levity, details of years of camaraderie, the sense of loss they were experiencing. Doyle watched Celia looking on attentively, sometimes nodding her head as if to encourage these tall, earnest, mournful men, long-time friends of hers and Bob's, who were struggling so mightily with their emotions.

The Saint James choir, bolstered by an organist who was holding nothing back, concluded the service with what

Monsignor Flaherty announced was "one of Bob and Celia's favorite songs."

Everyone stood as the organist played the first notes of "Bridge Over Troubled Waters." The silvery voice of the choir's lead soprano rose and rippled beneath the old church's tall ceiling. Two women in the row in front of Doyle wept, their shoulders shaking, their husbands reaching to console them. Doyle saw Celia briefly sit, then take Shontanette's arm and again get to her feet. Doyle had to tear his look away.

"Son of a gun," Doyle mumbled when the song had ended.

Moe looked up at him. "This a tough one, no doubt about it," Moe said.

Doyle and Kellman and the rest of the assemblage stood as Celia, Bob's parents, and four siblings, and Shontanette and Fidelia walked slowly down the aisle behind the coffin. Doyle wanted to reach out and touch Celia's arm. He did not. Celia walked past him, eyes down. He was looking for some kind of sign that what he felt for her had relevancy, even on this sad day, even in the midst of her powerful sorrow at her husband's passing. There was no such sign. That realization gave Doyle a hollowed out feeling that he knew he would have to live with.

Moe said, "Want to ride to the cemetery with me?"

"No, thanks. I'm not going there."

Moe gave Doyle's arm a squeeze as he moved past him. "Suit yourself, kid," he said.

Driving to his condo, Doyle imagined the cemetery scene, crowd a respectful distance from the carefully prepared grave, the monsignor intoning final words, the bits of soil being deposited on the lowered coffin, the widow's final gesture of farewell slicing gently through the autumn air. Then the slow walk to the many waiting cars. Some mourners would stumble over the horizontal grave markers in their haste to leave. Others would trip more lightly in anticipation of the catered luncheon they knew awaited them at Celia's Monee Park penthouse apartment.

He decided to go home, park the car, head for O'Keefe's Old Ale House. Nearing North Avenue, his cell phone rang. It was Morty. "Boss, I didn't see you at the cemetery. Where are you?"

"I'm kind of tied up with something here, Morty. Besides, I'm not much for those cemetery scenes."

"Well, are you coming to Celia's? There'll be a bunch of people there. Shontanette was wondering where you were."

He couldn't help himself. "Was Celia looking for me?"

"Not that I know. But you should come to the luncheon. Clarence Meaux put together the buffet. Tom Eckrosh, he was asking about you. Even if you're not hungry, it's for the family's sake, you know?"

"Morty, I'm sorry. I just can't make it," Doyle said harshly.

The phone was silent as he turned onto Wells Street. Morty said quietly, "Boss, what about next year? You going to be back at Monee Park? Once we get the slots going, the place will be jumping, you know?"

"I hope they do great with the slots," Doyle said, "but I'm not going to be around."

Morty was silent again. Doyle felt like just putting the phone down, but he didn't. He said, "Morty, I've got to get going. You take care of yourself. The job I had, I know you can take that over and do great with it, no problem."

"I get the picture," Morty said. "Aren't you going to say goodbye to anybody else? Celia? Shontanette?"

"No," Doyle said. "I've never been much good at good-byes."

Chapter Forty-Nine

SPRINGFIELD—In what was seen as a major triumph for the state's horse racing interests, the Illinois Senate on Friday passed by a vote of 32-27 a bill authorizing video slot machines at five of the state's six horse racing tracks. Governor Otto Walker is expected to sign the bill early next week. Getting the okay to install slots were Monee Park and Heartland Downs, thoroughbred tracks in suburban Chicago, as well as the city's three harness tracks. Cut from the bill in last minute negotiations were slot macines for downstate Devon Downs and a provision that would have brought a casino to Chicago.

An earlier version of the bill had previously passed the Illinois House by a narrow margin, then met stiff opposition in the Senate during hearings leading up to Friday's vote.

The bill's House sponsor, Representative Lew Langmeyer (D-Palatine), pronounced himself "jubilant" over the passage of this controversial measure, which had been solidly supported by the Illinois horse racing industry, but stongly opposed by an odd alliance of the state's nine casinos and a prominent anti-gambling organization.

"We didn't get everything the original bill sought," Representative Langmeyer told reporters, "but we got the portion that should guarantee the continued existence of horse racing in our state. Now, the majority of the tracks at least will be able to compete with the casinos."

The bulk of the new tax revenues expected to be produced by the racetracks will go to the state's education fund. A portion of the tracks' share of slot machine profits will be shared with horse owners in the form of increased purses. This is expected to attract better horses to the state and boost track attendance and betting.

Representative Langmeyer's enthusiastic reaction was echoed by House Majority Leader William "Willy" Wilgis. He had for months refused to take a public position on the bill, only in recent days announcing his "full fledged support." That support served to insure the measure's passage in its amended form.

According to Representative Wilgis, the bill "Ain't perfect, but it's a darn good start. The first potato chip is the one that empties the bag."

To receive a free catalog of Poisoned Pen Press titles, please contact us in one of the following ways:

Phone: 1-800-421-3976
Facsimile: 1-480-949-1707
Email: info@poisonedpenpress.com
Website: www.poisonedpenpress.com

Poisoned Pen Press
6962 E. First Ave. Ste. 103
Scottsdale, AZ 85251